# THE
# APPEARANCE
## OF
# IMPROPRIETY

**Also by Walter Walker**

The Immediate Prospect of Being Hanged
Rules of the Knife Fight
The Two Dude Defense
A Dime to Dance By

# THE
# APPEARANCE
## OF
# IMPROPRIETY

# Walter Walker

POCKET BOOKS
New York  London  Toronto  Sydney  Tokyo  Singapore

POCKET BOOKS, a division of Simon & Schuster Inc.
1230 Avenue of the Americas, New York, NY 10020

Walker, Walter,
    The appearance of impropriety / Walter Walker.
        p.   cm.
    ISBN: 0-671-74042-3 : $20.00
    I.  Title.
PS3573.A425417A85   1993
813'.54—dc20                                                      92-28746
                                                                      CIP

First Pocket Books hardcover printing February 1993

10   9   8   7   6   5   4   3   2   1

*To Jeffrey, my pride*

# CONTENTS

# The San Francisco GoldenGaters

| No. | Name | Ht. | Wt. | Yrs. Pro. | College |
|---|---|---|---|---|---|
| 33 | Tim Biltmore | 6'11" | 220 | 9 | Iowa |
| 35 | Curtis Clovis | 6'8" | 230 | 4 | New Mexico |
| 5 | Oliver Dawkins | 6'5" | 220 | R | NC State |
| 11 | Del Fuego Dixon | 6'9" | 225 | 8 | UCLA |
| 21 | Felix McDaniel | 6'3" | 210 | 9 | Louisville |
| 24 | Larry Miller | 6'5" | 215 | 2 | Oregon |
| 10 | Rynn Packard | 6'1" | 185 | 1 | Cornell |
| 45 | W.E.B. Pancake | 6'10" | 260 | 10 | Jones-Henry |
| 14 | Earl Putnam | 6'2" | 180 | 4 | Norfolk St. |
| 16 | Gilbert Rose | 6'9" | 235 | 7 | California |
| 50 | Chris Sarantopoulis | 7'0" | 270 | 5 | Wyoming |
| 54 | Zeke Wyatt | 6'10" | 240 | 1 | UNLV |

Coach: Booby Sinclair; Asst. Coaches: Mike Hacker, Mel Dykstra; Trainer: Dick Crabtree; Chief Scout: Woody Woodward

General Manager: Dale Rohmer

The GoldenGaters are proud to be a part of the Brandisi Corporation of Boston, Massachusetts.

# Tip-Off

Teddy Brandisi did not live in San Francisco, had never played organized basketball a day in his life, and cared very little about the city or the sport. Teddy, however, had made an absolute fortune in supermarkets throughout the Northeast, and after he had bought houses and cars and boats and racehorses, he awoke one morning and decided that what he really needed was a sports team. A franchise.

He would have preferred a baseball or a football team. He would have preferred a Boston team in any sport. But on that particular morning what was available was the San Francisco GoldenGaters, and Teddy Brandisi was an impatient man.

It was Teddy's original intention to be pals with his players. He envisioned himself as a benevolent owner, one who would be perfectly capable of inviting the guys on his team to join him and his friends for a round of golf or a day of deep-sea fishing. As it turned out, the Gaters' one and only visit to Boston to play the locals in Teddy's first year of ownership occurred in the first month of the season, and an hour before game time Teddy arrived in the locker room with a handful of his buddies, all men who looked remarkably like him, short of stature, well fed, and well dressed. He wanted his old friends to meet his new friends, but the visiting team's locker room in Boston Garden was very small, and his old friends soon got bunched together in a huddle of blue- and camel's-hair-colored cashmere while his new friends—most of them very large, and all of them in various stages of undress—tried to maneuver their way around them.

Teddy, who had been out to California to look the team over during preseason training camp, nonetheless found himself confused in the presence of so many large black men and resorted to calling each of the players "big fella," as in, "Have a good game, big fella," and, "How's it goin', big fella?" The one black player he did recognize was W.E.B. Pancake, and he called him Web and did not seem to notice when W.E.B. merely glowered at him in response.

Once individual greetings were out of the way, Teddy took the opportunity to address the team as a whole. He did it by standing on a bench. The men in the topcoats arrayed themselves along the far wall. Teddy's general manager, Dale Rohmer, and his coach, Booby Sinclair, took up positions slightly behind him. The players took seats in front of him, and Teddy smiled at them reassuringly and they listened politely. Except for the farts.

"When we have a product that people want," Teddy announced, "people will pay money for that product. I don't care if it's rebounds or rutabagas."

He paused there and grinned at his audience. It was a practiced line and he was awaiting a laugh. Instead, a long, low sound like a truck changing gears escaped from the satin-covered hindquarters of one of the athletic young men gathered before him. The players all grinned back at Teddy.

"The better the product," he continued, somewhat uncertain as to the meaning of the response he had received, "the more the people will pay for it."

A deep rumbling noise emerged from the audience.

"As an owner," Teddy said, his voice rising, his words coming quicker, "my product is the San Francisco GoldenGaters as a whole. The better basketball my team plays, the more people will want to watch it, and the more I will be able to sell it—not just to the live fan, but to the television audience."

It was at about this point that the noises began to rip one after the other. Little sputtering ones, strain-produced whistling

4

ones, an occasional big explosive one that sounded like a muffled cannon. And still the players sat unmoving, their eyes and their smiling faces trained on their now red-faced, nearly blubbering boss.

Teddy's tone grew more strident. "As players," he said, gesturing at them, "your product is your individual skill. The more you cultivate it, the better you display it, the more I want it. The more I want it, the more I'll pay for it. It's as simple as that."

A player named Neil Novaceski, a big forward generally regarded as one of the less mentally gifted men in the league, a man so guileless that he was sitting in the front row at his owner's inaugural speech, made the mistake of letting loose at that moment with his own anal blast.

Teddy, whose tolerance had been extended only by his unfamiliarity with locker room customs, leveled a shaking finger at Novaceski and demanded to know his name.

"Me?" said the big guy, pressing his hand innocently to his chest and thereby making everyone laugh out loud. "Neil Novaceski, sir."

Teddy, his face nearly scarlet, his pointing finger still quivering, said, "There are, I have noticed, a great number of men in this country, this world, who would love a spot on a professional basketball team where the minimum salary is over one hundred thousand dollars a year."

The mere mention of salaries caused the laughter almost immediately to die down to a titter. But Teddy continued on.

"Many of these men have a similar degree of talent. There are, I am told, two hundred thousand players on the college level. About forty of them make it into this league every year. A handful make it into other leagues, and the rest, including those whose skill may not be that much different, go home and look for a job with the phone company."

The smirk on Novaceski's face disappeared.

"There are rutabagas out there by the hundreds of thousands," Teddy railed. "Heads of lettuce and tomatoes by the millions. They all pretty much look alike and they all pretty much taste alike, and when that's the case, I don't care who I buy them from. If I get a real good grower, one who makes my customers come into my stores and ask for his tomatoes, then I'm gonna pay more to that grower. But otherwise, personally, I don't give a *shit* who's selling me their tomatoes, and since I'm not eating them, all I'm interested in is whether I can resell them at a profit. In other words, if I can get the same product anywhere, then I'm gonna get it from wherever I can get it cheapest."

Teddy paused then. He scanned the room slowly before adding his final words. "Got the picture?"

Then Teddy Brandisi signaled to his friends, his old friends, who had stood about looking alternately embarrassed and confused. He crooked his pointing at Dale Rohmer and stomped out of the locker room. Rohmer, who went six feet eight inches from the floor to the top of his red head, followed little Teddy and his friends out the door without a backward glance. Then Booby Sinclair, his face as white as if he had donated all the blood that had turned Teddy's face hematomic, moved to the front of the room and declared in no uncertain terms that if anybody thought Teddy's message was that individual statistics meant more than team effort, he was going to be on the next train to Palookaville.

*Palookaville* was not a term often used by W.E.B. Pancake and some of the other players, but the entire team nodded in unison. Then they went out and lost by 23 points to Boston. The next day Novaceski was put on waivers, where he went unclaimed.

Nobody laughed at Teddy Brandisi after that, and he never reappeared in the locker room for a pregame pep talk either. From then on, if Teddy had something to say, it was said through Rohmer.

It was, therefore, a matter of some significance to anyone in the Gaters' traveling party who happened to learn about it that Rohmer would be joining them once they got to Houston, the team's fourth stop on a grueling ten-day tour of the Southwest. The Gaters had by this point belonged to Teddy Brandisi for two and a half years, and their position in the standings was not even as good as it was the year before he had taken control. They were in fifth place in their conference, ninth in their division, had lost six straight games, and were showing no signs of improvement.

Rohmer's appearance on the road under such circumstances did not bode well for someone.

# 2

It was nearly two in the morning when the team arrived at their hotel in Dallas. They had a ten A.M. wake-up call, a late breakfast, and then they bused off to a practice session at Reunion Arena. There they shot around for about ten minutes and then did stretching exercises, some stretching more than others.

Booby Sinclair, standing in the middle of the court with his arms folded and a sheaf of papers in his hand, watched Oliver Dawkins study the drawstring on his shorts as if he were deactivating a bomb. He watched Zeke Wyatt make no effort to reach his hands below his shins. He watched Chris Sarantopoulis make the effort and still not get much farther than Zeke. But he said nothing until the stretching was over and he had them run some three-on-two fast-break drills. Nobody seemed to be running hard, and then he started to say things that were designed to draw this fact to their attention. The players ran harder, but they did not seem to be playing any better.

He blew the whistle and sent the five starters, Pancake, Del Fuego, Rynn, Zeke, and Larry Miller, down one end of the court to work with Hacker. He sent the remaining seven men, Sarantopoulis, Gilbert, Felix, Biltmore, Curtis, Earl Putnam, and Oliver Dawkins, to the other end to work with Dykstra. He told each group to concentrate on plays. He told Curtis and Earl Putnam to substitute in for Gilbert Rose and Oliver.

From his position in the middle of the court, Booby continued to watch both ends and gradually let his displeasure

8

become more and more obvious. "Don't bother improvising," he suddenly screamed. "Any Mary can score against no opposition. You think it's gonna be so easy against Dallas? They're not the guys who've lost six in a row."

Some of the players looked insulted, as if he, their coach, had a nerve throwing their disgrace in their faces. Booby blew it up again and ordered them into the transition drill. Hack would put the ball up, shooting it off the rim, and the team on the floor, the first team or the second team, running in heats, still without opposition, would grab the rebound, convert from offense to defense, race up the other end, and score. At least that was the idea.

Finally, Booby blew it up for good, ordered them each to shoot foul shots, and stomped off the floor. Even without opposition, the transition drill had resulted in shots being missed at least as often as they were made.

He looked neither to one side or the other, but went directly to the locker room, where he popped open the door and found his trainer reading the *Wall Street Journal*. Dick Crabtree dropped the newspaper to the floor and leaped immediately to his feet as if he had just been caught stealing wallets; but Booby did not give him a second glance. He simply grabbed his coat from its hook and walked back out of the room.

"Don't wait the bus for me," he said.

Booby Sinclair had grown up on the outskirts of Columbus, Ohio, which, at the time, he believed to be not just a major city, but one of the academic centers of the universe. His heroes were Havlicek and Lucas and Siegfried and Knight—in that order; and as a high school senior it had taken no more than an after-practice conversation with Coach Knight to convince him to sign a letter of intent to attend Ohio State.

In truth, it would not even have taken that conversation to get Booby Sinclair to become a Buckeye. He had never seriously thought of going to any other school. And as an A student who was president of his class, Ohio Christian Boy of the Year, and an ambidextrous guard who averaged 26 points a game for his highly regarded team, Booby could have gone anyplace he pleased.

All through his four years at OSU, Booby managed to maintain the conviction that it was the best, the only, place to go to college and that anybody who did not go there was (a) jealous, (b) mistaken, or (c) second-rate. He was stunned, to the point of refusing to accept the concept, whenever he heard that people from such places as Michigan, Indiana, Minnesota, and Wisconsin did not agree with him.

The fact was, however, that he did little to challenge his own thesis during his four years at OSU. He lived in the athletic dorm, studied physical education, and played basketball. He did not join a fraternity, go away on spring vacations, venture outside his prescribed course of study, hang around with students who were not athletes, or meet any girls who were not introduced to him in some way through basketball.

At twenty-two, he received his degree and an invitation to try out for the New York Knicks, an invitation prompted by the fact that he had been named All–Big 10 in his senior year and yet was not considered tall enough or fast enough to be selected in the annual draft of the nation's top college players. In his one week at the Knicks' preseason camp he shot over 50 percent, outrebounded men ten inches taller, and played tenacious, error-free defense. It therefore came as quite a surprise to him when at the end of that week he was handed his walking papers because he was too small and too slow.

Booby's perfect life—his faith in God, hard work, positive thinking, Ohio State, and the tenets of the Republican Party— came crashing to a halt. He was, in fact, nearly catatonic after receiving the news that his services were no longer desired. Eventually he called home, and when his father came on the line, Booby was not able to say a word. He simply blubbered. He stood in the phone booth sobbing, clinging to the receiver as if it were his father in person, and he continued to sob for an extraordinarily long time as he cried not only for himself but for the state of human existence. And his father, knowing what was happening, cried along with him.

Booby Sinclair returned to Ohio State in the autumn after his graduation and took a job for room, board, and spending money as assistant coach of the freshman team. He drilled the new players with the same work habits he had practiced himself. He attempted to teach them the same single-minded devotion with which he had played the game. The only difference was that he knew now that an errant shot, a blown defensive switch, a lost game, even a lost championship, was not the end of life, but was merely a lost chance of enjoyment. It was perceived by those who watched Booby that this was a positive attribute, this combination of fierce and intense dedication tempered by a perspective of transcendence. They thought it made Booby an excellent coach.

In a year he was put in charge of the junior varsity, where he showed neither undue exhilaration when his team repeatedly won, nor uncommon depression when it occasionally lost. In two years he was assistant coach of the varsity. At the age of twenty-five, he accepted a head coaching position at a state university in Kentucky, where basketball was felt to be very important and Booby was made an instant celebrity.

It was there that he came into contact with Meg Morgan, undoubtedly the finest woman in town between the ages of twenty-two and thirty; perhaps the finest thing in tight jeans within a radius of fifteen miles. She knew who Booby was. Indeed, she went to the party where they met just because he would be there. She spilled a drink on his leg and apologized profusely and gave him her name and address and telephone number so that he could send her the cleaning bill—thereby angering her girlfriends, all of whom worked with her at the town's leading department store, to the point that they refused to talk to her on the ride home.

But Meg did not care. Within twenty-four hours of Booby's calling her to say that dinner would be more than enough compensation for his slightly soiled trousers, Meg Morgan was his steady girl. Within a week he had made love with her more times than he had with every other woman on the planet, for Meg proved to be a wild, passionate, innovative lover, and Booby, for all his apparent success, was relatively inexperienced. The girls he had gone out with before Meg referred to

11

sex in phrases such as "getting to first base," "going all the way," "doing it," and even "sloppy seconds." Meg tended to use more direct, sometimes more graphic terms—particularly while the acts were going on. Six months after being introduced to Meg's world Booby married her, and Meg had her ticket out of Kentucky.

The Sinclairs moved on to colleges in New Jersey and Pennsylvania, and then Booby got his first professional job as assistant coach with Philadelphia. By the time the couple were in their midthirties they had two children in grade school and a fashionable ten-room home in Upper Darby. Meg had put on fifteen pounds, had a $100 dollar hairstyle, and a $40,000 Mercedes. Booby had a receding hairline, a slight drinking problem, and a stable of women located in league cities around the country.

After several years as an assistant, Booby's name began to pop up around the league whenever a coaching vacancy occurred. He was approached by Milwaukee, then Portland, then Washington; and then, to the surprise of everyone, he agreed to terms with the GoldenGaters, who at that time were known as the cheapest operation in basketball.

He told the press he had taken the Gaters' job because of the lifestyle in the Bay Area. This instantly endeared him to the basketball-caring public of Northern California, many of whom had themselves moved to the area because of the lifestyle, and all of whom neglected to note that Booby had spent most of the last four decades indoors. He publicly declared that he chose the Gaters because of the family atmosphere the team provided. This caused the media almost universally to applaud his sentiment and question his judgment. The Gaters, after all, were in trouble (and in need of a coach) largely because they were, at the time, owned by the Bancroft family, a civic-minded, genteel, bumbling lot who had bought the team in the days when owners only had to be rich and not megarich.

But Booby had his own ideas as to what was meant by family atmosphere. In San Francisco, Booby did not screw around. In Dallas he had a girlfriend named Kammy.

Kammy had a Porsche 928, a bubble blond hairstyle, an hourglass figure, and a penchant for wearing turquoise cowboy boots and tailored denim suits with studs on the arms and legs. She owned a hairdressing salon called GAL-erina's! And it was to the salon that Booby took a taxi upon leaving practice. He had not told her he was coming, but he was confident that she would be expecting his arrival, and that she would have scheduled her appointments in anticipation that he would be spending at least part of the afternoon and evening with her.

Kammy was, after all, a basketball fan. She knew when the Gaters came to town.

He was too early. She had heard about the practice and had not expected him for another hour, at least. Across the street was a steak-and-beer place with a bar that would be empty in the middle of the afternoon. He could wait there and she would join him as soon as she was done with her last customer. It was better for a professional basketball coach to be seen hanging around an oak-veneered, emerald-green-carpeted bar than the waiting room of a hair salon called GAL-erina's!

Booby sat alone in a booth next to a floor-to-ceiling tinted window. He had half a mug of beer in front of him, his second, and he had the *Dallas Times* open to the sports page. He was reading box scores and having occasionally dirty thoughts about Kammy when a familiar voice addressed him as "Coach."

Booby glanced up into the sparkling eyeglasses worn by Colin Cromwell. He tried not to act displeased at the sight of a San Francisco sports columnist at a nowhere bar in the middle of Dallas because he knew it would do him no good. Cromwell traveled with the team. He had been at the practice. It was not mere happenstance that he was within fifty yards of Kammy's business.

"Mind if I sit down?" Cromwell asked, gesturing to the empty bench on the other side of the booth.

Booby said yes.

Cromwell sat down anyway. He was used to being unwanted. He said, "Can I get you a beer?"

Booby picked up what he had. He swirled the beer around in his mug in silent response.

13

"Do you want me to leave you alone?"

Booby's pulse quickened. "No, Colin, I was hoping you'd drop by. That's why I came here. Some of the guys back home said this was your favorite place and I thought maybe if I hung out here long enough, I might see you and we could have a private little talk. Just the two of us."

Cromwell forced a grin. It was a thin grin, but it served its purpose. Obsequiously, he said, "You know, Coach, you can mess me up pretty well, if you want. Give me some bad information, make me look foolish when I write it up. You can freeze me out, even, give me nothing to write about. I'm not really interested in having either of those things happen. So if you tell me to, I'll just get up and walk away and there'll be no hard feelings."

Booby nodded solemnly. "Then why don't you do that?"

This time Cromwell flushed. "Because," he said, managing to keep his grin hanging in place, "I figured you'd appreciate the chance to tell my readers what's going on with this team of yours before I go making up all the wrong answers myself."

Booby sighed. "Yeah, I can tell you what's going on," he said, casually turning his head and trying to sneak a glimpse out the window toward GAL-erina's! "We're losing games. The season's not even half over and already we're worried about missing out on a play-off berth. You ready to start quoting me now? All right. We're playing one game at a time. Every team is tough. Our boys know it won't be easy, but it's gut-check time and we'll see who comes to play. That enough?"

Cromwell's brow furrowed. "Coach, you sound jaded. Burnt-out."

Booby's head snapped around. That was the kind of thing Cromwell liked to do, put words in your mouth, put labels on you, hit you with his own thought and then try to get you to adopt it. "Oh, no, you don't," Booby said. "Try this." He locked his eyes on Cromwell's and made his voice gush with enthusiasm. "I've never been so proud of a group of young men in all my life. Every one of them is out there giving a hundred and ten percent at all times. We've had some tough breaks, but these

14

boys never give up and we're going to surprise some people along the way."

"Coach, why is Dale Rohmer joining the team in Houston?"

Booby's attempt at riposte came to a sudden halt. No one had said anything to him about Rohmer arriving, and yet Cromwell, for all his faults, was not likely to make up a claim like that. He had to make a quick decision as to whether it was worse to know nothing or to let Cromwell see that he knew nothing. He tried a middle road, adopting a look of utmost sincerity and saying, "Because he loves to watch the game of basketball, Colin. And there's no better way to watch it than to watch the Gaters."

"Is somebody going to be leaving the team?"

"We're always out there looking for the best talent available, Colin. We think we've got that now, but you can't stand pat, and if we see a chance to improve ourselves, we will."

"There was an altercation between Del Fuego Dixon and Rynn Packard at the end of practice today."

Booby's lips moved in and out. This now, this didn't have to be true. Cromwell wasn't above interpreting things, shading things just to provoke a comment that he could use in one of his foolish "basketball players as human beings" columns. But a fight between the team's star and its playmaker?

Booby tasted his beer and decided to ask the question. He could ask about a fight. That wasn't as bad as not knowing his boss was coming. "What sort of altercation?"

"Just a minor one, but that was what was so strange. It was just a look, followed by a remark. Nothing you'd think a couple of guys like that would get so fired up about, but Del Fuego went after him."

Booby took another sip of his beer and put the mug down. "Road trips," he said. "Losing streaks. They can get everybody tense. Blowing off steam can be good for a team." He waited a beat or two. He made a gesture with his hands that was meant to convey that that was all there was to it.

Cromwell said, "All I know is what I saw. I was sitting up in the stands with a couple of Dallas hacks, just watching the guys do the foul shots you told them to do. But instead of shooting from the foul line, Del Fuego began practicing his

15

turnarounds, and instead of shooting his own shots Rynn began staring at him. You know Del's turnaround. Bing-bing-bing. It was going in every time. And then, on maybe his twelfth attempt, he suddenly spins in a full circle and comes up holding the ball in one hand like a grapefruit and looking directly at Rynn.

" 'What you staring at, Bill?' he says. You know how they call Packard 'Bill'?"

Booby nodded, telling Cromwell to get on with it.

Cromwell complied. "Rynn looks down at his sneakers. He starts to turn away, but Del Fuego doesn't let him. 'I got something on my face, or what?' Del says—and all of a sudden all the balls on the court stop bouncing. People had been shooting at six different baskets, and now nobody's shooting anymore.

"Del doesn't let up. He says, 'No, really, man, why you lookin' at me? Weren't you the one that missed those last two shots last night?' "

Booby knew that Cromwell was searching his face for a reaction. That was the reason behind all the theatrics, the dialogue; and seeing that, Booby was determined to give him nothing.

"Rynn looks at him," Cromwell said after a few moments, "he looks at him and he says, 'I shouldn't have had to take them.' "

The two men sat in silence pondering the significance of that statement and then Cromwell made the two-handed gesture that Booby had made a few moments before.

"Now, to me," Cromwell went on, "there was nothing infuriating about the words themselves. I'm thinking, okay, Rynn didn't give him the ball last night at the end of the game, so he's saying he's sorry. But apparently Del doesn't see it that way. All of a sudden he just springs toward Packard. He's within one step of nailing him when W.E.B. Pancake appears out of nowhere and gets between them."

Cromwell paused, surveying the effect his news was having. "I don't know what Pancake said," he admitted. "It was too soft for me to hear, but I saw his head motion toward where I'm sitting with the Dallas writers, and almost immediately Del Fuego stops." Cromwell used his two index fingers to trace

16

lines from the middle of his mouth to his cheeks. "Del's lips spread into a smile this big. He pats W.E.B. on the back. Then he reaches around him and taps Rynn Packard with just the tips of his fingers, like he's picking up a dime. 'Sorry, Bill,' he says, and Rynn gives a tight little smile of his own, says, 'No problem,' or something, and suddenly the whole thing's over with. Now, you tell me, Booby, what the hell was that all about?"

A flash of color across the street caught Booby's attention. He couldn't turn his head without Cromwell's noticing it because Cromwell was staring right in his face. He couldn't concentrate on giving Cromwell his answer because he knew what that flash of color was.

"You know what I think?" said Cromwell; and Booby hoped that whatever it was it didn't have anything to do with Kammy.

"I think when Rynn said, 'I shouldn't have had to take them,' he was talking about the fact that Del never once took that turnaround the whole fourth quarter last night. Check Dyk's stat sheets, you'll see. Del passed it up every time. Didn't make any difference if you guys were up ten or down two. Now we're talking about the bread-and-butter shot for a man who has consistently been one of the top scorers in the league. Why wouldn't he take it? Del's not the kind of guy who would pass up a shot under any circumstances."

Booby saw his opportunity. He threw a five-dollar bill on the table and quickly pushed himself to his feet. "I'll check into it and let you know what I find out. Meantime, buy yourself a beer, huh? I gotta run."

He tried not to run and the effect was a scurry that made him feel like a rodent. It was only good enough to get him out the swinging door in time to intercept Kammy on the sidewalk.

Without saying a word, he grabbed her by the elbow and turned her away from the entrance. With any luck, Cromwell would not be watching through the window. And if he was, Booby could always make up some explanation. He could say she was his investment counselor or something.

And if Cromwell—who knew enough to find him across the street from GAL-erina's!—pushed it, well, then, to hell with him.

17

# CROMWELL'S CORNER

## The Midwinter of Our Discontent
### by Colin Cromwell

In baseball, the dog days come in June. In basketball, they arrive in January. They hit particularly hard when your team is mired in fifth place, riding a six-game losing streak, and staring a multicity tour of the West and Southwest in the face.

In true team tradition, the GoldenGaters have met the dog days and succumbed. Gone is the heady promise of the off-season, when we were waiting for the spark that number one draft choice Oliver Dawkins was going to provide with his knifing drives to the basket, his laserlike passes, and his magical 20-foot jump shot. Oliver Dawkins, with his guaranteed three-year, $2-million contract sits on the bench and watches a $150,000-a-year free agent direct the team's offense. In Utah, Dawkins played just five minutes. In Denver he played but two (neither of them well).

Gone is the unrestrained optimism of the preseason, when Coach Booby Sinclair made us believe that with a year of playing together under their belts, W.E.B. Pancake, Del Fuego Dixon, and Zeke Wyatt constituted the most dominant forecourt in basketball. That trio was outrebounded by 21 in Utah; by 19 in Denver.

Gone is the excitement of the fall, when the Gaters ran off five victories in a row, including a Thanksgiving-eve shellacking of mighty Detroit. The boys with the bridges on their shorts have not won back-to-back games since then.

All of this has not been lost on owner Teddy Brandisi, who is interested in only one thing and that is winning. It is, after all, not half so much fun talking about the fluctuating values of his supermarket chain as it is discussing his team's fortunes—and there no doubt seems a lot more he can do to affect the latter. After all, there are only 12 players and one head coach.

When the team flies off to Houston after tonight's game, they will find waiting for them that son of New York, Dale Rohmer, whose job it is to make a glorious winter for Mr. Brandisi. The last time Rohmer joined the team on a mid-winter road trip, starting point guard Leotis Clark was shucked off to Indianapolis in exchange for a laundry bag, and Rynn Packard was handed the position—supposedly to keep only until a star like Oliver Dawkins arrived. Well, Oliver's here and Rynn's still playing and the team's still losing.

And the question on everybody's mind is, who will pay for the dog days this year? Before you answer, consider this: Not all 12 players are in a position consistently to make a difference in the team's play. On the other hand, none of the Gaters' strengths and weaknesses should have come as a surprise to Coach Sinclair. Indeed, only Oliver Dawkins seems not to have measured up to his expectations.

When expectations are met and success is not, an impatient man like Teddy Brandisi just might find it easier to change the one doing the expecting. As Richard III supposedly said, "It's just a hunch, folks."

# 3

Oliver Dawkins had the column read to him when he called back to San Francisco just before the team left the hotel for the game against Dallas. "You're not going to like this one, honeybunch," Petunia told him. "They're talking about your money again."

It sounded to Oliver that the article was more of a rip on Booby than it was on him, but he tended to defer to Petunia on these sorts of things. He was still paying for the last time he had disagreed with her.

Petunia was a year older than Oliver. She had stayed on at North Carolina State after she graduated, substitute teaching in a local elementary school, just so she could help him get through his senior year with all the distractions she knew he was going to have. She had sat in on the interviews he had conducted with agents, had asked the key questions about fees and percentages and annuities and deferred payments; and in the end she had advised him to pick the lawyer Rosenthal from San Francisco. But Oliver had disagreed. He had insisted on the guy Tresh from Florida who knew his father, the guy who only charged on an hourly basis plus expenses; and she had let him have his way, provided that he bear the burden of knowing forever more that he was making this choice against her better advice.

Tresh had seemed nice enough when he was taking Oliver and Petunia out to dinner and buying them wine and complementing Petunia on her clothes. He had seemed nice enough

20

when he was fronting Oliver a thousand dollars a week while holding him out of training camp. But as the hot summer days rolled by in North Carolina (half maddeningly slow, half inexplicably fast) and Oliver hung out waiting for Tresh to call, he began to like the man less and less.

The GoldenGaters' original offer was one year at $300,000, presented by Dale Rohmer himself. Oliver never actually saw the offer, but Tresh told him about it.

"Man selected as high as you in the draft doesn't take that kind of contract," Tresh told him.

Petunia, for once, agreed with Tresh. "Oliver wants three million for three years," she told him, and that sounded good to Oliver, who had never before had an actual salary and thought that a million a year sounded fair.

June passed, July passed, and the Gaters upped their offer to $500,000 for one year and then a million for two.

"That's going backwards," Tresh told him, and Oliver stayed home and shot in the school gym and sweated through pickup games on outdoor courts, where his friends gave him advice on how to deal with the Gaters and with Tresh, and with Petunia, too.

August passed and the Gaters' rookie camp opened and Oliver was an unhappy man. The Gaters said $750,000 for one year and Tresh said he had to have three years and Petunia said he had to have a million a year regardless of how many years they were willing to give him. Oliver got mad at each of them.

As his friends at the playground constantly reminded him, he was, after all, Oliver Dawkins, ACC Player of the Year, an all-American, most valuable player in the Pan-Am games. They didn't just cheer for him in Raleigh, they sang his name: "Ol-ee-ver Daw-kins," and then the drum would beat and the cheerleaders would dance. "Ol-ee-ver Daw-kins." And they would do it faster and faster until nearly every Wolfpack rooter in the stands was worked into a frenzy. A player of such accomplishments ought not to have his head messed with, his friends told him, and Oliver found himself agreeing.

Money was a matter of respect, and after a while concern

21

about it began to take up a fair share of Oliver's unoccupied time. A nationally known player like him was already a superstar and ought to have nothing but the best—a Mercedes, one of them big BMWs, maybe even a Rolls-Royce; a house with a room just for his pool table; a Rolex watch; designer-name clothes; Johnnie Walker Black, Wild Turkey, Rémy Martin, Heineken; and that fine white powder from Eddie Mac. It was just a matter of time until he could buy all those things. Meanwhile, he could get himself some clothes, drink Michelob instead of Bud, and that fine white powder was free to a guy like him. Everybody was willing to share a little white powder with Oliver Dawkins, and Eddie Mac was happy to give him whatever he wanted just for the privilege of hanging around with him. It was, Eddie Mac explained, good for business when folks saw that a celebrity was using his product.

During September and the first part of October, Oliver stayed away from the campus. The Wolfpack were back in training and it depressed Oliver to see them. He also did not want to run into Coach, who, last time he saw Oliver, told him he was overweight. Oliver did not want to hear it. He knew he was fast. He could feel it. He had never been faster. Quicker. Zoomier. He was zooming all over the playgrounds these days. Besides, he had to be bulky to bang with the big boys he was going to be posting up against in the pros.

Ten days before the season opener Tresh called and said he had done it. The Gaters had caved in, just as Tresh knew they would. Three years for $2 million, only part of it deferred—and the deferral was good because it provided for Oliver's future.

Within twenty-four hours Oliver was in California, where he met Booby Sinclair for the first time. And when he walked into Booby's office, Booby pointed at him, pointed somewhere in the general direction of his upper body, and said, "What's that?" Not "Hello," not "Pleased to meet you," not even "Who's that?" It was, Oliver thought, a no-class way of greeting somebody, and he did not plan to forget it.

Booby and Rohmer took him to a press conference, where Rohmer said they were thrilled to have Oliver in the family and that the terms of the agreement were very fair. Booby said it was going to be tough because Oliver had missed so much of training and the Gaters ran a complicated system of offenses, but all reports were that Oliver was a fast learner and Booby was sure that Oliver would be contributing before long. Oliver sweated under the lights and smiled for the photographers and said he was delighted to be in San Francisco and looking forward to the opportunity to showcase his talents. This last comment caused everybody to glance quickly at him to see what he meant, but he was smiling and sweating and doing his best to look sincere, and so the remark passed without comment or clarification.

That had been months ago, and as far as Oliver was concerned, he was still looking for his opportunity. Coach Sinclair didn't like him. Coach, in fact, was prejudiced against him. Coach liked Rynn Packard because he reminded him of himself. What never was. Short and slow little white boy running around charging into walls and shit like that.

Oliver wasn't playing and the team was losing and now the newspapers were blaming him when there was nothing he could do about it if he couldn't get off the motherfucking bench. Oliver decided, before he left the hotel, that he was going to confront that weasel Colin Cromwell and find out where he was coming from, printing all that bullshit. He decided, just in case he found the chump before the game, that he would do a line or two so that he would be thinking clearly. He knew you had to be quick with a guy like Cromwell.

Oliver listened to Wayne Brickshaw say, "We on? We on?" He stood there shifting his weight from one foot to the other and watching Wayne Brickshaw adjust the knot in his yellow knit tie and he realized that he had been tricked. He had made the mistake of moving in on Cromwell while the writer was talking to old Plastic Head, and the next thing he knew he was being forced into a Brickshaw radio interview. All he had wanted to do was get in Cromwell's face, find out why he was styling on him—and now here he was about to talk on the radio.

Brickshaw's eyes were not focused on anything. They were

23

just little nuggets fixed on distant-hold while he concentrated on listening for the cue that was going to come through the earphone he was wearing.

He got his signal and immediately broke into his announcer's voice—his trademark, good-guy, boy-next-door announcer's voice. "Good evening, everyone, and welcome to Texas, where the GoldenGaters are about to take on red-hot Dallas, in this, the twenty-eighth game of the season. With me tonight as my guest on 'Gaters' Warm-up' is the man who many say is the future of the franchise, number one draft choice and former North Carolina State all-American, Oliver Dawkins. Olivor, how arc you doing tonight?"

The microphone came under his mouth. He had to say something. "S'awright."

"Oliver, I know you were on some long road trips in college and on the Pan-Am team two summers ago and what have you, but this is the Gaters' longest road swing of the year and your first professional trip of any real duration. What's it like for you?"

What's what like? The trip? Not playing? The Pan-Am team? "Wha'chu mean?"

"Well, you know, a trip like this, six cities in ten days, can be exhausting for anyone, especially if it's your first time. How about you, any ill effects so far?"

"You mean, like, am I sick or anything, is that wha'chu saying?"

"Ho, ho! No, Oliver, I mean, like, is there anything about this trip that's different from trips you've been on before, when you were in college and so forth?"

He wanted to be careful. These radio guys made their livings getting people to say shit. "What'd be different?"

". . . Well, I know, for example, that you're recently married, have a beautiful wife, Petunia, who's back in the Bay Area and hopefully listening to our broadcast, and it can be hard on her as well as you. I know with my wife, Cindy, she's got to stay home with her husband gone, try to get the kids off to school in the morning, pick them up again at night, make them their meals—and I try to tell her that as hard as it is for her, it's even

24

harder for us on the road because we're constantly in strange surroundings. . . . Would you agree with me, Oliver?"

He wasn't going to get involved in that. He wasn't going to touch that one. No way. "I don't know what you tell your wife, man."

". . . No. What I'm trying to say, Oliver, and I'm sure you go through this with Petunia, but we have a lot of time to kill out here on the road. The fun part is going to the games, but the rest of the time is just spent traveling, waiting around, and you know, most of that time we're in strange hotels, strange restaurants, and our wives, as bad as it is for them, well, at least they're still in familiar surroundings and they're busy doing the things they have to do anyway. So while we both say we miss each other, I think the fact of the matter is I miss her a whole lot more than she misses me."

Okay, he could handle this. This was just common sense. "I don't know what kind of problems you havin' wit' your wife, man, but if she don't miss you none, I be lookin' into it, I was you."

"No—I'm only saying—I'm sure my wife misses me, Oliver. I'm only saying that these road trips like the one we're on can be very draining, and as tough as it can be for those we leave behind—"

And suddenly Oliver had a whole new vision of what Brickshaw was getting at. And just like that he lost his temper. "Hey, man, you want to get on the radio and talk about problems you havin' wit' your wife, that's your business. You don't need me to do that. I don't even know the lady."

Brickshaw was making a face. His mouth was twisting as if he had a lemon in it or something. Somebody had to speak.

"I thought you be axing me about my playing time. That's why I thought you want to talk to me, man."

". . . Well, folks, that concludes our pregame interview with Oliver Dawkins. Guests on 'Gaters' Warm-up' receive a free gift from Gensler Lee Diamonds, the store with a heart, and three hours of limousine service from Libra Man's Limousines, whose motto is, 'With a touch of class, you get there fast.' "

That was it? That was all he wanted to talk about—his wife?

Oliver was confused. "What am I s'posed to get? A gift certificate?"

"This is Wayne Brickshaw and I'll be back with tonight's starting lineups right after this important commercial message."

The Gaters lost to Dallas by 14 points. Oliver, to his surprise, was called on to play at the end of the first quarter. He tried not to let anyone know how pleased he was to get into a game this early and showed his ease at being on the court by promptly unloading a shot from halfway to the parking lot. It went cleanly through the hoop for 3 points, and some of the staggered Dallas fans actually applauded. By refusing to smile or even acknowledge his teammates' congratulations he hoped to deliver the message that he could hit 3-pointers like that all night if given the chance.

Coach let him start the second quarter and he lost the ball when he dribbled it off his foot. He lost it again on a traveling violation, but it was a bad call and he complained loudly about it. He then stole an in-bounds pass and threw an over the shoulder bullet that Del Fuego caught in midair and jammed through the rim. His teammates liked that. They leaped off the bench roaring and giving each other high fives, and he pretended he didn't notice.

The next time he got his hands on the ball he tried to pass inside to Biltmore, and stupid Biltmore didn't jump and the ball ended up three rows into the stands. Booby blamed him for that and sent him back to the bench, where he remained for the rest of the evening.

# 4

Wayne Brickshaw swirled mouthwash around his teeth and spit it into the sink. He carefully brushed his hair until every last strand was exactly where he wanted it. Wayne knew it was always important to look his best. He knew it was only a matter of time until he was tapped for television, and that he could be spotted anywhere, even in Houston.

He rode the elevator down to the lobby and walked into the bar. He wore a big smile on his face, ready to greet or be greeted, but the only person he even recognized was a woman named Maud, who served as Booby Sinclair's local love interest. Like Kammy in Dallas, Maud wore cowboy boots. Unlike Kammy, she had a New York accent. Wayne had done a double take the first time he heard that hard, nasal torturing of consonants emerging from her soft, barely lipsticked mouth, but it was the genuine article.

Wayne had also done a double take the first time he saw her walk. With her thick black hair and her incredibly tight jeans, she was an impressive-looking woman, and the men in her wake were practically bumping heads in their efforts to get a look at her from behind.

Word had it that she was the ex-wife of an oil baron, but that was an easy story to pass around, and Wayne did not know how much credence to give it. What he did know was that at eleven-thirty on the night the GoldenGaters had lost their eighth straight game, she was sitting by herself at one end of the team's hotel bar, and in Wayne's mind the only reason she could possibly have for doing that was if Booby was upstairs meeting with Rohmer.

Colin Cromwell had written in his column that day that Booby's job was in jeopardy. He had asked rhetorically if Booby hadn't grown weary of trying to motivate millionaires, adolescents, and egomaniacs. Wayne knew that Cromwell had good contacts, good sources of information, and that he often found out about things before they actually happened. He wondered if Colin's column meant that Booby was at that very moment up in Rohmer's room fighting for his survival. That would explain why Maud was being so patient, never checking her watch or doing anything more than sipping her drink and lighting an occasional cigarette.

Wayne liked the way she smoked cigarettes. He liked the way she put one in the middle of her lips and sucked deeply and then tilted her head back and blew the smoke out of everyone else's way. And Wayne was a man who hated cigarette smoke.

He wanted to approach her, and the more he drank the more lines he thought to use: "Hi, come here often? Nice seat you have there. This sure is a great bar. This sure is a crummy bar. This reminds me of the casbah. You waiting for someone? I'm Wayne Brickshaw, famous sports commentator. Broadcaster. Play-by-play man. Radio show host. You're one of Booby Sinclair's girls, aren't you? You're his mistress, aren't you? Say, do you like Hemingway? How about Bryant Gumbel? You look like someone I know. You look like my sister. My daughter. My sister and my daughter. You wouldn't know where a guy could get a nice leg of lamb around here, would you?"

A voice broke into his silent monologue, a male voice asking, "You from out of town?"

Wayne popped some peanuts into his mouth from a little bowl that was placed on the bar to make customers thirsty and took his time deciding whether to answer. He did not want to trade lines with some strange man. He wanted to trade them with Maud. He gave a quick glance at his inquisitor, nodded, and looked away again.

The man wore a light colored business suit. He was a friendly sort, of the kind that fill Houston hotel bars. He was not offensive looking by any means, but he reeked of alcohol. "Where from?" the man asked, as if he had every expectation that Wayne was dying to tell someone.

"San Francisco," Wayne said after an appropriate pause.

"Oh." The stranger fell back on his heels. It was, Wayne suspected, an involuntary motion and not entirely due to the fact that he was surprised. "You with the Gaters?"

Now it was Wayne who was surprised. "Sort of," he admitted. And then almost casually, he added, "I cover them."

"Do I know your name?"

Wayne, his mouth refilled with peanuts, said, "I give up. Do you?"

There was nobody to laugh at this little spot of cleverness, and after a moment or two Wayne glanced up to see the friendly man was still staring at him in a friendly manner, still awaiting a friendly response. He told him the truth.

The man smiled. He thrust out his hand and immediately Wayne regretted that he had not stuck to being rude.

"Trey Wilson," the man said. "Montgomery, Alabama."

Wayne had been in Montgomery once. He had covered a college all-star football game there, a Blue-Gray or a North-South game, and he made no effort to remember which because it would have given the game more importance than it deserved. What he did remember was that the city had a wheelchair ramp at every sidewalk corner, and he had wondered at the time if they had been put in to accommodate Governor Wallace. He chose not to mention those landmarks, as memorable as they were, and simply gave the man a handshake, one in which he did the squeezing and pulled back before the man could get in a squeeze of his own. He wanted the man to leave him alone.

But Trey Wilson was not finished with him yet. "You're the 'Voice of the Gaters,' " he said.

Wayne's head jerked around. The man was a fan.

Trey Wilson smiled. "I travel a lot," he explained. "I give seminars."

Wayne said, "That's nice," but he did not ask what kind of seminars Wilson gave because he still did not want to encourage the man—not when there still remained the possibility of

29

getting to meet Maud of Houston. It crossed his mind just to stand up, go to the end of the bar where Maud was sitting, and say, "Mind if I move down here? That loudmouth in the suit has been driving me crazy." She would know the feeling. Perhaps she would smile at him. Smile sweetly, and he could respond with all manner of *bons mots*: "So, where you from? Come here often? You wouldn't happen to know if your boyfriend is about to get fired, would you?"

"Yep," the undaunted Trey Wilson was saying, "I follow basketball. In fact, played a little hoops myself once upon a time." Then he laughed: "Har, har, har."

At that moment Colin Cromwell walked into the bar. Wayne instinctively raised his hand, but Colin had already focused on the dark-haired woman sitting alone at the end of the bar, and he blew right past Wayne as if he were not even there.

Somehow Trey Wilson had managed to signal the bartender, and Wayne, to his dismay, found himself being presented with another bourbon and soda while Wilson told him how he had played against a guy named Willie Smith when he was in high school. "Ya'll ever heard of Willie Smith?" Wilson wanted to know.

Wayne stared despondently at Cromwell as he wedged himself next to Maud, smiling the creepy smile he was always using to pick up women. "No," Wayne muttered.

He wondered where Cromwell got the nerve. He wasn't what you would call a good-looking guy. He was skinny and wore glasses and never wore ties or cuff links or shined his shoes. Yet there he was, walking straight up to beautiful women and engaging them in conversation, while Wayne himself, wearing a brand-new raspberry-colored, suede sport coat, sat talking high school exploits with a simpleminded rube.

He envisioned a scene: Cromwell leeringly drawing closer and closer to Maud until finally he was whispering obscenities into her ear, Maud drawing back in shock and distress, and himself racing the length of the bar to throw his body between them, to comfort her against his chest and protect her from the vile winds of Cromwell's heavy breathing.

Or better yet, he wouldn't need to wait for Cromwell to get

30

offensive. He could just walk down and issue greetings. Say hello to Cromwell and meet the luscious Maud. Except that Cromwell would hiss at him. "Hello, Waynie, old buddy," he would say. "How are your wife and kids?" Cromwell could be ruthless.

Wayne stared unhappily at his new drink. He hadn't asked for it and there was no reason why he had to drink it just to be polite. There was no reason why he had to treat the guy who bought it any differently from the way he treated phone solicitors who called him up and tried to get him to buy tickets for poor children to go to bogus circuses. "Look—"

But Wilson was talking again. "Yeah, well, you just ask W.E.B. Pancake about ol' Willie Smith. Just mention that name to him. See what he says."

Wayne caught a movement out of the corner of his eye. The raven-haired Maud was getting to her feet. Had Cromwell gotten lewd already? But no, she was saying good-bye to him, and he was trying to hold his smile, his I-got-the-devil-in-my-pants smile, and she was gathering up her purse. She looked to the front of the bar and Wayne spun in that direction. Booby Sinclair was standing there and his hand was in the air as if he had just beckoned to someone.

Booby's eyes slid from Maud to Wayne, but they showed no recognition when they landed, and they flicked away just as easily as if Wayne were a bus he didn't want. There was nothing about his demeanor that indicated whether he had just been fired or given a lifetime extension on his contract. He turned and walked out to the lobby, and a moment later Maud hurried through the door after him. Wayne could not stop himself. His own eyes went from Booby's back to Maud's behind. It was worth it. It was an absolutely exquisite behind.

Trey Wilson's hand closed over Wayne's biceps, summoning his attention. Wayne looked up angrily and Wilson smiled.

"By the way, Wayne, how old would you say W.E.B. Pancake is?"

Wayne tried to remove his arm, but the man still had hold of it. "I know how old he is. He's thirty-three."

Wilson nodded, almost sadly. "How old do you think I am?"

31

Wayne responded with a look designed to ask the man why Wayne could possibly care. Trey Wilson, however, was not easily put off. He slapped Wayne on the back and let loose with a hearty laugh that displayed all the good-natured bonhomie one could possibly expect from a drunk in a suit.

"Oh, don't go trying to flatter me now. I don't look much different from what I am, so this isn't gonna be one of them things where you have to say, 'Oh, wow, I don't believe it.' "

Wilson had sandy hair turning gray and receding leisurely from his forehead. He had lines etched into the skin at the corners of his eyes. "Forty," said Wayne meanly.

"Thirty-eight," said Trey, howling at the wonder of it all. "And I played against ol' Willie Smith three years running when I was in high school in Anniston. You tell W.E.B. that, now, hear? You tell him you ran into somebody who remembers Willie Smith from high school and see how he reacts."

Wilson's laughter grew as he tilted his head back and pointed his chin at the ceiling. Wayne would have been afraid that he was going to tip over, except at that moment Colin drifted by on his way out of the bar. Wayne's hand shot out and caught him. "What's the word on Booby?"

"No word," said Colin, which may or may not have been true. One journalist was hardly going to give another a lead. Even if they were in different media.

Wilson had stopped laughing and was listening, his eyes wide and rolling as they went from Wayne to Colin and back again. When Wayne saw that, he slid off his stool.

"Here," he said to Colin, "meet a friend of mine, Trey Wilson from Montgomery, Alabama. Take my seat. Have my drink. Ask Trey about ol' Willie Smith."

Then Wayne Brickshaw, the Voice of the Gaters, literally fled from the bar. He figured that was the least he could do to pay Colin back for sticking him with that freak Oliver Dawkins up in Dallas.

# 5

Rohmer said, "Sit down, Bill."

Rohmer was smoking a cigarette. He had a two-room suite that did not look big enough for him. The whole place was a mess.

Rynn Packard was surprised to hear Dale Rohmer call him Bill. It was a team nickname that he suspected was derogatory, and that had only come about because Marty Smart had once written a column in the *Chronicle* calling him the best player to come out of the Ivy League since Bill Bradley. After that, W.E.B. Pancake, who had gone to a very small and very black and very poor school in the South, had decided it was only right to call Rynn by the same name as the senator from New Jersey. The other guys had picked up on it, and Rynn had let it go on the off chance that having a nickname might somehow make him a little more acceptable to his teammates, and to W.E.B. in particular.

But when it came to Rohmer, who had gone to Syracuse and who presumably knew that Brown was not just a color, that there was a difference between Penn and Penn State, and that there was another Columbia besides the place that produced cocaine, Rynn would have liked to have been addressed by his real name. Except Rynn was not saying anything. He was too nervous.

He told himself that the worst that could happen was that the team was trading him. He had to be one of the lowest-paid starters in the league. Somebody had to want him. There were teams out there desperate for a white guy who could play this game. And a trade wouldn't be bad. How many teams were worse than the Gaters? He was single. He didn't own a home. He didn't have any particular friends in San Francisco. He could go anywhere.

"You want a drink?" Rohmer asked, peering through the smoke of his cigarette.

Dale Rohmer was a twelve-year veteran player with three championship rings in his wardrobe. His uniform hung from the rafters of two different arenas: Boston, where it belonged, and Cleveland, where they had once needed an event to celebrate in order to attract a crowd for a meaningless game in his final season as a player. He had served as head coach at Phoenix and later at Seattle before briefly retiring from the game because of an ulcer, and then returning as Teddy Brandisi's general manager. And he was a fearsome presence as far as Rynn Packard was concerned.

Rynn shook his head.

"Scotch? Bourbon? Gin? Vodka? . . . Beer? You like beer?"

Rohmer seemed anxious to get him to drink something and Rynn decided it was better to nod than to listen to him continue to recite the names of alcoholic beverages.

Rohmer walked behind a freestanding bar, pulled a green bottle from a refrigerator, inspected it for a moment, and then jacked off the top. "You want a glass?" he said, gazing around as if he knew that such things existed but was damned if he knew what they looked like.

Rynn surveyed the room because that was what Rohmer was doing. There were newspapers all over the couch; plates, coffee cups, warming covers, and an ice bucket on the coffee table; a sweater, a jacket, a coat, and a tie on the various chairs. There were a pair of spent socks lying on the carpet. A bulging wallet and a plane ticket were on a lamp table. But there were no glasses anywhere.

Rynn walked over and took the bottle out of Rohmer's hand. He went to the couch, pushed aside some papers, and sat down. Rohmer waited, staring at him thoughtfully. Rynn was sure now that he was about to be told his employment with the Gaters was at an end. He drank the beer without tasting it.

"You like that beer?" Rohmer asked.

Rynn nodded and then felt like a little kid drinking a milk shake. The thought chastened him. "What is it you want to tell me, Dale?" Rynn cleared his throat, illogically concerned for a moment that he might have jinxed himself with that question, that he might have hastened his demise. "Why did you call me up here?"

Rohmer took another deep breath of smoke and chemicals and grabbed the elbow of his smoking arm. "Bill, what's wrong with this team?"

Rynn, taken aback, said, "I don't know what you mean."

"You don't, huh?" Dale Rohmer suddenly seemed on the verge of apoplexy. It was one of his most familiar looks. He had an incredibly expressive face, and Rynn, who was used to watching him from a distance, was never sure whether it served as a mirror of his emotions or merely a tool of his act. "The team's lost eight in a row, we're practically in last place, and I hear you and Del Fuego nearly duked it out up in Dallas. What was that all about?"

Rynn took another sip of beer. The butterflies in his stomach had landed, but they were ready to take off again at a moment's notice. "Frustration."

He thought it was a good answer, but Rohmer literally roared in response. "Bullshit! I played over a thousand of these games, buddy. I know what a team looks like when it's disintegrating. This team, this fucking team's going through the motions. Mr. Brandisi, back in Boston, he gets the paper every morning. First thing he looks for is to see how his boys're doing. You know what he sees? He sees you lost. Dixon gets twenty-five points, Pancake gets a dozen boards, Miller's got three steals, and Packard's got ten assists. 'So how come my boys're losing?' he wants to know. You know what he thinks, don't you?"

"No," Rynn answered truthfully.

"Huh? Sure you do. He thinks it's Booby's fault. You think it's Booby's fault, Bill?"

"No."

"Then whose fault is it?"

The butterflies surged again. "Well, it's not mine."

Rohmer looked for a place to throw his cigarette butt. He opted for the ice bucket. "You got to think the way Mr. Brandisi thinks," he said, suddenly calm again. "He knows his team's losing and he knows it isn't his fault. He's pretty sure it isn't mine, out there in the home office. So he figures it's gotta be his coach's fault. If I tell him no—because no matter what that asshole Colin Cromwell writes in his paper, I happen to think Booby Sinclair knows his basketball as good as anybody I ever met—then Mr. Brandisi says, 'Well, if it isn't the coach's fault, then it's gotta be the field general's fault.' And that's you, bubba."

Rynn stared, unable to do anything but grip his bottle as tightly as he could.

Rohmer began pacing back and forth. "Now Mr. Brandisi, he doesn't really care whose fault it is as long as he can find it's somebody's fault. He'd love—what he'd love to do is find it's Booby's fault because he and Booby don't exactly see eye to eye on how to stock a basketball team, if you know what I mean. But I'm not about to let him get rid of Booby if I can help it because then he'd be all over me to coach and I'm not ever going to step into that pile of shit again." He stopped pacing and hitched his pants. "Ho, ho, ho, no," he said for emphasis, just as if it were Rynn who was trying to make him step into that pile of shit.

"Brandisi doesn't really have anything against you, Bill, not personally. But see, he's hardly ever heard of you so you don't mean that much to him, either. Besides, if he sits you down, he can play Oliver Dawkins, and he's got a couple of million rapped up in that kid."

Rohmer strode to the window and stopped there, perhaps for dramatic effect. "So, realizing I like my job and all just the way it is, what do you think I'm gonna tell him, Bill? You tell me what to say to him when he says somebody's gotta take the fall for losing."

Rynn Packard, knowing that he was being manipulated, knowing that he was playing right into Rohmer's hands, still went ahead and said, "You've got some alternatives, Dale, besides me and Booby."

But Dale Rohmer shook his big head. "None that I want to hear. You want to blame Pancake? He may have been around awhile, but it seems to me he's still playing as well as ever. Zeke, maybe. I've got my complaints about him, but we've got nobody on the bench to take his place, and none of the other GMs around the league been exactly chanting his name at me when I try to talk trades."

Rynn was silent. He rubbed the bottle between his palms.

"Larry Miller?" Rohmer asked, and then answered his own question. "Larry's a rock. Everybody should be like Larry."

The label was beginning to peel away on Rynn's bottle. He waited for Rohmer to go on to the next name.

"Well, you can forget it, Bill, if that's what you're thinking," Rohmer said at last.

He studied Rynn's reaction. He ran his hand through his red hair and left some of it standing on end. "You want to hear a story? . . . Good, I tell good stories."

He hitched up his pants again. He patted his chest pocket, then walked around the room feeling his clothes until he found an opened pack of cigarettes. "When Mr. Brandisi and I took over, and I say that with all due modesty, the Bancroft family had practically run this operation into the ground. For two years in a row they hadn't been able to sign their number one draft choice, and the only thing that was holding this team together was Booby, and he was doing it with smoke and mirrors—running ten, sometimes twelve men in and out of the game, playing three or four guards at a time, trying full-court presses . . . whatever it took to be competitive with a bunch of underpaid malcontents."

Rohmer got a cigarette in his mouth and then began pulling his pockets inside out in search of a match. "Mr. Brandisi tells Booby to go after whoever he needs to make a winner, and then sits back and waits for the results to put him on the cover of *Sports Illustrated*. So what does Booby do? He drafts a little-known defensive specialist from Oregon named Larry Miller, which only goes to show how brilliant the man is, but Mr. Brandisi—he shits. I don't suppose you got a match, do you?"

Rynn confessed that he did not.

Regretfully, Rohmer took the unlit cigarette from his mouth and tossed it onto the coffee table. "Mr. Brandisi explained that he could understand that players like Larry Miller have their value, but he felt that sometimes you have to sell the sizzle to get people to eat the bacon. Or something like that. Mr. Brandisi likes to use these little sayings that have food in 'em. So Teddy let Booby have his Larry Miller, and then he went out on his own and engineered a trade for Del Fuego Dixon."

Rohmer sniffed. "This did not make Booby very happy because Del Fuego is not exactly Booby's kind of basketball player. Booby much prefers what you call your overachievers. Booby complained, and that's putting it mildly. I explained to him that this was not my idea and he insisted on speaking to the boss himself. The conversation went something like this."

Rohmer made an elaborate pantomime of putting a phone to his ear. " 'Hello, Mr. Brandisi? This is Booby Sinclair, the coach of your basketball team? . . . Yes, sir, the GoldenGaters, out in San Francisco. I just wanted to tell you, sir, I can't have Del Fuego Dixon playing for me.' "

Rohmer shifted his imaginary phone to his other ear. He flattened his tone and commenced a parody of a Boston accent. " 'The name, Bob, the name alone is worth a hundred thousand seats during the coss of a yeah.' "

He shifted again. " 'Booby, sir, and we already got a guy with a funny name, Mr. Brandisi. W.E.B. Pancake. You can't get much funnier than that.' "

" 'I'm talking about a famous name, Bobby. Everybody knows who Del Fuego is. Why, I remembah hearing about him when he was in high school.' "

Rohmer let his Booby voice grow higher and higher. " 'Which is exactly why he's no good today, Mr. Brandisi. He was a star when he was sixteen and he never developed into a team player.' "

Rohmer's pale eyes grew wide with mock indignation. " 'He was an all-American at UCLA.' "

Rohmer grabbed a fistful of his hair as he shrieked, " 'Says a bunch of reporters. You get the entire UCLA publicity department jamming you to the media every day and you'll get some votes, too.' "

" 'Somebody liked him. He was the first draft choice in the whole league.' "

" 'And now his team is willing to trade him for three guys who have never even played a league game—the two draft choices that we couldn't sign and next year's number one, and they don't even know who that is. Doesn't that tell you something?' "

Suddenly Rohmer stopped his playacting. He put down his pretend prop and gazed intently at Rynn. "Am I getting through to you at all, Bill?"

Rynn, who had been watching in fascination, who had not expected to be quizzed at that particular moment, put his beer down and spread his hands uncertainly.

Rohmer looked disappointed. "Then let me give it to you straight, Bill. Del Fuego Dixon is here because Mr. Brandisi wants him. This is Mr. Brandisi's team and what Mr. Brandisi wants, Mr. Brandisi gets. You are not high on Mr. Brandisi's list of wants. You, we can sit down. You can drift off and nobody's going to get too excited. You, as long as you are starting, may think of yourself as a valuable commodity, but if I put your ass on the bench, if I tell Booby to put your ass on the bench, you are just another token white boy who's stealin' a seat that belongs to some poor black kid." He bent his elbow and cocked his finger as if he were throwing a dart. "Now do you understand what I'm saying?"

"Yes."

"What?"

Rynn could not come up with an answer. He had thought it necessary only to agree, but now Rohmer was staring at him incredulously. "Look, Dale, just tell me what it is you want and I'll do it." Rynn could hear a pleading note in his voice and did not like it. Once again he tried to clear his throat.

"I want you, Rynn, to pull this team together."

39

Rynn's tongue swelled in his mouth. It caught between his teeth. It flubbed the words he tried to use.

"The point guard is the quarterback of the team, the man who directs play on the court," Rohmer said. "To be an effective point guard you have to be a leader. And you can't be a leader unless you get along with the other players, Bill. To do that you have to become one of them. You have to stop being so standoffish and elitist."

Rynn's face flushed. He tried desperately to say something meaningful to this man who stood so confidently before him and who so completely misunderstood the situation. "Look, Dale, the players, the other guys . . . I think they trust me out on the floor, but . . . you know, to some extent this is Pancake's team and to some extent it's Del's—"

Rohmer cut him off. "This is not about Pancake. If you play hard, play well, he will respect you, and that's all you can ever hope to get out of him. But Del Fuego is a different matter. To run this team on the floor you cannot be at odds with Del Fuego because Del Fuego is our star. I know this because Mr. Brandisi tells me so, and Mr. Brandisi pays all our salaries. Therefore, if you are a smart boy, which I think you are, you will find a way to get along with Del. Because, my friend, Del Fuego Dixon is not sitting down and he is not leaving, and so if you don't want to sit down and you don't want to leave, you will learn to play to his strengths and cover his weaknesses. When you leave the court, you will give him high fives and tell him he has nice shoes and ask to borrow his rap music. You will, in other words, do everything you can to become Mr. Dixon's asshole buddy, and in the process you will gain his confidence and he will let you do what you have to do to make this team play winning basketball."

Rynn made one last attempt at escape. "What if Del isn't interested in becoming buddies? I mean, he's pretty tight with Zeke and Gilbert and Earl—"

Dale Rohmer folded his arms. "You leave that to me. All you need to know is that Del will have his own incentive to cooperate. A different incentive than yours, maybe, but an incentive nonetheless."

Rynn shook his head. "I don't know—"

Rohmer's arms exploded outward. "Of course you don't know. If you did, you could be the fucking general manager and there wouldn't be any need for me."

Rynn grabbed for his beer bottle, locked two fingers around its neck and tilted it to his mouth. When he was done drinking, Rohmer was looming over him, waiting for some kind of response. Rynn said, "Right, Dale." He tried to smile and hoped that the result looked like something more than just a crack in his face.

# 6

Curtis Clovis was well aware that he had never quite worked out. Of the twelve players on the Gaters, only Del Fuego Dixon and Oliver Dawkins had gone higher in the draft than he had. He had been the first pick of Milwaukee after a fine career at the University of New Mexico, where the team's offense had been built around his ability to muscle his way to the basket and where the team's defense had been nonexistent.

When Curtis had not been able to muscle his way through the bigger, stronger, meaner front courts of professional basketball, his poor outside shooting and his relative lack of experience at stopping other people from scoring had left him with little value to his team. When his "no-cut" contract ran out, so did Milwaukee.

Curtis, who had been a star virtually his entire life, who ever since he could remember had always had his time, his seasons, his living arrangements, scheduled for him by basketball and those who wanted him to play basketball, suddenly found himself without a thing in the world to do. He stayed in Milwaukee watching television and waiting for his telephone to ring. He waited for four months and the only calls he got were from San Francisco where his agent, Reynolds Rosenthal, was uniformly unsuccessful in placing him with any other team in the league. And so Curtis, not knowing what else to do, called his old college coach and asked for help. The coach, perhaps because it was his best contact, got Curtis a tryout with Boston, who did not exactly need a small forward, much less a former number one pick with a bad rep; and Curtis, to compound the situation, showed up at the team's summer camp twenty pounds overweight from his months of inactivity. He was gone in two days.

Back to Albuquerque he went, working out with the Lobos while he resumed pursuit of elusive credits toward a degree. Reynolds Rosenthal kept calling around and asking for tryouts. Any time a small forward went down with any sort of injury, Rosenthal was on the phone offering Curtis's services. And then, finally, Washington gave him a ten-day contract at the league's minimum salary.

They were surprised by him in Washington. They were expecting a prima donna and when they didn't get one, they watched him warily. He hardly played at all, but they signed him to a second ten-day contract and began to give indications that they liked him. Then someone unexpectedly came off the injured-reserved list and they told Curtis they were sorry, but that they were not going to be able to keep him. Six days later, Reynolds Rosenthal found Curtis living in a motel on the outskirts of the capital. It was not a very nice motel and by the time Rosenthal arrived Curtis had made it worse by accumulating empty beer cans, pizza boxes, and McDonald's styrofoam hamburger cartons.

Reynolds Rosenthal promptly threw all the food containers into the bathtub and pulled the shower curtain. He then took his camera and snapped as many photographs as he could of Curtis and the squalid room, and he made sure that almost every photo showed the beer cans—a dozen of them, arranged and rearranged so that there appeared to be three or four times as many as there actually were. Brandishing this evidence, he went directly to the commissioner's office and talked league officials into entering Curtis into a substance abuse program in Van Nuys, California.

Curtis, who had no particular substance abuse problem and nowhere else to go, entered the clinic gladly, and the league issued a solemn pronouncement about its commitment to fine young men of character and talent. A spokesperson looked into the nightly news cameras and announced that the league had a responsibility to rehabilitate Curtis Clovis.

Whatever public relations benefit the league scored with this humanitarian action was offset by the fact that it was suddenly inundated by requests from former players who insisted that the only reason they weren't still playing was because they had fallen victim to cocaine, crack, alcohol, or fatty foods. They all wanted a chance to be rehabilitated just like Curtis. None was given the opportunity, and after thirty days Curtis himself was back on the street, pronounced fit and dependency free, and now only in need of the chance the league spokesperson had mentioned.

Teddy Brandisi, likening Curtis to a cyclically depressed stock, ordered Rohmer to sign him—and suddenly there he was, twelfth man on a twelve-man squad, but back in the league again with nobody saying anything bad about him.

Unfortunately, two and a half months after his return, not too many people were saying anything good about him either. He was averaging about 3 points and 1 rebound a game, most of it coming in garbage time, and he sometimes went as long as a week without getting to play. He was, therefore, quite unprepared for the announcement that he would be starting the San Antonio game.

The announcer began speaking over the public address system. Sounding like a bass-voiced circus ringmaster, he went through some welcoming remarks and then proclaimed, "And now, the starting lineup for the visiting San Fran-cis-co Goldennn-Gaters!"

There was a smattering of boos as the Gaters gathered in something of a circle around Booby for the individual introductions.

"At center . . ." The announcer dragged the second word out, creating suspense where there was none. Then he began throwing out clues. "Standing six feet ten inches tall, in his eleventh year from Jones-Henry College . . . number forty-five . . . W.E.B. Pan-cake!" He accentuated the natural pauses between each of Pancake's initials and fell into the same cadence he would have used if he were saying, "Hip, hip, hip, hoo-ray!" And the crowd chanted right along with him.

"At point guard, in his second year from Cornell, standing six foot one, number ten, Rynn Packard."

No chant this time. There were only a few claps as Rynn jogged out to the visiting team's foul line and slapped hands loosely with W.E.B., who was still in his gold and white warm-ups, and who was rolling his neck and gazing disinterestedly around the upper reaches of the arena.

"At off guard, in his third year from Oregon, at six feet five inches tall, number twenty-four, Lar-ry Mil-ler!"

The reaction to Larry was about the same as it was for Rynn. He trotted out and pressed both hands into Rynn's and slapped loosely with W.E.B., just as Rynn had done.

"At one forward"—anybody who had been following the Gaters' season knew what was coming next—"at six feet ten inches tall, in his second year from the University of Nevada at Las Vegas"—but what they heard instead was—"at six feet eight inches tall, from the University of New Mexico, in his fifth year, number thirty-five, Cur-tis Clo-vis."

It had been a long time since Curtis had received that kind of introduction, and he was excited to hear his own name, excited enough to ignore the unmistakable mass shuffling of feet in the stands as people strained to see if they had heard correctly. Stripped to his shorts and game jersey, his limbs already damp with perspiration, Curtis lifted himself from the bench and ran out to join his three teammates. He was barely onto the court when a deep foghorn of a voice hollered, "Hey, Clovis, why don't you get a job, you lazy bum?"

There was no reason why that voice should have affected him. But one moment he was smiling and his eyes were seeking W.E.B.'s, and the next moment his toe caught and he stumbled. He did not fall, but a couple of thousand throats filled with laughter nonetheless, and the foghorn, delighted with what he had caused, laughed loudest of all.

"Write when you get work, Clovis," the foghorn shouted, and the laughter increased as Curtis, the sweat suddenly cold on his body, took his place with the other starters. He had forgotten to slap hands, and first Rynn and then Larry Miller reached over and gave him a little pop on the palm.

The public address announcer roared out the fifth and final introduction. "And at the other forward . . . standing six feet nine, in his ninth year from UCLA, num-bah eeee-leven, Del . . . Fuego . . . Dixon."

The noise that had started with Curtis surged into a swell of boos and cheers, and Del Fuego, moving with all the speed of an office worker going to sharpen a pencil, sauntered out, did the loose slap with W.E.B., high-fived with Rynn, higher-fived with Larry, and lightly passed his hand across Curtis's. Almost immediately he turned around and led the group back to the bench, and while the announcer was still calling out the names of coaches Booby Sinclair, Mike Hacker, and Mel Dykstra, Del Fuego went straight to Zeke Wyatt and double-high-fived with him. Then he turned and directed his tea-colored eyes into the impassive, pale-colored ones of Dale Rohmer, who stood like a monument in front of his seat, his arms folded, just three rows behind the Gaters' bench.

From where Curtis was standing he could see it plainly, see the unspoken messages that passed. Del had his friends, his crew, sure, and Curtis was not one of them—but he had never done anything to offend Del, and now here he was, caught in some sort of war he didn't understand between Del and Mr. Rohmer. He resolved he would just have to play hard, harder than ever before. Maybe look for ways to feed Del the ball. Del would like that. He wouldn't complain about Curtis if Curtis was getting him the ball.

At halftime the Gaters were up by 8. That was, Curtis thought with some satisfaction, the exact number of points he had scored. He had played most of the first quarter, and Zeke, who had 4 points at the half, had played most of the second. For the first time all season Curtis had made a difference.

In the third quarter, with Curtis back in, the Gaters increased their lead, helped by Earl Putnam, who came off the bench and hit a pair of 3-pointers. But in the fourth quarter San Antonio made its run.

Curtis knew that it was his fault. San Antonio's surge started as soon as Jerome Crown, its six-foot-eleven-inch bad boy, entered the game. Jerome, who, despite his prodigious talents, normally spent more time in his coach's doghouse than on the floor, posted up on him. Curtis did not score another basket the rest of the way. Jerome held his shirt. He held his shorts. He leaned on him, and when Curtis leaned back, he slid out of the way, causing Curtis to crash to the floor. He hit Curtis with an elbow and drew a foul. He hit him with his hips and got away with it. He hand-checked by driving his fingers into Curtis's ribs, and he kneed Curtis over and over in the exact same spot in the thigh. And all the while he was doing this, he jabbered at Curtis. He talked constantly, questioning Curtis's strength, his courage, his manhood.

Curtis pushed back. He held his ground. He said nothing in return. But his skin burned and his body ached from the abuse he was taking. By the time Booby removed him from the game, he had picked up 3 more points on foul shots and could not keep himself from limping. Jerome Crown, the man he was responsible for guarding, had scored 14 points and San Antonio had cut the gap to 4.

With two minutes left in the game San Antonio tied it up and Booby Sinclair walked down to the end of the bench, down to where Curtis was sitting with his warm-up jacket over his shoulders, a towel around his neck. Curtis's heart beat faster. If Coach wanted him to go back in to face Jerome with the game on the line, he would do it. Yes. That was what he was being paid to do. If Jerome elbowed him, he would just elbow back. If Jerome said bad things, he would ignore him. That's right. Play his own game. That was the best strategy with someone like Jerome.

But Booby walked right past him. Booby put his hand to his mouth. He looked at each of the players on the bench and then he pointed, not to Curtis but to the player seated next to Curtis, Earl Putnam. "Go in for Rynn," he said, and Oliver Dawkins spit out a cuss word and even Earl was so surprised that it took him a moment to react. Directing the team in the closing

47

moments with the game on the line was not something Earl Putnam was used to doing.

Earl ran to the scorer's table, ripping off his sweats as he went. The buzzer sounded and Earl pointed at Rynn, and now Rynn looked shocked. He started to protest, but then he held his tongue and Curtis was not surprised. Rynn was a good guy. He had probably never talked back to a coach in his life. When he came over and sat down in Earl's seat, Curtis patted him on the knee and said something nice to him. He knew how Rynn felt.

With a minute forty to go, Earl hit on his third 3-pointer of the game. The game was tied when he did that, and Curtis thought that a shot from beyond the 3-point line was not what the situation demanded. He exchanged silent glances with Rynn and knew that Rynn felt the same way.

San Antonio scored on its possession. W.E.B. missed a lay-up, and San Antonio got the rebound and went back down to its end of the court to score again and take the lead for the first time in the game. The Gaters played for the last shot. They kept the ball moving around until, with just seconds remaining on the clock, Earl saw what he thought was an opening. He drove, sprang high in the air, and Jerome Crown rose up (like Godzilla, Curtis thought) and swatted the ball right back in his face.

It bounced off Earl's forehead. It soared high in the air. Arms reached, fingers stretched. The horn blew to end the game and San Antonio had 108 points to the Gaters' 107.

The radio in the training room was tuned to the station that had broadcast the game, and San Antonio's play-by-play announcer was interviewing the star of the contest. "Jerome," he said, "for a while there the Gaters seemed to have things pretty much their way. Then the game turned around just about the time you went in to cover Curtis Clovis. Would you agree with that assessment?"

"Yeah, well, I know Curtis. I pretty much know what he like and what he don't like."

"You seemed to get pretty physical there at a couple of points. Was that part of the strategy?"

"Shhee . . . well, you know, I was just trying to keep him away from the basket. That's all."

"Of course, Curtis was getting a lot of playing time tonight that normally goes to Zeke Wyatt, and Coach Sinclair might have just been trying to shake things up on that Gater team, which has lost, what, nine in a row? But tell me, were you surprised to see Curtis Clovis out there when he was?"

"Well . . . shhee . . . I didn't mind, if you know what I mean."

Then Jerome laughed. The notes of his laughter filled the training room. One or two of the Gaters quickly glanced Curtis's way, but Curtis, who was getting the tape cut off his ankles by Crabbie, pretended he heard nothing.

"Ignorant bastard," said Crabbie. But he was muttering to himself, and Curtis pretended he did not hear that either.

# 7

In Phoenix fifteen minutes before the scheduled start of practice, only one man was shooting at the visitors' basket. The shooter's thigh was heavily taped. To those few people who were watching him as he moved around the court, it was quite obvious that he was testing his leg. It was also quite obvious that he was not happy with the results.

About the time Rynn Packard and Oliver Dawkins and Tim Biltmore came onto the court, the shooter gave up and headed back to the dressing room. He stopped long enough to exchange a few words with Rynn, to gesture with his open hand toward the bandage, and shake his head disgustedly.

Among those who saw this exchange was a very tall man wearing a thin, zippered jacket and an Irish country cap. He had a pockmarked face that made him appear older than he was, and a belly that looked soft and large and out of place, as if he were not used to carrying it around. He had been standing off to one side when Curtis was alone on the floor, but when the other men came out, he moved to a position behind the Gaters' bench, where he stood motionlessly with his hands in the pockets of his khaki-colored pants.

"Hey, Tim," he said after a while.

Rynn Packard glanced over. "Tim" sounded like "Rynn."

The man smiled a bit, a self-conscious smile. He indicated, mostly with his shoulder, toward Biltmore, who was directly under the basket and practicing his tap-ins. "Get Tim, will ya?"

Rynn stared. He had a ball in his hands and he bounced it warily. But the man was tall, tall as a player, and he seemed to know whom he was asking for, so Rynn called Biltmore's name and motioned with his head toward the bench.

Tim Biltmore turned, his face an open question. Then it blossomed into a grin so wide that Rynn looked again to see what was going on. "Goddamn," said Biltmore, "Neil Novaceski, how you doin', bud?"

Neil Novaceski watched Rynn Packard and Oliver Dawkins exchange looks. He figured they knew the farting story. He figured that's why they smiled when they caught each other's eye. He figured fuck them.

Biltmore loped across the floor and wrapped his long arms around him. Neil felt embarrassed, but pleased nonetheless. Biltmore was truly glad to see him, and up here where their heads were, they were all alone.

"What the hell are you doing, big guy?"

"Ah, I got a job with a restaurant chain." Neil had rehearsed it. That was just the way he wanted to say it.

"No shit? Doin' what?"

"I'm, like, their produce inspector."

Biltmore, who surely had no inkling as to what a produce inspector was, responded as if Neil had just told him he was president of the World Bank. "Really? That's great."

Neil nodded. He did not know what else to do. He hoped no more questions would be asked. They were still in a semi-embrace, still smiling directly into each other's face. "So how's it goin' with you guys?" Neil asked, and then, catching himself, he added, "Pretty rough, I guess, huh?"

Tim Biltmore said, "Eh, you know," and continued to smile without measurable concern.

Neil was the first to break physical contact. He dropped his hands to his pants pockets and rocked back on his heels. "What's the story with Zeke?" he said gruffly. "He hurt, or what?"

Biltmore looked surprised, as if he had just learned something that he had not known before.

Neil hastened to explain. "There's nothin' in the papers about

51

it, I just seen he didn't start against San Antonio and was wondering what was up. Then I come out here, you know, and I see Clovis gimping around, and I'm wondering, you guys hurting at forward or what?"

A smile crept over Biltmore's face. It made Neil go a little sick inside, especially when Tim leaned over and patted him on the belly. "You thinking of trying a comeback, Novo?"

Neil spun his trunk out of the way of Biltmore's pats. "Yeah, right. I just mean, maybe that's how come you're having some problems these days."

Biltmore shook his long, thin head. Everything about Biltmore was long and thin. His nickname when Neil had been playing was Needledick. He said, "I don't know what's goin' on there, buddy. Near as I can tell, Coach's just pissed at Zeke. But he's not hurt that I know of. What about you?" He grinned at Neil's physique. "You don't look like you're hurtin' none."

Neil tried sucking in some of his gut. He inched farther away. "Yeah, well . . . so what's the story? You guys're supposed to have this pretty good team—big board men . . . hotshot rookie. That him out there?" Neil nodded toward the court.

Biltmore glanced back, and Neil, knowing Biltmore's memory, didn't blame him for preferring to rely on his eyesight. "Yeah," Biltmore said.

"And what's the problem? He looks like he can shoot."

Biltmore turned his head left and right, as if checking out who was listening. He caught Neil's eye. In a gesture that was meant to be casual, he laid his index finger alongside his nose and pushed in one nostril until it was closed off. He inhaled quickly, sharply, then dropped his finger. Then he shrugged.

It took Neil a moment to get the message. "Oh," he said, and now instead of feeling a little sick, he felt a tingling of excitement. He looked out to the court, where Oliver Dawkins was raining bombs from just beyond the curve of the 3-point line, and almost sighed.

Before anything further could be said, Del Fuego Dixon emerged from the runway. Del glanced over and broke into a smile. He stopped long enough to pick up a loose ball and lob it toward the basket and then, still smiling, took himself in a little half-circle of a walk that brought him face-to-face with Neil. Without saying anything, he stuck out his hand. Neil stuck out his own hand and the two men shook, hooked thumbs, and then locked the first joints of their fingers.

"Aw-right," said Del.

"Aw-right," said Neil. "You're looking good."

"You're looking ..." Del let his eyes run up and down Novaceski's frame.

Neil squirmed. He faked a laugh.

Crabbie, dressed from head to toe in Gater gold, came scurrying onto the court like a little windup toy, and he, too, joined the group. A few moments later so did Earl Putnam and Gilbert Rose. Everybody touched Neil. Hand to hand. Hand to arm. Hand to shoulder.

"Where you livin' now, Neil?"

"Over in Scottsdale. Just east of here."

"Hey, that's it. You get to see the Giants in spring training."

"Giants and A's."

"The good life, man?"

"Can't complain. Miss you turkeys, though."

"You not playin' no ball?"

"Gotta work. Gotta work. Put the food on the table. The old lady don't seem to think it's okay for me just to play for fun. You know what I mean?"

"You don't wanna play for fun, you best be joinin' this team again," and the guys honked and bellowed with laughter and pushed and shoved each other around the little circle they had formed. All of the hilarity ended, however, when Larry Miller jogged onto the court.

Like Del, Larry had joined the team the season Neil was let go. Neil, however, had never gotten along with Larry. The man, even as a rookie, was too fucking serious. Too fucking intense. He needed to lighten up. He needed to live a little. He needed to stop staring at Neil as if he were a leper.

But already the guys were starting a last round of hand slaps. Neil tried desperately to think of something to say, something that would keep them talking for just a little while longer. As Crabbie stepped up to say good-bye, Neil absently took his hand

and spoke over his head, stopping the players' retreat. "Hey, you guys available to go out tonight or anything? Maybe get a beer or dinner or something?"

Looks were passed. There was a general hesitation, a general shifting of gazes until all eyes were on Del, who shrugged and said it was fine with him as long as Novo knew a place that wasn't filled with seven-foot Polish girls.

Flooded with relief, Neil laughed. "Don't worry," he said, "my sister is already married." He offered them Ricky's Hacienda, and the Gaters agreed that at least it didn't sound Polish.

Then Neil realized that he was still holding on to Crabbie's hand, that Crabbie was looking at him with wide eyes, waiting to see if he was included in the invitation.

Neil, feeling suddenly generous, rubbed the trainer's head gleefully. "You, too, you little tub of lard," he said; and Crabbie's round face lit up with pleasure.

It was only when Neil turned away, still grinning, still feeling electric inside, that he noticed Colin Cromwell sitting at the scorer's table, not ten feet away, writing steadily in the notebook he had laid out in front of him. He wondered if Colin had heard anything. He wondered if he had seen the gesture Tim Biltmore had made to his nose. He wondered if he should say hello. But Colin was in full concentration on what he was writing, and Neil had never liked the bastard anyway. He decided the best answer was no to all three questions.

# 8

Meg Morgan Sinclair worried a lot about her appearance. She did not consider herself a stupid, or even an average, person when it came to intelligence. On the other hand, she had never been burdened by the idea that her attractiveness to men had anything to do with her brain. As far as she was concerned, she had gotten where she was by virtue of her looks, and she was aware they were not everything they had once been.

She blamed her weight gain on the birth of her last child and continued to tell people that even after the child turned ten. She dealt with the problem by talking about it to anyone who would listen, by going on occasional diets, and by joining various health clubs. Mostly, however, she bought new clothes, clothes designed to accentuate her breasts, cinch her waist, hold up her buttocks. Meg had her hair done weekly, her nails manicured regularly, and facials performed whenever she felt like it. And somehow it was never enough.

The pictures Booby had from the days when they first met, the ones he kept in the bottom of his underwear drawer, showed a voluptuous woman whose breasts stood out straight and firm, whose butt rounded into seam-strained denim pants, whose legs were long and slim.

She felt that Booby should realize that breasts as large as hers would inevitably fall, droop, sag, and need support from an expanding waistline. She felt he should recognize that her seam-straining buttocks would eventually require, at the very least, larger pants. She felt he should know that legs that were smooth and shapely on a twenty-two-year-old would have to thicken in the thighs just to support the weight that a woman naturally added as she approached forty. And she was aware that Booby understood none of these things.

She sought to please him in other ways, and when those did not always work, she sought to please herself. She had the nice clothes, the nice hair, she drove a nice car, and she had affairs.

The affairs did not start in California but in Philadelphia, and they started with Booby's lawyer, who also happened to be his agent. He made love to her on the couch of his office, while she still had on her coat and he was wearing two of the pieces of his three-piece suit. She had hiked up her dress and pulled down her panty hose and lain back on the cushions with one foot on the top of the couch and one on the floor, and her eyes had filled with tears while she was doing it.

Later, she returned to the lawyer's office to warn him that what had happened before must never happen again, and this time she ended up getting down on her knees in front of him while he sat in the chair behind his desk. He patted her hair and even talked on the intercom, and the whole process seemed very exciting. Booby's lawyer appreciated her.

After the lawyer, she made love to the real estate agent who had the listing on their house in Upper Darby. He stripped her bare in the bedroom she shared with Booby, and he was very expressive about his feelings. "What tits!" he exclaimed, cupping them in his hands. "What beautiful skin! What long, sweet legs! I can't believe I'm doing this. I can't believe I'm screwing Booby Sinclair's wife."

She liked his appreciation, too. Even the part about being Booby Sinclair's wife enhanced her feelings of worth, of attractiveness, and she promised herself that once she got to California, she was going to make herself available to lots of men.

Things had, however, not worked out quite as she had anticipated. Once in the Bay Area, Booby and Meg had settled on a house in Moraga, in a planned community that had a swimming pool, tennis courts, and its own security force. The people whom she met tended to be professionals who spent too many hours working and commuting and who used their time off work to go on meticulously planned trips to places like Tahoe and Hawaii. The men, when they were around, looked tired and sad out of their business suits, and the women, those who did not work outside their homes, had different concerns from hers. Meg found herself being pressured into activities involving the children's swim team and Little League baseball and fund-raising for the schools. California was nice, it had everything she needed, and it was not at all what she wanted.

Life for Meg Sinclair was becoming increasingly frustrating, and she was not sure why it should be that way. She had a good home, two wonderful sons, plenty of money, and a famous husband, who, if he didn't pay that much attention to her, didn't exactly interfere with her activities either. She told herself that she had to take better advantage of her opportunities while she still had them.

It was for that reason, she supposed, that she had allowed herself to become involved with Colin Cromwell. God knew, he wasn't the type to whom she was usually attracted. She liked guys with big shoulders, broad chests, grace of movement; and Colin had a body that reminded her of an unbaked bread stick. She forgave him for that, and for his smart mouth and cruel wit, because she understood that he was an intellectual, a type with whom she had had precious little experience. But his appeal lay strictly in the fact that he was available. And if he, like the real estate man in Philadelphia, got a certain pleasure out of screwing Booby Sinclair's wife, at least he was interested.

Meg, however, was not feeling very kindly disposed toward Colin Cromwell as she waited at the San Francisco airport for the Gaters' plane to come in from Phoenix. She was one of several Gater wives gathered in the waiting area. Petunia Dawkins was there. So were Dawn Biltmore, Brenda Rose, Victoria Dixon, and Gayle Wyatt. But Meg stood a little apart from the rest. She was wearing an open green coat that was made of a parachutelike material and was of an ensemble with her slacks and blouse. On her face was a big welcome-home smile, and Brenda and Gayle and Victoria and Dawn, and particularly Petunia, kept cutting glances at her. She continued smiling nonetheless because she thought it was important for the coach's wife to appear upbeat, even in the face of disaster.

The door to the Jetway opened and the Gaters' party exploded into the waiting area. They were an impressive sight, obvious as to who they were just by their size and dress and racial mix, and other people automatically fell away from them, staring and commenting to each other as they passed by.

Oliver Dawkins was the first to emerge, and from the angry look on his face Meg suspected that there had not been enough first-class seats available and that he had been forced to fold his six-foot-five-inch frame into a coach seat. Airplane seats were assigned by seniority, determined by years in the league and then by draft position, and the one who ranked lowest in that regard was the team's only rookie. Oliver went immediately to Petunia, who planted a big and loud kiss on his lips and then guided him away without either of them looking at or speaking to any of the others.

Meg was watching this scene, her smile faltering but still intact, when she heard Colin greet her. She turned and smiled through him, as though he were a Hare Krishna hawking flowers.

Colin put down his valise and took up a leaning spot against the wall. "Tough trip," he said, "losing them all like that."

Meg kept her face pointed toward the Jetway. This was Colin's game. He would talk to her in public about the team and basketball and all the things a sportswriter could be expected to talk about, and then he would slip in some line that she was supposed to interpret as an invitation.

"I thought they had that one last night in Phoenix," he continued. "Up by twelve in the fourth quarter. You see it?"

The question angered her unreasonably and she was in the process of refusing to answer when Rynn Packard strode past her. Meg's hand fastened on the kid's sleeve and he stopped because the hand belonged to her and because she was practically singing his name.

"Hi, Mrs. Sinclair," he said, glancing cautiously at the hand on his arm.

"Sounds like it was a tough trip," she said, using the very

58

words Colin had used to her. "And if you call me Mrs. Sinclair again, I'm not going to bother getting dressed up when I come around anymore."

Flustered, Rynn said nothing. He smiled a smile that gave every indication it would disappear promptly if it was the slightest bit inappropriate. He was what, twenty-three? She would eat him alive. Mother him, smother him, make him cry out for mercy.

She held out her coat, opening it like a cape. "You like? Neiman-Marcus."

"It's beautiful," he said. But of course he noticed her breasts. He had to notice her breasts.

She pretended to be disappointed. "Seven hundred dollars and that's all you can say?"

Suddenly, Booby Sinclair was there, sparing Rynn from further confusion over how rhapsodic he was supposed to appear about his coach's wife's new outfit. Meg's welcome-home smile returned as she put up her cheek to be kissed and Booby did his duty, and Rynn, mumbling good-byes, stumbled backward, banging into Del Fuego and into Del Fuego's wife and apologizing profusely in the face of their obvious annoyance. Meg wiggled her fingers in a wave of good-bye, letting Booby see her do it, and Rynn, trying to wave back, tripped over the feet of a tall, stooped man with liver spots on his bald skull. "Careful son," said the man, and Rynn, seeing it was the Gaters' chief scout, apologized to him as well.

The scout smiled and stepped forward with his own set of apologies as he asked Meg if he could borrow her husband for just a few moments.

Her heart caught. She had not noticed Woody Woodward before. How long had he been waiting? Why had he not come up and said hello? And now that he was asking this stupid question, what was she supposed to say? No, I haven't seen the man in ten days? I've got to tell him about Sean's report card and the transmission on the Mercedes and the yardman's bill?

It made no difference anyway. Neither Woody nor Booby waited for her to respond to Woody's question. Already they were sliding off to the other side of the lounge and leaving her alone.

"Good kid," said the voice at her elbow, the voice of Colin Cromwell, goddamn Colin Cromwell. He nodded in the direction of Rynn Packard hurrying along the concourse.

Right at this moment she didn't care about Rynn Packard. Something was happening with her husband. Something bad.

"Yeah," Colin said, just as if they had been having a conversation, "the boys were looking good against Phoenix up to the point Del decided to administer the coup de grace by putting on a little show on a breakaway. Instead of just laying it in, he decides he's going to go through one of those fancyschmancy things for the highlight film. He cradles the ball in the crook of his arm, springs into the air, passes under the basket, and sweeps his arm back over his head for a reverse jam. It was an impressive move, but Phoenix didn't seem to like it too much. They went on a tear after that. Next thing you know, there's less than thirty seconds left and the Gaters are down by one."

Meg took a step away. Colin took a step with her.

"It was almost the same situation they had against San Antonio in the previous game, except this time they don't have Earl Putnam in there, thank God. Now anyone who's ever even seen a league game knows that a team's got twenty-four seconds in which to shoot the ball. Booby expects his players to know that. So he's imploring them to make every second count. Run the clock down. Then score. Give the other guys as little time as possible to come back."

She watched her husband bend his head as Woody spoke directly into his ear, and then watched his head jerk up sharply. A little bubble of noise escaped from her throat.

"Phoenix," droned Colin, "put on a full-court press, trying to keep Larry from passing the ball in bounds to Rynn. He has to pass to Zeke and Zeke gives it off to Del. Fine, they've used up about two seconds and Del's got his back to the basket. So what's he do?"

Meg knew. Meg didn't care. Meg wanted him to shut up.

"He puts a move on his defender that sends the guy leaping into East Nowhere." Colin was speaking out of the corner of his mouth now. Like her, he had his eyes on Woody and Booby. "He spins the other way, rises like a rocket into the air—got the picture?"

Booby began gesturing animatedly at the old man. Meg's whole body felt numb.

"From eighteen feet he sends a perfect rainbow of a shot that drops neatly into the net. *Phffft*. It was one of the most beautiful things you'd ever want to see. It was physical poetry, ballet, sheer perfection of human movement. It gave the ball back to Phoenix with twenty-one seconds on the clock."

Woody was shrugging. He was spreading his hands. He was trying to tell Booby something wasn't his fault.

Colin sighed. "Think Phoenix is going to do that? Shoot the ball as soon as they get it? Not them. They work it around the perimeter while the clock ticks down. They wait until there is one second left and then they shoot. Swish, buzz, that's it. Ten losses in a row."

Meg turned now. She looked him dead in the eye. "But I guess we can't blame that one on my husband, can we?"

Colin, who no doubt was about to mention how he was going home and would probably be trying to catch up on his sleep all day tomorrow (wink, wink), looked as if he had been smacked. His reaction made her reckless.

"What do you think happens to me if he gets fired, you asshole?" she hissed. "What do you think happens to my kids?"

Colin hesitated. His mouth opened as if he were about to answer. Then he changed his mind. His eyes moved slowly toward the two men on the other side of the waiting area. He let out a low whistle. "Is that what Woody's telling him? He's getting fired?"

"You ought to know. Isn't that what you've been asking for all week?" Meg wrenched her head away.

A moment later Colin was scooting across the room. Booby and Woody saw him coming and turned their backs. Colin touched Booby's arm and Booby drew it up high, and for one awful moment Meg was sure he was going to drive his elbow into Colin's face.

But Woody was there immediately. He got between the two

men and put his hands on Colin's shoulders. He was trying to say something to Colin and Colin was trying to say something to Booby, and all of a sudden Booby wasn't paying attention to either of them. He was looking directly at Meg. She tried to signal her helplessness, but he was glaring at her—as if Colin's being there were her fault—and she knew now that this was not going to be any different from most homecomings.

Maybe worse.

## 9

Ed Norbert picked up Colin Cromwell's column in one hand. He picked up the *Chronicle* sports page that contained Marty Smart's column in the other. He held each paper between a thumb and an index finger and he turned them around. "How come," he said, "Smart got the story right and you didn't?"

On the other side of Ed Norbert's cluttered desk Colin Cromwell sat in a wooden chair shaking his head. "We didn't get it wrong, Ed. We're just premature."

Ed Norbert caught the emphasis on the plural. He understood the meanings, the nuances, of even the smallest, simplest words.

He threw the papers down on his desk top. He put his hands behind his head and showed Colin Cromwell the sweat marks under his arms. He wanted Colin to know how hard his job was.

"Ed" Norbert's real name was not Edward or Edwin or Edmund or any derivation thereof. It was Augustus. The "Ed" was short for *editor*, a title he pretended to disdain and yet wore proudly. Editor Norbert was a spinoff from Emperor Norton, a legendary San Francisco character from the Gold Rush days. Norbert thought of himself as a character and wore suspenders to prove it.

He said, "You've just been on the road with the team for ten days, during which time you've presumably eaten, drunk, slept, and crapped with these guys. You return home and write a column that all but declares that Booby Sinclair is being terminated, and instead"—Norbert leaned forward and thumped Marty Smart's column with his finger—"the real news that comes out of the trip is that the Gaters have just made their biggest trade of the year. Gilbert Rose and Earl Putnam have been swapped to San Antonio, and I want to know, Colin, how come Marty got the story and you didn't?"

"I would say," Colin Cromwell answered in a tone that said he had given the matter a great deal of consideration, "that someone tipped him off."

Ed Norbert checked his temper. Unlike the other writers in his department, Colin Cromwell had not worked his way through the reporting ranks. He had been plucked by Norbert from the campus of Stanford University, where he had been writing a Ph.D. thesis on Conrad and picking up a little extra money writing biting articles about the Stanford athletic teams for the school newspaper. Norbert had gone after him because he had decided that what he needed, what his paper needed in order to compete with the morning *Chronicle*, was someone who could write about sports as culture. And Colin, with a $36,000 salary dangled in front of him, had taken Norbert up on the challenge. That had been almost a dozen years ago, and in that time the controversial nature of "Cromwell's Corner" had made it something of a fixture in the community. This, in turn, had made Cromwell a prickly character to deal with. He did not always seem to appreciate how fortunate he was to be a columnist rather than a reporter.

"Marty Smart," Norbert said, "is the laziest sportswriter in this city. Looking at you two guys, I can only assume that he's got some source on the inside that you don't have."

Cromwell shrugged. Norbert thought he did it rather smugly. "I've got my sources, Ed."

Norbert nearly popped out of his chair in his eagerness to zing Cromwell on that one. "Then how come your sources didn't tell you about this trade before it happened?"

"Because the only ones who knew about it were Rohmer and Brandisi and that's just my point." Colin Cromwell said it as if Norbert were an idiot. "The GoldenGaters have just traded two veterans whom Booby has kept on the team for years.

Traded them for probably the last professional basketball player in America that Booby would like to see on his team. What does that tell us, Ed?"

Norbert was silent. He did not like being talked to this way by one of his writers.

"It tells us," said Cromwell, "that Booby did not know about this trade, Ed. It tells us that Dale Rohmer, whose job is to make reality out of Teddy Brandisi's visions, is no longer concerned with keeping Booby happy." Cromwell laid his forearm on Norbert's desk. It was a casual gesture. A familiar gesture. It pissed Ed off.

"Do you remember the history here, Ed? Do you remember the last time the Gaters made a trade without Booby's involvement? It was for Del Fuego—who used to be the last player in America Booby wanted on his team. Booby threatened to quit and it was only because Rohmer worked out a compromise that he stayed. He had to keep Del Fuego, but from that point on all trades, drafts, cuts, signings, whatever, had to have Booby's blessing. That arrangement has lasted until now. What we're seeing now quite clearly marks the end of it."

Norbert was sweating behind the ears. This was his office, his lecture, his protégé arguing back to him. He closed his eyes and tilted his head back on his chair so that his face was pointed toward the ceiling. He tried to look contemplative. "You're saying," he said, "that the fact that the Gaters have just made this trade means that Booby is about to be fired."

"Yes. And I'm saying Rohmer and Brandisi didn't even tell Booby about the trade until he got back from the road trip."

"You don't know that."

"I know that Woody Woodward was waiting at the airport to tell him something he didn't want to hear. Now we know what that something was. Rohmer and Brandisi are making trades behind his back, bringing in players he would never have on his team. That can only mean one thing. The Gaters are no longer doing things Booby's way. He's out either literally or figuratively, but he's out."

"You're speculating, Colin."

"I am not," Colin Cromwell insisted.

Norbert picked up an edge of defensiveness in Cromwell's tone and it pleased him very much. Here, at last, was some semblance of the reaction he wanted. He sat forward, taking control of the conversation once again. "I think you're forgetting that the Gaters have a center who's getting on in years and a backup who's about as mobile as a redwood tree."

"I'm not forgetting anything—"

"And," said Norbert, talking over him, gesturing at him with his index finger to keep quiet, "I think that a sharp basketball mind like Rohmer's could figure that a talent like Jerome Crown is just what the team needs to turn itself around. And finally I think that Booby Sinclair is an eminently practical man who's capable of adapting to things that are beyond his control, because if his wife doesn't talk him into adapting, then I'm sure his girlfriends in New York, Seattle, and Washington will." Norbert wagged his head from side to side. "No, Colin, I can see this whole thing blowing up in our faces—"

"What whole thing?"

Norbert blinked. He did it deliberately. "This thing that looks like a campaign on your part to get rid of Booby."

Cromwell gaped at him. "I'm not on any campaign."

"Good," said Norbert. "Then you won't have any trouble finding something else to write about."

Colin Cromwell got to his feet looking very angry. Norbert smiled. Colin turned his back and Norbert let him go. Almost immediately the sweat began to dry under his arms.

January 16

# CROMWELL'S CORNER

## Desperate Times and Desperate Measures
### by Colin Cromwell

Nobody ever doubted that Jerome Crown could play basketball. It was, after all, the reason he was able to sign letters of intent to Maryland, Miami (Fla.), and LSU all in the same year—an amazing feat that clearly showed the breadth, if not the depth, of his appeal.

The fact that he showed up on the first day of classes at Maryland and then enrolled one week later at Miami caused many to question Jerome, including, no doubt, the battery of lawyers who were embroiled in the subsequent dispute between the NCAA and the University of Miami over whether Jerome's brief sojourn at another school was enough to make him ineligible for play his freshman year. (It was.)

Still, there were those who said that any young man who stood six feet eleven, weighed 260 pounds, could bring down backboards with his slam dunk, and had averaged 39 points a game as a high school senior deserved at least a few more chances. Not even the fact that he was ruled academically ineligible after his freshman year at Miami deprived him of all his supporters. They pointed out that he had only scored 500 out of a possible 1600 on his college boards, and there were a lot of distractions playing big-time college basketball—even for a guy who was not playing. Besides, they noted, his ineligibility was only for the fall semester, and that would allow him the time he needed to work off the 100 hours of community service he owed for that criminal assault on the woman in his dormitory.

And of course all that faith paid off. When Jerome finally did get a chance to play for the Hurricanes, he ripped down 14.5 rebounds and threw in 22.5 points a game. Not only were the 'Cane fans impressed, so was Jerome. He promptly announced (i.e., after less than one full season of college basketball) that he was ready for the big time and declared himself a hardship candidate for the pros.

New Jersey was willing to take the gamble and made Jerome its first-round draft choice. It was neither Jersey's fault nor that of Jerome that the state is, by a geographical fluke, located so close to New York City, and when this terribly unfortunate circumstance was realized by Jerome, it was agreed by all concerned that it was only fair to move his athletic ability a little farther away from the bright lights. Like to San Antonio, where he would not have quite so many opportunities to get arrested for street-fighting in Harlem at three o'clock in the morning. The fact that Jerome was traded for the rights to a guy playing in Israel merely stands as testament to the humanity of the Nets management.

And now we have him. We, of course, being the San Francisco GoldenGaters, without a victory in the last ten games and with the season on the brink of disaster. To quote Richard Dreyfuss in *Close Encounters of the Third Kind*, "This means something." To quote another star in the thespian firmament, "Uneasy lies the head that wears the Crown."

# 10

**G**ood evening, ladies and gentlemen, and welcome to 'Gaters' Warm-up.' In just a few minutes time, your San Francisco GoldenGaters will take on Seattle and try to end their ten-game losing streak. But for right now, our pregame guest is the newest Gater of them all, Jerome Crown. I'm Wayne Brickshaw, and I have to tell you, Jerome, this is a real thrill for me. Just the other day I was interviewing you in a San Antonio uniform and now here you are, wearing the gold and white. Jerome, welcome to the Gaters."

"Well, thank you very much, Wayne. It's nice to be 'preciated."

"Tell me, Jerome, that's an interesting comment. Did you not feel appreciated in San Antonio?"

"Well, you know, it's hard to feel 'preciated when you're sitting on the bench."

"What went wrong there? Anything you can put your finger on?"

"I guess you could say the coaching staff there and me just didn't see a little eye to eye, if you know what I mean."

"Why was that, Jerome? I mean, you're a guy who seemingly has all the talent in the world, and yet . . . I won't beat around the bush . . . God knows, Colin Cromwell didn't in his column today. Did you see that, Jerome?"

"Was it 'bout Jerome?"

"I should say it was."

"Well, I didn't read it. But any pub is good pub. You know what I'm sayin'?"

"Well, Colin's point seemed to be that everywhere you've gone, as talented as you are, you've been dogged by controversy. What is it about Jerome Crown that causes that?"

"You know, Jerome just want to play his game, and I'm not sure some of these people, some of these guys that goes into coaching, understand that. I mean, I feel like we grown men out here, and we don't need somebody always followin' us around sayin' do this, don't do that. Some of these guys, you know, I think they frustrated. I mean, they never was that good theirselves, and they thinkin', you know, to be a good basketball player you gotta be showin' blood, sweat, and tears all the time. It get to the point sometime, you know, I feel like that's what they want more'n they want you to put the ball in the bucket. It's like, they don't care so much did you win, as did you look like you was wantin' to win. You know what I'm sayin'?"

"Well, if you're not a blood, sweat, and tears sort of guy, how would you describe yourself, Jerome?"

"Me? I'm a nice guy. I'm a big guy and I'm a single guy. Any you girls that's out there listenin', you can get in touch with Jerome through the Gaters' home office. I answer all letters. 'Specially the ones with pitchers."

". . . Ha, ha. And you've got a great sense of humor, too, Jerome. That's a side not many people get to see of you."

"Yeah, well, I'm not really sure I been given a fair break by the media. A lot of stuff you see written 'bout Jerome is wrote by people who don't really know him, person-wise. I mean, Jerome got other sides to him besides basketball, and I feel like they don't want to hear too much 'bout that. I mean, they look at Jerome and they see he six eleven or whatever, and that's all they see."

"Tell me, then, if you weren't a basketball player, maybe if you weren't six eleven, what would you be? What would you like to be?"

"Be? Well, you know, I'd like to be in the movies, maybe.

Like Jim Brown or one of them guys. . . . Either that, you know, or I'd like to prepare tax returns. I think that'd be a good job."

". . . Did I hear you right? Did you say that you'd like to prepare tax returns?"

"Yeah. You know, I seen the way the dude works who does mine and, shhee . . . , I think he got a real good job."

"Well, there you have it folks. Your newest Gater, Jerome Crown, who just may prefer preparing tax returns to playing basketball. One thing's for certain, though. No one with the IRS is likely to argue with him.

"I'll be back with the starting lineups after this brief message."

When the game began, Jerome trooped to the end of the bench and sat down in the very last seat, next to Sarantopoulis. He remained there, except for time-outs and the halftime break, for the entire night. With three minutes left, Del Fuego Dixon pulled up lame and signaled to the bench. Nobody saw what had happened, but the whole arena saw him limp off the floor.

Jerome, still at the end of the bench, listened as the crowd chanted his name, sat immobile as coach replaced Del with Tim Biltmore, and then turned disinterestedly away from the action and watched as Crabbie guided Dixon back to the locker room. He was still watching when a skinny, bespectacled man got up from the press table and trailed after the trainer and the wounded warrior. Jerome wondered if that was the guy who had written about him. He wondered why he was heading to the locker room so early. He wondered if that little brunette who was sitting just above the passageway was really smiling at him. He waved. She was.

71

# CROMWELL'S CORNER

## Now I See Through a Glass Darkly
### by Colin Cromwell

So now it makes sense. The Gaters, reeling across the Western landscape, falling before everyone who stands in their path, have an excuse for a few of their more bizarre moves over the past several days.

Looking through the "retrospectroscope" (a fanciful instrument often invoked by doctors with a chuckle and a grin to explain something that looks as if it was malpractice but really wasn't), we can understand why Curtis Clovis was suddenly plucked from the end of the bench and hurled into a starting role against San Antonio. Curtis, former college wonder boy with the perfect basketball body and the gentle spirit, was being shopped to the opponent.

Now we can see why Earl Putnam, who came out of nowhere (or more precisely, Norfolk State) four years ago to make the Gaters as a free agent, who seemed to have more natural athletic ability and less basketball sense than anyone else on the team, was in there directing the offense in the closing minutes of the San Antonio game. He, too, was being shopped to the opponent.

Earl passed the inspection. Curtis did not. Earl went. Curtis stayed.

In the meantime, so what if the Gaters lost the game by one point? It was only one more notch in an already bulging loss column. The Gaters were looking to the future. When losses will be more meaningful.

The future, it seems, is to be the home of new Gaters' acquisition Jerome Crown, providing that Jerome does not decide to abandon pro basketball for the more lucrative and exciting career of preparing tax returns. Jerome, however, is a big offensive machine, a body-banger, who is most effective in a half-court game.

The Gaters, you might have noticed, do not play a half-court game. And they already have an offensive machine, a smooth and lithe shooter named Del Fuego Dixon, who needs to spread the floor and isolate his man one-on-one in order to maximize his great scoring ability. So if the future is the home of Jerome, what does that bode for Del Fuego?

Simply put, does the arrival of Jerome Crown mean that the Gaters are going to make Del Fuego Dixon the scape-goat for their present woes? Why, you might ask, would they do such a thing to their perennial All-Star?

Well, the team's record is 11 and 20, and Del Fuego is in the final year of his contract. He will no doubt be looking to double what he is presently making, given the current rates of pay around the league. Perhaps by bringing in Jerome Crown, Gaters' management is telling Del Fuego that it is preparing to live without his services next year.

But, you might say, Del Fuego Dixon is a proven com-modity and Jerome Crown is still a project. Management could not be writing the season off already, could it?

The answer can best be found by watching the type of game the Gaters elect to play as the second half of the season unfolds. If the team starts playing more and more of a half-court game, with Jerome in there in place of Del, then consider this to be a year in transition—and forget about those play-off tickets.

# 11

Mel Dykstra took a deep breath, fixed a small grin on his face, shifted his bottle from his right hand to his left, and rapped softly on the hotel room door.

The voice on the other side said, "Is that you, Dick?"

Surprised, he answered, "It's me . . . Mel."

Nothing happened. And Dykstra, realizing he was, after all, in Los Angeles, a place where there could be all kinds of guys named Mel who went around beating on people's doors after midnight, said, "Dykstra. Mel Dykstra."

"Oh, Dyk." Not Dick, Dyk. The voice said, "What do you want?"

"A minute." Dyk spoke with his mouth close to the door. "I want to talk to you for a minute."

The lock was unfastened. The door was opened just wide enough for Colin Cromwell to peer at him, to make sure that this was the real Mel Dykstra. It was only right that Cromwell be suspicious. Dyk had never visited Colin at this hour before. He had never visited him at any hour before.

Dykstra offered up the bottle of Harveys Bristol Cream in his hand. "Nightcap," he explained.

Mel Dykstra did not look like a professional basketball coach. He looked like an accountant. He stood five feet eight, his head was bald on top, his eyes were droopy and bore huge baggage under them, and his nose was long and beaklike. When he grinned, as he was doing now, his mouth twisted to one side.

Dykstra had been a high school mathematics teacher who

74

had become a basketball coach simply because his inner-city Philadelphia school had needed one. Eventually, when the right talent came along, his team had taken the city championship; and a few months later he and his two star players moved on as a package to La Salle. It was there that he had come into contact with Booby, then coaching at Penn, a rival in Philadelphia's vaunted "Big 5."

Dyk was the first in his area to use a computer, not only to keep statistics, but to determine the tendencies of other teams in particular situations, and Booby, who regarded computers as magic boxes, developed an appreciation for Dykstra's numerical approach to the game. Years later, when Booby was appointed to the head coaching position of the Gaters, he asked the older man to join him. Dyk, who had never lived outside Philadelphia in his life, accepted on the spot.

Dyk presumed all these facts were known to Colin Cromwell, and in Dyk's mind they gave him sufficient pedigree to allow him to stand outside Colin's door with a bottle of liquor in his hand—even if Colin was in his underwear.

"I'm not really up for a nightcap, Dyk," Colin said cautiously.

Dykstra looked up and down the hallway. He wiped his mouth, but kept his grin in place. "I can't talk to you out here."

Colin looked at him, looked at the liquor bottle again, looked back at him, and seemed to recognize at last that this was a business call. The liquor merely made it favor-seeking business. "I'll get my pants."

They took seats at a round table by the window, using the room's only two chairs. Colin remained shirtless and Dyk figured it was done as a reminder to him that this was an intrusive meeting. But Dyk did not care. He made space on the table by piling all Colin's papers on top of his portable computer, and then he poured an inch of liquor into each of two bathroom water glasses. "Here's to you."

Colin took a sip, a small sip, and waited.

"Tough game tonight," Dykstra said, licking his lips. "But it's L.A., you know? How many times you gonna beat L.A.?"

"So far, unless I'm counting wrong, you haven't done it even once this year."

Dykstra pretended to be amused. He glanced at the pile he had made on top of the computer. "Gonna slam the boys again, Colin?"

Cromwell heaved a sigh of annoyance. "I'm not a fan, Dyk. I'm a sportswriter and I have to report what I see. 'The boys,' as you call them, start playing well, I'll be the first to write about that."

"You ever think maybe the team couldn't be as bad as it's been sometimes?"

Colin shrugged.

"Lot of talent out there." Dykstra tipped his brow to let Colin know he was looking for agreement.

He got it in the form of a curt nod.

"I think the addition of Jerome has helped, don't you? He scored, what, forty that night against Portland?" Dyk chuckled. "You never seen a hamstring recover so fast as what happened to Del Fuego that next day."

"I thought it was a groin pull."

"That what it was? Yeah, you get over those faster, I guess. Tough to see 'em on X rays, too, you know what I mean?"

"You don't think he was hurt?"

"Oh, no. I'm certain he was. That's what made it all the more remarkable he was able to go thirty-something minutes two nights later against Indiana. But the human spirit, you know? A guy gets pressed and there's no telling what he's capable of. More Bristol Cream?"

Colin covered his glass with his fingers.

"You take me, for instance," Dykstra said, pouring himself another half inch. "I'm fifty-nine years old. I been in this pro game now only a couple of years and I guess I'm supposed to be eyeing retirement already. My wife, she thought I was supposed to be doing that before we left Philly. 'We have a beautiful setup here,' she said. 'You stay home with the Explorers. Our house is paid for, our kids are grown, we'll be able to afford a nice little place down the Jersey shore in a few years. What do you want to go moving out to California for?' " He laughed at the wonder of it all. "Women, huh? God bless 'em." He sipped, liked what he tasted, and sipped again.

"I says, 'June bug, I don't feel like getting ready for retirement. I don't wanna place down the Jersey shore. I wanna coach basketball.' You know the fooling, Colin? You discover, some point, what it is you really want to do in life, what it is you're really good at, and you say this is it. I figure, everything I ever done has been in preparation for this. All the crummy gyms I been in, all the sweaty clothes I smelled, all the ass-kissing I ever did to high school kids to make 'em come to my school, and suddenly I got the chance to make it mean something, and so help me, I'm gonna seize it."

If Colin was moved by this confession, he did not show it.

Dyk sighed. "Then I look at these kids playing basketball for us and I think, they don't even got a clue. Not a clue. They think they worked hard to get here? Doin' what they like doin' best in all the world and being good at it, great at it, on top of everything else? No way. They think, most of 'em, they got it tough where they come from? Wait till they see where they're going. And don't think I don't know. I been in their homes, recruitin' 'em. I seen the places where they live—no doors on the bathrooms, paint peeling off the walls, exposed wiring . . . rats and cockroaches everywhere. I'm not saying it isn't ugly, Colin. I'm just saying the day they crash it can be even uglier. How would you like to be a thirty-year-old has-been?"

Colin leaned forward, hugging his skinny arms around his bony chest. "There some point to all this, Dyk?"

Dykstra took his time. He was determined not to get rattled. "I can tell you this, Colin. There are guys playing today who don't appreciate the opportunity they have."

"I'll keep that in mind, Dyk."

Colin, his eyes open, yawned and delayed covering his open mouth. In the old days Dyk might have pasted a guy who acted that rudely, but this time he simply went right on talking. "And then there are other guys, nonplayers let's say, who haven't had everything they want come so young. And these guys know they gotta make an opportunity when they see one. They know there aren't going to be so many opportunities in life that they can afford to let one pass them by."

Dykstra poured himself more liquor. He did it slowly, deliberately. He tried to keep his hand from shaking. He had forgotten how much he disliked Colin Cromwell.

Colin, slumping back in his chair, said, "What can you tell me, Dyk, that's going to open up an opportunity for an aging assistant coach like you and a no-longer-youthful sportswriter like me?"

Dykstra felt a surge of hope. The hook was baited. He treated Colin to his best crooked grin. "What," he said, measuring his words, "would be the biggest possible story you could break on a beat like yours?'

"Booby's been canned."

Dykstra's grin faded. "You haven't been listening."

Colin gave it another try. "Somebody's been busted for drugs."

"Bigger, boy, bigger. Think Pulitzer Prize—winning stuff."

Colin gave a shake of his head. And then the shake stopped and his head stayed at a funny angle, an angle that would have been uncomfortable if he had been conscious of it.

Dykstra sipped his drink and managed to look both pleased and ashamed at the same time. He pulled the glass away from his lips, but did not lower it. "If I was to tell you something, Colin, something that could both make your career and bust mine up completely if it got out wrong, would you respect it?"

"Of course I would, Mel." Colin spoke with sincerity. "You know I would." And then he added, "I can protect you as a source, if that's what you're asking."

"What I'm asking is if you're prepared to make a deal for the story of your life."

"A deal," Colin repeated, and the words sounded hollow.

Dyk moved in fast. "You're what, Colin, forty? Somewhere around there? You got a good job, but you don't think of yourself as having peaked, not by a long shot. So where you going? You already got your own column for a good newspaper. But what you need," emphasizing each of the words, he said it again, "what you need is a little national exposure. Wouldn't you say that's true? I mean, you can write as good as anybody—I seen you always quoting Shakespeare and all a them, so that tells me, here's a guy who's just lookin' to bust loose."

Colin sat shivering in silence and the shivering gave Dykstra confidence. "That's the way I feel about me, you know? That's why I'm saying all this stuff. It doesn't do me much good to be all set to bust loose if nobody even knows who I am."

"You're a good coach, Dyk," Colin said softly.

"I am a good coach," Dykstra said, jerking his head up again. "But I'm in back of a man fifteen years younger than me on a losing team, and there aren't a whole lot of head coaching jobs made available to guys in a position like that. And in between me and Booby is Mike Hacker, so I can't even risk my mortal soul by thinking bad thoughts about the guy who gave me my shot at the big time because if Booby goes down, it's gonna be Mike who takes over. You know what I'm saying?" Dykstra fell back in his chair, wondering if he had said too much.

After a while, Colin asked Dyk what he thought Colin could do for him.

Dykstra ran his hand under his nose and pushed his lips around with the palm of his hand. It was now or never. "You were writing there for a while about how Booby was on mighty thin ice, coaching-wise. I don't know why you stopped, but I, personally, don't think the situation's changed all that much. I mean it's true we're not losing all our games anymore, but I still think it's only a question of time until that bozo back in Boston drops the ax on Booby . . . and when that happens . . . well, I'd like to have a shot at the seat."

Colin waved one hand bewilderingly.

"There's nothing dishonest about what I'm proposing, kid. I just want a few words that let people know that the old man on the Gaters' bench has a name and some history and can take a wild-ass bunch of prima donnas and mold them into a winning basketball team."

"Let me get this straight, Dyk. All you want is some good publicity out of what you're about to tell me?"

"No. In exchange for it. There's no good publicity gonna come out of what I've got. What I've got is so big the last thing I want is to have my name associated with it."

Colin raised his arms, wedging his hands into his armpits,

covering his heart. His mouth pursed. Dykstra watched. Neither man said anything for a long time. Then Colin nodded.

"We got a deal?" Dyk asked.

Colin nodded again.

Dykstra stuck out his hand.

Colin took his hand out from where it was tucked between his arm and his ribs. The instant their skin touched, Dykstra's fingers locked like a vise and wrenched Colin forward so that when he spoke his words went directly into Colin's ear. "Somebody on the Gaters is fixing games."

The words were out. Colin tried to pull back. Dykstra reeled him in tighter.

"The FBI's onto it."

Colin twisted his head enough to look directly into Dykstra's face. His eyes were wide. "How do you know?" he demanded hoarsely.

Dykstra cackled. "They've asked me to be their mole. They're counting on me to tell 'em who's doing it."

# Slam Dunk

# 12

Rynn Packard had first suspected something was wrong back in early January, at the start of the Southwestern road trip. During the Utah game, Del Fuego Dixon had let a pass go through his hands. It wasn't just that Del Fuego failed to catch the ball. God knows that had happened before. It was the way Del slapped his hands together afterward. It was the way he looked at Rynn to see if he was buying his sorrow.

For the rest of that game Rynn found himself watching Del Fuego closer than he ever had before. He watched a rebound roll off Del's fingers and fall out of bounds. He watched him miss an open ten-footer. He watched him reject a shot by slapping it a dozen rows into the stands when he could have kept the ball in play by tipping it to Larry Miller. And he wondered why Del Fuego was playing that way.

Rynn well knew that when the game was on the line, when a score was desperately needed, it was his responsibility to get the ball to Del Fuego. But against Utah, with the Gaters down by 4 and a minute and a half left to play, Rynn ignored Del Fuego breaking out from behind a W.E.B. pick and passed the ball inside to Zeke Wyatt instead. Zeke literally assaulted the basket and was slammed to the floor well short of his goal. The result was a two-shot foul by the team's worst foul shooter and Booby Sinclair shrieking from the sideline for a time-out.

"You know the play?" Booby howled at Rynn as the team gathered around in a huddle. "You know the goddamn three-set? DubyaBee steps outside, blocks off their four-man, and

Dixon gets behind him. You don't like that play we run forty million times? You got a better way of coaching this team? Or you just fucking blind?''

Rynn was not used to having a coach yell at him like that. He grabbed a towel from a ball boy and rubbed the perspiration off his face. It was a way to avoid looking at Booby while suffering his abuse. But when he took the towel down, he found Del Fuego staring at him, studying him really, from the other side of the circle of sweating men. Rynn caught the taller man's tea-colored eyes, then looked away quickly because he was not sure he liked what he saw in them.

The Gaters lost that game by 3, and afterward, in the shower, Rynn remembered all the questionable things Del had done, and he remembered in particular the way Del had stared at him during the time-out. It was a mind picture he could not shake. It stayed with him in Denver when Del Fuego continually passed up easy turnaround shots in the fourth quarter. It had been there during the following day's practice in Dallas when he watched Del bury that same turnaround jumper over and over until Del suddenly turned on him, challenged him, sprang at him as if he wanted to kill him. It was there now as Del entertained a group of his teammates at a corner table in the coffee shop of the Airport Marriott in Cleveland, Ohio. Rynn was not one of the people who, as Del told his tales, was leaning eagerly forward, ready to burst into raucous laughter. Rynn, instead, was sitting by himself across the room, pretending to be immersed in a book, trying to appear oblivious of everything around him.

Rynn had been there first, already seated when Del came in with Zeke and Felix and Oliver in tow. They had glanced his way, Felix had even waved, and then Del had led them to the table in the corner. Five minutes later Tim Biltmore and Curtis had come into the coffee shop, and Del had boisterously beckoned them over to join his gathering.

Six of them, half the team, yukking it up together, and Rynn was alone with his book. He could not focus on what he was reading. Indeed, he had not turned a page in minutes when he became aware that somebody was standing there, clearing his throat, waiting for him to glance up.

He did so very slowly, afraid that he was going to find himself confronting a stranger's face, one belonging to a frustrated jock-fan who wanted to talk with or at a professional basketball player. That had happened more than once, the worst time being in a restaurant in Secaucus, New Jersey, where the Gaters had been overnighting before playing a game at the Meadowlands. A tall, skinny, very red-faced young man had come up to the table where Rynn was dining alone and, in tones loud enough for all the other diners to hear, had denounced him as a "piece of shit." It had taken management a while to react, and Rynn had sat there with his head down while the angry young man spewed out a stream of vicious comments about Rynn, his heritage, and his basketball-playing ability.

This time it was not quite that bad. This time it was only Colin Cromwell, the bard of the boards. Cromwell was dressed in an overcoat and gloves and a scarf. His glasses were fogged, and he was sniffing and grinning and looking to sit down. Rynn closed his book and gestured with his open hand to one of the chairs on the opposite side of the table.

"Jesus, it's cold as a witch's teat out there," Cromwell said, dropping heavily into a seat. His skin was the color of strawberry ice cream. His eyes were watery.

Rynn watched as the sportswriter slipped his hands out of his gloves, unbuttoned his coat and pushed it back over his chair. Cromwell took off his glasses and shook them and grabbed a napkin and dabbed at his eyes and nose. "Cleveland," he said disgustedly. Then he put his glasses back on and glanced around the room.

"Looks like fun," he said, nodding toward the other table, where the boys were now engaged in blowing the paper wrappers off their straws and at each other.

Rynn looked and looked away again. He shrugged.

Cromwell, if he noticed, did not comment. He began searching for a waitress, doing so with a sense of mission, waving at any woman with a pencil in her hand. Suddenly he stopped swiveling his head and snatched up Rynn's book. He inspected the cover, front and back: *Sent for You Yesterday* by John Edgar Wideman. "This guy was a basketball player," Cromwell said, as if that explained why Rynn was reading it.

"I didn't know that," Rynn said, which was the truth.

"There's a lot of free time in this business," Cromwell said, tossing the book back onto the table. "But I haven't seen many guys using it to read. Watching TV, maybe. Hanging around the lobby, I've seen a lot of guys do that."

A waitress, one whose pencil was in her hair, appeared at their table. Cromwell ordered coffee and a bran muffin and she repeated the order to make sure she had it right. Cromwell assured her she did and winked at Rynn. Rynn turned up the end of his mouth to acknowledge the wink and nothing more, and the waitress, who was too tired to care what either man thought of her, wobbled away.

"I think that's the reason some guys get in trouble in this league, don't you? They've just got too much time on their hands."

Rynn shrugged again. "What are you going to do? You're on the road, you can't play basketball twenty-four hours a day."

But Cromwell was persistent. "Aw, you know what I mean, Rynn. The way it is these days, almost every player has plenty of money and too much time with nothing to do. Naturally they're going to start spending it on things they shouldn't be spending it on." Cromwell's arms were on the table. He was leaning forward. He was trying to talk casually, but there was something wrong with his presentation. He was a little too intense for a man making small talk.

"Like what?" Rynn asked warily.

Cromwell opened his hands. He tilted his head and widened his eyes as if searching for the most obvious examples. He took a moment, holding the pose. "Cocaine," he said at last. "Gambling," he added.

The waitress reappeared with a coffeepot. "Leaded," she said, turning over Cromwell's cup and filling it. Cromwell waited until she was done.

"The other thing is—don't you agree?—most guys playing ball are marks for any sharp operator who wants to take the time to seek them out. I mean, how much sophistication can a guy have who's come out of Podunk A and M and never done anything in his twenty-one or twenty-two years but play basketball? We won't even pick on Podunk." Cromwell lowered his voice and shifted his eyes. "Take a guy like Curtis. When he left New Mexico, what did he know about life? Look what happened to him."

Rynn looked. Curtis was watching in fascination as Biltmore very carefully arranged six laminated menus like a house of cards. But then again, everybody else at Curtis's table was watching the same way.

Cromwell, meanwhile, measured a little cream into his coffee and stirred it until it was just the right color. "What about somebody like Zeke?" he whispered. "He didn't even come close to graduating from Las Vegas. And hell, that was his fourth school. He was recruited from the Bronx to play at some junior college in Nebraska. Then the University of Alaska came along and asked him to play there. Zeke, God bless his soul, only had a vague idea where Alaska was. Jerry Tarkanian hears about him at the Great Alaska Shoot-out and knows he's got a fish out of water up there. Next thing—and Zeke doesn't talk about how this happened, but let's say he's miserable in Alaska—all of a sudden he shows up at some junior college in Glendale, which, by the way, he's also never heard of before, but which he attends for a year so he can transfer to UNLV."

Rynn was growing uncomfortable. He was generally willing to talk with Cromwell and to sit with him and even to agree with him if he could because he knew that having the guy like him was better than having the guy dislike him. Cromwell could make a player's life miserable if he chose to do so. But this particular conversation was getting strange, and Rynn's uncertainty as to what was going on was making him reticent.

"Now maybe I'm wrong," the reporter admitted between sips of coffee. "Maybe Zeke Wyatt graduated from Boys High or wherever he went and sat down with his mother and purposely worked out this peripatetic plan of global education that would take him six years and leave him thirty-seven units short of a bachelor's degree in general business, but I'm just cynical enough to suspect that there may have been people manipulating this guy, telling him where to go and how to get there and what he's supposed to do once he arrives. And when I suspect that, I also ask myself what happens to a guy like Zeke when he starts running into all these people who are aware that he's suddenly got a couple of hundred thousand bucks a year to spend."

It occurred to Rynn that Cromwell might be about to try to talk him into some sort of investment. That was happening with some frequency these days. People he met would push business cards on him, and he had received more than a few calls from people he had known in college who were now selling stocks or annuities and wanted to make sure he was aware that they could be of service. Often their pitches would contain elements of what Cromwell was saying: "making a lot of money now . . . but in the future. . . ."

As if reading Rynn's mind, Cromwell said, "I'm not just talking about the people coming around with business deals, mind you. But what about these guys you see who are always hanging about ready to get a ballplayer anything he wants: coke . . . women . . . lay down a little bet. You know what I mean?"

This was the second time Cromwell had mentioned cocaine, and the repetition was not lost on Rynn. "Is Zeke in some kind of trouble?" he asked cautiously.

Cromwell looked stricken, as though he had expected so much more, given the clarity of his lecture. He took too large a sip of coffee. It made his mouth do funny things. "I'm not talking about Zeke in particular. I'm talking about virtually any pro basketball player these days."

"Well, these lobby lizards you're talking about, they never approach me."

"No," said Cromwell after a moment, "I don't suppose they would. Not you, not Larry Miller . . . and probably not someone like Curtis or Sarantopoulis either, because what good could a scrub do for anybody? But these guys are around for some reason. They're making contact with somebody."

"I guess so," Rynn said, and just at that moment Cromwell's bran muffin arrived.

It was a distraction, a chance to get away, and Rynn seized it, grabbing his book and rising to his feet. Cromwell recoiled, and Rynn was suddenly concerned that by saying "I guess so" he had just acknowledged that the team was plagued by association with nefarious characters. He hesitated. "I mean, I don't know." Then, quickly, he added, "I've got to go rest up now, Colin. I'll see you at the game."

The waitress stopped with the muffin still in midair. A bubble of effervescence shimmied the length of her unsightly body. "Oooh," she said to Rynn, "are you a basketball player?"

Rynn admitted that he was.

Cromwell's muffin was waved and then ignored altogether. It dropped from an inch above the table, and when the plastic plate hit the Formica, it slid. The waitress dug in her pocket for a pad of paper. She pulled the pencil from her hair. "Can you sign an autograph for me? Just write: 'To Nina, It was great.' "

Rynn's cheeks flushed. He said to Colin, "You're my witness," and scribbled what the waitress requested. Then, with barely a half-smile on his face, he hurried out.

He passed the table of GoldenGaters just in time to see Tim Biltmore demonstrate how to hang a spoon off his nose. Rynn glanced back at his own table to see if Colin Cromwell was catching what was going on, but Cromwell was not looking.

He was busy squishing his bran muffin flat with an angry downward sweep of the palm of his hand.

# CROMWELL'S CORNER

## Let Us Now Praise
## Not-Yet-Famous Men
### by Colin Cromwell

The GoldenGaters, who have looked very, very bad on occasion this season, managed to look very, very good against one of the better teams in the league last night. Credit Del Fuego Dixon, who poured in 34 points on a night when he could probably have scored wearing boxing gloves. Credit Rynn Packard, whose passes were as true as heat-seeking missiles. Credit W.E.B. Pancake, who made the Clevelands feel as if they were having to run around a city block every time they made a move to the basket.

But those are old names. Those are the names of players who were seeing game after game slip through their hands just a few weeks ago. Let us also credit Jerome Crown, who came off the bench to spell Dixon in the first quarter and played like such a demon that Coach Booby Sinclair could not afford to take him out. When Dixon was fully rested, Jerome simply shifted to the other forward position and remained there for the rest of the game. In this land of giant men and giant egos, it may spark some controversy to say that Jerome spurred Del Fuego with his ferocious inside game, but no one can doubt that Jerome kept the Clevelands from concentrating on the Gaters' scoring machine.

Of even more surprise, however, was the play of newcomer Reggie Champlin, the journeyman who spent the past year and a half playing in Spain before signing a 10-day contract to fill the spot left vacant on the roster when the Gaters traded Gilbert Rose and Earl Putnam for Jerome.

Reggie does not look like the same man who bounced around the league playing for five different teams in his last three seasons before going abroad. Now he shows the poise we never saw before, the ability to exploit defenses and to make things happen when he gets his hands on the ball. When he replaced Rynn Packard at point guard, the Gaters' offensive attack did not suffer one iota. Indeed, it actually picked up some quickness.

Credit Dale Rohmer for taking a chance on a man whom many general managers had regarded as "washed-up." Credit scout Woody Woodward for making the recommendation to sign him. But most of all, credit assistant coach Mel Dykstra, whose project Champlin has become. Day after day Dyk has been working with Reggie on his shooting and his passing and his footwork, and last night his efforts paid off. "Keep an eye on him," Dykstra advises.

We intend to, Dyk. And you, as well.

# 13

In Atlanta, Dick Crabtree was the last member of the Gaters' contingent to leave the hotel lobby. He had his clipboard wedged between the fingers and biceps of his left hand and was busy checking off names and numbers as he directed the bellhops. It was bad scheduling when a trip went from Chicago to Cleveland to Atlanta to Miami in the middle of winter because all the different clothes that had to be brought meant extra luggage and extra luggage meant extra hassles—most of all for Crabbie.

It was not enough that he tended to the players' injuries, taped their ankles, rubbed their muscles, and iced their joints. It was not enough that he made their travel arrangements, hauled their gear, ran their errands, lied to their wives, shouted encouragement at them from the bench. He was also supposed to serve as everybody's general whipping boy. If something went wrong, Crabbie was damn sure he would be blamed for it—so it was best to take a few extra minutes to deal with something as open to error as delivery of the right bags to the right rooms.

Some guys—Del and his little clique of ignorant bastards came to mind—were worse than others. They acted like it was their God-given right to have somebody take care of all their problems. They acted that way and management acted like it didn't have a clue he did anything more than open the locker room and draw the water in the whirlpools. He got paid the least amount of money, put in the most amount of time, and no one had any appreciation.

A man in a lavender suit approached him. The man wore a matching broad-brimmed lavender hat and a ruffled shirt. He had a mustache that curled down on either side of his lips, and he had a gap between his front teeth. He was obviously pleased to be where he was and doing what he was doing, and yet he was obsequious in his politeness as he inquired as to the whereabouts of Oliver Dawkins.

Crabbie tried to wither him with a look over the top of his clipboard. "I can't give out that information," he said, his voice dripping with finality.

Disappointment showed in the man's face. He watched Crabbie return his attention to his room list and tried to twist his head to see what was on it. Crabbie snatched the list to his chest.

"Can you give him a message for me?" The man bent his knees when he spoke. He waved his hands.

Crabbie, still clutching his papers to his body, did not say no. He merely glared, as if he had caught the man stealing a glance at his private parts.

"Can you tell him," the man said, holding his bent-leg pose, "that Eddie Mac is here?" He straightened up. He pointed to a lobby chair. "I'll be waiting right over there, okay? Right there. You just tell him when you get a chance. Remember—Ed-die Mac. Okay? He'll be knowin' me."

Crabbie dropped his head and took a moment to darken something on his clipboard. Oliver Dawkins was one of the guys with whom he often had the most trouble. "Sir," he answered in the same tone that had been used on him at dozens of airport check-in counters, "I'll attend to your problem as soon as I am finished taking care of other people."

The man in the lavender suit said, "Oh, yes. Oh, sure. No problem," and retreated to the chair he had designated.

Crabbie resumed his tasks. But when the last bellhop had taken the last bag to the last room, Eddie Mac was still anxiously waiting, and Crabbie had no more excuses for avoiding him. Heaving a sigh, he walked over to the in-house phone and dialed Oliver's room.

"Wha'chu want?" asked Oliver Dawkins before Crabbie even had a chance to identify himself.

"Ah, Oliver, this is Dick Crabtree down in the lobby. There's a gentleman here who says he knows you and would like to see you. His name is Eddie Mac—"

Oliver simply hung up the phone. Crabbie, uncertain as to what this meant, turned and stared across the lobby at the little fellow in the bizarre clothes. It was possible that Eddie Mac was a nut and he should be calling hotel security. It was also possible that Eddie Mac was, like Crabbie himself, just another victim of Oliver's rudeness. Eddie Mac was nodding at him in a hopeful sort of manner, and Crabbie did not know what to say. He decided to nod back. The guy could interpret it any way he wanted.

Then, suddenly, Oliver Dawkins was in the lobby, bolting through it in a white T-shirt, gray slacks, and stockinged feet. Crabbie held up his hand to summon the player's attention, but Oliver blew right past him and found Eddie Mac on his own. The two men did a quick, familiar embrace, and then they were on their way back across the lobby: Oliver, big and muscular and graceful and only partially dressed; Eddie Mac, small and wiry, herky-jerky in his motions, talking nonstop, his eyes flitting all the while. They made an exceedingly odd pair, but they were, nonetheless, laughing, and Oliver did not seem to care who saw them or what anybody thought about their appearance. They passed in front of Crabbie, who stood with his clipboard at his side, waiting for some acknowledgment, some modicum of thanks. He got it only from Eddie Mac. He may as well have been a spittoon for all the attention Oliver Dawkins paid him.

The Gaters were in a good mood as a result of their victory over Cleveland. At ten o'clock Atlanta time, when Crabbie returned to the lobby to see what, if anything, might be going on, he found a number of players milling around, chatting with anyone who approached them. Zeke and Jerome stood together, an imposing duo, making certain comments to certain women and eventually attracting a crowd of female admirers. Biltmore and the Greek occupied another station in the lobby, where they were regularly approached by older people and youngsters in pursuit of autographs. Larry Miller came out of the newsstand with a couple of magazines under his arm and stopped to talk to Rynn Packard for a while. When Larry moved on, Del Fuego took his place, and he and Rynn stood together conversing, which was unusual, to say the least, but that was the kind of night it was. The only person who was not socializing was Colin Cromwell. The sportswriter was sitting by himself in a big wing chair, talking to nobody. That wasn't like Colin. He was always trying to get somebody in a conversation.

On a night like this, a night when everybody was up, Crabbie saw no harm in asking Colin to join him for a drink in the bar. He was surprised, and even a little offended, when Colin turned him down.

"I'm working on something," Colin said, and that was that. As if Crabbie didn't have eyes to see that all Colin was doing was looking around the lobby, watching people come and go.

Crabbie went into the bar by himself and sat with Brickshaw for a while, listening to him tell stories to some woman in spandex pants and a bouffant hairdo. When he saw that Brickshaw was moving in for the kill, leaning closer, describing the accoutrements of his hotel room, Crabbie excused himself and returned to the lobby. Not only was Colin gone, but so was everyone else connected with the Gaters.

A feeling came over him as if he had missed out on something: a notice, a meeting, a party. The guys got together spontaneously sometimes, and whoever was there got invited to join. His stomach gathered into a little knot. He cast his eyes around the lobby and they fell on three women striding toward the elevators. All three were extremely attractive, each in her own way. Crabbie had hung around enough lobbies of enough hotels inhabited by professional basketball players to know with absolute certainty that these women were here because of the Gaters. He could see *party animals* written all over them.

Only one of the women was smiling. She was small, round,

a lightly complected black woman. She was wearing a short jacket and she wore it open, revealing a green U-neck jersey that could barely contain her enormous breasts. Her breasts were bouncy. They made her look bouncy. One of her companions was very tall and very black, with hair that was waved and fell to her shoulders. She was wearing a long coat and an even longer dress that seemed to consist of diaphanous layers of maroon and gray and green and aquamarine. She looked quiet and intelligent and almost regal in her bearing. The third woman had a sullen expression on her face. She was dressed completely in white, white sling-back shoes, white jeans, white shirt, and she kept her hands in the pockets of her blousy white parka as she walked. He sought out each of them with his eyes. He greeted each with a welcoming smile.

The women, however, shimmied right past him, paying him no more attention than Oliver had earlier in the evening. He tried not to be discouraged, realizing that these gals probably did not know that he was part of the Gater family—they weren't expecting slightly rotund, pink- and white-skinned guys like him. He would just follow them and surprise them when he was welcomed into whatever bash they were attending.

But this thought had barely formulated in Crabbie's mind when suddenly the three women were involved in a disturbance. Seemingly out of nowhere a man appeared and intercepted them, a heavyset man with a sport coat that he wore like a uniform. He had his arms spread and he was trying to round up the women as if they were sheep.

"Oliver Dawkins, room eight oh eight," insisted the bouncy little one, getting right up in the man's face.

The man closed his eyes with great effort, as if he had heard it all before. "We don't allow visitors after eleven o'clock," he said, and the women knew as well as he did what he meant by the word *visitors*.

Crabbie stepped forward. This time his smile was benevolent, patient, understanding. "Ah, excuse me," he said, and all four people turned to him. "Dick Crabtree, trainer of the San Francisco GoldenGaters. Mr. Dawkins is one of our players."

The man in the sport coat looked Crabbie up and down. He dropped his arms. He lost a little of his self-importance.

"May I have a word with you?" Crabbie took the man's elbow and pulled him to one side. "You know who we are," he whispered. "You know your management likes having us stay here. You don't want to cause a scene."

The man said nothing. But now he looked at the floor between his black crepe-soled shoes.

"I'm here to make sure they get up safely," Crabbie told him, and this time the man nodded. "What's your name?"

"Mullins," the man said.

"There'll be a ticket waiting for you at the box office tomorrow night, Mullins." Crabbie patted him on the back, then turned and signaled the women toward the elevator. "This way, ladies."

The bouncy one said thanks. She told him her name was Tiffany and introduced the others as VaDonna and Inez.

"Dick Crabtree," he said, offering them each his hand.

"Oh, Dick. That's cute," cooed Tiffany, giving his fingers an extra squeeze.

The other two gave him their hands as if they were afraid they were not going to get them back. When an elevator car appeared, Inez and VaDonna entered and quickly slid to the back wall. Tiffany and then Crabbie followed them in.

"So, have you gals known Oliver long?"

Inez said, "Um—hmm." VaDonna looked away. Tiffany said, "Don't know him at all."

The door popped open on the eighth floor. They all tumbled out looking for numbers on the wall. "This way," directed Crabbie, leading them down the corridor. The women purposely slowed their pace, not wanting to appear to be in too much of a hurry, and Crabbie had to keep turning to make sure they were still behind him.

He was in the lead when they got to room 808, and while he made a big proprietary sweep of his hand, he wanted one of them actually to do the knocking. "Go ahead," he urged, his hand still extended.

Tiffany obliged him and almost instantly the door was thrown

97

open and a hard-thumping bass sound rushed into the corridor. "Hell-o, ba-by," crooned a voice. "Hell-o, sugar. And who is this exquisite creature you brung to make my acquaintance?"

But before the crooner got his answer, his eyes fell on Crabbie and clouded over.

"Hello, again," said Crabbie politely.

"Hey, what's happenin', brother?" said the man called Eddie Mac, but he neither looked nor sounded as if he really wanted to know.

"Little Dickie here got us in the place, Eddie," Tiffany said, and scooted past him.

Crabbie, without moving his feet, leaned at the waist and looked into the room. A cloud of smoke seemed to hang in the air. Oliver Dawkins sat shirtless, expressionless, motionless, in a chair against the far wall. Del Fuego Dixon sat on one of the beds, his back against the headboard, his long legs stretched far out in front of him. He appeared to be addressing someone, and as Crabbie peeked around, he was startled to see Rynn Packard perched uncomfortably on the edge of the other bed with his knees apart, his hands clasped in front of him.

Eddie Mac fumbled in his pocket for a moment and then stuck one foot against the door and stepped with the other far enough into the corridor so he could hold out his hand to Crabbie. "Thank you, brother," he said, and when Crabbie reached out to shake, he found himself being slipped a piece of paper.

Inez and VaDonna slithered inside the room. Eddie Mac stepped back. He winked and let the door swing shut in Crabbie's face.

Crabbie looked at the paper. It was a five-dollar bill.

Shortly after one A.M., Crabbie emerged from the hotel bar for the second time that night. He had spent Eddie Mac's five dollars and then some, and he was fairly well drunk. He was glad that there was somebody he knew in the lobby. Dyk and his old friend Colin—back from the dead, or wherever he had disappeared to. They were sitting together on a couch, right next to each other, talking quietly. Crabbie was sure it would be a good joke to sneak up on them.

He figured they would be discussing basketball, probably basketball esoterica, maybe something like the merits of the box-and-one defense. But as he crept closer, he realized that wasn't the kind of thing they were talking about at all. In fact, they seemed to be almost mad at each other.

Dyk was saying, "Is that the best you can do?" and good old Colin was getting huffy.

"You haven't exactly given me much to work with, you know. I'm beginning to feel like Inspector Clouseau."

Crabbie drew to a halt just behind their couch. He bent over, ready to grab them both by opposite shoulders, make them turn the wrong ways, and then stick his head in between them. Say, "Boo!"

"What did you expect," Dyk was saying, "somebody's gonna come up to you and confess? You gotta be looking for what these guys don't want you to see. Find out who's got something he doesn't want anybody to know about. You don't want to do it, I imagine I can get Marty Smart—"

Suddenly, Dyk spun around. It was too late to grab either of them. "Boo!" cried Crabbie, and Dyk nearly leaped off the sofa cushions. Crabbie grinned sloppily. "Got ya."

Both men stared, openmouthed.

"Well," Crabbie said as the moments ticked past and no friendly word was offered, "excuuu-se me, guys." He stood where he was for just a little while longer to see if they would invite him to sit down, but the two men might as well have been carved from wax. "Good night," Crabbie said, and when that got no response, he nodded and headed off to his room, wondering why it was that absolutely everybody seemed to be avoiding him tonight.

He boarded an elevator along with a handsome, well-dressed couple who looked as though they had spent entirely too much time in each other's company. Reasoning that anybody who was well dressed in Atlanta might work for Ted Turner, Crabbie grinned at them heartily. He was trying to think of a way to strike up a conversation when they were joined by two little foreign-looking men who arrived exclaiming in bizarrely accented English over their good fortune at finding an open car.

The doors closed and they whooshed upward. The foreign men wished to get off at the eighth floor, but there was confusion when they arrived at that level. As the doors slid open and they started to step out, they were confronted with the unmistakable sound of running footsteps and they paused. Coming toward them at what seemed to be full speed was a bare-chested man.

The man was grinning almost maniacally as he pounded down the corridor. He was perspiring, he was breathing like a water buffalo—and it took Crabbie a few seconds to realize that he knew who the man was. At about that exact same moment the man recognized him and came to a stop so suddenly that he had to throw his arms out in front of him to keep from falling over.

The foreigners stepped back into the car, escaping by inches the man's outstretched fingers. The man, however, was not looking at them. He was looking at Crabbie.

"Hello, Rynn," said Crabbie, and then suddenly everything was still.

The elevator doors started to close again. Rynn Packard seemed to gather up momentum, as if he were going to thrust his arm or his foot between the sliding panels. But the momentum was all working in the other direction. He was backing up. He was turning and running off the way he had come.

"Aiiii!" said the foreigners as the doors shut in their faces.

But the well-dressed couple said nothing. They merely looked at Crabbie as if he were somehow to blame for what they had just seen.

"Beats me," Crabbie said aloud. But he knew they did not believe him.

# 14

On the morning of the Atlanta game, the team had a brief shootaround and then returned to their hotel rooms to shower and prepare for lunch. Rynn had been back in his hotel room for just a few minutes when the phone rang. He was immediately fearful that when he picked up the receiver he would find Del on the line. They had not spoken at the shootaround about the previous night's activities. None of the participants had. Only Crabbie had asked questions, and Rynn had done his best to laugh off Crabbie's inquiries—telling him he had been out looking for an ice machine when they had seen each other, making it seem as though he had been entertaining a woman in his room.

But it was not Del who was on the phone. It was Eddie Mac, and he claimed to have something Rynn had left behind in Oliver's room. He was in the lobby, he said, and he could bring it right up.

Rynn was expecting his shirt. He did not argue when Eddie Mac said he could come up to his room because he was thinking it might look funny if he was handed something in the lobby by someone of Eddie Mac's appearance. But when he opened the door to Eddie Mac's knock, the thing he saw in his visitor's hand was not a shirt. It was a picture. A photograph, and Eddie Mac wanted Rynn to have it. He also wanted to make sure that Rynn understood the reason behind his generosity. "I've got more," he said.

\* \* \*

The Atlanta game did not go well. Booby shouted. He cajoled. He threatened. At the end of the first quarter he benched Rynn. That was not as much of a surprise to Rynn as was the fact that Booby replaced him with Reggie Champlin rather than Oliver Dawkins. With Reggie running the offense, the Gaters chopped 6 points off Atlanta's lead. That meant they were only down by 19 at the half.

Atlanta's superiority that night could not be blamed on Rynn's ineffectiveness alone. Jerome started in Zeke's place and Atlanta's forwards ate him alive. Unlike Cleveland, which had allowed Jerome to stay in close to the basket, his Atlanta counterparts kept shooting from farther and farther out, and when Jerome would finally go out to cover, his man would simply juke him in the open space and drive around him, laying the ball in, hooking it in, jamming it in until finally Booby had seen enough and Zeke was sent in to plug the hole. Zeke, however, was sulking because he had not started, and Atlanta's forwards continued scoring as they pleased.

It was only the outstanding play of Del Fuego Dixon that kept the Gaters from being completely humiliated. Del finished with 28 points, which was 26 more than Rynn, who returned at the start of the second half, played about ten minutes, and was benched again. Oliver Dawkins got to play for five minutes toward the end of the game. He put up a shot a minute and hit on three of them.

He also set a franchise record for speed in getting off the floor and into the locker room at the end of the game, and Rynn suspected he knew why. Seated not far behind the Gaters' bench was a small patch of Gaters' fans, and central among them were Inez and Tiffany and VaDonna and the ebullient little Eddie Mac, looking resplendent in a long black cloth coat with satin lapels and a matching hat with a satin hatband.

Rynn had noticed them during pregame warm-ups. Tiffany had called his name, called it in a short shout that smacked of familiarity, and he had chilled when he realized who it was, but he had waved and she had seemed enormously pleased. Throughout the game he had heard her voice, alone among ten or eleven thousand, sometimes making the same sounds she had made in Oliver's room the night before. She cheered lustily when her friends did well and made loud groans of dismay when they erred. She yelled, "C'mon, Oliver," and "Aw-right, Del," and even once or twice, "Yeah, Bill."

When the horn sounded to put a merciful end to a disastrous evening, Rynn was sitting at the very end of the bench. It was the seat with the clearest exit from the court. That was what made it all the more remarkable to arrive in the locker room on a dead run and find Oliver already there.

# 15

The game with Miami was a heartbreaker. A close loss, like so many of the Gaters' losses this year. It was a victory that had slipped away in the closing seconds, in unexpected fashion, and it left everyone in even a worse mood than the Atlanta game.

The flight back home left at seven A.M. But when the Gaters arrived at the airport, they found that the plane was delayed. Storm conditions had stopped all air traffic indefinitely, and the team was forced to hang around the waiting area at the gate. Some of the players wandered off to look for video games, some just to stretch their legs, but W.E.B. Pancake parked himself in a plastic molded chair, squeezing his hips into it until it fit as tight as a helmet.

W.E.B. did not read. He did not look at the people around him, especially not the ones who were looking at him. He simply stared straight ahead and thought about things he wanted to think about.

Greens and browns. Sometimes blues. He liked to get a picture in his mind of the piney woods, of a river or a lake. He did not work at creating these images. They came to him on visits and he explored them when they arrived, looking for good fishing spots, good shady spots, good resting spots.

He had just found one. He could feel the breeze off the water coming into his face—but the breeze was just a little sour—and then suddenly the whole image was snatched away from him and he was back in the airport again. It was loud and the colors were no longer natural and people were everywhere, walking, crying, shouting, laughing, complaining, smoking, dropping papers, staring. Someone was talking at him. Talking close. He turned his head. Colin Cromwell, that newspaperman, was sitting in the seat right next to him. What was he doing there? W.E.B. don't talk to the press. Don't he know that? Sure he do. In years Colin Cromwell hadn't once put himself this close to him, and now he was talking right at his face. What was he saying?

". . . plane hasn't even come in yet."

What did he care? Sit and wait, man, you got no choice. But what was that funny look on Cromwell's face? He had the bulging eyes, the twitching lip, like he was nervous. But he also had this shine to him, like he was excited about something. Okay, Cromwell, here your response.

"Better safe." Now beat it.

Cromwell looked relieved. He actually smiled. W.E.B. did not like to see that and looked away.

"That was pretty bad," said Cromwell, leaning his arm onto the plastic wing of the chair, leaning close as if they were friends, "what happened with Oliver last night."

W.E.B. wondered whether he should answer. There had been an argument after the game. Oliver Dawkins's father and his father's friends had been in the stands, but despite that, despite the fact that Rynn Packard was stinking up the joint, Booby had not chosen to play Oliver. Booby had, for the second game in a row, sent in Reggie Champlin instead. In the locker room Oliver had gone belly to belly with Coach, accusing him of trying to mess with his head. Coach had gotten this wild look in his eye and had shouted back, telling Oliver that it was time to grow up, that if he wanted to play he had to learn to cover a man who wasn't going to fall over just because he had read about the great Oliver Dawkins in the fucking paper. Something like that.

"He just a young kid," W.E.B. mumbled, and kept his eyes away from Cromwell's. Eyes could capture you. Suck you in. Read your soul.

"Not like you and me, huh, DubyaBee?"

W.E.B. tried to think. Cromwell had to be somewhere around forty. He had to know W.E.B. Pancake wasn't no forty years old.

Before he could come up with the right thing to say, Cromwell was speaking again. "And what was Booby saying about Oliver not having control of himself? What did he mean by that?"

"I don't know nothin' 'bout it."

This only caused Cromwell to inch a little closer. "Well, you have to admit, Oliver's been a major disappointment this year." Cromwell's voice dropped to a whisper. "Is he having some kind of substance abuse problem? Is that what that was all about?"

"I don't know nothin' 'bout that, neither. And if I did, I wouldn't tell you."

Cromwell sighed. "I've got to write that up, you know. What I saw."

"Figured you would."

"Won't look good for the team—the coach and prize rookie going at each other like that."

"Not my concern."

W.E.B. could hear Cromwell rattling around in his plastic chair. He had to look. Cromwell was shaking his head. "Oh, I don't know, DubyaBee. The team's been playing well lately, outside of this present road trip, I mean. Bad as you were for a while, you're still in the running for the play-offs, and here's the coach practically accusing one of his players of something, practically admitting that drafting him was a mistake—"

W.E.B. tried his glare, his hooded stare. "Wasn't no mistake. The boy can play."

"Then what's wrong with him?"

That old look of fear, the one W.E.B. had seen so many times in so many people, was in Cromwell's eyes, but this time the look was a little different. It came from surprise, from uncertainty, but not from intimidation, and when W.E.B. saw that, he felt fear himself, wondering why it was that a little punk like Cromwell suddenly had so much courage. "Look, wha'chu want from me, man?"

It took Cromwell no time to answer. The words were on the tip of his tongue. "A story."

" 'Bout what?"

"About whatever's messing up this team, whatever's keeping it from winning as often as it should. If Oliver's got some kind of problem, I want to know because that could affect his play, it could affect the whole team in a lot of different ways. What I saw last night tells me that's the direction I ought to go in. I'm asking you to tell me if I'm right."

"Why me?"

"Because, DubyaBee," Cromwell said, smiling the smile of a hungry man who had just been told lunch was served, "the only other lead I've got is you."

W.E.B. tried the stare again. He tried to burn holes through Cromwell's eyes. He tried to let the scrawny little bugger know that he could slap that smile right off his face. Make it fly across the airport, smack into the window, and drop to the floor like a lump of Silly Putty. But Cromwell, turning his head first one way and then the other, stayed put, and the smile did, too.

"Ain't nothin' 'bout me hurting this team," W.E.B. said defiantly.

Cromwell looked even happier than he had a moment before. "You know," he chirped, "I ran into a guy in Houston a couple of weeks back who said he knew you."

A tingling started someplace low in W.E.B.'s body. He recognized that tingling. He knew it was a warning that he was going to have to do something. What he needed now was time to think so he wouldn't go doing the wrong thing. "That right?" he mumbled, and began considering getting up from the chair.

"A guy from Alabama."

The tingling grew. It was electric now, running up and down his legs.

"Well, actually, I don't know if he knew you. But he seemed real anxious that I pass a message along to you."

W.E.B. did not want a message. Especially a message from Alabama. He tried to refocus his eyes on something straight in front of him. He wished Cromwell would burst into flame and disappear into cinders.

107

"The guy says he's thirty-eight years old and used to play high school ball in Anniston. Played for three years against a guy named Willie Smith. He seemed to think you'd know all about Willie Smith."

It was no longer just electricity that was coursing through W.E.B.'s body. There was screaming. It was in his head, ringing in his ears. It was in his chest, making his heart leap as if it were trying to get away. W.E.B. wondered for a moment if he had forgotten to breathe. He had to grip the chair with both his hands, and that made him feel strong again. He could pull the seat right off its stand. Pull it off and whack Cromwell over the head with it. See how he like that.

Cromwell somehow understood. He shrank back and his eyes popped like a frog's behind his glasses.

W.E.B. wanted time to think, but his mouth was flapping already. "Who told you to ax me that?"

Cromwell said hoarsely, "A guy named Trey Wilson."

White motherfuckers. Go around tell each other everything. "Fuck that guy."

Cromwell looked confused. Scared and confused. His body wanted out of there. His head was pulled back. But he stayed where he was. "Fuck who?"

The air rushed out of W.E.B.'s nostrils. "Fuck you," he growled.

But Cromwell still did not move, and now it was W.E.B. who was going to have to leave. He lunged upward. The chair stuck, catching on his hips, and he had to swat it away with the side of his hand. It sounded like the crack of a bullwhip. It made Cromwell cringe. That was all right. Let Cromwell know it could have been him. Give one last glare and be gone.

Don't bother me no more.

# 16

"Good evening, everybody, and welcome to 'SportsTalk,' where our guest tonight, joining us by telephone from his home, is the veteran forward of the San Francisco GoldenGaters, Tim Biltmore. Tim, how are you tonight?"

"Good. I'm good, thanks."

"Thank you for joining us."

"My pleasure."

"Tim, the team's coming off a four-game road trip, where you went one and three. You left on that trip looking like you were at last putting it all together. You lost to Chicago, you beat Cleveland, and then came the game against Atlanta, when the team looked—I'll put it bluntly now—miserable. What are your thoughts about what happened on the road trip?"

"Well, I had a good game against Cleveland."

"But I meant the team, Tim. Tell me, are the play-offs still a possibility?"

"Yeah, well, we think so. Eight teams from the West are gonna make it and we still think we got a shot. I mean, if we can get up around five hundred ball we'll be right in the thick of things, play-off-wise I mean."

"Still, Tim, you've only got thirty-two games left to play. In order to get to five hundred you're going to have to win nineteen of those thirty-two games. Seriously, now, think you can do it?"

"Well, jeez, you know, I feel like we got a real good

team and it's just a matter of having to overcome a few bad breaks."

"On the other hand, for a team that's gone this far into the season, the Gaters have been remarkably injury free, wouldn't you agree? What, exactly, have the bad breaks been, Tim?"

"Well . . . you know. . . . There've been a couple of games we coulda won except for a bad call or something. . . . Maybe just a rebound we didn't get or a ball that kinda bounced in and out of the basket."

"You mean, like, what happened the other night in Miami?"

"Yeah, that would be one example, Wayne."

"What exactly did happen there, Tim?"

"I guess Rynn didn't know how to miss, that's all."

"You're laughing now, but I know you didn't feel that way at the time. Let me set the scene for any of our listeners who were out of the country or delivering babies or had some other good excuse for not catching my broadcast of the game. The Gaters were up by one with one second left when Rynn Packard gets fouled. Rynn's the best free-throw shooter on the team. Hits about ninety percent and he's got two shots. Coach Sinclair calls time-out. Pick it up from there, Tim. What did Booby say in the huddle?"

"Well, the main thing, you know, he tells Rynn he's got to make the first shot and miss the second. That way he keeps the ball live, and by the time anybody gets his hands on it the game will be over."

"Let me stop you there, Tim. What you're saying is that if Rynn makes both shots, the clock is stopped, Miami gets the ball out of bounds, gets to call time-out, takes the ball in at half-court, and still gets off another shot. Isn't that right?"

"Um, yeah. Basically."

"So what happened?"

"Well, Rynn makes the first shot and misses the second like he's supposed to—except when he misses, the ball doesn't hit the rim. The ref calls it an air ball and the clock stays stopped. Miami calls time, inbounds at half-court, fires up a three-pointer, and it goes in."

110

"Miami wins."

"Miami wins."

"Is that the kind of thing that's been haunting the Gaters all season, Tim? Little mishaps like that? I mean, are those the sorts of things that happen to every team, or do they seem to happen more often to the Gaters? Let's speak frankly now."

"Well . . ."

"I mean, Tim, and I hate to put you on the spot, but the fans want to know. This team was picked by some preseason prognosticators—myself included—to be a real challenger this year."

"I feel like, you know, we just kinda hit a slump there for a while, but then we had the big trade, you know, and we seemed to come out of it—up until these last two games."

"So you would attribute the turnaround that we've seen in recent weeks to the arrival of Jerome Crown, is that what you're saying, Tim?"

"Well, Jerome's turned out to be a real good acquisition."

"Does that surprise you, Tim? I ask you that because I know a lot of people, my good friend Colin Cromwell in particular, speculated that Jerome and Del Fuego Dixon would not be able to play together."

"Yeah, well, I think it's been real good because, you know, Jerome's inside game has opened up Del's outside game, if you know what I mean."

"So you think it was a good trade?"

"So far, I guess, yeah. But, you know, I see where Earl Putnam's been scoring bunches of points down there in San Antonio now that he's been given a chance to play."

"Let's talk about Booby Sinclair, Tim. There've been a lot of rumors following the team around this season that Booby might be fired and so forth. Does that kind of thing affect the team's play?"

"Um, not really. When we get on the court, we try to put all that controversy stuff behind us."

"Well, does it add extra pressure? You know, the thought that maybe if we don't win this one, the coach might lose his job?"

111

"Well, I don't know. It might put extra pressure on Booby, game-wise, but, you know, he's a real good coach and he knows what it's like in this business, so I guess we all just go out there and try to do our jobs irregardless."

"So—"

"I mean, you can't let every little thing worry you."

"All right, Tim, we'll let it go at that and open up our callers' lines. We've got lines free in the South Bay, the East Bay, and marvelous Marin, and right now we've got Todd on the line from the City. Todd, how are you tonight?"

"Hello, Tim?"

"Yeah."

"How're you doin'?"

"I'm doing good."

"That's good. I just wanna know, I mean, what is it about Curtis Clovis? It seems like here's a guy who's too cerebral for basketball. You know what I mean?"

"Huh?"

"Well, Tim, I think what Todd is trying to say is that he sees Curtis as a guy who may be thinking too much out there on the court. Would you care to comment on that?"

"Well, uh, Curtis is a real good guy, you know, he's got a good shot. He's, I don't know, a quiet kind of guy. He kinda stays pretty much to himself."

"Do you think he's gotten over his alcohol abuse problem or whatever it was he had?"

"Oh, yeah, sure. I mean, I haven't ever seen him in a social situation really, but I'm sure all that stuff's behind him."

"So what's wrong with him?"

"Um . . . I don't know that anything's really wrong with him. . . ."

"Let me jump in here, Tim and Todd. We've got one more call and then we'll have to take a break for a commercial. Mary from Richmond, do you have a question for Tim Biltmore?"

"Yes, I do. How are you, Tim?"

"Good."

"That's good. My question to you is this. I've been a

Gaters' fan for many, many years, and so I've been watching you throughout your professional career and I'm a great admirer of yours."

"Thank you very much, Mary."

"Mary, now we've only got a minute before we have to break away. What's your question for Tim?"

"Well, it's this. Tim, you've been around a long time and you've seen a lot of things happen. And you know, I look in the paper every day and there's always this little box in it that tells you how much each team is favored over another team. The point spread, they call it. And my question to you is, how easy do you think it would be for a professional basketball player to fix a game?"

". . . Oh, jeez. I never thought about it, Mary. But, you know, you pretty much live with the other guys on your team, and if somebody was doing something like that— well, jeez, I think you'd know about it. I mean . . ."

"But you think it could be done?"

"Well, I don't know anybody who's ever done it, but I suppose . . . I don't know, somebody could miss a shot or something."

"The thing is, Mary—let me jump back in, Tim—what you've got to remember is that we're talking about professional athletes and I don't think there's a group with greater pride in the whole world. I mean, these guys hate to lose, but even worse they hate to get shown up. Once they get on that court they play for peer respect. And another thing—everybody talks about how much money these guys are making, and separate and apart from everything else, that acts as a preventive measure to just what you're talking about. You go back to 1919 with the Black Sox scandal and you could almost understand those ballplayers thinking it might be worth it—I'm not saying it was, mind you—but thinking maybe . . . may-be . . . it would be worth money to throw a game because I'm not getting paid enough to live on anyway. But with today's ballplayer that's not a possibility. Who could be bribed enough to outweigh his league salary? Wouldn't you agree, Tim?"

113

"Um . . . yeah. I mean, I guess so."

"I just wondered, you know, because everything you say is true, but still you hear about these young men throwing away their careers over drugs, and then you hear what big business gambling is in this country, and you have to wonder. I mean, when they put these little boxes in the newspapers just like with the racing forms, it makes you think somebody's got to be out there betting on basketball games."

"Mary, you've raised a fascinating point and what we really should do is devote a whole evening's show to it. But right now we've gone way over time on our commercial break, so we're cutting away and we'll be back in sixty."

# CROMWELL'S CORNER

## The Search for W.E.B. Pancake
### by Colin Cromwell

There are places in Alabama where one can find farmers who still plow their fields with mules, where homes are more often than not wooden shacks with kerosene heaters, where the vehicle of choice is a pickup truck—even if it has to be held together with baling wire.

Elisaville is such a place. Approaching on the two-lane state highway that is the only road in and out of town, a passing Hertz rental car can cause overall-clad men to look up from their toils and big-eyed children to stop their play and stare. One field blends into another, and then the rental car traverses a bend in the road, enters a grove of trees, and suddenly the business district appears.

The business district is not large by any standards. It is three blocks long and maybe three blocks wide. It contains a couple of gas stations, a post office, a café, a drugstore, an emporium, a tiny courthouse and jail, a lawyer's office and a bail bondsman, a couple of insurance agents, a feed store, and a grocery store. It also contains the campus of Jones-Henry College. Elisaville is able to hold the entire campus within its nine square blocks because Jones-Henry consists of only two buildings.

The two buildings are dignified and surprisingly attractive. They could have been transplanted brick by red brick from New England. In front of the one that houses the administration office on its first floor is a marquee such as those seen in front of Holiday Inns announcing the names of lounge acts or welcoming newlyweds. This one says, "Jones-Henry College, Home of the Mighty Thunderclaps." A few of the letters are missing.

### Walter Walker

Jones-Henry College is also the home, in a sense, of W.E.B. Pancake, stalwart center of the San Francisco GoldenGaters. This was where he was playing 12 years ago when discovered by the intrepid scout Woody Woodward. Given the small size of the school, given the relative dearth of other activity readily apparent to an out-of-towner's eye, given the magnitude of W.E.B.'s accomplishments since leaving his alma mater, one would expect to find some acknowledgment of his association. There is none. Indeed, it is not even clear where W.E.B. honed his slamming and jamming techniques because there is no sign of a gymnasium in the two buildings that house the Mighty Thunderclaps.

A clue appears to the out-of-towner as he exits his rental car and strolls across the lawn that serves as the campus commons. Not only is his the only white face, it is virtually the only male face. In the administration office the impeccably dressed, almost breathtakingly pure young lady who greets the out-of-towner is not familiar with the school's famous alumnus. Not even the added information that this particular alum stands six feet ten, earns over a million dollars a year, and is known throughout the breadth of this great land sparks a memory in her young mind of the man who made the Thunderclaps mighty back when she was just a little girl.

No, she explains, Jones-Henry is primarily a women's college. It is 75 percent women, most of them training to be teachers, and the men who attend are all commuter students. Yes, the school has a basketball team, but it plays out of Elisaville Community High School. A quick check with a senior person in the office confirms that the coach can be found working at Bubba's Garage on Main Street.

The coach turns out to be a Laverne Draper, who once played a bit in the ABA. He is himself six and a half feet tall and is easy to spot, even covered with grease and oil. An expression of wariness greets the out-of-towner, stays put when he learns the visitor is a reporter, and does not turn to a grin until the name of W.E.B. Pancake is mentioned. Here, at last, is somebody who remembers.

(To be continued)

116

# 17

Larry Miller was mad at everyone. On the night of the Detroit game, while he was getting sonar treatment on his thigh, he started in on Felix. He did it partly because Felix happened to be sitting next to him, waiting his turn with Crabbie, and partly because Felix was babbling away about things that had nothing to do with the game.

"I don't understand you, man," Larry said. "I really don't."

Felix grinned. He was always grinning and that was another thing that bothered Larry about him. "It's just a party," Felix said. "It's just a dinner they invited me to."

"It's a fund-raiser, man. Why you think they invited you? You don't think they coulda got Willie Mays or O.J. Simpson, they woulda invited him instead of you? Seriously, why do you think they want you?"

"I don't know."

"You don't know? Then, man, why're you going?"

Felix's eyes sought out Crabbie's and his grin intensified. " 'Cause they got good-looking women, why you think? Good-looking women always Republicans."

"Good-looking white women, you mean."

Crabbie, who had been grinning back at Felix, immediately dropped his head. This part of the conversation was not for him.

"Good-looking rich women," Felix said.

117

"What you need a rich woman for? You make more money than ninety-nine point nine percent of the people in this country."

"I do now," Felix agreed. "But how long that gonna be? You hear what they was saying about Novaceski? Novo's making about twenty-five grand a year working, what, some fast-food chain. Three, four years from now, I'm not playing ball, you see me still meeting all these people? No way."

"So why would you want to meet them now?"

"Because three, four years, like I say, I be looking for a job and maybe these people remember me then. Maybe they appoint me to something. They looking for a commissioner of something or other, and maybe one of them say, 'You remember Felix, what a nice guy he was? Let's appoint him.' "

Larry was on the verge of erupting. He felt like leaping down from the table and grabbing Felix by the throat. He would give one long and steady squeeze, thereby advancing the cause of black folks throughout America for a generation to come. But as the thought raced through his mind, Biltmore came striding up, goofy as usual. He wanted to know when Crabbie could set up some heat treatment for his lower back . . . just as if Crabbie wasn't already busting his fat little ass taking care of Larry.

"Hey, Needledick," he said, "you hear the shit you were saying on the radio last night?"

Biltmore beamed uncertainly, as if he were hoping to be complimented on his sorry performance.

"Why didn't you come down hard on that old woman who asked you if a game could be fixed?"

Biltmore hesitated, waiting to see if this was a joke. The guys played jokes on him a lot, but Larry wasn't usually part of that. Larry had no sense of humor. Biltmore shrugged.

"You let yourself get manipulated, man."

"I did not."

"You were agreein' with her, man. 'Oh, somebody could miss a shot or something.' What's that supposed to mean?"

"I didn't say that."

"You did too. I heard you. Tell him, Felix. You heard what the man said."

But it wasn't Felix who answered. It was Jerome, and he spoke in a booming voice that carried across the locker room. "Hey, whyn't you just shut the fuck up?"

For a couple of seconds the locker room was totally silent. Larry, who had barely even noticed Jerome, suddenly had a clear view of the man sitting in front of his cubicle with one sock on his foot and one sock dangling from his hand. He was smirking, as if he had said a very funny thing. Except nobody else in the room was smiling, not even Tim. Everybody was just staring at Jerome as if he were crazy, and Larry appreciated that.

Not since he was a kid had anyone addressed him that way, and he was not about to take it from some nappy-headed ghetto clown now. He got slowly to his feet, pushing Crabbie to one side without looking at him, staring hard at Jerome, challenging him to get his big ass off his chair. But Jerome did not so much as flinch. He never even lowered his sock.

"Fuck you, man," Larry said.

"Suck my dick," Jerome returned calmly, and he used his free hand to show Larry where it was and what a formidable task he was imposing on him.

Larry would have moved then. He would have taken that ugly thing and twisted it around Jerome's neck except that Booby suddenly appeared in the middle of the room, clapping his hands as loud as gunshots. "All right, all right, all right," he kept saying. "What is this crap? Fighting between ourselves? Calling each other names? What are we going to do next? Sleep with each other's women? Let's save our fight for Detroit, for chrissake. Let's get dressed and get the hell out there on the court." And then he was gone, clapping his way right out the door.

To a man, the Gaters were left staring at each other in shock. Larry sat down slowly. He would have liked to have kept his eyes fixed on Jerome, but the suck-my-dick grin was gone from Jerome's face and even he looked perplexed by the coach's bizarre performance. What had Coach meant about sleeping

119

with each other's women? Larry didn't sleep with other men's women. Coach did, but Jerome? Jerome would sleep with a dog, you gave him a chance. Was he sleeping with Coach's wife? Hell, not even Coach wanted to sleep with her. Was Coach saying Jerome was sleeping with Larry's wife? Is that why he figures they were fighting?

With all that was going on, nobody thought to mention Colin Cromwell's column. The rest of the team just assumed that W.E.B. was upset for the same reasons they were.

The experiment of starting Jerome in Zeke's spot was over. In Miami they had done the same as in Atlanta, using a small shooting forward to pull him out farther and farther from the basket until he was not only ineffective, but detrimental. Since Del already played away from the basket, that left only W.E.B. to do any defensive rebounding. Miami had shot and charged the basket, leaving Jerome trailing after his man, more often than not pushing him from behind.

Larry was glad that Jerome was not starting. That meant he did not have to shake hands with the chump when they introduced the starting lineup.

Of those who did start against Detroit, Larry was the only one who did not play well, missing six of his first seven shots. The worse he played, the madder he got.

When Jerome substitued for Zeke, Larry would not pass to him, not even when he was wide open. Jerome did not say anything, he just laughed and pointed to let Larry know that he knew what was going on and that Larry could expect some of the same. Shortly after that, however, Larry picked up his third foul. Booby replaced him with Reggie Champlin, and Detroit surged to a 10-point lead. Booby left Larry on the bench and sent in Felix McDaniel to take Reggie's place.

The Gaters slowly chipped away at the Detroit lead in the second half, finally going in front on a Del Fuego basket with thirty seconds remaining. Twenty seconds later Detroit went back into the lead by a single point. Booby took out Zeke and sent in Jerome, who promptly grabbed an offensive rebound off an errant shot by Rynn Packard and put the ball right back up. He jammed it into the basket, his hands and his forearms seemingly going right into the hoop, and the Gaters had the victory.

Once again, the only Gater who did not get to play was Oliver Dawkins, and afterward, in the locker room, he refused to change out of his uniform. Crabbie, whose job it was to pick up all the sweaty shirts and shorts and socks and jocks that the players threw into a pile in the center of the floor, who could not go home until he had all the uniforms (sweaty or not) stuffed into the laundry bag, begged Oliver to give him his clothes, but Oliver told him to eat shit. Crabbie had to go and get Booby.

With the coach standing over him, with everyone in the locker room looking on, Oliver loudly demanded to be traded.

For the second time that night Booby did a very strange thing. He began to laugh in a nonfunny kind of way, a "heh-heh-heh" that made Oliver demand to know what he meant.

"Oliver," Booby said, "with your contract and your lack of performance, there's nobody out there who's willing to take you off our hands."

Oliver leaped to his feet, furious. He flung out his index finger as if he were snapping open a switchblade and shouted, "Oh, yeah?"

But Booby's only response was to keep cackling "heh-heh-heh," until finally he turned and walked out of the locker room.

Oliver had to do something in front of all the people who saw this. Among the people his eyes fell on was Larry, but Larry neither blinked nor looked away. Oliver was messing up and it was time he learned it. Besides, he hadn't done anything to come to Larry's aid when Jerome was jumping down his throat.

So Oliver, after a moment, looked away. Then he threw himself down on the bench in front of his locker, muttering and tearing at the lacings on his sneakers. The sneakers were from a shoe company that paid him a great deal of money to wear

121

them. They had red piping and a bright yellow logo, and when they were off his feet, Oliver hurled them against the wall and screamed to anyone who cared to listen that he was going to get himself a new agent.

Larry picked up his shampoo and headed for the shower. He had his own problems.

# 18

Petunia Dawkins was a confident woman. That confidence had been bred in her throughout her childhood in Wilmington, North Carolina, where her father owned a drayage company and her mother was a school administrator. The fact that her father was a high school dropout and her mother held two degrees from Fisk University was something that Petunia took for granted as a little girl. It did not seem important because she knew her father's business was not insubstantial, and he was a physically large man with a good word and a handout for anyone who needed it. But the dichotomy was something that began to take on increasing significance as the years passed and Petunia's four older siblings drifted into early pregnancies, early marriages, and limited careers.

Petunia, the baby of the family, became the focus of her mother's aspirations. By the time Petunia was ten she knew that she was not only headed for college, but for great things in life. Important things. Her brother and sisters, far from resenting the inordinate attention she was receiving, came to think of her as a surrogate, someone who could make up for the disappointments they knew they had provided their mother. The more Petunia's mother devoted herself to her, the more her father stayed away from both of them until, by the time Petunia was fourteen or fifteen, her father virtually lived at his truck yard.

If asked, Petunia professed great love for her father, and she always described him to acquaintances as an owner of a trucking company who employed six drivers and drove himself around in a red Cadillac. She did it with a slough of her eyes, as if to say, "You know the type." But she maintained very little contact with him, particularly after she went away to college, and she tended to exclude him from references to her mother and her mother's house.

Oliver had only met Petunia's father twice, once at her graduation, and once at their wedding. Petunia's father, who, like nearly every other living North Carolinian, was a basketball fan, had been very pleased to meet Oliver, but their exchanges on both occasions had been limited to handshakes and nervous smiles, and Petunia's father never asked for the game tickets he would have loved to have had, and Oliver did not think of offering them because the subject of basketball never arose.

As with her father, Petunia would have been quick to tell anyone who needed to know that her husband was an intelligent man. It just never occurred to her that Oliver did not need her help in solving nearly every crisis that arose in his life. Perhaps, if challenged, if an Orwellian rat cage had been affixed to her head, she would have admitted that she considered herself brighter than anyone else she knew; but that was not the thought process that impelled her to be outspoken, to form immediate opinions, to implement plans for herself and others, and to seize on excuses whenever things did not work out precisely as she had anticipated. She was simply used to responding to situations in the unfettered belief that she was right.

Oliver had always been tremendously impressed with this approach to life. He had grown up with absolute, unthinking, undoubting confidence in his physical coordination, and it seemed to him that his wife somehow employed that same instinctive feeling when it came to intellectual problem solving. For him, nonathletic problems of almost any sort were a struggle. Multiple options, multiple points of view, invariably brought home to him how little he really knew; and that, in turn, made him feel weak, incapable, and to a certain extent that he would never admit—not even to himself—scared. He tried to learn from Petunia. He knew how it *looked* to be intellectually and socially self-confident, and he had an idea that

124

by asserting such self-confidence, by believing he had such self-confidence, he could blast right past the doubts and fears he did not want to have.

Paradoxically, Petunia herself made him feel doubtful and afraid. This sometimes made him rebel against her and her advice, but he had absolute, abiding faith in her wisdom—much as his mother had for her minister—and he always listened to what she said regardless of whether he followed it. That was why he sat patiently through all the reasons she gave as to why he should hire Reynolds Rosenthal as his agent.

"That man Rosenthal," she said, shaking her finger at Oliver as he sat alongside his kitchen table, "he knows how to work the angles. You think Curtis made it back into the league because he suddenly learned how to drive the baseline? Rosenthal, he made the league want Curtis back. And that's what we got to do with you."

She walked to the refrigerator and got out a can of grape soda. She put ice cubes into a glass, poured the soda over the ice cubes, and pushed the glass across the table and into Oliver's hand. "A year ago, every team in the league was dying to have you. Now you listen to that bull Booby Sinclair gives you, you think every team in the league was wrong and only he's right?"

Petunia put her hands on her hips and bent forward at the waist. She was wearing a red and black and green plaid skirt and a black leotard top. The outfit did not make her look particularly attractive, but it made her look solid. "He thinks you play half a year for him and now nobody else wants you? Why not? 'Cause they think so much of him as a judge of talent? Then how come Earl Putnam's starting for San Antonio and scoring in double figures every night? How come Leotis Clark's starting for Indianapolis? How come his team with his choice at point guard has lost sixty percent of its games this year? It's not 'cause of you, Oliver Dawkins."

"That's right." Oliver raised the glass to his lips. The carbonation bubbles spacked over the ice cubes and some of them landed in his mustache and for no other reason brought to his mind the thought that a nice line of coke might be just the

125

thing he needed to carry on this discussion. A nice fat line. Or maybe a bowlful. You fire up a bowl and you wouldn't even care about the discussion.

"You listening to me?" Petunia had moved closer. She was staring directly into his face.

"I'm listening."

"Well, where your eyes going then?"

"They're right here. See?" He spread them as wide as they could go. He poked two fingers at them.

"What I'm saying, Oliver, is that Booby Sinclair doesn't like your contract, you say, 'Fine.' You just buy it back."

"Buy it back?"

"See, I told you you weren't listening."

Oliver nodded, knowing that if he got past this minicrisis of attention he could catch on to what she was saying.

"I never liked that contract anyway, and you know it. Three years, that's too long for somebody like you. That man Tresh, he wasn't looking to get you as much as possible. He was looking to drag out negotiations as long as he could. You know why. He was getting paid by the hour and the more hours he put in the more money he put in his pocket. So he always knew he was going to get you to sign just before the season started. Most agents—I know, I talk to the other wives—they're on percentage. The more they get for you, the more they get for themselves. That's what you want, Oliver."

Oliver nodded again. It was the safest thing to do.

"Now you talk to Curtis and you make sure that's the way Reynolds Rosenthal works. 'Cause if he does, then we meet with him, tell him what we want. That's buy up your contract somehow. We play out this year and then we sell ourselves to somebody who'll give us the money we need to pay off the GoldenGaters."

Oliver laid his now empty glass to rest. "I don't think it works that way, honeybunch. Teams, you know, they don't just go letting number one draft picks walk away without gettin' sumpin' back for 'em."

"That's why you need an agent, Oliver. A real agent. We need a man who can figure out how they work these things, who can go to say, Sacramento, and plant a little bug in somebody's ear like, 'Hey, Oliver's unhappy in San Francisco and he'd be willing to rewrite his contract if he could come here.' That's one way to do it."

Oliver got to his feet. "Okay."

Petunia looked at him in surprise. "You'll talk to Curtis?"

"You bet," he said, leaving the room.

She watched him walk to the stairs that led down to his pool room. "I'd do it myself," she called out, "but Curtis doesn't have a wife or a girlfriend or anything and I barely know the man, myself."

"I'll do it," Oliver yelled as he shut the door behind him.

# CROMWELL'S CORNER

## A Web of Intrigue
### by Colin Cromwell

Laverne Draper, veteran of 23 games with the Virginia Squires of the defunct ABA, makes a futile attempt to clean his enormous hands with an oily rag and admits that he was indeed the last college coach of W.E.B. Pancake.

"W.E.B. just showed up one day," he says. Laverne is being serious, choosing his words carefully. He does not know this bespectacled Yankee who has just driven into town and started asking questions. He cares enough that the questioner claims to be a reporter that he is willing to answer, but he is not sure what there is to be gained by talking too much. Still, this point about an 11-year pro who had just shown up to play basketball for a school that is primarily known as a rural women's teachers college deserves some elucidation.

"It's not as though we recruit or nothin'," Laverne acknowledges. This makes sense. After all, the school has no gym and its coach works full-time as a garage mechanic in a gas station.

W.E.B. Pancake played two full seasons for Laverne Draper's Mighty Thunderclaps, but Coach Draper is surprised to learn that the Gaters' *Media Guide* says he went to high school in Okinawa. On the other hand, he says, it didn't much matter. "We just put up a sign, you know: boys' basketball tryouts at such and such a time on such and such a date. And one day, there he was."

Now Laverne laughs at the memory. "He knew how to shoot so I guess he'd played somewhere before."

"Didn't you ever try to find out where?" asks our innocent scribe.

128

Laverne shrugs. "He was from Anniston, as I recollects. But he didn't come right from high school to here. He'd been away for a while, I think. The army, maybe. Anyway, he knew how to play basketball, and that's all I cared about."

Before the reader leaps to his telephone to call the NCAA about such a seemingly callous attitude, it should be mentioned that Laverne Draper is paid $500 per year to coach the Mighty Thunderclaps. In addition to coaching, he often drives the team to away games, tapes their ankles, and occasionally even launders their uniforms. He has no connection with the college other than as seasonal coach, and he does this job for only one reason: "I like playing basketball."

What then, did he think of having a pro caliber player like W.E.B. Pancake suddenly appear on his team?

"What I liked best," he says, "is I had somebody to go one-on-one with. The team used to practice a hour and a half a day, after the high school was done. Then the team go home and me and W.E.B. go at it another hour. Every day."

Laverne Draper laughs only his second laugh of the interview. "I like to think I taught him some things. Course, he know'd a lot when he got here, but I like to think I helped him some, too."

Has Laverne been surprised by his prodigy's success?

He thinks about it. "We play about 25 games a year. We got boys who can play, but they mostly local boys and sometimes they got other responsibilities. We've had players miss games 'cause they couldn't get off work or couldn't get no baby-sitter. If we win 10 games, we consider we done good. When W.E.B. was here, though, we won 17, both years. We went to Birmingham and beat Samford and Birmingham-Southern. We beat Athens State and Mobile College and Mt. Saint Mary's. We even beat Alabama A. and M., and it wasn't 'cause of nobody else but W.E.B.

"I'll tell you how much he meant. After we beat all them teams, we go to Jacksonville State, up there near Anniston, and for some reason W.E.B. couldn't make the trip. We lost by 20 points and Jacksonville State didn't belong on the same court with A and M. Our team was Pancake and the other coaches saw that, you know. That's how he got in that all-star game down New Orleans where he got scouted.

### Walter Walker

"I guess you could say I knew he could do it if he ever got the chance. It's just, I seen a lot of boys around here who could do it if they ever got the chance."

He shakes his head ruefully, and it is clear to his visitor that Laverne Draper's mind is no longer on W.E.B. Pancake.

(To be continued)

# 19

Chris Sarantopoulis never said much to W.E.B., and while it was true that Chris never said much to anybody, he had more opportunity to never say much to W.E.B. than he did with most people.

It was Chris's job to play W.E.B. tough in practice and to spell him for a few minutes at a time during games. Chris did not aspire to W.E.B.'s position, and while that was recognized by both men, it still did not make them friends. W.E.B. was a player. Chris was a backup. And there was a gulf between them like that of an officer and an enlisted man.

Chris had twice been cut by the Gaters, just as he had been cut by Chicago and Portland. The difference was that the Gaters had resigned him each time after brief sojourns with minor league teams, and out of this series of signings and releases a general understanding had developed. Chris Sarantopoulis had a job with this team only as long as nobody better was available.

It was this understanding that caused Chris to try to make himself both invisible and useful at all times. He never complained. He cheered his teammates from the bench. He left his seat at every time-out and slapped the hands and patted the butts of the men who came off the floor. If Booby told him to go in and lean on someone, he went in and leaned. If he was told to take a charge, he positioned himself with his arms over his head in front of some rampaging opponent and let the man run into him. He did what he was told to the best of his ability, and he prayed each day that it was sufficient.

Yet Chris was realistic enough to know that the only reason he was a basketball player was because he was seven feet tall and 270 pounds. He was well aware that he was slow and awkward and that even W.E.B. wished he was better than he was. Chris Sarantopoulis therefore viewed each personnel change with trepidation. Most particularly, he worried about Jerome Crown, who not only stood six feet eleven inches, but had played center all his life until he entered the league. Chris lived with the certainty that it was only a matter of time until the Gaters' great basketball minds remembered this.

Chris nonetheless exulted when Jerome scored the winning basket against Detroit. He had done it at the power forward position, Zeke's position, and the more he could accomplish there, the less threat he was to Chris. For the first time since Jerome joined the team Chris actually meant it when he cheered Jerome's accomplishment. Indeed, he left the arena that night feeling nearly as joyful about Jerome's basket as Jerome himself did.

Chris's joy lasted right up until he returned to the arena the next day for practice and found Dale Rohmer waiting in the locker room.

Dale Rohmer was not a welcome sight to marginal players such as Chris. Dale Rohmer was the grim reaper.

From the instant he saw Dale the spring went out of Chris's step. He did not make the slightest attempt to acknowledge the general manager's presence, and yet, when he reached his cubicle, he undressed very slowly. If he was going to be released, he wanted as little humiliation as possible. He did not want to be wearing his practice clothes and then have the other guys see him have to strip them off. So he took his time with the buttons on his shirt and he folded his pants neatly and he tucked his socks into his shoes and arranged them on the floor shelf, and he gave Rohmer every opportunity to approach him discreetly.

The players came in, one or two at a time, and no matter how garrulous they may have been in the corridor, each went about his business quietly when he saw Dale. W.E.B. walked in with a newspaper under his arm, and when he sat down he

132

spread the newspaper out on his knees and stared at it, and Chris remembered that Colin Cromwell had written a column that he had meant to read, one that was all about W.E.B.'s college or something like that. Chris would never have asked W.E.B. what was in the column, but he particularly was not going to mention it now, not while Dale Rohmer was in the room and anything he said might draw attention his way.

So Chris was silent, and W.E.B. was silent, and off to one side Rynn Packard was silent because he had been in a funk for days. Zeke was silent because he knew his starting position was still on the line. Larry was silent because he was mad at Jerome. Oliver was silent because he was mad at everybody. Tim was silent because he thought everybody was mad at him. Jerome tried a few jokes, but nobody laughed and then he acted hurt and fell silent himself. The door opened and into this tomblike atmosphere walked Curtis Clovis and Reggie Champlin.

Reggie was in the middle of telling what must have been a good story because Curtis was grinning from ear to ear, and then they saw Dale and Curtis stopped grinning and Reggie stopped talking. Dale took a step toward them and Chris looked away.

He pulled on his practice shirt, pulled on his shorts, crammed his feet into his sneakers, and as soon as he was done tying and tugging at the laces, he started for the door. It was only then that he saw what damage Dale Rohmer had done. Reggie Champlin was seated on the bench in front of his cubicle, his head buried in his hands. Rohmer was bent over him, touching his shoulder, whispering in his ear.

Crabbie glided up. He hovered for a moment, then darted forward, slipping an airline ticket between Reggie's splayed fingers. Reggie grasped it without raising his head. He knew what it was.

Chris remembered that Reggie was from the Midwest somewhere, Kansas City maybe, and they would be flying him back home. That was the worst message of all. Sometimes when they needed to open a spot on the roster they would tell a player he was hurt, tell him he had back spasms or something like that, and then they would carry him on their injured-reserve list. But plane tickets, they were walking papers.

Reggie had been through the league before. He had gone off to Europe and worked his way back for one more chance. He was twenty-eight years old and had a wife and some kids, and this was, most likely, the end of his career. As he watched Reggie press the ticket to the side of his head, Chris felt immensely sorry for the man. And glad at the same time.

Booby whistled them up and they gathered in the middle of the court. All but Oliver. He had been the last to arrive on the practice floor, and now he kept shooting by himself, just as if he were not with the rest of them. Booby ignored him, ignored the bouncing ball, the soft squeak of sneakers, the thumps and clangs and *phhts* as Oliver's shots hit the backboard, the rim, the net.

"We've got a new player joining us," Booby announced.

Some of the ten men in front of him sat on balls. Some held balls on their hips. Some spun balls on or between their fingers. The only players making contact with each other were Del and Zeke. Zeke was bent over, his hands on his knees, and Del was leaning on him.

"Woody's very high on him. Six-seven, which means he can play swing, and averaging about eighteen and a half points, so he can shoot—"

Oliver stopped shooting and wandered over, as if he were half-curious to see why the crowd was gathering.

"—twelve, thirteen assists a game, and I'm told he was leading the Continental Basketball Association in steals, so he should be an asset on defense."

"Coach?"

Booby looked up as if he were not sure but that maybe the Lord was calling him from the rafters. "Yes, Oliver?"

"I thought you told us a big number of steals don't mean much. I thought you told us it just means a guy's reaching in a lot. When a guy's reaching in three things can happen, and two of 'em's bad. That's what I thought you said."

Booby stared unblinkingly at Oliver, who stared back the

same way. Chris quickly riveted his eyes to the floor. All around him guys were shifting their feet. Someone coughed.

It was Biltmore who broke the ominous silence. "What did you say his name was, Coach?"

Heaving a single exaggerated sigh, Booby said, "Jonnie, spelled funny, Martin. Jonnie Martin."

"Kentucky?"

"Georgetown?"

"I think I played against him, man. Southwest Missouri State, right?"

Booby said, "I'm told he went to Irvine."

Some of the players hastened to pick up the banter. "What's Irvine, man?"

"I knew a dude named Irvine."

"Irvine Berlin, man. He wrote the 'Star Spangled Banner' or something."

"The University of California at Irvine," said Booby, dragging out each word. "Small school program, near Newport Beach. Volleyball school."

"Maybe it was 'America the Beautiful.' "

"He a volleyball player, Coach?"

"He's a goddamn basketball player. He just went to a small school and nobody picked up on him and now he's jumping over goddamn buildings for the Albany Patroons of the CBA."

"Volleyball guys do that. I seen 'em in the Olympics, man."

"I never heard of him, Coach," Oliver said, raising his voice above the others. "I never heard of him or his school."

There was only a moment's pause. Then someone said, "They jump so high, how come you never see no brothers playin' volleyball?"

"Wilt Chamberlain, I heard he played volleyball."

"I heard he could snatch silver dollars off the top of the backboard."

"Who? Jonnie Martin?"

"No, fool. Wilt Chamberlain."

"I don't believe that, man. Who go puttin' silver dollars up there in the first place?"

"Shut up!" Booby Sinclair's shout was so sudden and so loud

that everybody froze. In all the practices and all the games that he had played under Booby, Chris had never heard him shout like that. Never a shout that was so out of control. Never a shout that was so unnecessary. The guys were only goofing to cut the tension.

Chris watched as Booby slung a few long strands of hair out of his eyes, but Booby did not look at any of them. He seemed about to say something and then, instead, he signaled to his assistant: "Hack, run them through some plays." Then he turned and stalked off the court.

Chris watched him go. He did not watch Hack as he rolled over a portable blackboard and threw himself into the task of tracing patterns of X and O figures.

Hack was excited. "All right," he called out. "San Antonio's coming in and they've got a whole new look since Earl Putnam's taken over at point guard." His chalk hit the board with the sound of clacking typewriter keys.

Chris did not understand what was going on with Booby. In the old days, in Chris's first tour with the Gaters, even in his second, Booby would have reamed any player who was acting the way Oliver was. He would never have allowed a team meeting to get out of hand. But now he no longer seemed to care.

It was all so crazy. Here was a man who had everything. He had a great job and he was great at it. He had the respect of his players, his peers, his GM. He was handsome and smart and rich and famous. He was even the right size. Chris would have taken any of those things as a gift from God. Yet there was Booby Sinclair, acting as if none of it were good enough.

Hack was diagramming San Antonio's plays. He was drawing lines and pointing arrows. He kept up a running dialogue about how to play Earl Putnam. Then he smacked the chalk into the board one final time and demanded to know if there were any questions.

Tim Biltmore raised his hand. "This guy who's joining us . . . is he going to be getting any minutes at forward?"

136

# CROMWELL'S CORNER

## A Web of Intrigue—Part II
### by Colin Cromwell

In Jimmy Dean's great song of years gone by, "Big Bad John," he told us "nobody knew where John called home. He just drifted into town and stayed all alone."

In Elisaville, Alabama, nobody seems to know where Big W.E.B. Pancake called home when he went to school in this tiny (pop. 1,843) town slightly more than a decade ago. He just drifted into town and stayed all alone.

The administration at Jones-Henry College was unable to tell me anything about him, other than the fact that he is on their alumni list and is not shown to have received a degree. The school's records from beyond the past four years are not computerized, and I was told it would take days to do a hand-check of files in storage.

The basketball program, consisting of one underpaid, overworked, part-time coach, was unable to tell me anything about W.E.B. other than it was thought he came from Calhoun County and had been somewhere else between high school and Jones-Henry. Your intrepid investigative reporter was thus forced to begin tracking down other potential sources of information.

A former teammate of W.E.B.'s, Gerald "Goosey" Goggins, was located in town working as a deliveryman. "He never associated much with the rest of us," said Goosey. "Seems to me he didn't live too close by." Goosey thought W.E.B. had a family somewhere and would just come to town for games and practices. He could not ever remember seeing him at classes.

Goosey referred me to Clarence Tatum, another teammate, a man whose seriousness is projected by his black

137

horn-rimmed glasses. Tatum is now a science teacher at Elisaville Community High, and he is the first person in town to whom W.E.B. does not seem a total mystery.

"He was," Tatum says in no uncertain terms, "older than the rest of us. Goosey, Phil Winslow, and I had all gone through school together. We'd known each other all our lives. We were still kids when we were playing at Jones-Henry, and when W.E.B. arrived, he was to us a grown man, somebody closer to Coach Draper in terms of age and experience. I mean, when we were on the court with him it was like, 'Yes, sir. No, sir.' And after we got off the court he'd go his way and we'd go ours."

I asked Clarence Tatum if he had ever discussed W.E.B.'s past with him, and Tatum shook his head. "Not really. I know he'd played ball at some other school, but he just said it was up north and he wasn't the kind of guy you pressed too much for information." The subject of Okinawa, of being born and raised overseas, never came up—at least not to Clarence Tatum's recollection. He, too, was under the impression that W.E.B. came from Anniston.

Clarence, like Goosey, could not ever remember seeing W.E.B. in class, had never been to his home, and vaguely recalled his having a family. This, however, is the extent of the information Clarence Tatum will give me. "You know," he explained, again using the no-uncertain-terms tone of voice that has probably terrorized a generation of Elisaville students, "you're asking questions as though W.E.B. has done something wrong. I may not have known him well, but he was a teammate and I'm not going to say anything that could possibly get that man in trouble."

Pleas for the public's right to know thereafter fell on deaf ears. Clarence Tatum, the college boy who had been impressed by his more mature teammate, will tell me only something about himself. He is, he says, now 33 years old. That is the exact same age listed in the Gaters' *Media Guide* for W.E.B. Pancake.

(To be continued)

# 20

At the end of every practice, Gaters shoot foul shots. Zeke hated shooting foul shots. Ball didn't go in. And if it did, so what? Have to do it again. Ten, twenty, twenty-five times. Dudes like Rynn Packard shot a hundred a day. Every day. Nothing better to do. Like playing darts. Anybody could do it if he didn't have nothing better to do all day long. Didn't have to be big, strong, quick, mean, or nothing. Just have to like being bored. Zeke had been bored enough in his life.

He threw up a shot and it bounced out. Rynn, who was his shooting partner this day, fetched it for him. Zeke threw up another. It missed everything. He wasn't paid to shoot foul shots. His percentage, Coach Dyk had told him, was .574 or something like that. Wasn't worst in the league.

Some noise started up behind him. He looked over his shoulder and saw a couple of the San Antonio guys coming on the court for their practice. There was Earl the Put, first one out, slapping hands with his old teammates. The San Antonio team was on their Northwestern swing and they had come down this morning from Portland.

Zeke took the ball one more time from Rynn, fired up a last shot that hit the backboard hard and then ricocheted into the net, declared, "Twenny-five," and walked away from the free-throw line even as Rynn Packard was giving him the kind of funny look that said he had been counting and knew that Zeke had done no more than fifteen.

He met Earl Putnam at the half-court line, where he stood in his silver and black sweats talking to Del Fuego. Earl held a ball between his forearms and his crotch. Del was poking him. Both men were smiling.

"Earl forty-points-per-game Putnam," Del was saying. But they stopped their fooling so that Zeke and Earl could get their greetings down.

"Howyoudoin', babe?"

Earl said he doing all right.

Zeke asked him, "Howyoulikenit,SanAntone?" and Earl said, "I'm gettin' to play."

"And kickin' ass." Del took a swipe at Earl's head, which was shaved bald on the sides and brushed straight up on top. "You look like a plumber's helper," said Del.

Earl ducked out of the way. That put the spark in Del and he went after the dude to box his ass, but Earl kept dancing away until both men got laughing too hard to keep it going.

"That's great, man," Del said. "It really is. We look in the paper every day, see how you doin'. I have to read it aloud to Zeke, here, you know." Quickly, Del curled his shoulder to protect himself from the rap he knew Zeke was going to give him. "I say, 'Yep, there's twenty-six points we coulda had—if only Earl had learned to do a two-handed bounce pass.' "

Zeke laughed along with Del and Earl at that one, but he threw a look over his shoulder just to make sure Booby wasn't still standing around. Trouble enough with Booby playing Jerome in his minutes. No need to create more.

Earl said something about Jerome. He called him "ole bad-ass Jerome."

Del said, "He is a weird dude, man. I steer clear of that guy."

Earl said, "You ought to hear the stories they tell on this team, man. Like, you know he wasn't taking no showers after practice?"

"You shittin'."

"Swear, man. He said nobody on the team liked him. So after practices he just put on his sweats and go home."

Zeke spoke up. "Youhearhedrivin'limonow?"

"Big one?"

"Bigasamotherfuckin'bus."

140

"You're right," Earl said, rolling his eyes at Del, "he's a weird dude, man."

"How about Gilbert? We don't hear nothin' about him."

"Not so good. He's riding pine."

Del put his hand to his brow, like a sailor, and looked all over the court. "Well, where is he? Why isn't he out here?"

"He's not a happy dude, man, and he's lettin' folks know it. You know what I'm sayin'? Things ain't going right and he's makin' 'em worse."

"Sounds like Oliver, man."

"You got it."

Zeke saw Del make a face and he made one along with it. Del said, "Okay, gotta cut this fraternizin' 'fore Larry comes out and does a nasty on us. Tell Gilbert I see him later. We'll go to Leon's and get some barbecue."

Zeke thought that was it. He turned to jog off the court, but after a few steps he realized Del was not with him. He looked back and saw that Earl had him by the arm. Earl was pulling him close, so close that Del's ear was right next to his mouth.

As Earl whispered, Del's forehead wrinkled. After a moment he pulled back and stared into Earl's face as if he couldn't get something figured out. Enough space was between them that Zeke could hear Earl say the word *Phoenix*. He could hear Del say, "I don't know what you're talkin' about."

Earl let go of him and said to forget it, but this time Del grabbed him and whispered something hard. Earl tried to back away, but Del kept holding and Earl kept trying to shake free. The movements were not what they were when the two men were faking combat a few minutes ago. Earl hacked at Del's arm and Del let go. A look passed between them as Earl backed toward his own team's end of the court. Zeke had seen that kind of look plenty of times before, back home on the streets. It was the look men gave each other before they killed.

A long moment passed. Del said, "Fuck you, man," and Zeke was glad because guys who said it usually didn't do it.

Earl, still backing away, had an answer. "I put it in your face tomorrow. We see who says fuck you."

Then Earl spun toward his team's basket, took a running step or two, and let fly with the ball he had been holding. Zeke watched it sail through the air, watched it bang off the rim, watched Earl dissolve into the middle of a group of San Antonio players who were bunched under the hoop waiting for rebounds. It was only then that Zeke ran after Del to find out what was happening.

He caught him just outside the locker room. But Del said it wasn't about nothing, and then he hurried away before Zeke could ask anything more.

# CROMWELL'S CORNER

## A Web of Intrigue—Part III
### by Colin Cromwell

In Calhoun County, Alabama, the largest city is Anniston. In Anniston there is but one high school. No one named W.E.B. Pancake ever went there.

"I would know," insists Rose Anne Stanky. "I been here 25 years and the school's only got 1,100 students. I would know if there was a boy with that name. Especially if he was a star basketball player."

Just to make sure, I ask the confident Ms. Stanky to check the archives of Anniston High School. Those records bear out her memory. There has never been a student named W.E.B. Pancake at Anniston High School.

"Perhaps," she says, "your young man went to some high school in the Anniston area. There are nine in Calhoun County, you know, although a couple of them are K through 12."

"Perhaps," I say, but I go to the local newspaper, *The Anniston Star*, instead. I ask to see the *Star*'s winter and spring issues from 16 and 17 years ago, when, presumably, a 33-year-old would have been playing. I peruse the sports pages. I search for the names of local stars. I read the box scores, and I, too, find nobody named W.E.B. Pancake.

I go back further, to the sports pages of 22 and 23 years ago. Again there is no reference to a Pancake. What I do find is that the Calhoun County hotshots of that era were named Fox and Wilson and Dinwiddie and Brewer, and that there was a boy named Smith who was dominating his league. I dig deeper. I study pictures. I learn only that Wilson and Dinwiddie are white and the other three are black.

I push my way into the sports department of *The Anniston*

143

*Star,* flashing my credentials and my portable word processor. The sports editor is unimpressed. He is, perhaps, even a trifle suspicious. "Yes," he admits, he is familiar with W.E.B. Pancake of the San Francisco GoldenGaters. (What do I take him for? He's a sports editor, for gosh almighty sake.) "No," he confesses, he was not aware that W.E.B. comes from Calhoun County. "In fact," he concludes, after giving the matter considerable consideration, "it isn't true." If W.E.B. Pancake came from Calhoun County, he, like Ms. Stanky, would surely know. After all, he has been covering high school sports in this county for 19 years—and Pancake himself is only 33.

(To be continued)

# 21

Ida Pancake did not often attend her husband's basketball games. She was indifferent to the sport itself, and W.E.B. liked it that way. He liked going home after a game and being able to say that the team had won or lost and that he had done well or not done well without having to spend a great deal of time talking about all the things that had happened.

But Ida knew what was going on at all times in her husband's career. She read the papers and listened to the radio, and she watched for the little signs her man gave when things were troubling him.

She had been watching particularly hard ever since the team returned from its road swing and W.E.B. told her about his conversation with Cromwell in the Miami airport. He had told her how the plane had been delayed and how, when they finally boarded, Cromwell had not boarded with them for the trip home; and she and W.E.B. had waited with equal anxiety to see what, if anything, Cromwell would do.

When the first column came out of Elisaville and it was not as bad as they had feared, she tried to offer her husband hope. "Anybody could have checked out your college anytime," she told him; but W.E.B.'s response was that nobody had ever had any reason for going there before now.

The second and third columns appeared and she pointed out that his friends back in Alabama were good men and that they had said all the right things. W.E.B., however, refused to be

145

comforted. "Cromwell ain't through yet," he warned her. And of course W.E.B. had proven right.

And with the fourth column, she had seen a change come over her husband. "Don't take no genius to figure out where Cromwell going next," he said. "He found that boy Wilson. Won't be long till he find Willie Smith."

"He won't find Willie Smith," she assured him.

"He will, and when he do, you can kiss my black ass good-bye."

W.E.B. had said the words sadly, without anger, and she had reacted to that, snapping at him. "He won't find him, W.E.B., and I don't want to hear nothin' more about it. What's more, nobody cares anyhow. Alls we got is one crazy-ass reporter running around the country trying to stir up trouble. Your team-mates don't care what he's saying, do they? No, they do not, else they be sayin' somethin' theyselves. So you just stop wor-ryin' 'bout this and pretty soon Cromwell go on to fry bigger fish."

But she had, nonetheless, come out to the San Antonio game, come to see how her husband was holding up away from home. The other players' wives hid their surprise when she arrived in the section of the stands that was reserved for them, and they went out of their way to make her feel comfortable. They greeted her warmly, Victoria Dixon, Gayle Wyatt, Barbara Miller, Dawn Biltmore. They told her how good she looked, they told her about the visit they had just had from Gilbert Rose's wife, Brenda, who had come here to see her husband's first game at the arena since he had been traded—but they said nothing about the columns. It was, she felt, as though her husband had a disease and everybody was afraid to mention it.

So she sat and listened to the others agree as to how unhappy the Roses were. She listened to them discuss the fact that Brenda and the kids were staying in the Bay Area so that the kids could finish the school year, the fact that Brenda was hav-ing a hard time selling their house, and the fact that Gilbert was living in a San Antonio hotel. They talked about how Gil-bert wasn't getting his minutes with his new team and how difficult it would be to move the family down to southern Texas

146

if there was a chance that he wouldn't be with San Antonio again next year. They all felt that they should give Brenda a call and try to get together.

Then, since Meg Sinclair was not there, they talked about what she had been wearing the last time each of them had seen her. Somebody asked if the others had heard that Booby had been acting weird lately. Somebody asked if Meg and Booby were having trouble, and Victoria said, "No more than usual," and they all burst into laughter.

Finally, the game started and Ida Pancake stopped paying attention to what the other women were saying because her husband was putting on a sensational show. In forty-five minutes of all-out running, W.E.B. pulled down 18 rebounds and scored 24 points, his best numbers of the season. When he left the game late in the fourth quarter, the entire crowd rose to its feet to applaud him, and she felt so proud that her eyes welled with tears. It was only then that anybody acknowledged that she might be having any difficulties of her own. Victoria Dixon leaned over and hugged her to her cheek. Dawn Biltmore reached out and squeezed her hand. "That shows them," Dawn said, and for some reason that made the tears actually roll down Ida's face.

Later, as she stood in the corridor outside the locker room, she wished she could feel better, more excited, happier. And when W.E.B. emerged from the locker room, she could tell by the look on his face that he felt the exact same way. "Don't worry, baby," she murmured. "Mama won't let nothin' bad happen out of this."

# CROMWELL'S CORNER

## The Web Draws Closer
### by Colin Cromwell

There's a fellow in Montgomery, Alabama, who has never met anyone named W.E.B. Pancake, and yet he knows W.E.B. Pancake quite well. William "Trey" Wilson III played against the man known as W.E.B. Pancake six times in official high school games alone. According to Mr. Wilson, he cannot count the number of times they played against each other in unofficial games.

"Only, he wasn't known as W.E.B. Pancake back then," says a smiling Wilson, now a successful businessman and father of four. "His name was Willie Smith, and at the time I was playing he was quite possibly the finest schoolboy basketball player in eastern Alabama."

And what time was that, Mr. Wilson?

He ticks the years off on his fingers. He runs out of fingers. He is talking over 20 years ago. "I'm 38 years old," he says, "soon to be 39. And I played against Willie Smith my sophomore, junior, and senior years in high school. I never asked him his age, but I know he graduated the same year I did."

And where did he go, this Willie Smith?

Trey Wilson shakes his graying head. "He was supposed to go to Oklahoma State, is what I heard."

And did he?

The crow's-feet at the corners of Wilson's eyes crinkle in consternation. "I never heard what happened to him. I played a couple of years at Davidson, myself, and I'd ask around sometimes, check the college basketball magazines and so forth, but he just seemed to have dropped off the planet. That is, until about seven or eight years ago when

148

I turned on the tube and saw him playing for the San Francisco GoldenGaters."

But not as Willie Smith.

"Heck, no. But it was the same guy all right. Bigger, bulkier, you know, and he keeps his hair short now and wears a mustache where he used to have an Afro and be clean-shaven, but it's the same guy. I'd bet my life on it."

Trey Wilson has not verified his discovery with anyone back in Anniston. He was a service kid, he says, his dad stationed at Ft. McClellan, and he did not stay in touch with former teammates or opponents.

"And what the heck," he says. "Ol' Willie wants to pass himself off with a name like W.E.B. Pancake, what do I care? It's not as though he's hurting anyone. I'm just happy to see him hustling up and down the court like he does. It's kind of inspiring, you know?"

It may be. But it is also intriguing, because regardless of the admiration we may feel if in fact W.E.B. Pancake is the 38-year-old Willie Smith, we are nevertheless left with certain haunting questions: Why the name change? What did happen to Smith after high school? Where was he during all those years before he resurfaced at Jones-Henry College? And what is the secret that he has kept hiding all this time?

(To be continued)

# 22

In Sacramento, they played taped music designed to pump up the fans. It filled in whenever there was no action; it entertained and occupied and reminded any spectators who may have forgotten how much money they paid for their tickets that they were at an event, a nonstop, whirling happening in which they were actual participants, in which their energy could be cranked up to the point where it arced from the seats to the gladiators on the floor. Because the seats in Sacramento were close to the floor, the arc did not have to be very long.

On the night of the Gaters' visit, the music became driving just before team introductions. Then it cut abruptly to a simmering, stalking, deep background rhythm of anticipation as the cheery-voiced announcer made known his intention of introducing the visitors from down the highway.

He called out Rynn's name and the stalking music kept playing and the fans booed. He called out Larry's name and the fans booed louder. He called out Zeke's name and the music itself grew more intense and the fans' boos became a steady sound of accompaniment. They were still booing Zeke when the announcer called out "Del Fuego Dixon," and Del, surprised not to be called last, looked around to make sure there was no mistake before he trotted onto the floor.

"And at center, in his eleventh year from Jones-Henry College, at six-ten, numbah forty-five, W.—E.—B.—Pan-cake!"

Immediately, the driving rhythm of the music broke and was replaced by the familiar sounds of a rock classic. The segue was seamless. All of a sudden, with W.E.B. not halfway between bench and foul line, The Who were belting out "Who Are You?"

If W.E.B. was affected by the joke, it was not apparent to Mike Hacker, who was standing on the edge of the circle of players. He never saw W.E.B. complete his journey to clasp hands with his teammates, however, because Booby Sinclair nearly knocked him over in his effort to get down the sideline. The Gaters' coach was pointing at the announcer's table almost before Roger Daltry was done singing the word *who*. And he was yelling.

Hack saw the announcer grin. He grinned as if he and Booby were the best of friends and a good time was being had by all. The grin faded only a little as Booby closed in on him. It faded more as he realized what it was that Booby was shouting. It disappeared altogether when Booby kicked over his table.

There was pandemonium. The announcer went flying backward into the crowd. His microphone, his large Coca-Cola in a wax cup, his papers and pencils and his headphones—all went into the air along with him. People in the first row of seats, people walking in the aisle in front of the first row of seats, screamed and tried to get out of the way. Security guards rushed forward, confident only in grabbing the fans and unsure as to what they should do about Booby, whose arms were flailing, whose white shirt had pulled out of his pants, who was bellowing a nearly unbroken stream of obscenities at the bewildered and terrified announcer as the poor man lay where he had fallen, his bottom still affixed to his folding chair.

The only one who beat Hack to Booby was W.E.B. Two of the referees were right behind, and one of them managed to pull the tails of Booby's sport coat over his head. Booby, now a headless animal, began to punch blindly with his fists and kick with his heels, and nobody wanted to get too close. W.E.B. was trying to speak to him, trying to whisper in his ear that it was all right, that he didn't care, that it was just a joke. But Booby was snorting and yelling "Son of a bitch," and Hack had to shove W.E.B. out of the way. He had to throw his arms around the coach's chest and hoist Booby's feet off the floor by wrenching himself backward. Then one of the refs seized Booby's legs, and together he and Hack held Booby like a rolled carpet.

The Sacramento crowd, gasping just a moment before, now roared with the excitement of a lynch mob. Every person in the arena was on his or her feet straining to get a look, trying to figure out if this was some sort of staged act, yelling advice that grew progressively more savage with each new voice.

Booby was expelled from the game before it even started. Hack and Crabbie escorted him off the floor, each holding an arm, and by the time he got to the locker room he was quiet. He did not start to cry until the door of the locker room closed behind them with a security guard stationed out front to keep everyone else away.

Hack did not know what to do. He wanted to get back to the court because he was first assistant coach and if he wasn't there, Dyk was going to take over the job of running the team. But Booby, his boss, his friend, was sitting on the end of the trainer's table sobbing like a baby. Booby's sport coat was hanging off his shoulders, his tie was loose around his neck, his shirt was spilling like a napkin over his lap, and other than covering his eyes with his thumb and forefinger, he was making no effort whatsoever to control himself.

"You want a drink of water, Boob? A Coke? You want a towel? Want us to call Meg?" Hack asked. Then, when he did not get any normal kind of answer, he looked to Crabbie for help.

Crabbie, although no doctor, no doubt knew more than he did about nervous breakdowns. Crabbie squatted down in front of Booby and put his hands on both of the coach's knees and tried to talk directly into his face.

"Calm down. It's okay, Boob," he said. "Want some water? Want a Coke? Want us to call Meg?"

From out on the court, Hack could hear the sounds of the game getting started. Something happened right away, something that had the crowd roaring and individuals yelling as if they were in a fever.

Hack cocked an ear. For five seconds there was no discernible sound, and then the crowd burst out again as if it had just witnessed a game-winner. The noise made Hack glance at his watch. It made him ask Crabbie what he thought.

The trainer, his round face filled with concern, was saying, "You've got to pull yourself together, Booby. It was no big deal, that song. DubyaBee didn't care. Really, Boob, nothing bothers DubyaBee. It was just a joke."

Hack leaned in. "You okay now, Boob? You gonna be all right by yourself?"

Booby continued to cry.

Hack, for a fleeting moment, wondered whether there was any other woman they should ask about calling—anyone geographically closer than Meg. But he did not voice the thought. He gave a facial shrug to Crabbie instead. He was trying to convey his reluctant acquiescence in case Crabbie was thinking that it might be okay to leave Booby alone.

A whistle shrieked so loudly that the sound made its way to the locker room. Feet stamped over their heads. The building began to shake. Mike Hacker once again checked his watch.

"I think," said Crabbie, issuing his diagnosis, "we ought to get him to a hospital. I think he's suffering from exhaustion."

"Think we should both go?" asked Hack hesitantly.

"I'm not going to any fucking hospital," said Booby; and Hack breathed a sigh of relief.

"Well," said Crabbie, speaking from his squatting position, "at least you're talking. That's one good sign."

"I don't want any press. I don't want anybody seeing me like this."

"Oh, no," agreed Hack. He fought back an urge to check his watch yet another time.

Suddenly there was a banging on the door. A hard knock of the kind that demanded to be answered.

"What is it?" Crabbie shouted.

The security guard answered. "It's one of the ball boys. Needs to talk to the trainer."

153

"I'm the trainer," Crabbie shouted back.

"It's Pancake," a young voice called out. "We think he may have just got his nose busted."

Crabbie slowly raised his eyes until they rested on Hack.

Hack took a long, slow inhale. "Ah, go ahead. I drove my own car up here. I can get Booby home."

Crabbie nodded and rose to his feet, unsure about leaving his patient, but pleased to be so needed. He patted Booby on the knee. He told him he would be okay in a few minutes, and he repeated that Hack would be taking him home. Then Crabbie hoisted up his drawstring GoldenGater sweatpants and hurried off to attend to the nose of W.E.B. Pancake.

And so it was that halfway into the first quarter of the Sacramento contest, the Gaters' fifty-third game of an eighty-two-game season, Jerome Crown, with Mel Dykstra coaching, made his debut at center. Before the final buzzer sounded, Packard, Miller, and Zeke Wyatt would all foul out, and yet the Gaters would still win by 6. Jerome, finishing with 5 fouls, led the team in scoring, rebounds, and blocked shots.

All this became known to Mike Hacker from the car radio as he drove back to the Bay Area with Booby Sinclair curled up against the passenger's door. For well over an hour he had to suffer through Wayne Brickshaw's repeated praises of Mel Dykstra for the deft and incisive way he was handling his depleted forces.

Logic did not affect Brickshaw. He seemed to think it was brilliant of Dyk to move Jerome to center, as if there were any other choice, as if anybody in his right mind would play Sarantopoulis. "A new era of Gaters' basketball may have been born tonight!" Brickshaw crowed.

Hack was, therefore, not surprised when Booby suddenly said out loud, "I'm gonna kill the bastard."

Hack felt the same way.

154

# CROMWELL'S CORNER

## by Colin Cromwell

(There will be no column today by Colin Cromwell, who is on special assignment.)

# 23

The reason that Dale Rohmer was the GoldenGaters' general manager was that Dale, like the team itself, was available when Teddy Brandisi went shopping. The league's Board of Governors, while more than satisfied with the color, width, depth, and expanse of Teddy's money, had been a little concerned about Teddy's knowledge of their sport when he submitted his application to buy the team. They did not want anyone coming into their ranks who might tarnish their image or screw up their television contracts, and Teddy, after all, was an unknown quantity to them.

Dale Rohmer, on the other hand, was a part of the great league family. And the reason he was available when Teddy needed him was that he had retired from the coaching ranks upon developing a serious ulcer, and had gone home to his wife and teenage daughters—only to discover that as a result of his having spent the better part of the previous nineteen years on the road, his family had grown quite accustomed to doing without him. Indeed, his day-to-day presence had proven to be an uncomfortable, even unnecessary intrusion into their lives, and while his ulcer disappeared, he put on thirty-five pounds and began to suffer depression.

Thus, when Teddy got word as to what was bothering the Board of Governors, he called Dale, whose name he knew from Dale's playing days with Boston, and Dale promptly opted for the return of the ulcer. Teddy got his team, his franchise, and Dale's family packed him up and sent him off to San Francisco to live in a hotel and drink Maalox and smoke cigarettes and get home for three or four days at a clip whenever he could. Just like the old days.

Rohmer liked being a general manager. It did not require the incessant travel, the pressure, and the inherent feelings of guilt that went with being a coach. He particularly liked being Teddy Brandisi's general manager because Teddy—at least since the uproar that had occurred when Booby threatened to quit over the Del Fuego Dixon trade—let him run the team whatever way he wanted.

But Teddy, as Rohmer knew better than anyone, was willing to wait only so long to be delivered a winner, and after three straight years of being eliminated in the first round of the play-offs, time was running out as far as Teddy was concerned. He needed something to brag about to his friends. He needed some return on his money.

Dale had tried to impress this upon Booby when he met with him in Houston during the disastrous road trip back in January. He had tried to explain that from Teddy's perspective he had let them draft defensive players Larry Miller and Zeke Wyatt and pay a fortune for Oliver Dawkins, only to end up with the same mediocre record the team had when he bought it. Dale had come right out and told Booby that if something did not turn around soon for the Gaters, it was going to be their jobs that were on the line—and that he, Dale Rohmer, owed it to his wife and daughters to make sure it was Booby's job that went before his own.

Booby had listened, he had nodded in agreement, he had even gone along with Rohmer's directions for the San Antonio game—starting Curtis, playing Earl—but his compliance had been disconcerting. Rohmer had expected a fight, an argument, a denunciation of the meddlesome Brandisi and his basketball ignorance, but he had gotten none of that. And while Rohmer had been loathe to believe that Booby might have lost his intensity, his desire, his will to win, the fact was that Dale had had enough doubts that he had gone ahead and made the Jerome Crown deal on his own, without consulting Booby.

Now he could no longer so much as pretend that Booby did

not have problems. Booby's screaming, uncontrolled tantrum had taken place in front of over ten thousand people. It was on videotape. It had been broadcast live by that idiot Brickshaw. From what Rohmer could tell, it had all the earmarks of a nervous breakdown. He needed to know why it had happened. He needed to know what he had to do about it. He needed some answers from the three men assembled in front of him.

"It's the Pancake thing," said Hack.

"What, exactly, is the Pancake thing?" Rohmer asked. He was seated behind the desk in his too small, windowless office. The walls were empty of everything but the seal of the San Francisco GoldenGaters. The men facing him were squeezed shoulder to shoulder in a lineup of chrome-and-leather sling-back chairs that carried their asses so close to the carpet that only big Hack did not have to look up in order to see over the desk.

"Booby's loyal to his players," Hack said, speaking as though he were responding to a preliminary examination question to which he was expected to give a rote answer.

Rohmer reached down to the floor next to his feet and came up with a stack of newspapers that he thumped loudly onto his desk. "I'm asking," he said slowly, making each word louder than the one before it, "what the ever-loving fuck that asshole Colin Cromwell is writing about."

The three men stared at the newspapers as if they were so many severed heads.

"I think," Hack said at last, "that Cromwell's telling us W.E.B. is not the man we think he is."

Rohmer was not sure which he resented more, being talked to like a moron or talking to morons. To keep his temper under control he spoke very deliberately. "So who is he and so what?"

Mel Dykstra tilted forward. His baggy eyes took on a sincere cast as he confidently said, "Colin Cromwell is a shit disturber, Dale. I think it's clear what he's got hold of here. W.E.B. Pancake is apparently this guy Willie Smith, and what's more important to this organization, he's apparently a good deal older than we thought." Dyk smeared his nose with his hand. "Okay, that's bad for Pancake. But it's good for us to know. It explains why my computer sheets show how much his produc-

158

tion tends to fall off in the fourth quarter. It explains why my stats show he consistently plays better on two days' rest than when we have to go back-to-back."

The men on each side of Dyk turned to stare at him. The looks on their faces hovered somewhere between surprise and incredulity.

Dyk inched a little farther toward Rohmer's desk. "Booby, like Hack says, is incredibly loyal to his players. He's especially loyal to W.E.B., who's been the rock of this team ever since me and Booby got here. He knows that day in and day out W.E.B. Pancake shows up to play ball, and it hurts him to see that W.E.B.'s being hurt." Dyk paused. "It hurts him to see that W.E.B. is all through."

"Come again?" demanded Hack.

Dyk did not return his gaze. He kept his baggage-laden eyes on Rohmer.

Hack said, "The guy got eighteen boards against San Antone the other night. He was tearing fucking Sacramento apart until he caught that elbow in the nose—an elbow which, by the way, the films clearly show belonged to Jerome Crown."

Rohmer's head snapped back. He was unsure if Hack was saying what he thought he was saying. He was unsure Hack meant what he was saying even if he was actually saying it.

Hack nodded. He did it with a funny look on his face. "Jerome wanted to play center, I'll tell you that much."

Dyk broke the silence that followed, steering the conversation back to his subject. "If W.E.B., or Willie, is really thirty-eight, as it appears, then we have to think about moving him out. Some of the things that we've been seeing that we thought were merely—what do you call them?—aberrations, we now maybe have to recognize as something else. Something permanent."

It was up to Rohmer to say something. He found himself asking the question that he knew Dyk wanted him to ask. "You think Jerome's ready to replace him?"

Dyk shrugged as if he merely had an opinion. "He played pretty good once I put him in there last night."

The word *I* smacked around the walls of the room. It made

Hack snort like a horse. "Jerome's a head case. We're never even sure if he's going to show up half the time."

Dyk shrugged again. This shrug said many things, not the least of which was that Dyk didn't have any trouble handling him.

Hack burst into a belly laugh. "Jerome's got a new toy now, in case you haven't heard. A stretch limo. He drives it himself and calls it his party machine." Hack threw up his hands. "It seems he was quite impressed with W.E.B.'s Rolls and thinks he's gone him one better." He laughed again. "That was his excuse yesterday for almost missing the bus to Sacramento. Claims he got on the freeway and drove all the way to San Jose before he realized where he was. Claims the car's so big that he gets places before he knows it."

Dyk shrugged a third time, slaughtering Hack's laughter in the process.

"I don't care what you say," Hack said petulantly. He made a little jabbing motion with his finger. "The day we call practice at ten in the morning after a midnight flight you can bet your balls there will be no stretch limo at ten in the fucking A.M. There will, however, be a brown Rolls-Royce, because W.E.B. Pancake, no matter how old he is, no matter how many families he has, or where he was before he stumbled onto Jones-Henry College, will be on that floor and he will be practicing his hook shot and his foul shots, and there will be sweat dripping down his face by the time everybody else is assembled."

Hack was a big, earthy, simple guy who generally made it very clear where you stood with him. Aware that some sort of dispute between the two assistant coaches was unfolding before him, Rohmer favored Hack by asking what he proposed they do.

"I say," Hack replied, "we call in DubyaBee and give him a big vote of confidence. We tell him we don't care what Cromwell says about him, he's our man."

"I think," said Dyk suddenly, "we might consider one other factor."

Rohmer turned his attention to the older man and raised his eyebrow quizzically.

"W.E.B. Pancake has been carrying around a secret. I think we can all agree"—Dyk waved his hand disinterestedly at Hack—"that it's not good for a professional athlete to have a secret. It makes him—what would you say?—vulnerable?"

"To what?" Rohmer asked, being purposely obtuse, not wanting Dyk to slide out of this situation with the safety of any ambiguity.

"To people who know his secret. People who know he doesn't want the secret to get out. People who might try to influence him by promising to . . . keep that secret if he does a little something for them."

There was silence in the room.

Finally Hack spoke. He explained what he thought of Dyk's suggestion. "You're fulla shit, Dyk." He looked at Rohmer for concurrence and Dale would have given it to him if he had not then said, "I think the best thing we can do is call DubyaBee in and give him a new contract. Tell him, tell the team, tell the whole world, 'You play hard, and it will be recognized. Nothing else makes any difference.' "

The words *new contract* chilled Dale Rohmer. Such words were not anything that a general manager of a struggling team would like to say to the team's increasingly dissatisfied owner, particularly when they pertained to a guy who was already getting $1.2 million and still had an option year left on his contract.

Dale said, "We, ah, have a problem in terms of changing anybody's contract until we work things out with Del Fuego Dixon, who, as you know, is eligible to be a free agent at the end of this season. So far, the only numbers we're hearing from Del's camp have seven digits and the first one is a three." He cleared his throat. "Mr. Brandisi's position has been that he's only one man with a limited amount of resources, and it's going to strain him to have to go as high as two to sign Del. I don't see him weakening that position by giving anything away to anybody in the meantime."

"I'm not asking you to give anything away, Dale," Hack complained. "I'm asking you to consider something that dollar for dollar will probably buy you a lot more basketball than whatever you end up paying Dixon."

Dyk said, "The fans would kill us if we let Del walk away and sign with somebody else. They'd murder us."

Hack said, "Dixon's gonna test the free agent market no matter what you offer him. 'Member all that business in Cromwell's column a while back about how the trade for Jerome probably meant that Dixon was going to be leaving the team? You don't think that was all a plant? You don't think Dixon was protecting himself in case his precious scoring average dipped any, so he could say to the other teams, 'Hey, the Gaters saw I was going to leave so they started working me out of the offense'?"

"His scoring average is actually up one point three five points a game since Jerome joined the team," offered Dyk.

Rohmer leaned forward. "Of course," he said, speaking carefully, delivering his words as though he was running both their arguments through his mind, "there is a problem if Pancake really is five years older than we thought. If that's the case, we don't want to get stuck with any kind of long-term deal."

Dyk brightened. "That's right."

"I'm thinking," Rohmer went on, "that maybe this little injury to DubyaBee might be a blessing in disguise. He's going to be out a few days, so let's give Jerome a shot at his position."

"Booby doesn't want to use Jerome at center," said Hack. "He won't pass the ball."

"Booby . . ." Rohmer shifted his gaze to the third man sitting in front of him, the only one who had been quiet throughout the discussion. "What's the reading on Booby, Dick?"

The little trainer cleared his throat. He looked as though he were caught in the leather sling-back chair, like a baseball in the pocket of a catcher's mitt. "I talked to Meg a little while ago. She said Boob spent the whole morning sitting in the middle of the living room floor with the headphones on listening to record albums that he had back in college."

"What did she say about him?"

"I think she's worried, Dale."

162

Rohmer nodded while Dyk and Hack and Crabbie waited. "I guess I'd better have a little talk with the team," he told them.

Dale Rohmer was well aware of the reaction he normally generated in the locker room. He wanted it to be different this time. He wanted the players to see that he was on a mission of goodwill. He therefore did a lot of smiling. A smile was not a natural look for him. It made him appear as though he were in pain.

He stood in front of the team with one hand on his hip and one on his forehead, and he tried to speak with his lips wide apart. "You know, all things considered, you guys have been playing really good ball lately. I mean, that game last night, you played one *hell* of a game."

He gazed around the locker room in admiration. His smile was beginning to hurt. "We got some media attention out of what happened up there in Sacra-Tomato and that isn't all bad. People believe what they read in the papers and that tends to make them forget what they see with their eyes. And that means whatever problems we're having just may distract our opponents more than they distract us."

A few of the guys nodded. Tim Biltmore was particularly demonstrative in his assent. His enthusiasm didn't count.

"I suspect that'll be the case tomorrow with Charlotte," Rohmer continued. "I suspect they'll be expecting us to self-destruct, and I further suspect that by the time we're done with them we'll have won our last four games—and that, gentlemen, ain't bad."

Most of the team sat in front of their cubicles. Most were in practice shorts and shirts. Most had their knees spread and their hands clasped. W.E.B., in a sweatshirt and sweatpants, leaned against a pillar. He had a bandage across his nose and his face was puffy and disfigured.

Rohmer said, "Booby, it looks like, is gonna sit out for a week or so. His doctor tells us he needs a rest and we're gonna coincide that with the suspension he's probably gonna draw. But that's all right, because what he did up there in Sacramento, boys, he did for you—and I hope each and every one of you appreciates the fact that that's the kind of coach you have. . . . As for DubyaBee, he's out for the rest of the week with that nose of his and we'll just have to make do. But both he and Booby should be with us when we go back east again and that's what really counts. D.C., Philly, New Jersey, and Boston. That may be the key trip of the season for us. It can make us or break us in terms of our play-off hopes. It's that crucial." And to show how crucial it was, Rohmer, to everybody's relief, stopped smiling.

"In the meantime," he said, "until DubyaBee is ready again, we'll go with Jerome at center and Del and Zeke on the wings, and I don't see any problems there." His eyes searched for any signs of disagreement.

Finding none, he turned to the subject that he presumed was on everybody's mind. "Okay, so let's talk about this thing that Colin Cromwell's been doing. I don't like going around making a big deal out of what some reporter writes in his paper, but I suppose in this instance something ought to be said. Now I got my own opinions about Cromwell, but he's a fact of life on this team and like you I got to learn to live with him."

Rohmer stroked his face. He loosened his tie. He smoothed down his hair. "He hasn't been around since we left Florida, and it doesn't take any genius to figure out where he's been. I called his editor this morning, trying to find out when he'd be back, saying I'd like to have a little sit-down talk with him, see if we couldn't straighten some things out. The editor, who's name is Norbert—maybe some of you know him—gave me some good news and some bad news. The good news is that Cromwell's left Alabama, so I'm not anticipating any more of these shots at DubyaBee that have been upsetting all of us. The bad news is, however, that now Cromwell's gone somewhere else."

The players watched Rohmer. Only their eyes moved as he paced two and three steps in each direction. He had expected some cry of outrage, but there was silence. He wondered if he had been clear enough. "I expect," he added, "that means he's gone to somebody else's hometown. If I interpret Mr. Norbert correctly, it seems that Cromwell has decided to do a series of these up-close-and-personal columns."

The grumblings started then. They started with profanity,

164

then turned into whines. It was Del Fuego, of course, chorused by Zeke and Oliver, who had the most complaints. Rohmer thrust up both hands. "There is nothing we can do about this," he said, raising his voice. "We have no choice but to just press forward—business as usual. But that in itself may be our best solution to this problem."

He waited until the noises died down. "Guys, I've given this a lot of thought, and I am here to tell you that Colin Cromwell is nothing more than a reporter looking for a story. I also happen to believe that the best story he could come up with would be the one about the miracle GoldenGaters who go all the way to win the championship this year. What I'm saying is, if we start winning, the story is right here with us—it's not out there in our hometowns. I mean, you don't watch soap operas when the play-offs are on another channel. You only watch the soaps because there's nothing else on."

Rohmer was uncomfortable in using even elementary analogies with this group, a feeling that was brought home to him as he looked around at the array of mostly blank faces. "I have talked this over with Mr. Brandisi, and he is very much in agreement with me that the best way to distract Colin Cromwell is to give him something better to write about. Now Mr. Brandisi is also mindful of the fact that there's been a lot of stress on the team lately and that this business of Cromwell's is adding to it. He is very pleased that you guys have been handling things as well as you have and he wants to reward you."

Heads lifted. The blank faces suddenly turned keen with appreciation at the mention of rewards. There was a general stirring among the athletes.

Rohmer tried his smile again. "So," he said, filling his voice with exuberance, "when we arrive in Boston on this next road trip, Mr. Brandisi has decided to throw a little party in your honor. At his house."

His smile became genuine. "Attendance is mandatory."

Jonnie Martin was sensitive about being a twenty-seven-year-old rookie. It made him stand out, sure; it gave the reporters something to write about; but it did not garner him much respect. If he did something well, people tended to say, "Yes, but . . . ," as though he was expected to be mature and yet was obviously lacking in some essential skill or it would not have taken him so long to get to the league.

He was hoping, once he read Colin Cromwell's Alabama columns, that he would get a little empathy from W.E.B. Pancake, whom he now understood to have entered the league at an age even more advanced than his own, but the big center had yet to acknowledge that Jonnie was even on the team.

In the eight days he had been with the Gaters, precious few people had talked to him about anything. At first he had suspected that his ten-day contract had much to do with the coolness of his reception. Players came and went on these mini-deals during the course of a season, and there was probably no sense in getting too close to a guy who was only going to be around for a couple of games. But the Gaters had won all three games since he had arrived—San Antonio, Sacramento, Charlotte—and Jonnie had been on enough teams and in enough locker rooms to know that this particular team was not responding as it should. Not to anything. In fact, the one thing that Jonnie was sure of was that there was something dreadfully wrong with the San Francisco GoldenGaters.

Thus, instead of being overjoyed at finally being in the league

166

after a year in Portugal, two in Spain, and two more in Albany, the most prominent feeling Jonnie was experiencing was one of tension. Most of that tension was in the locker room and at practice sessions, but it was there in the games as well.

Larry, he noticed, would go to almost any lengths to avoid passing the ball to Jerome. Del Fuego, who did not pass much to anyone, most particularly did not pass to Rynn. Zeke and Curtis would readily give the ball up to Del and W.E.B., but would not give it to Jerome in the same situations.

And yet the team was winning. From what Jonnie could see, this was due almost entirely to the efforts of two players. He had heard how selfish a shooter Del Fuego Dixon was, had even seen this for himself on television, but in the three games since Jonnie had arrived, Del had been on a scoring binge, and whenever the Gaters needed points, Del had gotten them. For his part, Jerome Crown, since taking over at center, had been a monster on both the offensive and defensive boards.

But as for the rest of the team, Jonnie had not been that impressed, particularly at guard. Larry Miller was primarily a defensive player. Felix McDaniel had lost a step and was playing on guile. Oliver Dawkins was clearly a head case. But the biggest shocker was Rynn Packard, who, while skilled in all phases of the game, excelled at none except free throws. If what Jonnie had seen in his first three games was any indication, he was certain that it would only be a matter of time until he wrested the starting spot from Rynn.

All he needed was the chance. And another ten-day contract. Given the fact that his coach had gone crazy and his general manager would not be joining the current road trip until after Jonnie's present ten-day had expired, neither of those things was a certainty. It was, Jonnie decided, necessary that he get noticed. Very noticed. Very quickly.

Washington, a team known neither for its offense or its defense, matched the GoldenGaters point for point through forty-eight minutes and the game went into overtime. Jonnie, who had scored on his only two shots in the second quarter, was sent in to spell Rynn for a minute. He hit an open 18-footer

167

and then he hit a driving lay-up with Washington players hanging all over him. Hack left him in.

Washington went up by 2. Del scored, and with just seconds left the Gaters put on a full-court press. Jonnie, reading the eyes of the man he was guarding, stole the inbounds bass. He immediately looked to pass off, but there were no Gaters free. Jonnie dribbled back outside.

Del yelled, "Hey, hey," and with his hand in the air slammed his butt into the pelvis of his defender and backed step by step toward the basket. "Yo," called Jerome, and spun away from his defender, swatted at the man's clutching hand, and spun away again. But Jonnie waited, and as the clock ticked down, he calmly popped in a 20-footer that proved to be the game-winner.

Jonnie was the center of the postgame media attention. He gave interviews to Marty Smart and a guy from the *Washington Post* and a guy from *USA Today*. He talked with the local television cameras and acknowledged that he was very fortunate to have been in the right place at the right time. He told each of the interviewers that he hoped he would have many more opportunities to help the Gaters before the season was over.

Jonnie did not even take off his uniform until after the last question had been asked and answered. By then most of the other Gaters were already dressed in their street clothes, and somebody yelled at him not to hold up the bus.

He stripped and went off to a long shower. When he came out again, there were only three other people still in the locker room: Crabbie, Del, and a thin, bespectacled man with pale skin, who was talking with Del. Jonnie had not noticed the man before, but he was clearly a reporter, so Jonnie smiled at him as he walked by holding his towel to his still-dripping body.

"Hi," the stranger said, and when Jonnie said "Hi" back, the man stuck out his hand. "My name is Colin Cromwell." He laughed softly at the reaction he got. "I see my reputation has preceded me."

Jonnie laughed with him and hung about to see if Cromwell

had any questions. But unlike the other reporters, Cromwell seemed content just to compliment him on his game.

Crabbie, meanwhile, had the last of the team bags under his arm and was staggering out the door. "Bus is leaving," he called.

Del nodded Jonnie's attention to the departing trainer. "Better get a move on."

Thinking to ingratiate himself, Jonnie shrugged and said, "I figure I'm safe as long as you're still here."

He did not get so much as a smile out of this flattery. Del, despite the victory, did not seem to be in a smiling mood, and Jonnie wondered if it was because he had not delivered him the ball on that last play, or if it was because he, rather than Del, had gotten all the postgame attention.

But then Del said, "Except I already told them I'm not going back on the bus. Mr. Cromwell here is taking me out to dinner," and Jonnie stopped wondering about anything except how fast he could get into his clothes.

Nobody on the Gaters was going to hold the bus for him. Not yet anyhow.

# 25

Wayne Brickshaw, his hair slicked, his tie knotted, his hop-sack blazer brushed clean and blocked at the shoulders, gazed resolutely into his guest's eyes and in his most stentorian voice said, "Now, you don't fuck with me, all right?"

The tall young man nodded.

Wayne pointed his notes at him and said, "Because if you fuck with me, I'll cut you right off. Hear? You just answer the questions and don't give me any of your bullshit."

He got another nod in response.

"This is my show, my turf, and I can make you look like dead meat if I want. Got that? You don't believe me, ask that wise-ass Dawkins what happened to him after he fucked with me on my show. He doesn't ever get mentioned by me on the air anymore, and now he sits on the bench letting ten-day wonders like you come along and take his minutes."

Wayne believed it was necessary to be firm with first-timers, especially kids who were called up in the middle of the season and meant nothing to anyone. They were not the kinds of guys he had to chase after, cajole, approach through an agent, or make an appointment to interview. He would have given the young man even more lessons in on-the-air etiquette except that suddenly his signal came through his headphones.

"Good evening once again, everybody, and welcome to 'Gaters' Warm-up.' I'm your host, Wayne Brickshaw, and we're coming to you live from the Spectrum in Philadelphia, where your red-hot San Fran-cisco GoldenGaters are about to get under way in this, the second game of the final Eastern road swing of the season. My pregame guest is something of a Cinderella story. He's Jonnie Martin, and not too many days ago he was playing in the wilds of Albany, New York. General Manager Dale Rohmer took a look at him, liked what he saw, and signed him to a ten-day contract. Last night Jonnie found himself thrown into the Washington game in overtime to replace a slumping Packard, and not only did he steal an inbounds pass, but he transformed that steal into the game-winning basket. He's a very articulate young man and I'm delighted to give all of you out there in radioland a chance to meet him.

"How are you tonight, Jonnie?"

"Good, Wayne. I'm sitting on top of the world right now."

"That's terrific, Jonnie. Tell me, that shot you made, how confident were you that it was going in?"

"Oh, I wasn't confident at all, Wayne."

"Why is that . . . Jonnie?"

"Well, to say I was confident implies that I was thinking I could do it, and that isn't really what was going on. I guess the best you could say is it never really occurred to me that the ball wouldn't go in if I could just get the shot off."

"Well . . . isn't that confidence? Whatever word you want to use, it amounts to the same thing. Now, tell me, Jonnie, I've had players over the years say that sometimes when they get into a situation like you were in last night, there's a certain something that happens so that all of a sudden the basket looks as big as the ocean. Is that the way it was for you?"

"I don't know if that's true, Wayne, that the basket looks any bigger. Maybe it's just a way of saying something else. I can only tell you what happens to me is like you get this feeling deep inside that you know the ball is going to go in. It's like a message that goes backwards, from your hands to your brain, instead of the way messages normally go. It runs right up your arms, and I suppose if I think about it, I can almost trace it through my shoulder, my neck, my head. And it's all done in, what, a hundredth of a second? A thousandth? I don't know. I can only tell you that there are times when I am certain what

171

the ball can do and I know where the basket is and exactly how much strength I have to use, how far I have to shoot it, where I have to aim it. Now that may be a thinking process, like you implied earlier, but it's not one that I'm thinking about."

"So what you're saying is—"

"The thing that's so fascinating about this process, Wayne, is that if I break down one little bit, if I give one single extra thought to what I'm doing, the certainty of the ball going through the rim is no longer one hundred percent. Now maybe it never was one hundred percent, but I felt it was, and if all of a sudden I add a thought or a worry, my chances of scoring could drop all the way to fifty percent, which is still big league shooting—but it's a heck of a long way from perfection."

"So your theory is that there's no room for thought in shooting a basketball, is that it?"

"Oh, no, Wayne, that's not it at all. Thought is there, but conscious thought is not the most productive part of shooting. That's all I'm saying. The amazing thing is, some people can shoot naturally without conscious thought and others have to work for that ability."

"Well, thank you, Jonnie, for that most—"

"Of course, what I'm talking about now is shooting from the field under pressure, and that's different from shooting free throws from the foul line."

"Of course—"

"Free-throw shooting is almost strictly a matter of mechanics, Wayne."

"Perhaps we can get to that another time—"

"When you're at the free-throw line, that's where you can work that 'big as an ocean' theory you were asking about. You've got time to zone-in on the basket until it's just you and the hole, until all you have to do is drop the ball into it like it was coming off a conveyor belt. That's why you see foul shooters staring at the basket, Wayne. They're making the basket bigger, whether they know it or not. Watch the great foul shooters, watch their concentration. That's the key. Not the dribbling or the twisting of the ball that you see them do. That's just getting comfortable so they can get in a position where they're

172

zoning, and once they're zoned, then it all comes down to doing it the way they've done it five hundred thousand times before."

"All right, so if we accept what you say, is there any reason why you can't shoot one hundred percent from the free-throw line?"

"There's no reason why somebody can't. I'd sure like to, but just because I want to do it doesn't mean I can."

"So, what you're saying is, you're not perfect. All right, Jonnie, I think some of our listeners will agree with that—"

"See, but that's another thing, Wayne. As good as the players are in this league, nobody's perfect. When I first came up, I was real tentative, almost like I felt the pressure of the game. But I stayed aggressive, and it's helped me learn that everybody's human, you know? Even the guys playing at this level, and that's really helped me with my confidence."

"Well, there you have it, ladies and gentlemen, the philosophy of young Jonnie Martin—and it all comes around to just the word I was using earlier: *confidence.* We'll be back after these brief messages."

Once the game got started, it did not take long for Wayne to observe that Philadelphia was going to be no match for the Gaters on this particular night. W.E.B. Pancake, playing for the first time since his nose was broken, raised the level of intensity beyond anything Wayne had seen this season.

Early on, Wayne dutifully reported the riding W.E.B. was taking from the Philadelphia fans and the Philadelphia players. He told his listeners about the fans' chants of "Willll-eeee," and the players' taunts of "Dad" and "Pops." He explained how, in the bumping under the basket, the Philadelphians said, "Watch it, old man, watch it"; and he repeated the better lines delivered by the fans, such as when W.E.B. leaped for a rebound and a leather-lunged rooter screamed, "He flies like a jailbird."

Still, when Jonnie Martin replaced Rynn at the start of the second quarter, Wayne Brickshaw all but forgot about the W.E.B. Pancake Show. He introduced Jonnie as "Zen-Master Martin" and used every break in the action to comment on his "remarkable" pregame interview. When Jonnie missed his first shot, Wayne wondered aloud if his synapses were firing too rapidly. When he missed his second, Wayne delightedly informed his listeners that clearly Jonnie was thinking too much and that soon league teams would be defensing him just by making him think. "Who fought the battle of Waterloo, Jonnie?" he called into the microphone. "What's the square root of thirty-seven?" And then, while Wayne was still chuckling, Jonnie took a stutter step, made a twisting, turning drive to the basket, faked a pass, and laid the ball in with a move so deft that even Wayne had to compliment it. "Oh!" he gasped before collecting himself. And then, very calmly, he explained, "Martin clearly wasn't thinking on that one, ladies and gentlemen."

# 26

**D**yk was disgusted. Because he had gone off to visit his daughter and her family, he had missed the party that W.E.B. had spontaneously thrown after the game. W.E.B. had never thrown a party after any other game, but on this, the night of his triumphant return, he had stomped into the middle of the locker room floor, spread his legs, jammed his hands on his hips, and announced that he was taking everyone on the team to Bookbinder's to celebrate. And Dyk had been unable to go.

He had not gotten back until this morning, in time for the bus that would take the team to Sccaucus, where they were scheduled to meet up with Booby and Rohmer and prepare for that night's game against New Jersey. The bus was to depart at ten, and when he arrived at five minutes of ten, the only people on it were Wayne Brickshaw and Marty Smart. They had not been invited to W.E.B.'s party and were looking relatively chipper. They were discussing their buddy Cromwell, who had shown up in D.C. for the game and then had disappeared again. In response to Dyk's questions they did not know why the players were still in the hotel.

Dyk went into the lobby and saw for himself. Jerome, in particular, looked very ill. Dyk found him sitting in a huge easy chair, wearing dark glasses and holding both arms of the chair as if he were riding in a tub on the ocean. Tim Biltmore, as white as a ghost, leaned against a pillar sipping from a huge cardboard cup of black coffee. Two or three others stood around looking as if they were about to be led off to their execution.

175

But the one who most disgusted Dyk was Mike Hacker, hotshot undefeated interim coach, who, at some minutes after ten o'clock, positioned himself at the door of the bus with his hair still wet from a shower, his face seemingly only half-shaved, his eyes bloodshot. He was wearing an overcoat over an open-necked white shirt with no tie, and he glanced from time to time at the bus as if it were a traveling cesspool. On his last day, before returning the reins to Booby, Hacker had gotten drunk with his players.

Next to Hack stood Crabbie, holding a clipboard in his hand. IIis cheeks were glowing red from the coldness of the air, but they shone like bloody wounds against the pallor of the rest of his skin. Eventually, and with some effort, Crabbie raised his wrist in front of his eyes. He held it there a while before saying, "It's ten-thirty, Hack."

Hack inhaled and nodded once.

Crabbie turned, inhaled just as Hack had done, and hollered, "Okay, let's load her up."

Hack ducked away from the sound as if he had been shot. His obvious pain was the only thing about the whole sorry situation that gave Dyk any pleasure.

Slowly people began emerging from the lobby. Even though the sky was extremely dark and overcast, a number of players besides Jerome were wearing sunglasses. As they mounted the steps, Crabbie checked off their names on his clipboard and at last he announced to Hack that three men were still missing and that it was now ten forty-five.

Hack raised his arm in the direction of the lobby. He took a breath and spoke while holding it. "Go look."

Crabbie handed his clipboard to Dyk and stumbled off to do as ordered. Shortly after that Wayne Brickshaw stuck his head out the bus door and complained about the delay. Hack looked at him as if he had just thrown up on his shoe and Wayne quickly pulled his head back inside.

There was a commotion at the revolving door leading from the hotel to the sidewalk. A huge dark mass of moving parts gradually revealed itself to be Oliver Dawkins, held up on either side by Curtis Clovis and Felix McDaniel.

176

It took some minutes to get Oliver up the stairs, down the aisle, and onto the backseat, where he was laid out like a stiff, and when it was finally done, Hack surveyed the bus and gasped, "That everyone?"

No one answered.

"Start it up," Hack told the driver.

Dyk, who still had the clipboard, said, "Crabbie," and it seemed to take Hack a moment to remember. Then a look that was more relief than anything else came over Hack's face and he settled slowly into the front-row seat, the one traditionally occupied by the head coach.

Dyk dropped the clipboard into Hack's lap and announced that he would go get him. Hack seemed relieved at that, too. "Lobby," he said.

But Dick Crabtree was not in the lobby, and Dyk, on arriving there, wondered if perhaps Crabbie had gone back to his room for something. He decided to try calling on the house phone and, seeing none, followed the signs that pointed to the pay telephones. It was there that he found the trainer, wedged into a booth, whispering into a receiver.

Dyk approached. He intended merely to rap on the window of the booth to get Crabbie's attention, but something about Crabbie's posture, the hunch of his shoulders, the angle of his head, made Dyk hesitate. And when he hesitated, he distinctly heard Crabbie say the letters "FBI."

And then Crabbie glanced up, saw Dyk, and his little pig-eyes flared. He mumbled something hurriedly into the receiver and hung up. "Oh," he said, scooting out of the booth, "time to go?"

Dyk caught him by the collar and asked him if he was talking to the FBI and what about. But Crabbie would not even admit he had said what Dyk had heard. "I never mentioned the FBI," he insisted, and Dyk thought that at least at that moment he no longer looked hung over. Dyk let him go.

He followed the little trainer out to the bus and watched his gait gradually become a shuffle and watched him make a production out of hauling himself up the bus stairs, but Dyk said nothing more.

Hack was in a stupor when Dyk passed him, and Dyk had to shake him roughly by the shoulder to get him to acknowledge that they were at last ready to roll. Then Dyk sat down in the row directly behind Hack, the one the two assistant coaches usually shared and that he now had entirely to himself. He stared out the window at the traffic and wondered if now the FBI was using somebody else—or worse, if they had taken to spying on him. He told himself that he had to come up with something good to report, and that he had to do it fast.

# 27

At Boston's Copley Plaza, Jerome Crown found not one but two stewardesses. At least he told Felix they were stewardesses. He also said they would not ride in their fancy sequined dresses in the bus that Mr. Brandisi had provided to transport the team to his Wellesley home. That was why Jerome had rented the limousine that was parked directly in front of the hotel at seven-thirty at night. He asked Felix if he wanted to ride with him and the "stews," but Felix, feeling resplendent in a red-and-blue-plaid dinner jacket with matching bow tie, had discovered that the bus Mr. Brandisi had provided was no ordinary bus. It had plush seats, a multispeakered sound system, and a bar stocked with Mumm's champagne, and Felix was not about to miss that.

While the liveried chauffeur posed next to the open doors of the limo, Jerome sat inside with Veronica and Sally. He was wearing a white double-breasted suit with a deep red silk shirt, a white tie, and white boots, and he called to each of his team-mates as they came out of the hotel, asking if they wanted to ride with him. To everyone's surprise, it was W.E.B. Pancake who accepted the invitation.

Del Fuego and Zeke, when they saw that, asked if they could go, too. But Jerome said it was just a two-man, two-girl party machine, and so Del and Zeke discussed ordering their own limo, and then their discussion turned into an argument as they stood on the sidewalk and tried to tell each other how they could get a car to the hotel before the bus left. Finally they agreed on a cab. But then Oliver, who had been standing nearby, said he wanted to go in the cab as well, and a new argument broke out because Del said it wouldn't look cool to pull up to the party with three big guys crammed into the backseat or one guy sitting up front with the driver. He told Oliver to pair up with somebody else and get his own cab, and Oliver, sulking, went onto the bus and tried to talk Felix into getting off.

Felix, however, said no. He had his seat, he had his glass of champagne, he was ready to roll. Then Oliver asked Biltmore and Larry and even tried Jonnie Martin, but none of them would agree to ride in a taxi with him. He did not ask Rynn or Chris or Curtis.

Booby boarded and said nothing to anyone. His assistants boarded and so did Rohmer and Marty Smart and Brickshaw. Crabbie was about to declare everyone accounted for when all of a sudden someone appeared behind him on the stairs, tugging at his coattails, forcing him to step out of the way. It was Colin Cromwell and he was grinning as if he were sure everybody would be glad to see him.

Felix, who had heard that Colin had been present for the Washington game, but who had not seen him, stopped calling out insults to his teammates, and everybody else went quiet as well. But Colin, wearing a white dinner jacket that did not quite fit, a ruffled shirt, and a hand-tied bow tie, gave no sign that he noticed. He just proceeded up the aisle and sat down next to Marty Smart as if Marty had been saving a seat for him.

The bus started off with its load of eight players, three coaches, a general manager, a trainer, two sportswriters, and a radio broadcaster. Following behind the bus was a gray limousine containing two players and two women, and directly behind the limousine was a yellow cab with two more players. In this order the caravan snaked through the narrow streets of Boston until it reached the Massachusetts Turnpike, and then the three vehicles shot off to the west.

The ride was not particularly long and they were moving rapidly. The bus had come equipped with tapes, and Rohmer, to be clever, plugged the Beatles' *Magical Mystery Tour* into the cassette player. He kept looking over his shoulder to see if

180

everyone "got it," and Felix gave him the thumbs-up sign to acknowledge how clever he was, but as soon as the first song ended the players began clamoring for what thoy called real music. The bus was stocked with nothing that met the players' shouted specifications, but eventually a compromise was reached when a Smokey Robinson tape was found.

Felix moved up and down the aisle with bottles of Mumm's, making sure every glass was constantly refilled, even Cromwell's, and by the time they were off the Turnpike some of the riders were already lit. The bus navigated a series of narrow, country roads, and Smokey was replaced with Aretha Franklin, and Felix managed to get Tim Biltmore and Curtis Clovis dancing. He got Curtis to sing "R-E-S-P-E-C-T" in falsetto and everybody laughed, even Oliver, and by the time the song ended everyone on the bus except Booby and Dyk and maybe the driver was jiggling around and waving his arms and singing "R-E-S-P-E-C-T."

The bus driver turned through a stone gate and some of the people on the bus said "Ooooh" and "Look at this" as they drove up a drive that took them past evenly spaced trees of virtually identical size and shape until it eventually hooked in front of a large porticoed home with awnings over each of the front windows. The awnings were blue and on each one the letter *B* was carefully detailed in fancy white script.

Felix immediately decided he would do that. He would get awnings for his house and script on them the letters *FMD*, mix them all up the way the initials of some cities were mixed up on baseball caps.

The area directly in front of the house was rectangular and paved, and in the exact center of that area was a fountain lit by multicolored lights. The rest of the area was, at the moment the caravan arrived, filled with vehicles—Jaguars, Mercedes, BMWs, Cadillacs, Lincolns, and two strategically located Rolls-Royces—so that only a single lane led around the fountain and back down the driveway, and that lane was not going to be wide enough for the bus to make its turn.

Tim Biltmore stood in the aisle, bent at the waist, gaping out

181

the window at the brilliantly lit structure awaiting them. "Holy shit," he said.

Felix said, "Amen," and experienced a rush of excitement that he was actually going to be a guest in such a place.

A bald butler was perched rigidly at the top of the half dozen brick stairs leading to the set of front doors. He was grinning wildly and seemed personally delighted at the Gaters' arrival. The doors behind him opened without his help, and out came the master of the manor, moving somewhat faster than a walk, but not quite at a flat-out run.

Teddy Brandisi was wearing a black tuxedo with a gold bow tie, a gold cummerbund, and a gold carnation in his lapel. On his head was a gold paper top hat, and stapled in the center of it was the team logo, a basketball zooming out of the cross-span of the Golden Gate Bridge. He was there to meet Rohmer the moment the general manager stepped off the bus. "Hello, Dale," he cried, pumping Rohmer's hand in both of his own. He turned, without letting go of the hand, as if to introduce Rohmer to an entourage, but halfway into the turn he noticed the gray limousine and the yellow cab behind the bus and he paused long enough to throw Rohmer a curious look.

Rohmer shrugged. Mr. Brandisi looked again. Then he looked behind him and saw nobody was there. Instead, a large group of people remained clustered at the threshold of the double doors, where they were jammed like a human wall, not one of them stepping outside the house, all of them tilted slightly forward in anticipation of what they were about to see.

The clustered men, for the most part, wore dark suits; a few were in tuxedos or dinner jackets. The clustered women tended to be in cocktail dresses. Nearly all the people at the doors were in the forty-to-sixty age range, and nearly all held some sort of drink. By the way many of them were bobbing their heads around to get a better view, they reminded Felix of spectators in a golf gallery.

"Dottie," Mr. Brandisi called, sweeping his arm urgently. "Dottie!"

One woman disengaged herself from the group as if she had just been selected for a prize. She had hair that was too richly dark brown for her age and that was set in a top wave that was designed to make her appear taller than she was and that only succeeded in making her head seem out of proportion to the rest of her body. She wore a dark green, strapless satin dress that covered her breasts with stiff, flaring shields and that exposed her shoulders and upper arms—showing them to be skinny, unseasonably tanned, and goose-bumped from the March-night air. Felix thought that if she were his wife he would throw a sweater over her.

Dottie Brandisi held the loose skirt of her dress with one hand, held a cocktail high with the other, and scurried down the stairs and the walk to put up her cheek for a kiss from Dale Rohmer. Dottie Brandisi's face was thin and her mouth and jaw were narrow, but she had wide, expressive eyes and a constant look of concern that told people she would like to help as much as she could—if only she could figure out what the problem was.

Rohmer actually appeared glad to see her and smiled appreciatively at her effort to hurry to him. In the meantime, Teddy Brandisi was taking Booby's hand and peering deeply into his eyes. "How are you, son?" Mr. Brandisi asked, and when Booby said, "Fine," he said, "Hmm?" so that Booby had to say it again.

Mr. Brandisi turned then to Hack, who was next in line to get off the bus. With his right hand he pumped Hack's right and with his left he grabbed Hack's biceps. "Good to see you, Hack," he said, and then promptly discarded him so that he could throw his arm around Dyk's shoulders and pull him into a handshake. "Hey," he said, flinging Dyk to one side and grabbing at the hand of the next man descending.

"Dick," said the descender, and when Brandisi looked confused, he added, "Dick Crabtree. Crabbie. The trainer."

"Oh, yes, of course. How nice of you to come. And who's this? Is this Zeke?"

"No, I'm Larry Miller."

"Larry, of course. I couldn't see you. It's dark in there. Good to have you. And is this Rynn?"

"Hello, Mr. Brandisi."

"Rynn Packard, how are you? Hey, you're playing great ball there, son. I listen to Wayne Brickshaw talking about you and I'm just tickled pink. Say hello to my wife, Dottie.

"And this must be the new guy. Jonnie, is it? Jonnie Martin? Heard we just signed you to a second ten-day. Keep up the good work, boy, keep it up. Who's next there? Chris—is that you? You bet, who else could it be? Hey, get in there. I've got a big old ham, half a steer, lobsters, scallops, a whole swordfish—wait'll you see it.

"Who's this? Tim? Right. Good to see you, Tim. Where's Del? He in there? Del, you in there?"

"I'm Felix McDaniel, Mr. Brandisi."

"Hell-o, Felix, and welcome to Casa Brandisi. Lot of folks inside still remember you. Go on in and say hello. Is this Del?"

"Curtis Clovis, Mr. Brandisi."

"Hey, Curtis. Is that it? You the last one?"

And then Mr. Brandisi encountered one more figure on the steps of the bus. The figure appeared suddenly and made him jump back. "Who's this? Who's this? Who's this?" he said. "Oh, Oliver Dawkins. 'Oll-eee-ver Daw-kins . . . ,' " he sang.

Felix found himself alone on the driveway, smiling around as if the driveway were a perfect spot to stop and rest for a few moments. His smile fell on Mrs. Brandisi. She tentatively put out her hand. "I'm Dottie."

Felix took her hand and did a little bow that brought his lips closer to her hand than he meant. He straightened up quickly and told her his name. There did not seem to be much else to say. "You have a lovely dress," he offered. She said, "Yes. Thank you," and, "I'm glad you like it."

Felix said, "I bet it cost a fortune," and then wanted to bite his tongue because Mrs. Brandisi looked startled.

Marty Smart and Brickshaw and finally Colin Cromwell followed Oliver, each one outdoing the other at showing how easy he felt tagging along with the team. Teddy Brandisi extended a warm welcome to Smart and Brickshaw and then mistook Cromwell for the bus driver even though Cromwell was wearing his dinner jacket. Felix thought that was good. He thought that Mr. Brandisi had not really mistaken Cromwell, particularly

184

since the moment Cromwell identified himself, Mr. Brandisi said, "Ah, yes," and walked away.

The group from the limousine and the cab had gathered on the brick walkway leading to the steps, four men standing six-eleven, six-ten, six-ten, and six-nine, and two women—one black and one white—wearing spangled dresses and looking as if they were loaded to the eyeballs. Felix, following along in the wake of everyone else, happened to be right behind Teddy when the owner encountered this gathering. Cranking back his head, Mr. Brandisi said, "How's it goin', guys?"

The four men agreed it was going all right. Jerome tried to exchange sly grins with the rest, but he was unsuccessful.

"You," said Mr. Brandisi, snapping Jerome's attention back, "must be Jerome Crown."

Jerome admitted he was and Del Fuego belatedly mangled an introduction that started with Mr. Brandisi shaking Jerome's hand and ended with the players shaking hands with each other and Mr. Brandisi embracing Del.

"Del," Mr. Brandisi said, gazing up at him with complete sincerity, "you are having one hell of a year."

Del said thank you several times and then Mr. Brandisi turned to W.E.B. and looked at him sincerely. "And Web, I've been reading about your troubles and I just want you to know, you don't have a thing to worry about. You're a Gater for life, as far as I'm concerned."

W.E.B. seemed only capable of giving a small indication of how grateful he was for that information.

"And Zeke, you're looking well," said Mr. Brandisi. He put his hands on the elbows of Zeke and Jerome and turned the group toward the house. "You four guys, you are the heart of my basketball team—"

Felix hurried after them.

"Mr. Brandisi," interrupted Jerome. The group stopped; Felix stopped with them. "These are my friends Veronica and Sally. I brought them along. They's stewardesses."

"Oh, how nice. Who do you girls fly for?"

"Delta," said Veronica.

"United," said Sally.

185

They both giggled. They both launched their upper bodies forward, bending at the hips and turning their giggles into hard laughs.

"Those are both good airlines," said Mr. Brandisi, strolling the group toward the doors. "But as I was saying a moment ago, you four fellas are the heart and soul of my team and I'm counting on you. I really am. The way we been playing lately— I don't mean the New Jersey game, of course, we really got blown out there. What was it, jet lag that finally caught up with you guys or what? I read where Oliver was sick, didn't even leave the hotel and all that—but what was it with the rest of you guys, something you ate? Because you looked tremendous against Philly. Absolutely tremendous. Play like that every night and I don't see any reason why we can't go all the way. I mean it. Sure, we've gotten ourselves in a bit of a hole, but we're right on the verge of a play-off spot right now, and once we get in the play-offs I think we're going to surprise a lot of people along the way."

The players said "Yes, sir" and "I think so, too" and "You bet." Felix said a combination of all three, but Mr. Brandisi apparently didn't hear him because he never turned around.

# 28

By ten o'clock Jerome had lost one of his women to Oliver. Del Fuego noticed that Oliver had been talking to the one called Veronica in a corner of a room that had high, beamed ceilings, a walk-in fireplace that was in full flame, sand-colored stucco walls, and a set of paneled-glass doors that led to the grounds and the swimming pool and the cabana and the tennis court. One moment they were standing in the corner talking and the next the paneled-glass doors were open and they were gone.

A bar had been set up in that room and there was a Steinway baby grand at which a pianist in tails worked in relative solitude. Del recognized that he was playing Cole Porter and Hoagy Carmichael, but when Zeke asked Del what that shit was, he said he didn't know. Rather than let anybody think he liked that kind of music, Del left the room shortly after he noticed that Oliver and Veronica were gone.

There was an open door on the main hallway. It led down a set of carpeted stairs to a huge "party" room with a tiled floor and a multispeakered sound system that was playing dance music. But it was disco dance music and nobody was dancing. Del heard shouts from another room and found Curtis and Zeke playing video games on a wide-screen television. He watched them for a minute, then wandered off. Video games weren't Del's thing.

He found most of the partygoers congregated in the dining room, where the food was laid out in an elaborate buffet overseen by uniformed chefs, or in the adjoining living room, where there was another fire and another bar and a number of caterers passing out hors d'oeuvres from little silver trays. There were about 150 guests, and aside from the basketball contingent, nearly all of them had come in couples. No one seemed to have taken into account the fact that a group of twenty men, unescorted except for two women in shimmering dresses, would throw the balance of the party completely out of whack.

Del, who was used to being a focal point of social gatherings, felt alienated as he wandered from room to room. He wondered where all the Brandisis' black friends were. He wondered why so few of these people who had come out to honor a basketball team seemed interested in meeting basketball players.

The players, for the most part, drank and ate and moved about the house like tugboats in the midst of a sailing regatta. Chris Sarantopoulis sat alone on a couch and drank Pepsi. W.E.B. and Jerome and the woman called Sally occupied a corner as if they were guarding it from intruders. Two girls, still in their teens and daughters, obviously, of some of the other guests, attached themselves to Rynn, but seemed to be spending all their time talking to each other in his presence. "Oh, my God," they said, "oh, my God," and Rynn kept a half smile on his face and studied the ice cubes in his nearly empty glass.

Only Rohmer and Booby and Felix seemed to be successfully interacting with the folks who had gathered in their honor. Rohmer was entertaining a group of mostly older women with an animated story that had their faces glowing. Booby had a very attractive blonde casually leaning her shoulder into a wall while she crossed her legs at the knees and gazed raptly at him over the champagne glass she held to her lips. Felix was explaining to two silver-haired men in pin-striped suits his admiration for President Bush.

When Del passed by Felix, he distinctly heard him make reference to a thousand points of light.

"And I can count them," Felix said earnestly.

Del stopped to catch what the response would be.

One of the silver-haired gentlemen looked away.

The other, after a moment's silence, said, "Do you play golf?"

Del hated them. He hated each and every person there. He

188

was about to tell Felix he should let these sorry-ass men know what they could do with their golf sticks when he noticed Dottie Brandisi approach Rynn Packard. Dottie had in tow a black-haired, blue-eyed woman with skin that was tanned dark and made up to look even darker. The woman's legs were sleek. Her black dress was cut low and held her breasts in pockets of soft cloth through which Del was certain he could make out her nipples. Del forgot about being angry.

Dottie got between Rynn and his teenage admirers and laid a bony hand on Rynn's forearm. "Rynn," she announced, "I want you to meet one of my oldest—"

The other woman was aghast. "Don't say that, Dottie!"

"You know what I mean." The two women laughed and flicked their hands at each other the way rich white women do, and then Dottie said, "Anyhow, one of my dearest friends, Tory Brewer. Tory's husband owns the largest office-furniture rental company in the Northeast and is a very big contributor to Harvard." Dottie Brandisi nodded with satisfaction. "Rynn went to Harvard."

"Cornell," corrected Rynn, shaking the woman's hand.

Tory Brewer literally fell into him. She laughed and pulled herself back and covered her mouth, but she did not let go of Rynn's hand. "I'm so sorry," she said. "But I had to get myself tanked to work up the nerve to meet you."

"Tory and her husband flew up from Florida just for the party," Dottie Brandisi explained. "Isn't that grand?"

Rynn allowed that it was.

Del moved in closer. The kid wasn't going to be able to handle this woman. She had at least fifteen years on him—fifteen years of getting her way with people who didn't know what she was doing to them. Her black hair was soft and shimmery and Del wanted to run his hands through it. Her eyes were blue, but they were narrow and expertly marked with black eyeliner and blue shadow. She smiled and showed teeth that were even and white and wet and expensive looking.

"I wanted to see all the beautiful young men," she said.

"Well, they're here," Rynn responded, sweeping one hand around the room and blushing as he did so.

Tory picked up Rynn's uninspired line with an ease that came only from a great deal of practice. "Which ones are they?" she gasped, and when Rynn blinked, she laughed again and pitched her forehead into his chest. She snapped it back almost immediately and covered her mouth as she had done before. Her blue eyes sparkled. "I'm sorry," she said from behind her hand. "I'm really going to have to get some air to straighten up a bit. Will you take a walk outside with me?"

Rynn looked at Dottie Brandisi. It was obvious he did not particularly want to go for a walk with this woman whom he had just met, who was making lovely but drunken eyes at him—and Dottie responded to his silent plea.

"Oh, now, Tory, it's freezing cold out there and you've got to remember that these California boys aren't used to such temperatures."

There was more gibberish, but Tory, having made her pitch, was doomed to move on alone. That was when Del moved in.

A waiter passed with glasses of champagne on a tray, and Del scooped two of them without the waiter's even slowing down. Holding one in each hand, Del tracked across the room until he caught up with the raven-haired beauty. "I'll go outside with you," he said, holding out one of the glasses.

Tory Brewer inspected him coolly. Her eyes ran the length of his body, and somewhere along the way they softened so that by the time they reached his face they were showing every bit as much interest as they had shown Rynn. "Are you a player?"

"I'm the star," he told her matter-of-factly.

"Ooh," she said, "are you W.E.B. Pancake?"

"No, I am not W.E.B. Pancake," he snapped. He was about to add, "And neither is he," when he realized she was laughing. She knew who he was. She had made a joke and he had missed it. He blushed because he did not want her thinking he was not smart enough to appreciate her sense of humor.

"My husband is here, you know," she said.

"He definitely won't go out in the cold with you."

"You know my husband?"

"Sure. Rich guy. With a tan."

Now it was her turn to catch on slowly, and Del felt better. She tapped a fingernail thoughtfully against a lower lip and then downed her champagne in two sips and said, "You pretty adventurous, star?"

"With a name like Del Fuego," he told her, just in case she didn't have it right, "my mama didn't give me much choice but to be adventurous."

She nodded. "Okay. Then let's go out to the pool." She grabbed his hand, held it very loosely between her thumb and fingers, and led him along a hallway that took them past the Steinway room. They went past the door to the stairs going down to the party room and past the door to the room where Curtis and Zeke were still playing video games. They entered the kitchen, where three or four workers were hurrying back and forth between a walk-in freezer and an industrial-size stove, between a walk-in pantry and a large double sink, between the sink and the butcher-block table that occupied the center of the room. Tory hooked a champagne bottle from a couple of dozen that were sitting on a counter and opened a door to the backyard.

The door led to a small flight of steps and a flagstone path that meandered between two low hedges and down a slight incline to a six-foot hedge that screened the pale blue light and rising vapor of the Brandisis' heated swimming pool. She skipped down the steps, and Del, who refused to appear in a hurry, nonetheless had to take long strides just to stay with her. She flung open a wire gate in the hedges and her heels tapped on the concrete of the pool deck.

The pool was long and lined with lanes laid out in black and white tiles that could be seen through the water as clearly as if they were painted on the surface. It was impressive, but after a few seconds of looking at it, after a few swigs of champagne, there was nothing more for them to do. Tory seemed to have her mind elsewhere. She might even have been listening for something.

"Let me show you the pool house," she said suddenly. "It's not like a cabana at all. It's more like a guesthouse."

Del followed her across the deck to a series of doors. Tory

191

went directly to the one on the far left. "Wait till you see this place," she told him, and twisted the handle.

The door opened and the room was dark. She reached inside for the light switch and a man's voice said, "Don't touch that."

Del froze. His first thought was that they were caught. Tory's husband, the furniture man, was going to leap out with a shotgun and blast holes in his body. He wanted to run. He could see nothing inside and his heart was thumping.

Tory, however, was unafraid. "Who's in there?" she demanded.

The voice said, "Just a guest." And Del's heart resumed its normal rhythm. He recognized the voice now.

"You, man," Del said.

"Leave us alone for a minute, will ya, man?"

"Yeah, sure." Del tried to reach around Tory to close the door, but she held it firm.

"Are you in there, Marcie?" she wanted to know.

It was left up to Del to tell her that it was not Marcie who was in there. He pulled the door shut.

Tory spun on her heel and her face was furious. "I wonder who he's with. I bet it is Marcie. She's been talking about basketball players for two weeks." She looked out at the pool. She gazed around and her eyes settled on a second door. The anger seemed to drain from her and she slid her free hand under Del's arm. "Let's," she purred, "go one up on them. Let's go in the pool."

A ripple of panic ran through Del. "I don't have a suit," he protested. He also could barely swim, but he thought it best not to tell her that.

"Don't worry," she said, patting him reassuringly. "We'll go skinny-dipping."

She guided him toward the second door; pulled him actually, like a mule being dragged into a barn. They entered what was almost an alley of a room. The walls were lined with hooks and beneath the hooks were benches, but the walls did not go to the ceiling. Del could see his breath.

"It'll be fun," she urged, and Del bobbed his head in an attempt at enthusiasm. He was interested in this woman's white butt. He was not interested in going in that water.

A moment later she was naked and he saw a flash of what he wanted as she opened the door and ran for the pool. He heard a splash as the door swung shut. He stood alone in the narrow room, silently debating whether he was actually going to take off his clothes.

"Hey," she called after a few moments. "Don't leave me out here by myself."

He undressed quickly. He opened the door, took two or three giant steps to the edge of the pool, and stopped there. He wanted her to see him. He wanted her to appreciate him. She did. She said, "Oh, my." And Del felt a whole lot better.

He looked around for depth markers. The highest number he saw was six. That gave him nine inches to breathe. That was enough. He crouched down and slipped over the side, groping for the floor with his feet before letting go with his hands. It was fine. It wasn't deep here. Three and a half, four feet, maybe. And it was warm.

Tory Brewer, looking pleased, appeared in front of him, her black hair clinging to her skull and hanging to her shoulders in long, looping curlicues. As he tried to smile at her, she took his face in both her hands and covered his mouth with hers. Their stomachs, their legs, their skin—all came together. She was slim and smooth and finely toned. She tasted of sweetness and sparkling wine and he thought fantastic thoughts of tigers leaping through the jungle. Immediately he was aroused. Immediately she knew it. But she kept kissing him.

His eyes were closed and his ears were filled with the sounds of the slap of the water against the sides of the pool and the panting of Tory Brewer and the far-off strains of music from the main house, and he did not immediately realize that he was also hearing footsteps on concrete. When at last the message did come through to him, he looked up to see Oliver Dawkins and the alleged stewardess named Veronica slipping across the deck. Oliver had her by the hand, and he was looking right at Del and giving him the sly look.

Mrs. Brewer stared after them as Oliver and Veronica passed through the gate. "That wasn't Marcie," she said.

Del did not see what difference it made, but she broke out of his arms and swam to the far end of the pool.

"We forgot towels," she said as she pulled herself up and out of the water by grabbing onto the rim and pressing down with her palms. Her back gleamed and her muscles went taut as she hung for a second before landing on one knee. She pushed to her feet and ran to the room Oliver had just vacated, moving lightly and gracefully and shedding a trail of water drops and wet foot marks.

A minute passed and Del was alone in the water, wondering what had happened and why he no longer felt as warm as he had. He crossed his arms in front of his chest in an effort to keep from shivering, and while he was standing like that the gate creaked and a man in an ill-fitting dinner jacket stepped onto the deck. "Del," he said in surprise, "what are you doing?"

Del said, "Hi, Colin," and could not think of an answer. Of all the people in the world, maybe the last one besides his wife that he wanted to see at that moment was Colin Cromwell. This was not a good way to be found by a nosy reporter, standing alone, naked, in Mr. Brandisi's swimming pool.

"You just swimming all by yourself?" There was a note of skepticism in Cromwell's voice as he moved closer to look.

"Hell, no." No, of course not. He was getting whirlpool therapy. But the door opened and Tory Brewer emerged carrying two large folded towels as if they were fireplace logs.

She was still naked and showed not the slightest bit of concern that Cromwell was there, that his mouth had fallen open and his eyes had popped wide behind his glasses. "It's cold," she said, as if that was all Cromwell needed to know, and then she threw down the towels at the edge of the pool and dived into the water—one slim leg scissored out from the other.

She landed with a gentle splash that took her deep under the surface. Without coming up for air, she swam silently across the pool until she was behind Del, and then she rose and pushed the hair out of her eyes with both hands so that her breasts flared when she did it. "Are you a player?" she asked.

Cromwell, his mouth sliding around impishly, said, "You bet."

194

Tory Brewer looked dubious. She continued holding her hair back. "What position do you play?"

"Right field."

"What do they call you?"

"Righter. Sport Righter."

"Well, Sport," she said, "would you mind running into that little changing room over there and getting us our bottle of champagne? And then why don't you get your clothes off and jump in with us? It's great, isn't it, Del?"

Del told him it was. He told him in such a way that he would know he was not to accept Mrs. Brewer's invitation. But it did no good. Colin Cromwell came out of the changing room with a bottle in his hand, still wearing his ugly jacket, his glasses, and not another thing else. His legs were skinny and hairy and pale, and when he took his jacket off, the rest of him was skinny and pale, too. But Mrs. Brewer must have been looking at something else because she said, "Oh," just as if he were a halfway decent physical specimen.

Cromwell handed Tory the bottle, laid his glasses down on the edge of the pool, and pranced into the water. He kept his head from going beneath the surface even as he stroked his way up to where they were standing, and Del hoped that Cromwell wasn't going to do anything crazy such as splash water at them or propose they all go dashing down the other end in some sort of butterfly race that was meant to show Del up. But then there was a commotion at the gate and all three of them turned in that direction. The gate rattled, shook, and was wrenched open to admit Oliver Dawkins, Zeke Wyatt, and a somewhat bewildered looking Curtis Clovis.

Del Fuego, assessing the situation, immediately took control. "Oliver!" he cried. "Curtis. My man, Zeke. Wha'chu doin', babes?"

Del did not wait for them to tell him. He mushed through the water to the side of the pool and, when he got there, held out his hand in Mrs. Brewer's direction. "Meet my friend, Toeree," he announced. "God's gift to man."

Tory Brewer did not seem to dispute his assessment. She fluttered her eyes and stepped away from Colin so that she was considerably more exposed than she had been, although she did sling her right hand over her left shoulder so that her arm partially covered her breasts.

Zeke introduced himself. "Zeke Wyatt, number fifty-four." He stood with his hands in the pockets of his pleated pants, and his hands were actively moving about as he smiled a smile that gave every indication he had put away his share of the boss's liquor.

Oliver, who had hung back at first, developed a burst of energy and crashed into a squat next to Del. He demanded the bottle. He had to demand it twice because Mrs. Brewer's eyes were on Curtis.

"And who," she said, "might this big, strong, beautiful man be?"

"Curtis," he answered, and turned away as if he were going to retreat.

"Why don't you get in here, Curtis?" Mrs. Brewer asked, stopping him.

"Curtis doesn't swim," Del Fuego said. He was telling Curtis that, but Curtis reacted defensively.

"I do so."

Annoyed, Del Fuego challenged him. "Then whyn't you get in here?"

Mrs. Brewer said, "Why don't you all get in here?"

Oliver and Zeke looked at Del. He had to make a quick decision. He said, "Why don't you get out and we'll party some?"

Coyly, she smiled and said, "What do you have to party with?"

"Oh, one of us might be able to come up with something."

She cocked her head. Her eyes sparkled. Her teeth flashed. "Like what?" she asked invitingly.

"Well, wha'chu like, woman?" Oliver interjected.

"Tory," she corrected him, but already Oliver had dropped down on one knee and was leaning forward, his head stretched out over the water so he could whisper something in her ear that only she could hear.

She put her wet hands on Oliver's shoulders. She held her

196

face next to his, and when she heard what he had to say she cried, "What?"

Oliver put his finger to his lips. "Shhh!" He glanced at Colin Cromwell.

Then he began whispering again and Tory Brewer smiled as she listened, and Del Fuego took this as a sign that he should issue instructions. "Ezekiel, you get the towels for these people. And Curtis, how about you doin' us a favor and maybe goin' back up the kitchen and gettin' us another couple bottles of bubbly? We'll be in the pool house, Curtis, when you come back. Just knock, you know, three times or something."

Zeke made a production of picking up a towel and holding it out for Mrs. Brewer. He pretended not to look as she rose from the water, but he looked nonetheless and she pretended not to notice and wrapped the towel tightly around her and knotted it under her arm. With a lascivious smile plastered on his lips, Zeke stepped back to admire the final product and promptly crushed Colin Cromwell's glasses beneath his size-sixteen shoe.

He was sorry, genuinely apologetic, but it was too late. The frames had snapped at the nose bridge, and what was once a single unit was now two distinct pieces. In the minicommotion that ensued, Del managed to get Mrs. Brewer hustled off to the beckoning warmth of the pool house. They left Colin alone on the deck, trying to fit the two halves of his glasses back together.

The room in which Del and Zeke and Oliver eventually found themselves with Mrs. Brewer had a four-poster bed, a woven rug on the floor, a couple of bureaus, a desk with a mirror over it, and a couple of wicker chairs. It was nothing to get Tory Brewer to sit on the bed, and then Oliver got down on his knees in front of her and opened a little brown vial and jammed a little silver straw into the vial and told her to take as much as she wanted. She looked at Oliver as if she wanted him to think she never had done such a thing and then inhaled enough to snap her head back on her neck.

The motion made the towel slip down her breasts. Del moved quickly, dropping down onto the bed next to her and fumbling with the knot so that he could pretend he was tightening it

197

while he was really just getting his fingers under the cloth. He was faster than Zeke, who had to settle for the other side of her, the side without the knot, but Zeke was smart enough to catch up a handful of Tory Brewer's black hair and say that he had to keep it from getting tangled in the towel that Del was fixing. That gave him an opening to start nibbling on her neck. He needed only one hand to hold her hair, and so he let the other rest on her knee. Zeke had big hands.

That was the way everybody was arranged when the door suddenly popped open and in walked Colin Cromwell. He had his stupid jacket on again and half his glasses hooked over one ear, and he was carrying in his arms two pairs of shoes, his pants and shirt, a black dress, a lacy bra, and a pair of black panty hose.

Oliver spun his back to Cromwell. Tory Brewer, who did not understand what he was doing, pawed at Oliver's hands, trying to peel open his fingers. But Oliver was holding his fists to his chest, and she eventually got the idea that if she didn't stop he was going to murder her. Zeke was staring, his lips frozen in place on Tory Brewer's neck.

Once again, it was up to Del to say something, and when he spoke, he did so slowly, reassuringly, as if he were talking to a Doberman pinscher. "It's all right. It's fine. Colin's cool. He parties. He's been here and there once or twice before, haven't you, my man?"

Colin's eyeglasses dangled from his ear. His exposed body was shimmeringly white. It was thin where it should have been thick and thick where it should have been thin. He was holding an armful of women's clothes and a head full of champagne. The beauteous Mrs. Brewer, in her struggle to open Oliver's fingers, had completely lost the knot on her towel and did not seem to care that her breast, her side, her hip, her thigh, were exposed for all to see. Three members of the San Francisco GoldenGaters sat so still in front of Colin as to be nearly inanimate.

He nodded. He told Del he was cool.

198

# 29

Booby Sinclair lay on the king-size bed and tried to recall the name of the woman next to him. She reminded him of Kathleen Turner, but Kathleen was not her name. Her husband owned a Cadillac dealership and a horse that had once run in the Kentucky Derby, and he had gone off to New York for the week to meet with important people. Developers. Financiers. People who were going to help him build something somewhere. She had come to the party anyway and she had agreed to give Booby a ride back to Boston so he would not have to ride on the bus. They had gone in her Jaguar and she had agreed to go into the hotel for a nightcap. And then she had agreed that it would not look right for either of them to be seen sitting with each other in a public bar that late at night.

That was how he had gotten her to his room, and into his bed, and maybe it was why he could not remember her name. He knew that she had once played intercollegiate tennis, that she had been to Africa and had gone to school in Paris and had a home in St. Bart's. He knew that he wished she were gone.

He had, at some point, decided he wanted a woman like this. Perhaps he had gotten the idea from a magazine on an airplane or a movie in a hotel room. He had wanted to accompany such a woman to a fancy restaurant, or maybe a ballet. He was not really sure where such people went, but he had seen their pictures in advertisements and knew they went somewhere that required them to look elegant and commanding and self-possessed.

In Ohio, the best-looking girls had always been the wholesome, clear-faced, fluffy-haired, slightly rounded ones. But those Ohio girls from his youth would never have made it in the Northeast, where the women he saw had a different kind of beauty, a more sophisticated kind, a kind that made him feel they knew more than he did. So he had wanted one of those women and now he had one and he was disappointed.

It was always that way. There had been a time when Meg had seemed to know so much about so many things that mattered. But then they moved from Kentucky and he had seen that she was even more out of place than he in a world where different things were important to different people, where not everybody was striving for the same goal, where success was so often marked by what you had instead of what you did. He had wanted one of Meg's kind of women and he had gotten one, and she had not been what he had thought she would be.

And neither was this woman. She was long and slim and pretty, but out of her clothes she was boyishly cut. Instead of being fun, she had lain still and stared at him for an uncomfortably long time so that he would know she was not used to cheating on her husband or going to hotel rooms with unsophisticated basketball coaches. He had been quicker than he had intended to be and she had not been forgiving or understanding or reinvigorating. She had looked at him as if he had crashed her Jaguar into a tree.

Booby lay next to the blonde whose name he could not remember and thought about girls from Ohio whom he remembered very clearly, and then the phone exploded next to his ear. Its piercing, heart-stopping jangle made both him and his companion virtually leap into sitting positions.

"It's my husband," she said, clutching the sheet to her egg-sized breasts and staring at him as if he could do something about it.

"More likely it's my wife," he said, swinging his legs off the bed.

The phone jangled again and it occurred to him that there

200

was no reason for a phone ever to be so loud. He glanced at his watch and saw that it was after two. He watched the receiver dumbly, and when it shrieked a third time he picked it up and said, "Yeah?"

"Booby . . ."·

He did not immediately place the voice. It was too out of breath, too strained.

"Booby, it's Colin Cromwell."

But it wasn't Colin Cromwell's voice. It was Mike Hacker's.

"Hack, is that you? Where the hell are you?"

"Here. In the hotel. The cops are here, Booby."

"Why?"

"They're all over the place."

"Why?" Booby said again. He could say it all night long.

The blonde was grabbing her clothes from the floor, the chair, wherever she could find them.

"Because of Cromwell. He's gone off the building."

"Gone off—what's that mean?"

"His room was on the top floor, Booby. He went out the window."

This did not make any sense. Booby, watching the blonde run into the bathroom, hesitated. "Well, is he all right?"

"Is he all right? He went off the sixth story, Booby. He's splattered all over the street, for God sakes."

# Buzzer

# 30

For Ed Norbert, it was embarrassing to be seated in the first row. He had come alone, wearing a gray herringbone sport coat because he had nothing darker. He had expected just to mingle with the crowd, listen to the eulogy, pay his respects, and get the hell back to the paper. But Colin's brother Carl ("We're all Cs in this family, Mr. Norbert") had been greeting people in the foyer, and when Ed introduced himself, Carl insisted that Ed join the family in the row of honor. So there they sat: mother Catherine, brother Cole and his wife, a seat for brother Carl, sister Candace and her husband, a cousin somebody-or-other, and Ed.

The Cromwell family understood that Ed had been Colin's best friend. Carl told them so. And there seemed to be nobody else present to claim the title. The family members looked into Ed's face and could see that he felt distraught, and they were comforted by that. They did not realize that Ed was in equal parts upset because he was going to be delayed in getting back to work, because he was wearing an inappropriate sport coat, and because he was the best they could get to personify what a great guy Colin was. Ed had not even liked Colin.

Sitting in the front row, Ed had to keep looking over his shoulder to check out the other mourners. There were a fair number, but they did not fill the chapel, and no one sat in the second row, behind the family.

Ed recognized a few people from the paper. He nodded to Marty Smart and the beat writers from the *Oakland Tribune* and the *San Jose Mercury News*. He figured the tentative-looking folks who came in wearing nylon jackets or ski parkas or raincoats were fans or readers, and that gave him some amount of satisfaction, but he noticed a pair of impeccably shaven young men with square jaws, short haircuts, broad shoulders, and wrinkle-free suits and wondered what connection they could possibly have had with Colin.

"We're from Michigan," cousin somebody leaned over and whispered.

Ed nodded. He said he knew.

"That's why there aren't more of us here. If it were back in Michigan, this place would be packed."

Ed nodded some more.

"I live in Monterey now, myself," the cousin said. He handed Ed a business card. It identified him as a real estate agent.

"Came out for the Summer of Love in 1967, and now look at me."

Ed looked. He was not sure what he was supposed to see. The man was balding and bearded and looked anxious to please. Other than that he was totally unremarkable.

"Isn't it funny how life works sometimes?"

Ed agreed that it was and glanced once more over his shoulder. Rynn Packard and Dick Crabtree had just walked into the chapel. No one was guiding them, and after a moment's hesitation they took seats along the side farthest from Ed. People were looking at them and Rynn held his head rigidly, looking neither to one side or the other. From what Ed could see, Rynn and Crabbie were the only representatives of the Gaters who had shown.

"My cousin came out to Stanford to get a graduate degree in literature. Was gonna teach, I guess. Teach and write the great American novel. Now look at him."

It was not an easy thing to do. The casket in front of them was closed. Ed, however, was spared any further discussion because there was a general disturbance in the back and everyone turned to see the mayor of San Francisco entering in grand fashion. With the mayor was a city supervisor, San Francisco's most famous newspaper columnist, the publisher and the editor in chief of Ed's paper, and, at the heels of the others, Wayne Brickshaw.

The cousin whispered the roll call of luminaries to sister Candace and her husband and they passed it along. As the mayor and his entourage seated themselves in the second row, everyone in the Cromwell family except mother Catherine turned to beam at them. Ed, however, caught only the eye of the editor in chief, who looked startled to see Ed where he was. Ed shrugged.

The service began. A minister talked about carpe diem. A screen was lowered against the wall behind the casket. Slides showing Colin Cromwell were projected onto the screen. His sister burst into sobs.

Eventually, brother Carl strode to the podium. He said he had known Colin almost all his life, which Ed interpreted to mean he was a little older than Colin. He said Colin was the brains of the family, the smart one. He got out some notebook paper and read, "I have no doubt that Colin would have been just as good an athlete as Cole and I were—maybe better, because he had so much determination—but Colin was an asthmatic and he had to spend much of his formative years in bed.

"We had a big backyard and there were a lot of kids around, and between Cole and myself and even our sister, Candace, it seemed there was always something going on and always something for Colin to observe.

"I can still remember his little face watching from behind the screen of his bedroom window while Cole and myself and the other kids in the neighborhood played football in the backyard. Sure, he wanted to play, he wanted to be out there with the rest of us, but even back then I remember admiring him for making the best of the situation.

"Sometimes he would announce the games as we played them, and sometimes he would watch closely and tell us what we were doing wrong. Which, of course, we did not always like to hear."

Carl paused in case anyone wanted to laugh, but perhaps because he was reading, nobody responded.

207

"At night we would hear him in his room listening to Big Ten basketball games on the radio. He would keep charts and statistics on the various players, including, I am sure, the present coach of the San Francisco GoldenGaters, Booby Sinclair."

People turned to see if Booby was in the audience. Heads went one way and then another, and in a space of a few seconds a good many people were staring into a back corner. They were not looking at the coach of the GoldenGaters, but at a blond woman wearing dark sunglasses and a coat with its collar turned up against her cheeks. She was sitting by herself and she refused to acknowledge that she was the focus of anyone's attention.

"Who's that?" demanded the cousin in a whisper, and when Ed told him that it was Meg Sinclair, the cousin grunted and said that he guessed the coach couldn't make it and had sent his wife in his place.

Ed picked up Carl's speech again when he was close to the end. "There remains a great mystery about what happened to my brother the other night in Boston. My family does not have answers to give you, nor have we received the answers we want. If, in fact, his death was an accident, then we all must be moved by the surprises that life has in store for us. For if it can happen to my brother Colin, it can happen to any of us. If, on the other hand, it was not an accident, then we are, as individuals, affected even more, because Colin, then, died for all of us, for our right to know."

Carl paused, momentarily overcome by the enormity of what he was suggesting. "It is true," he went on haltingly, "that Colin was a sportswriter and not a foreign correspondent or a political commentator or even a muckraker, but his job was to bring us information, and if he had something to tell us and if he died because someone wanted to prevent us from learning what he had to say, then we have lost more than just a brother, a son, a friend, a coworker. We have lost a freedom.

"On behalf of my family, I call on the authorities of this country to put every means at their disposal to learn why it was that my brother died, to expose whatever it was that he may have been about to tell us, and to insure that whoever is responsible is brought to justice."

"Amen," said the mayor, startling Ed Norbert, causing him to turn to see if the man was serious and turning just in time to see that his editor in chief and his publisher were solemnly chorusing with "Amen" 's of their own.

Ed quickly faced front again. "Amen," he said loudly.

# 31

Ida Pancake looked at the dark-haired, narrow-faced man sitting in the giant maroon leather chair on the opposite side of the cherrywood desk from her and her husband and waited. The man was reading the papers they had presented him. From time to time he would glance up, and whenever he did so, Ida would grow more anxious. She knew a thing or two about patience, but right now she was leaning on one arm of her chair as though she were about to be catapulted into space.

W.E.B. was putting her to shame. He sat as if he were in a train station, waiting for a train that was not expected to arrive for some time. Unlike Ida, he was not watching the lawyer they had come to see. He was staring at a space of tongue-and-groove hardwood floor between the edge of the red Oriental carpet and the bookshelves that lined one wall.

The man sighed. He put the papers down. "Where, exactly," he said, pausing for emphasis, "were you on the night Cromwell died?"

It was immediately clear to Ida that the man understood the situation. She allowed herself to relax just the tiniest bit. Jewish lawyers, she thought, were every bit as smart as people said.

W.E.B. drew in a rattling breath and announced, "I was at Mr. Brandisi's party, 'long with Cromwell and all the rest of the team."

"What time," the lawyer asked, "did you leave?"

"Same time as most other peoples."

"But you didn't go back on the bus."

210

W.E.B. shook his head. "Went back with Jerome in his limo," he mumbled.

"And who else went with Jerome?"

"Some friends of his'n."

"I see," said the lawyer. And Ida was grateful that he seemed not to want to embarrass anyone unnecessarily. She liked the man without actually liking him. She wanted him to like them.

The lawyer asked, "When was the last time you can be absolutely sure of seeing Colin Cromwell?"

"I saw him . . ." W.E.B.'s hooded eyes glazed in concentration. "I saw him absolutely at the party. Um-hmm. He seemed like he wanted to talk to me, but I stayed mostly put in this one part of the big living room, the corner, with Jerome and his friends."

W.E.B. would have left it there, but the lawyer kept staring at him as if he knew he had more to say, and finally W.E.B. spread his hands and explained, "I didn't want him comin' up tryin' to talk to me."

"So you never did speak to him that night?"

"That's right."

"And if somebody says they saw you with him . . . ?"

"They'd be lying."

The lawyer said, "Okay, Mr. Pancake, then your thought is that the only reason the FBI has questioned you is because of these articles that Cromwell wrote." He thumped the articles they had brought him with his long, perfectly manicured fingers.

Ida was trying to guess what it cost a man to have a manicure like that when she realized that W.E.B. was looking to her for assurance. "That's right," she said for him.

The door to the office opened and a secretary came in carrying a silver tray with a coffee service on it. Also on the tray were two tall glasses filled with ice and three cans of soda. One was a can of Coke, one was of diet Coke, and one was some sort of fruit soda. The secretary was young and blond and extremely good-looking. Her blue jacket and skirt were made of rough silk and they fit tightly, particularly around the hips. Ida wouldn't wear a skirt like that. She was too big a woman.

And once this little cutie pie had a couple of babies she wouldn't be wearing it either.

The young woman asked what she could pour them, and Ida gave her a very quick smile. The smile was meant to freeze Miss Cutie Pie and tell her not to dare to so much as raise an eyebrow at her husband. "Coffee," she ordered. "Cream and two sugars."

W.E.B. refused to look up from the floor.

"What would you like, Mr. Pancake?" the secretary asked sweetly.

"Diet," W.E.B. said, still not looking up.

The young woman worked efficiently. She set cups of coffee in saucers on coasters in front of Ida and her boss, and she poured W.E.B. his diet Coke in a way that made the ice snap and the soda break into singing bubbles. Then she took her tray and slipped out of the room, and nobody's eyes moved from wherever they had been when she was passing out the refreshments.

They all sipped and sipped again. "What bothers me," said the lawyer, "is that it was the FBI." He watched their reactions. He was looking to see if it bothered them, too. "The report that I heard was that Colin Cromwell was drunk and had fallen out the window, perhaps as he was trying to open it."

He carefully replaced his Royal Doulton china cup in its saucer before continuing. Ida knew what it was. She had been to Harrods in London with W.E.B. and she had looked at all the china patterns. She had bought Wedgwood, but W.E.B.'s niece had put the whole set in the dishwasher one Thanksgiving and a lot of it had gotten broken.

"When an unusual death like that occurs," said the lawyer, "you can expect that the local police will at least look into it. The FBI, that's a different story."

"Why, Mr. Rosenthal?" Ida asked.

He turned to her with genuine interest, and while Ida was grateful that he treated her question as important, something about his look, like the fragile Royal Doulton cup and saucer in her hands, made her feel big and dumb and awkward.

"Because," he said, "the FBI is interested only in federal matters. The things they generally go around investigating are

212

bank robberies, kidnappings, issues of civil rights, matters involving interstate commerce."

Ida had started nodding as soon as he had started speaking, and she was mad at herself for that. She picked up on the most available option he had given them. "A newspaperman traveling with a professional basketball team across state lines," she said, "doesn't that count for interstate commerce?"

"What often qualifies as interstate commerce, Mrs. Pancake," the man said bluntly, "is gambling. Particularly if it involves a professional sports team."

Ida Pancake felt as if she had just been slapped in the face. "What are you trying to say?"

"Look, Mrs. Pancake, you came to me because you"—he gestured—"your husband is worried. Two FBI agents contacted him and started asking him a lot of questions about where he was and what he was doing at the time Cromwell went out his window. So you've come to me for advice. Why? I'm not a criminal attorney. My specialty is contracts and entertainment law. I must assume you've sought me out because I also function as a players' agent. Now, given who I am, given who your husband is, what is it I can really do for you? That's the question, isn't it?"

There was an edge to his words, a sharpness to his tone, that made Ida and W.E.B. exchange glances. People had talked to them like this in the past, but not for a long time. Still, they were here, and this man was supposed to be the best, and maybe that's what you should want from a lawyer—the ability to cut right to the bone.

"W.E.B.'s contract is up at the end of this season," Ida said slowly, measuring each word to make sure there was nothing about it that the man could throw back at her. "One point two million a year, which isn't much, the way some people get paid these days, but W.E.B. signed a four-year deal with a option clause back when Mr. Brandisi first bought the team, and it seemed like a fine deal then."

"Leigh Rossville was your agent at the time, wasn't he?" Mr. Rosenthal asked. The man seemed to know Leigh. He seemed not to hold him in high regard.

"That's right," she admitted. "But Leigh's not getting nowhere now. We expect, this year, some time long before now, Dale Rohmer would want to sit down and negotiate a new contract. The way it is, the Gaters can exercise their option and pay W.E.B. the same for next year that they paying him now. But if they do that, he becomes a unrestricted free agent at the end of next season and can sign with anybody he want."

"Or," said Mr. Rosenthal, "they can refuse to exercise that option and he becomes a free agent as soon as this present season is over."

"That's next month," added W.E.B., his voice loud, "and they haven't done nothing."

Ida irritably moved the cup and saucer from her lap to the lawyer's desk and missed the coaster. Mr. Rosenthal's eye went to where the saucer sat on the bare wood, but she wasn't going to jump for him. She was the customer. She was the one who was supposed to appreciate his unique desk. Not keep it clean. "Back in February, Leigh was talking to Dale Rohmer, tellin' him we want three years, six million," she said. "Dale Rohmer was saying something like three years, four point five. We wasn't that far apart."

Mr. Rosenthal smiled encouragingly. But his beady brown eyes kept going back to the cup and saucer.

"Then these columns started to appear and all of a sudden Dale Rohmer's a ghost. Leigh can't get through to him. No more negotiations of any kind."

"What," said Mr. Rosenthal, finally able to stand it no more, reaching out and moving the cup and saucer to the coaster, "makes you think I can do any better?"

"We know what you did for Curtis." Ida let it sink in. "We been seeing how you can turn a problem into a advantage. And we have a problem."

She had her husband's approval on that one. The vibration from his nod practically made the floor shake.

"I'm not a miracle worker," Mr. Rosenthal said, his fingers doing a little dance. "If W.E.B. did something wrong . . ." He left the rest hanging.

Ida knew right away what he was getting at, but before she

214

could react, her husband, misinterpreting, spoke out, "My real name is Willie Smith."

"I know," said Mr. Rosenthal softly, his fingers alighting on top of Cromwell's columns.

"I played basketball against that Wilson boy in high school, jes like he says."

"I figured that, too."

"Well, then I guess you must know'd I got in some trouble back when I was eighteen."

"That part I didn't know."

"All right." W.E.B. looked at Ida, pleased that the man didn't know everything. "The thing that so bad, I was actually on my way to college when it happened. I mean, en route. I mean, the school sent me a plane ticket to fly there, but my brother Luther, he just got a car, a GTO."

Ida interrupted, taking nothing for granted. "And that was dumb of Luther because that was considered a white boy's car where we come from."

"But he got it," said W.E.B., "and he talked me into cashing my plane ticket so me and him could have some fun 'fore I left. He promised me I did that, he'd drive me to school. See the country, he said." W.E.B. paused to wipe his mustache out of his mouth.

"Well, we see Mississippi and then Mississippi sees us and pulls us over."

"For speeding, they say," Ida added.

"They put me and Luther up on the side of the road and they don't seem to believe that Luther own that nice car, and ole Luther can't keep his mouf shut when they start goin' through it. One thing lead to another and all of a sudden ole Luther gettin' the shit beat outta him with nightsticks, and I jumps in to try to get the troopers off my brother."

"He was a big boy even then, Mr. Rosenthal."

"So you might say Luther and me was more than holding our own until the guns get drawn and one of 'em starts goin' off. You might say we was lucky they wasn't goin' off into us, but, you know, some of them cops got hurt and you wouldn't believe what their fellow officers done when they seen that."

Fearing that her husband was going to get off track, Ida picked up the story. "It turns out they wasn't a star basketball recruit being driven off to college by his brother. They was drug dealers deliverin' marijuana. Least according to them troopers, who claimed they found a key of grass in their trunk. Time have changed some since then, Mr. Rosenthal, but you didn't grow up down there like we did. That was a big crime."

W.E.B. grimaced. "A couple of poor black boys from Alabama dealin' marijuana? Who we s'pose to be dealin' to?"

"My husband's making a joke, Mr. Rosenthal, but in this case the joke was on them because Luther and him ended up spending forty-two months in prison in the great state of Mississippi."

Reynolds Rosenthal inclined himself slightly forward. "Is that why you changed your name? Why there's all this secrecy about your past?"

W.E.B. turned to her with question marks in his eyes. She nodded. He nodded back and began his explanation.

"When I got out of prison, I was twenty-two years old. I'd spent most of the past four years locked up, and I damn well didn't want to go home and get in no more trouble like my brother was gone do. What I'd been doin' the whole time I was in the joint was playin' basketball, and that's all I wanted to keep doin'. I heard about this factory up in St. Louis that would hire you if they thought you could help them in their industrial league, and your whole job was just sorta punch the time clock and go to practice. You know what I'm talkin' 'bout?"

Rosenthal assured him he did. He asked him how long he'd played there.

"Long enough to see I was good enough to cut it wit' most anybody I went up against. Not so long as to make me lose this other idea in my head that I could still play college ball. So I went to this junior college 'cross the river in Illinoise and I started playing there until somebody learnt I was playing in the industrial league at the same time. It turned out there was some kind of rule 'bout playin' for pay and I wasn't eligible for college ball no mo'."

W.E.B.'s upper lip twitched violently, the way it did sometimes when he got extra mad, and Ida put her hand on his arm

216

to keep him from swiping at it and maybe coming into contact with his nose. His hands were so big that that could easily happen, and his nose was still tender from where it had got broke.

She said, speaking to Mr. Rosenthal, "By this time, you know, me and him was together and we had a little girl we was trying to raise and we had to do something fast. I come from down in Alabama, just like W.E.B., only over the other side of the state. I told him about Jones-Henry, and we decided we could go back there and give it a try. But now he wasn't just thinkin' about college, he was thinkin' how he could best get him a shot at the big time. And that's where the name thing come in."

W.E.B., taking up the story, said, "I couldn't play under my own name no mo', 'specially in Alabama where somebody might 'member me from high school and know I wasn't no kid jes comin' along. But I'm also thinkin' I need som'pin' that gonna get me attention. You see, I figgered out people had a habit of 'memberin' certain athletes' names even more than they 'membered their excellence. I'd figgered out that guys in the press had to have som'pin' to work on and was actually lookin' to build up players with names that's kinda catchy, like I. M. Hipp, Elvis Peacock, Baskerville Holmes, Fennis Dembo. Wasn't none of them that good, but they all got a lot of pub when they playin' in college."

"Well . . . ," Mr. Rosenthal said, and Ida could see W.E.B. didn't like that at all. W.E.B. didn't claim to know much, but certain things he did know and he didn't like having them stepped on.

"Well, shit." W.E.B. turned his head to the side and clenched his cheek. But then he went ahead and said what he had to say anyway. And Ida was proud of him for that. "So I come up with W.E.B. Pancake and I hope somebody notice. W.E.B. for W.E.B. DuBois, and Pancake 'cause I figger it was jes plain fun. I'm playin' at a school where nobody axes no questions and everything's cool as long as I don't play no place near Anniston, and Lord, I up and get drafted by the Gaters. By this time I am twenty-eight years old and has two kids and my woman's working as a nurse's aide, and I ain't gonna let nothin' stop me from the one thing I wanna do in life. Nothin'." The last word escaped from his mouth. It came out with a boom almost loud enough to crack the windows, and Ida's pride slipped a little.

Dropping his own voice, Mr. Rosenthal said, "Being in prison, playing for money while you were in college, playing under a false name, even trafficking in dope isn't going to keep you out of the league."

"But age do, Mr. Rosenthal," said Ida evenly. "You may think what he makes is a lot of money, partic'ly for a poor black boy from Alabama, and you would be right. But he now has five children and he supports not only his family, but his mother and his grandmother, and even his worthless-ass brothers and they families when they need it. Since he got his first money from this team, he has paid for nine nieces, nephews, and cousins to go to college, and one of 'em to go to law school. He has that car everybody talks about, I have a Cadillac, we got a nice house, a boat, and hardly nothin' in the bank."

Ida paused, stared, and held off Mr. Rosenthal by speaking again. "The reason we don't have hardly nothin' in the bank is that until these columns started, we thought W.E.B. was doing just fine. We figured that the worst that could happen was that he'd get one point two for next year and then sign with somebody else for what was fixin' to be considerable more than one point two because his bio would show he will be thirty-four years old, a twelve-year starter in the league, with probably four good years left to play. So he was a secure man, Mr. Rosenthal, until Colin Cromwell come along and start raisin' all this stuff 'bout his age."

The lawyer picked up a black and gold pen and began writing down a few notes. "What I'm hearing, W.E.B.," he said to him and not to her, "is that you're afraid no team will pay you the money you were expecting if they perceive you're really thirty-eight or thirty-nine years old."

"I do not never stop keepin' in shape, Mr. Rosenthal," W.E.B. said by way of an answer. "The day after the season ends I am workin' out for next year, 'cause I cannot afford to lose my hold on even one rung on the ladder I have climbed. But that is not gonna mean shit to the people who run this game if they

218

thinkin' I don't fit in their percentages. You know what I'm sayin'? They businessmen, and they don't know from nothin' 'bout nothin' but business."

"But this is the point, Mr. Rosenthal," Ida said, and waited until he put down his pen before giving it to him. "Now that W.E.B.'s story out, now that people pretty much know who he is and how old he is, he wouldn't have had no cause to kill Colin Cromwell. The damage is done."

"Revenge," said Mr. Rosenthal, and for Ida it was as though he had just set off a little explosion in the room. She had to struggle to keep from showing any reaction as he said, "By Cromwell revealing what he did, he may have cost you several million dollars. Some people might be mad enough to kill over that."

"I was gonna get revenge," W.E.B. mumbled, "I'd a busted open his head."

"Isn't that exactly what happened to Colin Cromwell?"

"W.E.B. was gonna kill him," said Ida, her eyes springing from one man to the other, "why wouldn't he do it right away? Why wait so long for him to come back?"

"Maybe he didn't know where Cromwell was," Mr. Rosenthal offered. Then he smiled. He was not being accusatory. Not argumentative. Just cautious. And Ida Pancake no longer liked him.

"Shoot," she said, "he was in Alabama, wasn't he? How hard it be to find him there? Jes start calling hotels and motels in Anniston."

Mr. Rosenthal shrugged to show that it was something he would be willing to think over. "Do you have any idea what Cromwell was doing after his last column appeared? What was it? March the third?"

Ida shook her head as her husband said, "I don't hear another thing till we get to Boston and he leaves a message on my phone saying he at the ho-tel and would like to see me. I don't know what he's got this time. I don't know what to say to him. I jes know'd he's trouble. That's why . . . you know. . . ." He wound down and, just when Ida thought he would say no more, started up again. "When Jerome axed me if I wanted to ride in

219

his limo with him and his friends . . . I figgered it was better'n havin' to ride in the bus with Cromwell. . . ."

Ida held her pose. She wasn't going to let this part of the story get to her.

But Mr. Rosenthal knew what was being said and was kind enough not to drag it out. "All right. What is it you want me to do?"

"Do like what you did for Curtis. Turn a bad situation into a good one." Ida spoke positively, confidently. The specifics were up to him. If she knew those, she wouldn't need a tricky lawyer.

"The FBI is treating you as a suspect, is that right, W.E.B.?"

"They's asking me questions."

"And have you been able to answer them all? To their satisfaction, I mean."

"We think, Mr. Rosenthal," Ida said, "that you can best advise W.E.B. as to how he should answer these questions."

"Advise him as his attorney, you mean."

Ida fixed Reynolds Rosenthal's eyes with her own so that he had to look directly at her and not at her husband. "And at the same time let Gaters' management know they best be signin' W.E.B. and signin' him fast, 'fore he goes talkin' to the FBIs 'bout all the reasons other people on the team might have had for wanting Colin Cromwell to go out that window."

"Ah," said Rosenthal, "then you also want me to be his agent."

"What's the difference?"

"As an attorney, I charge two hundred fifty dollars per hour for my services. As an agent, I take a percentage of what I get for you."

"And if you both?" she asked.

"I take whichever is higher."

"In that case," Ida said, "I hope it's the percentage you get, Mr. Rosenthal. For all our sakes."

# 32

Rohmer stood in the runway beneath the stands with his arms folded, watching the practice scrimmage. The gold team took the ball up court, Miller to Packard, down into the corner to Crown, back out to Packard, inside to Pancake as he crossed from one edge of the key to the other. The white team pulled a switch and Zeke left off guarding Del Fuego and knocked the ball loose from Pancake's hands. It hit the floor and Jonnie Martin scooped it up before Pancake could react. Jonnie passed to McDaniel and Felix took it all the way to the basket.

"When it rains it pours," a voice said, and Rohmer looked down. Reynolds Rosenthal had stepped up next to him. The agent was wearing a black trench coat belted tightly at the waist. His hands were thrust into the coat's pockets. He stood head and shoulders beneath Rohmer.

Rohmer looked at him with surprise. He wondered how Rosenthal had gotten into the arena. He wondered why he was there and what he wanted. He acknowledged his comment with only a grunt.

"Thinking of making any changes?"

Rohmer measured his answer. He hated agents. He had never had one as a player, and now that he was in management he regarded them as exploiters of youth, quintessential parasites of the system. "If I were, I sure as hell wouldn't tell you, would I?"

"The reason I'm asking, Dale, is I'm representing W.E.B. now."

Rohmer studied the man for a moment and then turned back to his team. He was trying to digest this news. As far as agents went, Rosenthal was probably the best of the lot. He was intelligent and actually seemed to care about his clients, but he was a hard guy to get to know. He drove one of those Japanese luxury cars that Rohmer believed were causing the country's economy to go down the drain, and he was rumored to fly his own airplane. Rohmer was suspicious of any agent who traveled so much that he had to have his own plane. While he knew that Rosenthal had neither a wife nor kids to keep him home, Rohmer did not consider it normal that he appeared to work all the time. Rohmer much preferred to deal with the guy who used to represent Pancake, Leigh Rossville, particularly after Leigh had had a few martinis at lunch. "I'll need written notice on that, Reynolds," was all Rohmer could think to say.

Rosenthal handed him an envelope. Rohmer did not bother to open it. He just jammed it into the inside pocket of his sport coat. He hoped the message was clear. Rosenthal had delivered his mail. Now he could leave.

"He'd like me to sit down and talk with you about next year," Rosenthal said.

"We've still got to finish this year, my friend. Fourteen games to go. We go eleven and three, maybe ten and four, we're in the play-offs. See what happens there. Then we talk."

"W.E.B. told me you were talking before. Then you stopped."

"Concentrating on this year, buddy. One thing at a time." Rohmer started to step away, but Rosenthal stepped with him and caught him by the arm. Rohmer looked down as if he were being bitten by a dog. He expected Rosenthal to let go, but he merely loosened his grip.

"He seems to think you don't feel he's as valuable as you did back in February. He needs to know if he's still a part of the Gaters' plans or if he should be making some of his own."

Rohmer had been around. He understood the way agents talk. But he moved his face down close to Rosenthal's anyway and said, "Just what is that supposed to mean?"

"W.E.B. has always considered himself a team player, Dale. But he can play one-on-one if he has to."

Rohmer rolled his eyes. "Good basketball talk, Reynolds."

"I'm not necessarily talking basketball, Dale."

It took only a moment for Rohmer to get the full import of what Rosenthal meant. He drew away. Out on the floor, Jerome hooked in a one-armed dunk over Biltmore and laughed. It was an ugly sound, coming all by itself amidst the squeak of sneakers and the slap of rubber on wood, and it rolled across the open space that separated Rohmer and Rosenthal from the players. Rohmer would have shouted at Jerome then, if only to escape from Rosenthal, but the agent, perhaps seeing that Rohmer was about to make a break, said, "You know about the FBI, don't you, Dale?"

The feeling that came over Rohmer was one of complete weariness, and he more or less toppled to his left so that his shoulder fell against the wall of the tunnel in which they were standing. On maybe ten thousand occasions since becoming a general manager he had realized that basketball just wasn't as simple as it used to be. Never before had that realization been so clear as it was now.

Rosenthal moved half a step closer so that the two men were almost touching. "Have they been asking you about him?" Rosenthal did not wait for an answer. "That's what he's afraid of, you know—that the FBI told you he's a suspect and that you're not going to talk to him about next year until you're sure he's cleared of any involvement in Colin Cromwell's death. He's afraid that in order to get you back to the table he might have to tell the FBI everything he knows that could have given anybody else a motive to kill Cromwell."

Rohmer's sudden anger propelled his shoulder off the wall. Because he was such a big man, people usually shrank back when he moved like that. But Rosenthal, slimy little Rosenthal, held his ground even as Rohmer's hands flew out from his sides and did everything but make contact with him.

"See those guys out there?" Rohmer demanded, pointing toward the court without looking. "Nearly every one of them had some reason for hating Cromwell. But kill him? You think any of them hated him so much they would have thrown him out a fucking window?"

223

His voice had gotten too loud. It echoed in the tunnel. It made him glance in alarm at the players on the court. But Oliver Dawkins was clanging a shot off the rim and then getting beaten to the rebound, and nobody was paying any attention to the two men arguing in the tunnel.

Rohmer reached inside his coat and fumbled for a cigarette. No smoking was allowed in the arena, but nobody was here to tell him not to do it. He was the general manager of the god-damn GoldenGaters, and his team, his company, had rented the goddamn arena.

Rosenthal, watching Rohmer's hands shake, said, "I don't believe anybody threw Cromwell out the window, Dale. I'm just trying to keep other people from believing that if anyone did do it, it was W.E.B. Pancake."

Rohmer made him wait while he searched for a match. The process took a while because Rohmer didn't want his eyes straying from Rosenthal's. "Has the FBI accused him?"

"They've just been asking a lot of questions. About the Alabama columns, who he really is, why he changed his name, what he felt like when he saw Colin was closing in on him."

The match fired on its second strike and Rohmer squinted through the sulfur and the smoke. "If that's all it is, you can tell him to relax. They've been questioning a lot of people."

"Like who, Dale?"

Rohmer raised his eyebrows. "You don't know?"

Rosenthal was a bright guy. He caught on fast, and when he did, his own eyebrows shot up as well. "Are you saying they've talked to Curtis?"

Rohmer bobbed his cigarette up and down between his lips. He enjoyed surprising the sanctimonious son of a bitch. "You come here threatening me with all W.E.B.'s revelations about his teammates," he said mildly, "and you didn't even know that Curtis was the last person seen with Cromwell that night. The Brandisis' butler loaded them into a cab together and sent them back to the hotel. He said they appeared to be fighting, that Curtis was all upset and that Cromwell appeared to be arguing with him. The doorman at the Copley Plaza remembers them entering the hotel together. He remembers them because

224

he thought Curtis may have had tears in his eyes and he wondered what could possibly be wrong. See, the night doorman is six-five and never got off the bench for a school called St. Michael's in Vermont, and he can't figure out what could possibly make a professional basketball player so unhappy that he would have tears in his eyes when the alternative is to be standing around in a silly-looking uniform opening doors for people at two in the morning." Rohmer took the cigarette out of his mouth. A moment later he sent a cloud of smoke rushing after it. "Can you?"

Rosenthal looked for his answer on the court. There was Curtis, substituting on the white team, bobbing, weaving, positioning himself beautifully for a rebound, but never actually getting his hands on the ball. "They got any more suspects, Dale?" Rosenthal asked quietly.

"Oh, do they got them. They got 'em coming out their ass. They got guys Cromwell screwed in print, guys he screwed in life, and at least one guy whose wife he screwed. You think W.E.B.'s the only one who's scared? These boys are walking on eggs. They lost to Boston. They flew home and lost six of eight since then. You look at them today and they can't even beat themselves. But can I get any one of them to tell me what's going on? Nah. Not until now. And now you tell me—hallelujah, Lord God Almighty—W.E.B.'s willing to talk."

Rohmer snapped his unfinished cigarette against the wall. "So I'll tell you what I'm gonna do, hoss. I'm going to take you up on your offer. Only, you tell W.E.B. he doesn't have to go talking to the FBI to improve his chances of coming back next year. Tell him anything he's got to say about any of his teammates he should bring directly to me and I promise I'll give it every consideration when we sit down to talk about his future."

Rohmer reached out and patted Rosenthal on the shoulder. He smoothed a wrinkle from Rosenthal's trench coat. "That's one way he could help the team. No matter what age he happens to be."

225

# 33

Curtis moved swiftly through the restaurant. He was wearing a dark green polo shirt that clung tightly to his arms, black-and-gray pleated slacks that emphasized the narrowness of his waist, a pair of slick, black Gucci shoes, and brown Revo sunglasses. Most of the rest of the men in the lunch crowd at Stars wore suits and ties. No one else wore sunglasses. No one else was black. At virtually every table he passed, one or more diners glanced up at him. Some turned to watch him over their shoulders and Curtis knew that. He was used to standing out and being noticed in places like this. He expected it, he would have been disappointed if he was not noticed, and yet he still resented it. He kept his sunglasses on.

Mr. Rosenthal was seated at a corner table. He sat with his back to the wall and a view of the room. Curtis would have nothing to look at but him and the wall behind him. If Curtis had had any doubts before, he was sure now that he was in trouble.

Mr. Rosenthal rose from his seat as Curtis approached. He extended his hand and smiled and nodded at the open chair all at the same time. He said, "Don't worry about being late. I've had a pleasant fifteen minutes drinking vodka and grapefruit. Would you like one?" He gestured to his glass, which was half-empty.

Curtis understood what Mr. Rosenthal was saying. He hadn't meant to be late. He hadn't known where the restaurant was and he hadn't been able to find a parking space. Now he looked at his watch, his gold-and-diamond chronometer with the many hands and the minifaces that assured him he would know the right time no matter where he was in the world or how far beneath the surface of the ocean he happened to be, and saw that he was, indeed, fifteen minutes late. He apologized. As always, Mr. Rosenthal had him at a disadvantage.

Curtis wondered if the offer of a drink was a test, and he said no, he would have only an ice tea.

Rosenthal waved his hand and the waiter came just like that.

"How you doin'?" the waiter said, and Curtis looked over the top of his sunglasses. The waiter was looking at him. He was grinning. He was an angular, loose-haired young man, handsome in a wild, what-the-hell kind of way, and Curtis was disconcerted by his familiarity. Did he know him? Couldn't the man see Curtis was on business? That he was with somebody important?

"How you doin'?" Curtis responded cautiously. He mentioned the ice tea. The waiter's eyes lingered for just an instant too long, and then he dashed away without even addressing Rosenthal.

Curtis turned to sit sideways on his chair and crossed his knees carefully so as not to take the press out of his pants. He waited for Mr. Rosenthal to let him have it.

His agent leaned forward. "You didn't tell me about the FBI, Curtis."

Curtis was almost relieved. The FBI could be explained. The FBI ask you questions, you got to answer.

"I'm assuming," Mr. Rosenthal said, "you're willing to tell me about it now."

Curtis nodded, but he said nothing. He was thinking that if he talked about the FBI he would have to talk about the party, and once he talked about the party he was going to have to talk about himself. He had never talked about himself with Mr. Rosenthal before. Not really. He stopped nodding.

Mr. Rosenthal said, "You never should have spoken to them without me, Curtis."

Curtis averted his face. He was, in a way, letting Mr. Rosenthal know he was ashamed. Unfortunately, the waiter arrived

227

with his ice tea just at that moment. He thought Curtis was turning to him and he responded with a smile that sent shivers throughout Curtis's chest. The ice tea was placed in front of him with a maximum of fuss while Curtis concentrated on searching for patterns in the tablecloth.

The waiter was eager to know if they had had a chance to check the menu. He went away disappointed.

"What were you and Colin Cromwell fighting about on the night of the Brandisis' party, Curtis?" Mr. Rosenthal whispered, and Curtis kept his head hung down, hoping Mr. Rosenthal would just tell the story and let him agree with what he said.

But it was not to be. Mr. Rosenthal said, "You have a good place to begin, Curtis?" and Curtis, figuring that Mr. Rosenthal knew everything anyway, said, "I guess it started when I was playing video games with Zeke at Mr. Brandisi's house."

Curtis looked up, but it was not enough. It was silly to think that it would be. He was going to have to go all the way through.

"Oliver came running in and said he had something to show us. Well, Zeke, really. I was just there. I was just following along, see what they was up to. That's when I made my first mistake, Mr. Rosenthal."

The agent's face was blank. This, too, was not enough. Mr. Rosenthal did not just want an apology. He wanted a full confession.

"What it was, was Del was in the swimming pool with this lady, one of Mr. Brandisi's guests. Colin Cromwell was there with them. And none of them had on any clothes." Curtis shrugged. He wanted to be blasé. "The lady didn't seem like she was the least bit embarrassed that we caught them. Fact, she said she wanted us all to get naked and get in the pool."

Mr. Rosenthal took a long taste of his grapefruit drink. He said, "Did you, Curtis?"

Curtis shook his head. "I don't really know what happened, Mr. Rosenthal, but somehow it got decided that instead of everybody going in the pool, everybody would go in the pool house. Del Fuego tell me to go up the main house to get some champagne, and me, like a fool, I go." A thought came to him.

It was a thought that had come to him ten, twenty times before, but its familiarity did not make it any less burdensome. "I should have just took off," he said sadly.

Mr. Rosenthal maneuvered the glass of ice tea over closer to Curtis. He wanted Curtis to drink it and Curtis did.

Curtis was not sure how he would tell the next part. He did not want to offend Mr. Rosenthal and he was concerned about what words he should use. In the end he spoke with his eyes closed. "I thought I would just bring them a couple of bottles and scat, but when I got back there . . . well, Mr. Rosenthal, it was sort of like what they call a gang bang."

Mr. Rosenthal was silent for a long time. When Curtis opened his eyes, he expected to find his agent cringing. But nothing about his face had changed. "Was Cromwell there while all this was going on?"

"He was, like, watching."

"He was watching Del, Zeke, and Oliver have sex with this one woman?"

Curtis nodded very slowly. "That's right. Although it was mostly Del and Zeke."

"Was she passed out, Curtis?"

Curtis's head rocked back. There was some sort of major problem here. Some sort of major misunderstanding. "Oh, no, Mr. Rosenthal, it wasn't anything like that. She was doing stuff to them as much as they was doing stuff to her."

The waiter floated up. He wanted to tell them about the day's specials. Salmon, he said, with a brandy-dill sauce. Rosenthal flicked him away and he went, unwillingly.

"Tell me what happened, Curtis," and Curtis had no choice because Mr. Rosenthal's head, shoulders, and upper body were extended across the table, trapping him without touching him.

Curtis leaned back onto the rear two legs of his chair. It was better when there was more room between them. He said, "The lady was lying on the bed like a Roman goddess or something."

Still Mr. Rosenthal stared in, as if he thought Curtis were not telling him the whole truth.

"Look, Mr. Rosenthal, I was there and I didn't want to be

there, and if you were there, you could of told the difference
in a minute between me and her.''

He waited. But so did Mr. Rosenthal. He took off his sunglasses and spoke directly into Mr. Rosenthal's face. ''She was
doing things to both Del and Zeke, and Oliver was doing something to her. Now do you know what I'm saying?''

Mr. Rosenthal simply waited some more.

Curtis gestured impatiently. He tried to use his hands to show
what he was describing. ''Zeke and Del had one foot on the
floor, and they was sort of like kneeling with one leg on the
bed near her head and she was like going back and forth
between them.''

''But you weren't doing anything, is that what you're telling
me, Curtis?''

His heart racing, Curtis said, ''She started making a big deal
about me not joining in. She was saying things like, 'My, aren't
you the shy one.' And that got the guys to start saying, 'C'mon,
Curtis. C'mon, Curtis,' and all of a sudden Oliver gets up from
what he's doing and starts pushing me from behind.'' Curtis
got angry at the memory. His hands balled into fists as he
explained, ''He was trying to get me up next to the bed like
Zeke was.''

He showed Mr. Rosenthal one of his fists. ''I was still wearing
my suit, you know, and my hands was like this in my pockets.
But Oliver's behind me and the lady's touching me in places
where she's not supposed to touch me and I just freaked out.''

Curtis realized his breath was coming in rapid little spurts.
He tried to get it under control by moving his fist to his mouth,
but then his fingers spread out on their own, forming a cage
through which he spoke. ''Seemed like everybody was shouting
at me, grabbing at me, and I had to do something. It was too
much. It was just too much.''

Mr. Rosenthal reached out and tried to lower Curtis's hand.
He resisted until he realized that other diners might be watching him, that he might be making a spectacle of himself. ''I
screamed something,'' he whispered as his protective fingers
gave way.

''What did you scream?''

230

"I screamed"—Curtis hesitated—"I screamed, 'I don't do women.' That was all I did. I jumped back and I screamed. Then everything just went quiet. Nobody moved. Nobody said nothing. I started backing toward the door and nobody tried to stop me. I got there and I said, 'I just don't, see?' and I turned and I ran."

There, it was out. The confession was over and Mr. Rosenthal still sat across the table from him, just as he had before.

The waiter approached, tentatively this time. "I have to tell you that we're very low on the linguine with chicken livers in a light cream sauce." He waited a few moments. "Hello?"

Rosenthal ordered cream of winter-melon soup and a Caesar salad, and Curtis ordered a cheeseburger, rare. Neither man looked at the menu.

"And Cromwell followed you, is that what happened?" Mr. Rosenthal asked when they were alone again.

"All I wanted to do was get out of there. I ran to the front of the house and told the man at the door to get me a taxi. While I was waiting, Colin showed up wanting to talk about it."

"About what had happened, you mean?"

"About being gay, Mr. Rosenthal. It wasn't nothing I wanted to talk about, but he insisted. He said he knew now and he had some sort of obligation to write about it. He said he didn't want to blow me out of the closet or nothing, so he wanted me to give it to him my own way."

"What did you tell him?"

"I told him, he wasn't about to write about the other guys' sex lives, all the things we just saw, why should he write about mine?"

"So you argued?"

Curtis thought about it. "He was drunk, Mr. Rosenthal. Real drunk and he kept trying to make me talk to him. I wouldn't. Maybe that's an argument."

"Did you get angry?"

"Not angry. I was upset."

"Then what happened at the hotel?"

"We went up the elevator together. He went to his room and

231

I went to mine. I figured, drunk as he was, he was just gonna pass out."

"And did he?"

"I don't know. I never saw him again."

"How are we going to prove that, Curtis?"

It took a moment for Curtis to appreciate the importance of that question. This conversation, this concern on the part of Mr. Rosenthal, wasn't about his sexual orientation at all. Curtis's back became very stiff and suddenly he was the one leaning forward, he was the one getting right in the other man's face. "Why should we have to prove it? I didn't kill the man."

"Didn't you get the impression that's why the FBI was questioning you, Curtis?"

"They only asked me about the party."

"Why did you think they were asking you about that?"

"Because of the woman."

"The Brandisis' friend?"

Once again it occurred to Curtis that there was something terribly wrong here. He paused for a second, but Mr. Rosenthal only waited for him to talk, just as he had been doing ever since Curtis sat down.

"Tory Brewer," Curtis said. "The one who says she's going to sue everyone for raping her."

Finally, he had a reaction. Mr. Rosenthal's mouth fell open, revealing two full rows of crowded little teeth. "But," he sputtered, "I thought you told me she was a willing participant?"

"She was, Mr. Rosenthal. First I heard she wasn't was when her attorney contacted me."

Mr. Rosenthal had to lick his lips before he could speak again. "You talked to her attorney, too?"

"He said he understood I was the one who give her name to the FBI, and I figured I probably was since two agents talked to me before we even left Boston."

"So you admitted it?" Mr. Rosenthal seemed incredulous. He seemed as if he would be angry as soon as he got over being so surprised.

"I couldn't tell a lie, Mr. Rosenthal."

"But he was an attorney— Look, what else did you tell him?"

"Well, he said I shouldn't have mentioned her name because now the FBI had been to see her to ask about Colin Cromwell, and until that happened she had been in shock and hadn't told anyone what we done to her."

Curtis made a face to show Mr. Rosenthal how ridiculous the claim was. "I tried to tell him I hadn't done nothing to her, but he said she had what the Vietnam vets got—"

"Posttraumatic stress disorder?"

"That's right. And he said now that her husband knew what had caused it he was going to sue all of us for everything we got."

Mr. Rosenthal's mouth was hanging open again. His little teeth didn't have a drop of spit on them. They looked as dry as piano keys.

"Oh," said Mr. Reynolds Rosenthal.

# 34

Norbert took no pains to make him feel comfortable. The man had arrived in his office without an invitation, and Norbert saw no reason why he should be concerned if the newspaper's old wooden chairs might leave a few splinters in a $2,000 suit. It wasn't his suit.

But Reynolds Rosenthal was not complaining. He sat in front of Norbert's desk as if he liked sitting in old wooden chairs, and he peaked his fingers under his nose and almost looked as though he meant it when he said, "My condolences, Ed, on your loss. Colin Cromwell was a fine man."

Norbert twitched one shoulder. "He was a talent and I'll miss him. As to whether he was a fine man or not. . . ." Norbert twitched the other shoulder.

Rosenthal pondered the significance of what Norbert had just said. "Did he have any family, Ed?" he asked after a moment.

"Michigan. The whole shebang came out here for the funeral. Didn't see you there, though. Were you a particular friend of his, Reynolds?"

Norbert leaned back in his swivel chair with the little pillow on its seat, hooked his thumbs under his red suspenders, and waited for Rosenthal's answer. He knew they had not been friends.

"No, Ed," Rosenthal said, holding Norbert's eye. "I barely knew Colin. He'd call me once in a while when he wanted something regarding one of my clients, and sometimes I'd give it to him and sometimes I wouldn't."

Norbert grunted, his image of the integrity of lawyers momentarily shattered by Rosenthal's honest answer. Then he brightened. "Depending on what you thought was in the best interest of your client, of course."

Rosenthal agreed. "Of course."

That made Norbert feel better. He had the picture now. "And that's what brings you here today, to see me, the best interest of one of your clients."

"I hope so."

Norbert turned to a computer and rapped out some letters on his keyboard. He pressed a key, read the message that appeared on the video display screen, and announced, "And since your only client on the Gaters right now is Curtis Clovis, I'd say that I owe the honor of your visit to him."

"You've got yesterday's news, Ed," Rosenthal said, and Norbert, remembering what a smart ass Rosenthal could be, simply stared at the screen that had betrayed him.

"I recently began representing W.E.B. Pancake, and for purposes of this meeting, I could also be here representing a former Gater, like Gilbert Rose."

Norbert's eyes still did not leave the screen. "But you are here looking for something," he insisted.

"That's right."

Norbert sniffed. He pushed back to face Rosenthal. "What?" he demanded, wiping his nose, jamming his hands into his suddenly damp armpits. He did not like guys like Rosenthal. He did not like their clothes, their airs, or their condescension. He did not like lawyers and he did not like player agents. And all of that made Reynolds Rosenthal about the most unlikable man he could think of.

"I'm here to find out what Colin Cromwell was working on at the time he died." Rosenthal, seeing Norbert's reaction, quickly thrust up his palm. "Oh, I know he was with the team. But he hadn't been traveling with them since he'd gone off and done those pieces on Pancake. He'd been on something that you were calling a 'special assignment.' I'd like to know what that was."

Norbert dropped his hands beneath his belly. His faded, pin-striped, button-down-collared shirt was stretched enough that he could see the white cotton of his undershirt between the buttons. That embarrassed him: the faded shirt, the undershirt, the belly that stretched it into prominence. None of that had mattered when he came into work this morning, but Rosenthal probably only wore his shirts once and then threw them away. He probably had his own personal trainer to keep himself in shape.

Norbert hunched forward. He put his elbows on his desk and pulled his belly in close to the drawer so that Rosenthal could not get a clear view of it. "You think one of your clients might have had a special interest in what Colin was working on at the time he died, counselor?"

"That falls within what we call attorney-client privilege, editor."

"My answer falls within what you call quid pro quo."

Rosenthal looked out of the tops of his eyes. His surprise at a newsman's familiarity with Latin legal terms made Norbert chuckle. Norbert did it meanly.

"Let me get this straight, Reynolds. You're here on behalf of a client. Somebody who's paying you money for your efforts. Your client, assuming he is a professional basketball player, is making an extraordinary amount of money himself—so whatever he pays you he can damn well afford. Now I am not sitting here entertaining you because it's making me rich—so why do you suppose I am doing it?"

"Why," said Rosenthal, his dark eyebrows arcing skyward, "you're not asking me for money, are you, Ed?"

Norbert felt like smacking him. He let Rosenthal know it by glaring for a rather long time. Then he said, "All right, Reynolds, let's cut the crap. You want something from me, you've got to give me something back. And I'm not talking about money. Coin of the realm around here is information."

Rosenthal offered a gentlemanly shrug. "I think we both have an interest in learning the truth about how Colin Cromwell died. He was your writer. I'm sure you feel some responsibility for him—"

Norbert bristled. "And the FBI thinks that W.E.B. Pancake is the one who pushed him onto the fucking bricks."

Rosenthal stopped talking. He looked like a boxer who had just taken a tremendous shot in the ribs. "How do you know that? How do you know what the FBI is thinking, Ed?"

In an instant, Norbert realized his mistake. He cast about for an escape and, seeing none, elected to retreat. "The only thing I'm going to tell you, Reynolds, is that there's no way on God's green earth that Colin Cromwell killed himself."

But Rosenthal was after him in an instant. "From what I read in the Boston papers, there were no signs of a struggle and Cromwell's blood alcohol was well over the legal limit. Why couldn't he have just opened a window for some fresh air and then leaned too far forward?"

"People in Copley Square said they heard him yell on his way down."

"That could still have happened if he fell. I mean, six stories isn't so high up that a killer could be positive he'd die when he hit."

"It's far enough that it can break your neck, crush your skull, and smack your face as flat as a nickel—which is exactly what happened."

Rosenthal had no immediate comeback to that, and Norbert was just beginning to feel the glow of triumph when his visitor leaned forward and said, "That's not how you got the FBI involved, Ed."

Norbert pushed back his chair, no longer caring about his belly, his shirt, or the wet spots under his arms. He held the edge of the desk at arm's length. "Tell me," he hissed, "a young guy, forty years old, a guy with his own newspaper column and an unlimited future, a guy with no financial problems, no family problems, no known psychiatric history, comes home from a fancy party and goes out a goddamn hotel window. You don't think somebody ought to be investigating a thing like that?"

Rosenthal nodded very slowly. "Somebody, Ed, but not the FBI. Not unless you called them and told them that at the time of his death Colin was working on something that interested them."

Norbert saw that he had been trapped. He searched the lawyer bastard's face for signs of triumph, but the man was concentrating too hard on getting a response. Norbert said, "The question really is, why are you so concerned about the FBI?"

When Rosenthal did not answer right away, Norbert pulled himself back to his desk and thrust one finger at Rosenthal's face. "It seems to me that just the fact of you being here gives me enough to make mention in my paper that the FBI is questioning W.E.B. Pancake in connection with Colin's death."

"Only," argued Rosenthal, "if you can explain how you know the FBI is out there questioning anyone—because I certainly didn't bring it up."

The two men sat looking at each other until finally Norbert was afraid that they would sit that way all day. "What's in it for me," he asked warily, "if I answer any of your questions?"

Rosenthal did not even hesitate. "I'm going to be out there looking for information that is going to help my client," he declared. "I'm going to need a forum for whatever I get. That forum can be Marty Smart, it can be the *Boston Globe*, it can be *Sports Illustrated*, or it can be you."

"In other words," Norbert responded pointedly, "you've got nothing to offer me right now. None of that coin of the realm I was talking about."

"What I've got is an abiding belief that Pancake is innocent, and"—Rosenthal played the pause and then dropped his voice—"a suspicion that this could shape up to be the biggest sports story of the twentieth century." He studied Norbert's reaction before adding, "Not just the biggest sports story, the biggest story to come out of sports."

Norbert, who well knew that the man was pandering to him, nonetheless indicated his willingness to listen some more.

"And it's right in your own backyard, Ed," Rosenthal said obligingly. "You don't want to get scooped here. So you're going to have to throw in your lot with someone who's got inside information. I'm suggesting W.E.B. Pancake is as good a candidate as anyone."

Rosenthal waited for a sign of acquiescence. Norbert spread open his hands. Rosenthal said, "Just tell me what it was that Colin was working on when he died."

More than anything else, Norbert did not want Rosenthal putting one over on him, and he sensed that he was dangerously close to having that happen. "I'm not going to tell you anything that might clear the murderer of one of my writers," he said adamantly.

But Rosenthal was reassuring. "I know that, Ed, and I wouldn't ask you to. In fact, you don't even have to believe me to get the benefit of what I'm offering here." Rosenthal inched closer in his chair until just the desk itself was separating them. He dropped his voice even further until it was a conspiratorial whisper. He spoke without blinking. "Let's assume you're right and the FBI really is talking to my guy. Why would they think he'd push Cromwell out the window? Because of the Alabama columns, obviously. Well, what would those columns have to do with them? My guess is that they would only be interested if they thought the columns had to do with something more than W.E.B. Pancake's age or his background or his ego."

Rosenthal waited. Norbert refused to respond. Rosenthal filled in the answer for him.

"Like fixing the outcome of professional basketball games."

Rosenthal watched closely to see how he would react. Norbert tried to be stone faced.

Rosenthal held up his fingers and ticked them off. Norbert was distracted by Rosenthal's manicure, by his Lucien Piccard wristwatch, but he got the gist of what Rosenthal was saying: If the FBI believes Colin died because he was about to expose a game-rigging scandal, then the logical suspect is Pancake; unless whatever Colin had been working on in the ten days before his death gave somebody else an even more pressing motive for wanting him dead. "If there was another motive, I intend to find it," Rosenthal concluded. "And I will if you just point me in the right direction."

Norbert reflected on the offer. He took his time, playing with his lips, plucking them like banjo strings as he eyed Rosenthal, letting him know that he was wondering just how much he could trust him; and when he thought he had gotten the message across, he leaned forward and spoke with an exaggerated movement of his mouth. "Phoenix."

239

Rosenthal said it back.

Norbert nodded.

"Are you telling me Colin was in Phoenix between the time he left Alabama and the time he showed up in Boston?"

"He had a tip, a lead," Norbert explained.

"What was it?"

Norbert felt his behind sliding around on his seat cushion. "I don't know. I presumed it had something to do with Pancake. I mean, he hadn't finished the series on him."

"Didn't Colin have to get authorization to go there?"

Norbert's behind moved some more. It itched. He could not control it. "Colin and I had a special relationship. I gave him some latitude and he usually produced."

"So he must have reported in. He must have told you what he was working on."

"He left a phone message for me. Said he was leaving Alabama and going to Phoenix."

"And that's all he had to do?"

Norbert decided that the momentum of the conversation had to change. He stopped sliding around. He took off his glasses and polished them with his tie. "I kept expecting to hear from him again." He squinted. "But I didn't."

"You knew he went to D.C.?"

The glasses went back on. The perspiration rolled down Norbert's sides. "I got another message. Said he was rejoining the team. Then I never heard another thing."

Rosenthal tilted his head. "You mean to say that you got a call from Alabama telling you he was going to Phoenix for some unexplained reason, and then a call saying he was going to Washington, D.C., and the next thing you knew he was dead in Boston?"

Norbert raised one shoulder in a semishrug.

"So you don't know what he had been doing? Where he was between Washington and Boston?"

"We're still waiting for his credit card receipts to come in."

"What about his notebooks?"

Norbert looked away. "There was nothing in his hotel room. Nothing in his luggage. His portable computer was still in his room, but every single disc was gone." Norbert sniffed, he rubbed his nose. He spoke to the incredulity that was written all over Rosenthal's face. "That's another reason we know it was murder, Reynolds."

Rosenthal very slowly drew back into his chair. He got to his feet, put his hands in his pants pockets, and studied Norbert for a long moment. "Ed, do you really think that W.E.B. could have done it?"

The lawyer's uncertainty gave Norbert a whole new shot of confidence. "I'd say"—he smiled magnanimously—"that W.E.B.'s as good a candidate as any of them."

"But you've seen no evidence he was involved in any game rigging."

Norbert admitted that was true.

"Then, with all due respect, Ed, how did you manage to convince the FBI to get involved?"

"I didn't, Reynolds. They contacted me."

# 35

Since Colin Cromwell's death, the Gaters had dropped into a tenth-place tie for the eight play-off spots that were available to Western Conference teams. There were grumblings in the press and among the fans, not only about the losses, but about the uninspired play. Marty Smart pointed out that the problems had not started with Cromwell's death, but with the return of Booby Sinclair, and he began to wonder in print if Booby was still the right man for the job.

Rynn Packard, reading Marty's ruminations on the morning after a 24-point blowout by Portland, was surprised by the criticisms Marty was leveling. He knew that what was happening to the Gaters was not the fault of the coach, and yet here was Marty, making up things to criticize. Booby, Marty said, was to be commended for his loyalty, but was too much wedded to the past. The game, he said, was constantly evolving, and players and coaches had to evolve along with it. Booby, he concluded, had lost either interest in or control over his players.

Then the phone rang and Rynn was reminded that he had troubles of his own. He put the paper down.

"Hello?" he said, and the sound of his mother's voice greeting him, calling him "honey," stunned him and filled him with guilt. He had not talked to her in—he tried to calculate the number of weeks—four, five—since February 21, when she had come to see him play in Cleveland. She and his grandmother. They had closed up their bed and breakfast and driven the two hundred miles from Bernardston to Cleveland and he had put them up in a suite at the Hilton. He had had a good game, 12 assists, the Gaters had won, and he and Mom and Nana had all been in good spirits when they parted. But then the team had flown off to Atlanta and he had not contacted them since.

"Hi, Mom."

"Is everything all right, Rynn?"

His mother was young. He had introduced her to his coach and had been surprised to see Booby's eyes light up.

"Yes. Fine. Everything's great. How are you? How's Nana?"

"We're all fine here, Rynn, but we hadn't heard from you in a long time and I just wanted to make sure everything's okay."

"Sure. Absolutely."

"Did anything come of that story that man was going to write about you?"

Rynn was confused. He tried to remember which story he might have discussed with his mother. "Which man?"

"The one who came here to see Nana and me. He stayed at the B and B, you know. Did he tell you? He saw your high school coach, talked to some of your teachers. You must know the person I'm talking about. I wouldn't say he was really a nice man, but he seemed fascinated by you."

Rynn felt as though he were entering a dark chamber and were groping about the wall for a light switch. He could not recall any writer ever expressing any interest in his hometown. "I don't know, Mom. I don't have the faintest idea who you mean."

"Oh, here's where he signed the register. Cromwell, his name is. Colin Cromwell."

The idea of the chamber was gone. He had stepped into a hole and he was falling. "When?" he said, and he was falling too fast for his voice to stay with him.

"The date he checked in was March twelfth."

"March twelfth."

"Checked out on the fourteenth."

"Mom, he died on the fourteenth. Or the early hours of the fifteenth. That night anyway."

"Died?" The word did not make sense to his mother. She had seen Cromwell live that day.

243

"He went out a window in our hotel in Boston. Didn't you read about it?"

Rynn heard her speaking off the phone, trying to explain to his grandmother what had happened. "Mom," he called to her. "Mom! Mom! Will you get back on the phone, please?" He waited. He sensed her return. "Will you tell me what Cromwell was asking about?"

"Well, he wanted to know what you were like as a kid, what kinds of things you did, how you started playing basketball."

"And what did you tell him?"

"I told him the truth. I told him how you were almost obsessed with the game from the time you first started playing it—how you used to go and shovel off the court in winter so you could play by yourself. And I told him about the time you made me drive you to Buffalo and drop you off at that tough neighborhood playground where all the black kids were. You remember, where they stole your sweater and punched you in the eye—"

"What was he looking for? I mean, did he seem to be trying to dig up dirt or—I mean—" What did he mean? His mother didn't seem to be catching on. He had to come right out and say it. "Did he ask anything about my father?"

Rynn's mother hesitated. "He asked, and I told him it was nothing we ever talked about in our family, so I sure wasn't going to go putting it in any newspapers."

"Mom, you can't talk to these guys about anything. They won't respect any kind of limitation. They've got a job to do and they think that justifies them doing whatever they want in order to get a story that people will read. You tell them there are things you won't talk about, that just gets them all excited to go ask somebody else."

"Who would say anything?"

"Coach Garrity, for one. Big-city sportswriter starts asking him questions, he'd tell him in a minute all about the night I got the school scoring record and how I kind of had that breakdown when they stopped the game for that little ceremony. And Cromwell would have kept asking questions until he had the whole story about you and Jack 'the Shot' Foley and how everybody for twenty miles was at the gym that night except for the guy whose record I was breaking—"

"Rynn." IIis mother's voice cracked over the line, shutting him up just the way it had always shut him up when he got excited like this. "Don't talk to me like an idiot and don't lecture me on things I have no control over. The man came here and started asking questions. What was I supposed to do? Make up a story? If people want to dig up old dirt, there's no way either of us is going to be able to stop them. All we can do is hold our heads high and not make trouble for other people. Are you listening to me?"

Rynn said he was. He said nothing more.

"If Coach Garrity wants to go speculating on things that are none of his business, the shame is on him, Rynn. And before you go letting yourself get any more worked up, just remember that whatever he may have said, it hasn't been publicized, and now that this man Cromwell is dead, chances are that it won't be."

"Mom, Mom," Rynn said, striving for patience, "can't you see that that's one of the problems? The talk going around is that Colin Cromwell didn't fall. He was pushed. If anyone's looking for a motive for killing that jerk, he can find it right there in the exposé Cromwell was about to do on me."

"Rynn," his mother said firmly, "nobody cares about that kind of thing. How many of the guys that you've played basketball with over the years since you left Bernardston have come from two-parent families?"

"No, Mom, that's not it. The story usually is about the poor ghetto kids who don't know who their father is. This one would be about how much tougher it is for the small-town boy to know perfectly well who his father is—to have everybody in town know who he is and nobody acknowledge it because the father has another family of his own with kids that bear his name right in the same school with the son he gave to the queen of the senior prom."

"Stop it, Rynn," his mother said, and once again he did as he was told.

For some moments the only sound he heard was his own

245

breathing into the receiver. Then his mother said, "I'm sorry, Rynn." Her voice was faint and far away. "I'm sorry I've caused you so much pain."

"Oh, Mom," Rynn said, throwing his head back to try to keep his eyes from filling with tears, to try to keep the tears that did come from overflowing his sockets and rolling down his face. "I just don't want you to be embarrassed anymore, that's all."

"I made my decision almost twenty-four years ago, Rynn, and I've never regretted it for one minute. You're the achievement of my life and you don't go around being embarrassed about achievements." She paused. "Humble, yes." She meant to inject a little humor into what she was saying, and when Rynn did not respond, she added something more.

"Besides, Mr. Sensitivity, he was far more interested in asking questions about your social life than mine." She made a laugh. "I told him you didn't have one. That basketball was your only love."

But Rynn did not laugh with her. Colin Cromwell, who spent from October through April in his company, was asking his mother about his social life? "What was he asking about that for?"

Rynn's mother, her tone announcing that she was getting tired of not being able to say the right thing in this conversation, told him she was sure she didn't know; she assumed it was the kind of thing they asked in profile pieces.

But Rynn knew. He was suddenly filled with a clarity of understanding that went far beyond suspicion. "He asked about drugs, didn't he?"

"Well, yes. And I told him you were never involved, not even when the other kids were experimenting or called you chicken. You didn't care—"

"Oh, Jesus, Mom. I know what he was after. I'm in so much trouble now I can't even begin to tell you."

# 36

It was Marty Smart who broke the story of the FBI investigation. He did it on the day following the Gaters' loss to Utah, their sixth loss in a row, a 44-point drubbing on their home court, where they had never before lost by so great a margin. He used the details of the Utah game to exemplify the demoralized condition of the players, then explained that it was no wonder they could not put the ball in the basket, bounce it off the floor, or deliver it to one another with any consistency. Hanging over their heads, he said, without so much as hinting at the source of his information, was the uncertain specter of an FBI investigation into the mysterious death of Colin Cromwell, an investigation that was probing into the innermost secrets of everyone connected with the GoldenGaters.

"The finger of suspicion now points everywhere," he wrote. "Best friends are looking askance at one another. Words are being interpreted, reinterpreted, and then stored away for repetition to spouses, agents, attorneys. A missed shot, an ill-timed foul, a double dribble, are suddenly grounds for questions of integrity, and as a consequence missed shots, ill-timed fouls, and double dribbles have never been so plentiful as they were last night."

Marty took pains to assert that he did not want to be or to appear callous. "But like it or not, the issue of the play-offs still confronts the Gaters. Twelve regular-season games remain to be played, and Denver, Dallas, and San Francisco are still fighting for the last play-off spot. Players' futures, fans' much

247

needed enjoyment, and yes, even a great deal of money is at stake. It goes without saying that Coach Booby Sinclair has been having a difficult time personally this season, as best exemplified by his outburst in Sacramento a few weeks back. It is too much to expect him to deal with the kind of pressure of a play-off race when he, just by virtue of the position he has held up till now, may have to weather investigative scrutiny himself."

The solution Marty offered, "without casting any aspersions whatsoever," was to make a temporary change in leadership. "It is better for Booby, better for all concerned, that he entrust the reins to someone else until the present crisis is resolved."

And Marty had just the person in mind. "It must be someone totally familiar with Booby's system, and yet someone who himself has wielded no power over games, scores, or player transactions." By deductive reasoning, he concluded that an assistant coach was the logical choice. He then whittled down the possible choices by noting that first assistant Mike Hacker was necessarily tarred by the same brush as his boss. And while that was also true for the second assistant, the tar grew thinner by the time it got to "the wily old college wizard from Philadelphia." He thought Mel Dykstra was a good choice. After all, Dyk had been the one who had first come up with the idea to play Jerome Crown at center, "perhaps the single best strategic move the Gaters have made all year."

And what could Dyk possibly have done to merit investigation into his activities? "Not hand Booby his clipboard during crucial time-outs?"

The woman who came to see Reynolds Rosenthal brandishing a copy of Marty Smart's article was dressed in leather. She had on navy blue leather boots that went to the tops of her calves and a white leather skirt that stopped well short of her knees. She wore a shimmering blue silk blouse that could barely contain her chest beneath its overlapping lapels, and a white leather jacket that matched her skirt. Her legs were a little too pudgy to attract attention on their own, but the result of the peekaboo effect was to draw one's eyes to that uncovered area

248

between skirt and boots, and a less fastidious man than Reynolds Rosenthal would have been mightily distracted as she seated herself on the other side of his cherrywood desk.

"To what do I owe the pleasure of this visit, Mrs. Sinclair?" he asked as he waited for her to make herself comfortable.

She crossed her legs. The skirt rode higher. The curve of her thigh became more pronounced as more skin came into contact with the tufted seat-bottom of her chair. Despite the March weather, she was not wearing any stockings. Rosenthal pretended not to notice.

She pulled a newspaper from a large bag that she wore over her shoulder. "What," she said, "is that bastard driving at?"

Rosenthal thought it funny the way she said *bastard*. He did not believe that in Kentucky they pronounced the word similarly to the word *Basque*. He kept his funny thought to himself.

"I interpret what he's saying to mean that there are rumors circulating that someone connected with the team has been fixing games," he said matter-of-factly.

"Where," she said, throwing the newspaper contemptuously onto Rosenthal's desk, "does Marty Smart get off blaming that on my husband?"

Rosenthal straightened out the newspaper. "You don't seem to be shocked at the idea that anybody connected with professional basketball could have anything to do with fixing games. May I ask why?"

"Mr. Rosenthal, I am a basketball wife. I have been for almost eighteen years. When my husband changes jobs, I pack up the family and move after him. When he goes on the road, I wait at home and try not to ask too many questions about what he does. When he comes back snarling, I fix him dinner and get out of his way. But every now and then he has to talk, if only because I am always there, in his house, in his bed, washing his clothes, raising his kids. And when the FBI comes around questioning him, why, that is the very kind of thing he tells me." She ended with a smile on her lips. A hard smile.

"So they've been to see him, too."

"They've been to see him, too. And they've been to see Del, and Oliver and Zeke and Curtis. And now I understand from

Boob, who got it from Dale, that they've been to see DubyaBee. Is that right?"

"Mrs. Sinclair, I am W.E.B. Pancake's attorney. I couldn't tell you that even if I knew the answer."

"I like your style, Mr. Rosenthal," she said, slapping the arm of her chair. His chair. "And the other thing I like about you is that you're the only one who seems to be trying to do anything for anyone." She shifted her weight onto one hip so that her skirt rode up even higher. So that it showed even more skin. He wondered if it would ever stop.

Rosenthal sat up straighter in his chair, hoping that she would follow suit. "I'm not sure I understand you, Mrs. Sinclair."

"I'm sure you don't," she said, but it was unclear if she was being argumentative. She gave a halfhearted tug at her skirt and then tilted back into a position that was more normal for people visiting a lawyer in his office. "But I'm like you in some ways, Mr. Rosenthal. I'm not just going to crawl into a little hole and pretend this isn't happening. Everybody connected with this team is walking on eggs right now, afraid somebody is going to find out something that links them up to Colin Cromwell's death in some way. You're the only one who's out there trying to get to the truth."

"I'm flattered, Mrs. Sinclair, but I'm not sure what it is I can do for you."

"The same thing. I want you to expose the truth and I'm here to help." She leaned forward and what she exposed was an acre of cleavage. A rose could have been placed between her breasts and it would have stood up straight.

Rosenthal, steeling himself to look only at Mrs. Sinclair's face, said, "Why?"

"Why?" She threw herself around in the chair. "Why?" she said again as if it were the most ridiculous question she had ever heard. "Because, quite frankly, Mr. Rosenthal, neither my husband nor I can afford to have him lose his job under circumstances like the ones we've got here."

"Meaning Cromwell's death."

"Meaning," she said, her eyes flashing, "the team not only

250

losing, but playing like shit. Meaning those damn FBI men coming around asking Booby why he did what he did at various times in various games. Meaning if he gets fired under a cloud of suspicion, he isn't ever gonna get another job coaching anything but CYO."

"Suppose I find that somebody has been throwing games, Mrs. Sinclair?"

"Then my husband doesn't have any more explaining to do, does he? Then all those losses haven't been his fault, have they?"

"And suppose I don't?"

"But," she said, pulling a thick spiral notebook out of her bag and placing it in her lap, "I think you will." Her knees were together, her feet were apart, and her face was set almost primly as she waited.

"What have you got there, Mrs. Sinclair?"

"Colin's notebook."

"I see." But he could barely see because more than anything else Reynolds Rosenthal was conscious of the chill that had run up his spine. "Is it," he said after a moment, "the one that was taken from his hotel room on the night he died?"

A genuine look of surprise crossed Meg Sinclair's face. She lifted the spiral notebook in both hands. "This is an old notebook, Mr. Rosenthal. I brought it 'cause it covers the games the FBI's been asking my husband about. Games back in January."

"May I ask where you got it, Mrs. Sinclair?" he asked cautiously.

"Let us just say that I knew where it was."

Rosenthal shook his head. "Mrs. Sinclair," he said sternly, "it is my job to establish that my clients did not have anything to do with Colin's death. That's my only interest. To the extent that your husband can benefit from what I'm doing, that's fine— but I'm not working to help your husband. Do you understand what I'm saying? If anybody other than my clients took that notebook from Colin's hotel room, that's a pretty strong piece of evidence that I can use in their behalf."

Meg Sinclair stood up very suddenly. She stepped forward and plunked the notebook down on Rosenthal's desk. Her breasts, which were eye high when she bent over, shimmied and shook from the force she used as she placed it directly in front of him. "For chrissake, Reynolds," she drawled, "I went and got this myself from Colin's apartment the moment I heard what happened, and now you've gone and embarrassed me."

But it was Rosenthal who blushed. "You had access to Colin's apartment?"

She swayed her way back to the chair and sat down. Her skirt made a special noise as it touched the tufted seat-bottom, like skin on skin. "Yes."

"Does your husband know?"

"He suspected. He saw us talking together one day at the airport when the team got back from a road trip. He thought I told Colin something and he wanted to know why." She shrugged. "He never believed my explanation."

"But you never admitted it?"

"I never admitted anything. But after that—and it was really nothing, what he saw. I don't know why he got so worked up about it—he began looking at me different. He began calling me at strange times just to see if I was home. That's why"—she pointed to the notebook—"I went and got that. I knew that somebody would be going through his stuff eventually, and I didn't want them finding anything that might say something about me. That covers the whole first part of the season up to the time me and Colin stopped seeing each other."

"Which was?"

"Which was the end of January when they got back from that road trip and my husband got suspicious." She made a face. "Besides, I was mad at Colin after that."

Rosenthal looked at the inconspicuous cover. "Does it mention you?"

"No. It's strictly basketball. It's all notes about the games and his interviews and his observations and his ideas for columns. Doesn't say anything about game-fixing, but if you want to know what Colin was thinking about the players and what they were doing"—she pointed with her chin—"it's all in there."

"Does it," asked Rosenthal, turning his head ever so slightly, "happen to mention anything about Phoenix?"

252

"The Phoenix game is in there. A long thing, talking thing, where he's writing down what everybody was saying about going to a party with Neil Novaceski."

Reynolds Rosenthal smiled and opened the book. "In that case, Mrs. Sinclair," he said, flipping the pages, "I'm delighted for both of us."

# 37

The boys went off to the Northwest, Seattle and Portland, and Reynolds Rosenthal headed in the opposite direction. He put on an off-white linen sport coat and a black silk shirt and he flew his own Cessna down to Palm Springs, where a limousine was waiting to whisk him off for lunch at a country club with a client who had once been a premier basketball player and was now a color commentator taking acting lessons and looking for film roles that called for a middle-aged man six feet seven inches tall. When the man had been playing, he wanted the media guides to report him as being six foot nine. Now he wanted Rosenthal to convince Hollywood he was only six feet five. And that he could sing. After lunch, where Rosenthal promised to see what he could do, he was limousined back to the airport, where he reboarded his plane and continued on to Phoenix, Arizona.

The taxi driver at the Phoenix airport knew his destination well. He turned in his seat and gave Rosenthal a wicked grin. "Oh, yes," he said, "very nice place," and Rosenthal almost expected him to reach into his glove compartment and produce either a badge or a box of prophylactics.

Ricky's Hacienda turned out to be a Mexican restaurant cum singles bar. The dining area was dark, with oilcloth covers on the tables, little candles in red ball-shaped jars, and high, ladder-backed chairs with cane seats. Because it was just after five o'clock when Rosenthal arrived, the restaurant was empty, but already the bar was filling up.

The interior walls of the bar were made to look like cracked and broken adobe. A couple of serapes and Mexican hats were nailed high up above the bottles, and in between a few of the shelves were black-and-white wanted-poster drawings of grinning bandidos that lent the place an air of devilry.

The bartenders were moving about rapidly and calling out orders as seriously as if they were in a hospital emergency room. The happy-hour crowd was there for margaritas, which were served in huge glasses and came mixed and frozen, with salt and without. Nearly every woman in the place had a margarita in front of her. A few of the guys had them, too, but mostly the guys had bottles of Mexican beer, which they dangled by the necks from between their fingers.

There were speakers in the four corners of the bar, and a tiny parquet dance floor was in front of one wall, but at this hour entertainment was being provided by a series of strategically placed television sets, each of which was tuned to some sporting event: wind surfing, motocross racing, exhibition league baseball. For the most part, the televisions seemed to be ignored by the patrons in favor of hearty and sometimes boisterous conversation. "And then she fell right on her butt!" roared one guy in a business suit and cowboy boots, and a tableful of people burst into laughter.

Rosenthal took a seat at the end of the bar and ordered a Corona so he could dangle its long-necked bottle like the rest of the guys. He ate chips and salsa because they were there, and when he got a chance, he asked questions.

"I'm looking for Neil Novaceski," he said to the bartender who took his money. The bartender was little more than a kid, and his black hair was long and stylized. On his pocket was a plastic tag that said his name was Jason. "You know who he is?"

"Sure," Jason said, scooping up the bills. He made a point of not looking at Rosenthal. "Big Neil. Great guy." Then he was gone.

"You seen him around lately?" Rosenthal tried on Jason's next trip into his end of town.

"Not lately." Ice was slapped into a glass.

The questioning process was harder than Rosenthal had anticipated. "How long you been working here?"

"A while." Jason was still not looking at him. Liquor was poured, mixed, stirred, taken away. Rosenthal had already assumed that he had reached the end of that particular route of inquiry when Jason, on his way to the other end of the bar, decided to throw a cryptic remark over his shoulder. "I didn't talk to him myself."

"I'd like to ask you some questions about an evening when he was in here a couple of months back," Rosenthal called after him. The noise from the music and the people around them was loud, and it was possible Jason did not hear what he said. It was possible that Rosenthal imagined that Jason's step actually quickened. But he clearly saw him get into a whispered conversation with another bartender, and the second bartender definitely leaned back so that he could get a look at Rosenthal.

The second bartender was stockier and older than the first. He had a scar over one eye and a bristling ginger mustache. As he steamed down the length of the bar to make Rosenthal's acquaintance, he carried with him an air of authority that suggested it was backed up with more muscle than experience. His tag said BUCKY on it. "Can I see your credentials?" he demanded.

Rosenthal spread his hands.

"Your papers," Bucky said impatiently. "Your badge, your identification."

With his hands still spread Rosenthal looked down at his tieless shirt and his $425 sport coat. He looked up at Bucky again and screwed one eye shut in a quizzical expression.

Bucky got the message. "Oh, shit," he said, and stared off at the kid who had spoken to him.

Rosenthal leaned forward and whispered, "I gather the FBI's already been here questioning you."

"No." But Bucky's face was flushed and he had to take a moment to hand-drag his mustache into place. "Jason just told me—he got it wrong, that's all."

"What did he say, 'Another one of those FBI guys is here asking questions about Neil Novaceski'?"

Bucky the bartender had time to regroup and grow tough

again. Unfortunately for Bucky, subtlety was not his strong point. "You a reporter?" he demanded.

"You mean a newspaper reporter? No, I'm not one of them."

Bucky would clearly have liked to say something clever, something definitive, something that would erase this conversation from the annals of human history. He settled for "Oh, shit," again.

Rosenthal said, "The difference between me and these other guys who may have been in here asking questions about Neil is that I can make it worth your while to speak to me."

The idea was to talk Bucky's language, but Bucky said, "Excuse me," and skipped off. He skipped all the way out of the bar.

Rosenthal was left alone with his nearly untouched beer. He did not particularly like beer and he had grown tired of dangling the bottle. But he waited and, eventually, as he knew would happen, he was approached by yet another man. He could hear the man's footsteps come up behind him, and he spun around on his barstool to confront him. Their eyes locked.

Standing before him was a black man with very broad shoulders and a neck like a tree trunk. It was a neck made to look all the thicker because his hair was cut close to his skull. He was not particularly tall, but his chest was huge and his arms rippled from shoulder to wrist. "Hello, Ethan," Rosenthal said, and the man moved in close to him, grabbing his elbow and pulling his head forward so as to speak into Rosenthal's ear. "What are you doing here, Mr. Rosenthal? I'm supposed to throw you out."

"You're the bouncer?" Rosenthal asked in surprise.

"It's just a temporary thing till my knee comes around, man. But I need the work so don't gimme a hard time."

"Did you know it was me you were supposed to throw out?"

Ethan stayed close so that they could continue to converse in whispers. "They just told me to get rid of you, man. I didn't ax no names."

"Who's they?"

"The owner, man," Ethan whined. "Him and Bucky didn't tell me what it was about, they just ax me to take care of it. Now do me a favor and make it easy for me because I'm working on a deal that's gonna get me a invite to the Phoenix Cardinals' preseason camp, and I don't wanna see you saying nothing that's gonna fuck up my shit."

Rosenthal had to look in the man's face to make sure he was serious. Ethan had not, to his knowledge, run with a football in competition for three full seasons, not since he was carried off the field during an exhibition game in which he had torn a cruciate ligament.

"Listen, Ethan, I'm willing to trade favors with you. If you get any kind of contract from the Cardinals, I'll review it for free. All you have to do is go back to the owner and tell him you know who I am. Tell him that I'm a lawyer, and that I'm a straight guy, and that if I can talk to him now, I might be able to save him from being served with a subpoena. Okay?"

It was probably not possible for Ethan's arms to become any tauter, but Rosenthal definitely became more conscious of their remarkable strength as the man thought over the proposition.

"Wait here," Ethan said at last, and then he got into a spasm of finger-wagging. "And don't say nothing to no one."

Twenty-five minutes later, the onetime footballer returned and Rosenthal was taken on a walk through the restaurant. They entered a short corridor through a door marked EMPLOYEES ONLY. The corridor led to another door marked PRIVATE. Ethan knocked and gained them admittance to a small room equipped with a desk and a safe and a television and a couch.

On the couch, her eyes glued to a television movie depicting gladiators with glistening skin and huge pectorals, was an attractive brunette with a little mole on her lip. Rosenthal did not get much past her mole because his attention was almost immediately summoned to a man sitting behind the desk.

The man, like Rosenthal, was wearing a sport coat and an open-necked shirt. Unlike Rosenthal's, however, this shirt was boldly striped and seemed but a prop for a pair of enormous gold cuff links that blocked the sleeves of the man's sport coat from reaching their natural destinations. He was blessed with a full head of dark hair that was just beginning to show traces of gray, but he had bags under his eyes. Heavy bags, no doubt awaiting plastic surgery.

Ethan said, "This here's Mr. Rosenthal," and promptly disappeared.

Rosenthal's host did not bother to get up. "I understand there's some sort of problem," he said. His expression indicated that he had not invited Rosenthal to resolve the problem, but to receive his outrage that such a thing had been brought into his establishment.

Rosenthal, giving his full name, walked to the desk and extended his hand.

He was surprised by the gesture, this don of Hacienda, and he glanced toward his friend on the couch before he reluctantly took the offering. The glance told Rosenthal what he needed to know.

"Ricky Purcell," the man muttered. "And I'm the owner here."

Rosenthal looked at the woman, but Mr. Purcell did not bother to introduce her and she kept her gaze on the gladiators. She was wearing black slacks, a white blouse, and flat shoes. There was nothing flashy about her clothes, nothing that screamed out, "Hey, look at me," or at this or at these. She was not like Ricky Purcell's cuff links in any way.

"What is it," Purcell said cautiously, "that you want to know about Neil Novaceski?"

"I'm not so much interested in Neil as I am in a sportswriter named Colin Cromwell, who I believe was in here looking for Neil about two weeks ago."

"Well, he wasn't." Purcell's eyes started toward the couch and then rocketed back. "At least to my knowledge."

"I have his notebook," said Rosenthal. He did not say which notebook. He did not say why the notebook was significant.

But it was enough. This time Ricky could not keep his eyes from the couch. He was an amateur at the game that was being played, and Rosenthal turned to the woman and waited for her to acknowledge what was now obvious to everyone in the room. She sighed and used a remote control to shut off the television. She stood and regarded Rosenthal with narrowed brown eyes

259

sunk in features set so firmly that it was no longer possible for him to think of her as being pretty. He had to think defensively instead.

A business card appeared in her hand. "I'm Judith Dominguez," she said, holding out the card, "and I am Mr. Purcell's attorney."

Rosenthal fished in his inside pocket and came out with a card of his own. They exchanged. They studied each other's office addresses.

"Mr. Purcell was informed that you were looking to cut some sort of deal. I rushed right over to hear what it is."

Surprised, Rosenthal said, "I didn't mention anything about a deal with Mr. Purcell."

Purcell squealed. "Did so. Ethan said you promised to keep me out of this if I talked to you now."

"Be quiet, Rick," Ms. Dominguez said sharply, and crossed over to Purcell's desk. She perched on its front edge so that she was dangling one foot off the ground. The dangling foot showed white stocking between black slack leg and black shoe. It showed a more workmanlike ankle than Rosenthal might have expected. "Who do you represent, Mr. Rosenthal?" she asked, her leg kicking back and forth.

"A couple of players who have been questioned by the FBI in connection with Cromwell's death."

"And how does that bring you here, to Ricky's Hacienda?"

"Colin Cromwell's dead."

"We know."

"It seems the FBI thinks Cromwell might have died because of a story he was working on about possible rigging of professional basketball games. Cromwell's editor says he was in Phoenix just before he died. The Phoenix entry in his notebook leads me to believe he came to Ricky's Hacienda, probably asking questions about Neil Novaceski and the time last January when Neil brought a bunch of the GoldenGaters in here."

Ms. Dominguez's foot slowed, but still swung like a pendulum. "And why should Rick want to tell you anything about anything, Mr. Rosenthal?"

"Because one of the basketball players who came in here that night in January was my client, and that, it seems to me, gives us a commonality of interest that my client doesn't go saying the wrong things—things that either make him appear to be a liar or bring the FBI back to the Hacienda's door."

"Are you saying we should be working together, Mr. Rosenthal?"

Judith Dominguez spoke coolly, enunciating distinctly, and Reynolds Rosenthal was instantly on his guard. He wondered if the room was bugged, if there were government agents hanging about in the closet or behind the couch. He wondered if he had said too much already. "I'd say we lawyers should always be working together when it comes to the truth, Ms. Dominguez," he told her, but his voice was stronger and clearer than it needed to be in order to carry across the few feet of space that separated them.

She understood at once and smiled. "There's nobody here but us, Mr. Rosenthal. No listening devices, no hidden cameras."

"Ms. Dominguez, if Colin Cromwell managed to get here, and if I managed to get here, I have to assume the FBI's been here as well. They may not have Colin's notebook, but they have infinitely more resources than he or I."

"Well, I'll tell you what Rick's interest is," she said, pulling her hands out of her pockets and folding her arms in front of her stomach. "It's in keeping any and all investigations as far away from this restaurant as possible."

"How did Colin Cromwell respond when you told him that?"

"He didn't," piped up Purcell. "I wouldn't even talk to him."

The provocatively dressed restaurateur was once again shushed by his thick-ankled lawyer.

"But he was here?" Rosenthal asked, deferentially addressing Ms. Dominguez.

She took a moment to decide whether to answer. "Cromwell came in one night a couple of weeks ago looking for Neil. Nobody would answer any of his questions, but he left his business card with Bucky Baker, the bar manager."

"And the reason nobody would answer Cromwell's questions," Rosenthal said, interpreting, "was because the FBI had already been here."

Ms. Dominguez's face grew cold and hard, colder and harder

than it had been at any time before. Rosenthal recognized that they had reached the bargaining point. He forced his own face to soften. He tilted his head in the slightest of shrugs. He spoke gently. "I'm offering you the chance to eliminate any misunderstandings that could land Rick in the middle of a whole different kind of criminal investigation. Things have changed since Colin Cromwell was in here. There's reason to believe he was murdered and that the murder was directly related to the story he was working on when he came looking for Neil. If you've already been cooperating with the FBI, and I think you have, then clearly you believe you can minimize Rick's involvement. I may be able to help you do that, Ms. Dominguez, if I'm not confused about what he knows and what he doesn't know—what he's going to say and what he isn't going to say."

She thought about it and then swiveled her upper body toward Purcell. "Rick," she said.

Her client, like a racehorse out of a starting gate, bolted forward in his chair and said, "Neil Novaceski is a fuckin' bum. I don't know what he was like when he was playing, but he's worthless now."

Invigorated, Ricky rose to his feet, a big man, soft in the stomach, with his pants pulled high in an attempt to hide the bulge. "Neil started hanging out in here about a year ago, and Bucky Baker and some of the guys knew who he was and let him run up a line of credit that got so enormous he never had a prayer of paying it off. We eighty-sixed him. We told him he wasn't welcome back until he paid down his line."

Ricky looked to his lawyer. She was gesturing at him, telling him he did not have to speak so loudly.

"Okay." He ran his fingers through his hair. "But he'd gotten lucky with the chicks in here a few times on account of he's an ex-jock and all, and he really wanted back in. He calls Bucky one night and says his former team is in town and is it okay if he brings them around. Bucky figures that's not bad, get some real pros in here, and so he says yeah.

"And sure enough, Neil shows up with—" Purcell held out his fingers and checked with Judith Dominguez. When she gave him permission, he started ticking off the names. "Dixon, Earl

262

Putnam, Tim Biltmore, Gilbert Rose, and, um, W.E.B. Pancake. Oh, yeah, and the trainer, the little fat guy. I guess it was all the guys that was on the team with Neil. They pay for their dinner, but Bucky comps them on their drinks, and pretty soon Neil, the schmuck, comes up to me and says, 'If I give you a tip, I mean a tip that will make you a lot more than what I owe you, will you let me off the hook?' "

Purcell grabbed hold of his pants. He jerked them up higher on his stomach simply by hoisting his shoulders. He began circling around the room so that Rosenthal had to pivot to follow him.

"I tell him to get outta my face. But I'm thinking, you know, the guy used to be a professional basketball player, he comes in with professional basketball players, he's whooping it up with professional basketball players—and now all of a sudden he's got a tip for me? So I don't walk away or anything. I mean, I'm still willing to listen, and he gets up real close to me, looking over both his shoulders, the whole bit, and he says, 'I got five hundred bucks I'm gonna put down on this thing myself, that's how sure I am of it.' I say, 'You got five hundred bucks, you shoulda made a payment to me,' and he says, 'This is outta my paycheck. I don't come home with this money tomorrow, it's divorce city.' "

Purcell stopped and extended his arms to encompass the whole world and all its combined knowledge. "Now, what am I supposed to do when he tells me that? Tell him, 'No, no, don't share this tip with me?' "

Ricky Purcell flexed his arms, tugged at his collar, and craned his neck. "He says to me, 'Put your money down on Phoenix tomorrow night.' "

Now Ricky jabbed his lapels with a full set of fingers from each hand. "I didn't just fall off the turnip truck. I ask him what the spread was. He says, 'Don't take the spread, just Phoenix.' I say, 'Where can I make a bet like that?'

"He says, 'I got a guy who can make book on anything, anywhere. He's giving me three-to-five on Phoenix and he'll do the same for you.'

"I say, 'Three-to-five isn't my idea of great odds.'

"He says, 'It is on a sure thing and I got it on the best possible authority that the Gaters are gonna lose tomorrow night.' "

Ricky raised his hands, palms up. It was all so easy, what could he do? "I give him a grand to put down with his five hundred on Phoenix and we win, okay?—and I pick up six hundred bucks, which is about half what Neil owes me. So I'm trying to get him to give me his three hundred and he's telling me instead that he's got another sure thing that will make me ten, twenty, a hundred times what he owes me. So I go for it, you know? I bring in Bucky, who's my manager, and we put down everything we got on Seattle to beat the Gaters. We take the odds again, no points, which is lucky because the spread was six and Seattle won by six, so it was a push for everybody but us."

"How much did you put down?"

Before Ricky could answer, Judith Dominguez declared that the amount was none of Rosenthal's business. "Immaterial," she said in a most lawyerlike way.

"A lot," was all Ricky would allow.

"You place it with the same guy as before?"

"So far as I know, yeah."

"You mean because you relied on Neil to place it."

"That's right."

"How long did this go on?"

"The next game was Portland, I think. Me and Buck are all set to go again. In fact, we got about ten guys ready to kick in, but something went wrong, and when Neil pays us off after the Seattle game, he tells us it's a no go for Portland. Sure enough, the Gaters went out a night or so later and broke their losing streak by blowing Portland out of the gym. They got a new guy on the team, Crown, and he goes and scores forty points or something. That was it. That was the last tip we got of any kind from Neil."

"Do you still see him?"

"Not since he told the fuckin' FBI it was us that got him to make the bets. I put out the word to all the people up front that I never want to see that prick in here again." Ricky glanced—quickly—at his attorney. "Pardon my French, Judith."

264

"How do you know he did that, Mr. Purcell?"

Ms. Dominguez answered for him. "The FBI, as I presume you know, Mr. Rosenthal, is not exactly a fountain of information. They ask questions. They don't answer them. But from what they were asking Rick, we gathered that the bet that was made on the Seattle game somehow came to their attention. And when it did, it generated a great deal of suspicion—both because of its size and its nature."

"A win-lose rather than a points bet, you mean." Rosenthal was not sure if he had the terminology right, but she understood what he meant.

She nodded and continued, "They traced it to Phoenix, apparently to this guy that Neil Novaceski said could make book on anything. From that guy they traced the bet to Neil, and Neil, apparently, pointed to Rick and Bucky and said he was just a conduit for them."

"Would it be fair to say that your client agreed to cooperate, Ms. Dominguez?"

She hesitated. "It would be fair to say that the FBI threatened to close down the restaurant and go through every single financial record, receipt, and expenditure Ricky's Hacienda has ever had."

"I see the restaurant's still open."

"Nothing wrong with your eyesight, Mr. Rosenthal."

"You look to me like a practical person, Ms. Dominguez. Under the circumstances you've described, it would appear that the only reasonable thing to do would be to explain to the FBI the source of the tip Mr. Purcell had received."

"Like I said, Mr. Rosenthal, there's nothing wrong with your eyesight."

"And who did you say was the source of Neil's information?"

"We didn't," said Ms. Dominguez.

But her client was not quite so judicious. He tilted back on his bootheels. Looking down, Rosenthal saw that they were extraordinarily high heels, that they added at least two inches to his height. "I could guess, though," Ricky said. "I saw the Phoenix game live. That little trainer give me a ticket that had

265

me sitting just a little ways up behind the Gaters' bench. I saw
what happened at the end."

"But," interjected Ms. Dominguez, holding out her hand to
stop her client from saying anything more, "there's no need for
Rick to be speculating. You want anything more, I suggest you
go directly to Neil."

"You have his address?"

From out of her pocket, Judith Dominguez took a folded piece
of paper that she held in front of her chest with both hands. "I
assume we have an agreement that if I give you this, there'll
be no more bothering Mr. Purcell?"

"There shouldn't be any need for Mr. Purcell ever to see or
hear from me again."

She dropped the paper into Rosenthal's open palm. He
turned for the door and turned again when he reached it. "By
the way, Ricky. I think you made a mistake when you told me
the people who were here. You had W.E.B. Pancake on the
list."

Purcell's chin moved very slowly from side to side, but once
again his lawyer was quicker than he. "We know who you are,
Mr. Rosenthal. And you said yourself one of your clients was
in here that night with Neil."

"Just hoping to get lucky, Ms. Dominguez."

"Try the lottery, Mr. Rosenthal."

It took a while for his taxi driver to find Neil Novaceski's
home because the address Judith Dominguez had provided was
in a trailer court. Once inside the court they cruised little
byways with cute names (Annie Oakley Lane, Red River Valley
Lane, Whiskey Pete Lane) until they found the one she had
identified. Rosenthal bade the driver wait for him and walked
up to the mobile home that he believed to be Novaceski's. It
was dark, but he had no trouble making out the smallness and
the shabbiness of the structure. He also had no trouble making
out the new Jeep Cherokee parked in the set of ruts that served
as the structure's driveway.

What he did not see was the tricycle and the tiny wading

pool. He stumbled over one and stepped directly into the other before he reached the steps.

He knocked on an aluminum-framed door, and after some seconds an outside light came on and a round-faced woman with stringy blond hair pushed open the door. She was wearing off-pink shorts and a sleeveless blouse that bore a pattern of the same off-pink interspersed with white checks. On her feet were flip-flops. On her face was a worried expression.

Rosenthal tried to remember if he had seen her before, if she looked at all familiar. "Mrs. Novaceski?"

"Yes."

"I'm Reynolds Rosenthal."

The name meant nothing to her.

"I'm a players' agent from San Francisco and I knew your husband when he was on the GoldenGaters."

Her dull blue eyes went to the taxi waiting in the distance. "What do you want?"

"I'd like to ask your husband a few questions."

"He's not here." Her voice was every bit as dull as her eyes.

"Might I ask when you expect him back?"

Rosenthal could hear a television and the sounds of children, several children, at least one of whom was crying and one of whom was yelling. He watched as Mrs. Novaceski played with the spring latch on the door. He knew what was coming long before she burst into tears and said, "Oh, Mr. Rosenthal, I don't expect he's ever coming back."

# 38

Something happened in the Northwest. In Seattle, Booby replaced W.E.B. with Jerome Crown in the second quarter, then benched Larry Miller in favor of Jonnie Martin. With Jonnie feeding him lob passes, Jerome went wild and dragged the rest of the team into their first victory since Philadelphia. The next night Booby tried the same maneuvers, but Portland sagged onto Jerome and nullified his inside game. The more Portland sagged on Jerome, however, the more Jonnie was left open. He hit fifteen of twenty shots from the floor, and Portland fell far enough in the hole that it was unable to catch the Gaters despite a furious end-of-the-game rally that so totally exploited Jonnie's defensive weaknesses that Booby had to put Larry back in. The Gaters returned home with a record of 33 wins and 39 losses, with ten games still to play. They were now ensconced in tenth place, one game behind Dallas and three games behind Denver, which was clinging to the last play-off slot.

The Gaters took on Chicago, mighty Chicago, in its only San Francisco appearance of the season, a guaranteed sellout regardless of the Gaters' dwindling play-off hopes. W.E.B. managed to get the opening tap and directed it to Del, who gave it off to Larry, who sent it right through the hoop. Chicago then ran off 12 straight points and the fans began to boo.

The Gaters called time-out and the catcalls rained down on them from around the arena. Booby inserted Jerome at center and W.E.B. came out. It was the earliest W.E.B. Pancake had ever sat down in all the time Booby had been his coach.

Play resumed and things improved only slightly. At 20 to 10 Booby replaced Rynn with Jonnie Martin. Rynn started for the end of the bench, but Booby grabbed his jersey and forced him to sit next to him, on the chair that was usually occupied by Hack. Booby talked and Rynn listened. Jonnie got burned over and over and Booby pointed as he talked, and Rynn's head went up and down as he listened.

At 40 to 18 Rynn returned to the game. He did nothing that was immediately spectacular. He scored on no long bombs and made no inhuman moves, but as the minutes ticked off, the score gradually narrowed, and in an even more gradual sense it became apparent that Chicago was no longer in control of the game.

Rynn knocked a pass away and then got a partial block on a shot. Going one-on-one with Chicago's point guard, he forced his man farther and farther away from the basket until the Chicago players had to come outside to help. On one occasion, Rynn got his man so isolated that he tried to bounce the ball off Rynn's legs and out of bounds, but Rynn stole it instead. On another occasion, the Chicago point guard tried to make a crosscourt pass and Larry Miller intercepted it on the dead run and went the length of the court to score.

Rynn's defense was relentless, and then in the third quarter he went on a scoring jag of his own. Two, four, six, seven points, and suddenly the score was 88–83.

The boos died when the gap narrowed to single figures. And when, with less than two minutes left, the Gaters closed to within 3, they did so to a prolonged ovation that charged the arena. The feeling expressed by thousands of voices was a mixture of gratitude, welcome, surprise, and even pride. Chicago called time to regroup and the fans kept right on roaring. The entire Gaters team gathered around Booby, and the guys on the bench gave up their seats to the guys who were playing, and everyone leaned in close and draped his arms across the others, and when the buzzer sounded there was a simultaneous clasping of hands.

Chicago passed the ball inside and tried to muscle it to the hoop. Jerome Crown went skyward, and when the shooter tried

269

to release his shot he found that Jerome's outstretched fingers were already occupying the flight path.

The sound of the block reached twenty rows into the stands, yet the ball went neatly, deftly, to Zeke, coming in from the corner, and Zeke, in one fluid motion, whipped it to Larry, who was already racing for the other end. Larry had one defender to beat, but as he made his move to the inside and as the defender committed with him, there was a flash of white uniform trailing the play and the ball that had been in Larry's right hand went behind his back so that the defender had to fall away. He threw himself at the flash, but the flash no longer had the ball either. Rynn Packard had given it right back to Larry as fast as if it had come off a backboard, and Larry, untouched, jammed the ball home. Pandemonium reigned. The Gaters, once down by 22 points, had moved to within 1.

Chicago again called time-out, their last, and this time the crowd remained standing right along with the players. Chicago substituted and the Gaters did not. From the bench, W.E.B. Pancake was waving a towel round and round his head, and the crowd was responding as if it were a cavalry call. In the midst of this noise, Chicago, taking the ball back up court, tried to pass inside. The ball was swatted toward the rafters, swatted again like a beach ball, and then Zeke Wyatt plucked it out of the air. The Chicago coaches and players screamed for a foul, but the refs paid no heed.

The ball went back to the Gaters' end and then went around the perimeter. Rynn to Larry to Zeke to Larry to Rynn to Del. Quick-quick-quick. Del did a head fake and moved inside to release his shot. The ball bounced off the back of the rim. It seemed to hang in the air for seconds. A dozen hands reached for it, bodies smashed together, and a chorus of huge men grunted from the effort of giving every last ounce of strength. For one curious moment the crowd's cheers grew reed-thin and almost disappeared as the ball stayed just above a blur of outstretched fingers, and then Jerome Crown snatched it away from the rest and hurtled back down the floor. He landed in a crouch, his elbows flailing. His head jerked as if he were going back

270

up again, but when the red uniforms of the Chicago players rose into the air, he fired a bounce pass outside to Rynn.

There were four seconds left on the clock as Rynn drove from the outside. Del picked off one man and Rynn would have had a clear path to the basket if it were not for the fact that Chicago's center had stepped directly in front of him. Rynn's transition from moving horizontally to moving vertically occurred seemlessly, almost magically. But the Chicago center went with him, and there was no way Rynn could even see the basket. He let the ball loose from behind his head, and it arced in a parabola of absolute geometric precision, reaching its apex high above the attempted block and then plummeting straight into the net.

The Gaters were 34 and 39 with nine to play.

## 39

**W**.E.B. Pancake took the call on his car phone on his way home from the game because he thought it would be his wife. It wasn't. It was his agent.

Reynolds Rosenthal had just heard the score and wanted to congratulate him on the victory. W.E.B., keeping both hands on the wheel, mumbled that he hadn't done much, and Rosenthal asked him what he meant.

"Only three minutes in the first half, five in the second. I think the man's getting to him."

"What man? Getting to whom?"

W.E.B. snapped his lips and for a moment wondered if his agent was jerking him around. Agent's supposed to know things like that. "That Marty Smart," he grumbled. "Keep writin' 'bout how Jerome should be playin' 'stead of me. Today he had these statistics in his column. You see that? Says my e-ffectiveness is off in the fourth quarter and when we play back-to-back games. E-ffectiveness, my ass. What's some computer know about e-ffectiveness?"

"I was curious about that myself, W.E.B. Where do you suppose Marty got the stats?"

"From some computer, like I said."

Rosenthal came back at him with, "And who is it on the Gaters who's best known for his computer work?"

"Front office, man." But W.E.B. was guessing. He didn't feel like thinking. Rosenthal, he was paid to think.

"It's Dyk, W.E.B. Dyk fancies himself as having single-

272

handedly brought the computer to basketball. I don't know if those are his statistics, I can't prove it, but everything I'm seeing in Marty's columns these days looks to me like it could have been spoon-fed by Dyk."

W.E.B. was confused. "Me and him never had no problems. Why would he want to do something like that?"

"I'm sure it's nothing personal, W.E.B." Rosenthal's voice grew very distant over the cellular connection. W.E.B. had to strain to hear him say something about how Dyk was the first to use Jerome at center, and if Jerome looked good playing that position, Dyk looked good.

"Then how come he don't push to get Jerome in there?" W.E.B. shouted back.

Rosenthal's voice became clear again. "That could be part of his plan. I'm speculating now, but if Dyk wants to be the head coach—and what assistant doesn't?—then he could be saying one thing to Booby's face and another behind his back."

W.E.B. was silent for several moments. "That why you calling me, man?"

"No. I'm calling you because I just got back from a trip and I needed to ask you some things so I can try to piece together what I've learned. You remember a game you guys played in Phoenix in January?"

W.E.B. felt a twinge at the mere mention of the city. It almost made him step on the brakes. "I 'member all my games, man."

"Tell me what happened."

"Lost by one. Last second."

"Anything funny happen in that game?"

W.E.B. was approaching his exit. He slowed and very deliberately put on his blinker. Yeah, there was something funny. And there was something funny about Rosenthal managing to track it down.

"Hello?" Rosenthal called. "You still there?"

"How you know 'bout Phoenix?"

"I've been working." The man paused, as if he thought maybe W.E.B. were going to thank him. Or congratulate him. Then he said, "Cromwell's editor told me that's where he went after he left Alabama. Then a sort of girlfriend of Cromwell's showed me a notebook where he talked about Phoenix."

"So you know what happened there?"

"You tell me."

W.E.B. turned onto his street. "Instead of working the clock, Del puts up a crazy shot. It go in, but Phoenix get the ball back with all the time in the world to score. Which they do. No excuse for Del's shot, man, 'cept it went in."

"You think the game was fixed?"

"I don't know nothing 'bout that."

"A big bet was made on that game by Neil Novacoski."

Rosenthal had not even finished the sentence before the curse was out of W.E.B.'s mouth. He swore again and then a third time, and Rosenthal didn't say any more after that.

W.E.B. wheeled his car into his driveway, punched the automatic door opener, and drove into the garage so quickly he just managed to avoid scraping the roof. Reynolds Rosenthal was still on the line when he snapped off the engine and bolted up the stairs to his house.

Ida heard him coming. She approached him head-on from the kitchen, her shoulders hunched, her hands in front of her, her face ready to be slung into fear, sadness, anger, concern— whatever it was that was making her husband run at her.

"Shit, woman," he yelled, "you told him, didn't you?"

"Told who? What? What are you talking about?"

"Told somebody som'pin'." He was close now, close enough to shake her by the shoulders. "Don't lie to me, Ida Mae. That Colin Cromwell got to Phoenix and now Rosenthal's got there, too."

She tried to shrug away from him. She was a big woman and she had shrugged away plenty of men before. But when his hands slipped he was still quick enough to catch her by the wrists.

"Leggo of me, Willie, or so help me, I'll—"

"You'll what? You already broke your word to me."

"I would do whatever I have to do to save your ass," she shouted, still struggling, bending low, trying to rip at least one arm loose.

"And what did you do, Ida Mae?" he shouted back, pushing his face up close to hers.

Somehow she managed to do it. She flung herself backward and she was free. "I did," she said, panting, "just what I told Rosenthal anybody coulda done. When those articles was coming out that had you so upset, I got a damn phone book and called every hotel and motel in Anniston until I got hold of Cromwell." She pushed the hair out of her face. W.E.B. knew that if her eyes were fire, he would be burned to a cinder.

"What did you tell him?" W.E.B. demanded. But he didn't go after her. The woman was crazy.

"I told him," she said, her voice pumping out between breaths, "that if he would leave off of my husband, I would give him the story of a lifetime."

"And that story was that somebody on the Gaters had tipped off Neil Novaceski that we was going to lose to Phoenix."

"It got the man out of Alabama."

"You tell him who it was?"

"Only thing I told Colin Cromwell was if he really wanted to know who was fixing games, he'd best be starting with Neil."

"Don't you think he told Neil it was you that sent him? And don't you think Neil woulda passed that along?"

Ida's face looked sorrowful, but her body looked defiant. "I'm sorry, baby. But it was the only way I could make sure he'd go."

W.E.B. Pancake crumpled slowly into a cross-legged position on the floor. He looked up at his wife and his eyes were blurred with misery. "Oh, my God, Ida. How'm I ever gonna be able to look at that man and act like neither one of us don't know nothin'?"

# 40

Orlando and Washington, two teams out of play-off contention and dragging themselves through their final West Coast swings, came to town and dutifully laid down in front of the Gaters. Del Fuego went on a scoring rampage, hitting 18 of 21 shots against Orlando on Friday night and accounting for 47 points on considerably more shots against Washington on Sunday afternoon. Rynn Packard fed him constantly, getting 14 assists in the first game and 16 in the next. Jerome kept playing center in relief of W.E.B., and he outmuscled and outleaped everyone who tried to go up against him.

At 36 and 39, the Gaters flew off to play Minnesota, yet another team that was already eliminated from the play-offs. Marty Smart, for the first time in anybody's memory, did not accompany them on the road trip.

The Gaters arrived in their hotel rooms in Minneapolis, turned on their televisions, and learned that they had no sooner left town than Marty had broken the story that a Washington, D.C., attorney named Fenwick had been appointed by the league commissioner to investigate certain unspecified charges against certain unnamed members of the San Francisco GoldenGaters. Fenwick's investigation, Marty reported, would start in Boston.

The next day the Gaters lost to Minnesota 114–91.

In Milwaukee the team was met by the biggest contingent of reporters they had seen all year. People flew in from around the country, virtually forcing Booby to hold an impromptu press conference.

"What do you have to say about the rumors that Fenwick's investigation involves game-tampering?" shouted a member of the assemblage.

Booby looked dully into the television cameras and said, "I do not believe there is any substance to such rumors."

"What then is Mr. Fenwick investigating?" demanded a reporter with a British accent; and Booby said he was sure he didn't know as Mr. Fenwick had not yet seen fit to contact him.

"How is this investigation affecting the team?" someone wanted to know; and Booby assured the questioner that the team wasn't feeling the effects at all.

"We've already moved ahead of Dallas," he reminded the gathering. "Now we just need to go five and one the rest of the way to get that last play-off spot away from Denver. Maybe four and two."

That afternoon, Booby ordered the Gaters to close ranks. He gave strict instructions that nobody connected with the team was to talk with anybody connected with the press about anything. The Gaters' locker room was made off limits to outsiders, and all media people, even Wayne Brickshaw, were banned from traveling on the team bus.

The Gaters emerged from their seclusion only long enough to beat Milwaukee 97–84. Then they went back to their hotel to await the morning flight to Indianapolis.

Reynolds Rosenthal's secretary said there was a woman on the phone who wouldn't leave her name, but insisted on talking to him. Rosenthal took the call because his secretary had good intuition and thought he should. He was glad he had done so when the caller identified herself as Petunia Dawkins.

"My husband ever come to see you?" she wanted to know.

Rosenthal assured her he had not.

"He promised me he would."

"I would remember if he had."

"He was supposed to talk to you about buying out his contract."

"I would particularly remember that, Mrs. Dawkins. It's not something that you normally can do."

"Well, he got a bad deal with the contract he signed last summer."

"They often seem that way in hindsight, Mrs. Dawkins."

"That's all right, because now I'm just trying to save what he's got. That's why I'm calling you."

"He has an agent, doesn't he?"

"We fired him. That much I'm sure of because I wrote the letter and mailed it myself. That's the best way for me to get him to do anything—do it myself."

"Are you calling on his behalf now, Mrs. Dawkins?"

"I just got off the phone with Oliver," she said, her words tumbling over each other. "You know about this investigation the commissioner's got going on?"

Rosenthal said he had heard about it.

"You know that investigator's back in Boston?"

He admitted he had heard that, too.

"This man, this Fenwick, he's looking for trouble. All of a sudden, everybody's talking about point shaving and game fixing and trying to find out who all's involved. Where's Fenwick go? He goes to Boston, the only place where the team ever had a problem. You know what I'm saying, Mr. Rosenthal?"

"I have an idea."

"Seems to me that if the man's looking at point shaving, he shouldn't be looking into a party where some of the fellas got out of hand. I mean, he's looking to find the one thing, he comes up with the evidence of the other, what good will that do anybody except Rohmer and Brandisi?"

"I'm not sure I follow you on that, Mrs. Dawkins."

"Why, they find out what went on, they'll have an excuse to kick my husband off the team, get out of paying him what they promised."

"Mrs. Dawkins . . . ," Rosenthal said, and then he backed up and tried again. "Mrs. Dawkins, the Gaters have a lot of worries right now. A lot. My guess is that their disappointment with Oliver is not their number one concern."

"Oliver's contract's guaranteed for three years unless he's

278

suspended. That's the first thing that came to my mind when I heard about this investigation into what they call 'unspecified' charges, and that's why I called Oliver. I said, 'Oliver, anything at all that they can get you for?' I said, 'Anything they can get you for in Boston?' And he comes clean with me, Mr. Rosenthal. He told me all about Boston."

"What, exactly, did he tell you?"

Mrs. Dawkins made a noise of exasperation. "He told me there was a party at Mr. Brandisi's house, that some people went off in another room and that there was a woman there, and that she was trying to get Curtis in bed with her and Curtis wouldn't go. He says Curtis got real upset and told everybody he was homosexual and ran out."

"That's all Oliver told you?"

"He told me there was some sex involved between the woman and some of the others. Some sex and some drugs." She did not elaborate.

"Doesn't sound to me as though Oliver's likely to be singled out in that situation, Mrs. Dawkins." Then, because he was feeling a little put upon by the demands of this wife of a nonclient, he added, "Unless he was involved with the drugs."

"Oliver doesn't do drugs, Mr. Rosenthal," Petunia snapped. "But I wouldn't put it past anyone to blame him. They're going to need a scapegoat for whatever this investigator comes up with, and they sure don't want the commissioner's office focusing on any of their star players. So it's either Curtis or Oliver who's going to take the fall for this one, the way I see it. I thought you might be willing to do something to prevent that."

"Like what, Mrs. Dawkins? What is it you think I can do?"

"Head off this investigation. Get that man Fenwick pointed in the right direction. And get him the heck out of Boston."

"And how do you propose I do that?"

"I can tell you, Mr. Rosenthal, but you've got to promise on your word of honor that you won't ever tell where you got it from, and you most especially won't ever let anybody connect what you're about to hear with Oliver. Can you do that?"

"Yes."

"Word of honor?"

"Word of honor."

Reynolds Rosenthal could hear Petunia Dawkins take a deep breath. Her exhale rushed through the receiver. "Tell that investigator to go to Raleigh, North Carolina, and check out a man named Eddie Maclean. Tell him to check out his bets, and tell him not to get stuck looking at any history of Eddie Mac being a friend of Oliver's. Oliver's never played enough for this team to go fixing any games."

Long after he hung up, Reynolds Rosenthal was still staring at the telephone. Eventually, he took it off the hook again and dialed a number. It was not, however, the number of the commissioner, or the commissioner's investigator, Mr. Fenwick. It was the number of Marty Smart.

## 41

**D**enver did them a favor, falling to Houston, and when the Gaters took the floor against Indiana, they were just a game back in the standings. Once again they held their opponent to less than 90 points, and when the final buzzer sounded, they had closed to within a half game, with the Gaters still having four to play and Denver five.

Teddy Brandisi was so pleased with this push for the last play-off spot that he chartered them a jet to fly home. Two days later they took on Sacramento. The Sacramento players were talking trash, remembering the last time the two teams had met, and five minutes into the contest somebody said something about Booby. Jerome Crown knocked the man down and then kicked him for good measure, whereupon he was promptly ejected. W.E.B. went back in at center and proceeded to play forty-three minutes straight. He played viciously: banging; leaning; throwing elbows. The Gaters won going away.

Since New York, on its way out to the Coast, had stopped en route long enough to thrash Denver, the Gaters found themselves in sole possession of eighth place, with a record of 39 wins and 40 losses. Denver stood at 38 and 40.

Rosenthal asked Marvin, the uniformed guard, and because it was late and Rosenthal was the only one still around, Marvin checked for him and said Coach Sinclair, Coach Hacker, Coach Dykstra, Crabbie, Del, and Rynn were all who remained in the locker room. Rosenthal told Marvin he would wait just around the corner of the corridor, and because he gave him five bucks Marvin agreed to say good-night by name to each person who left.

Rosenthal heard, "Good night, Rynn. Good night, Mr. Sinclair. Hack, good night to you, too, sir," and then he heard several sets of footsteps, but he remained where he was. Not long after that he heard, "Good night, Dyk. That was a good one, yes, sir."

He waited until Dyk was gone, and then he returned to Marvin and for another five bucks got him to go inside and ask a few questions. When he came out, Crabbie was with him.

"You know it's still off limits, Mr. Rosenthal."

"What's he say?"

"He asked me to take a walk."

"Can you make it a fifteen-minute walk, Dick?"

Crabbie looked at Marvin, who looked away.

"A favor, Dick."

Crabbie shrugged. "They did well tonight, didn't they, Mr. Rosenthal?"

"They did great."

"I've got to check on some things at the office. After New York comes in we go right off to L.A., and then we finish up in Phoenix." Crabbie sighed. "The traveling, it gets to you after a while."

Rosenthal nodded. "I just had to go back and forth to Phoenix myself."

Crabbie looked surprised. "You did? But Phoenix has been playing on the East Coast for the past week."

"Yeah, I was there on some other business."

"I thought you just represented athletes, Mr. Rosenthal."

"But I try to serve all their legal needs, Dick—contracts, taxes, investments, divorces."

"Criminal, you don't do any of that, do you?" Crabbie's brow narrowed, as though he were hearing about an illness Rosenthal had. Then he smiled. "Oh, I imagine you've done a few drunk drivings, that sort of thing, for some of the guys."

"Those things happen, Dick. Every now and then."

"But you do them yourself?"

"Usually."

"Gee, I'll keep that in mind, Mr. Rosenthal, in case I ever need you."

"Let's hope you don't, Dick."

Crabbie laughed. He glanced at his watch. "It should take me about fifteen minutes, these things I have to check on." And then to Marvin he said, "You can go, Marvin. I've got a key to get back in."

Rosenthal entered the locker room and found Del dressed in a long-sleeved gold shirt, powder-blue Jockey shorts, and black socks that covered his calves. He had a pair of dark green suit pants laid neatly over a bench, and he was busy brushing his hair in a mirror that was set up at the back of his cubicle. He used the mirror to watch Rosenthal approach.

They were not friends. They had never even been introduced, but Del Fuego knew who he was. "Word is," Del said, "you wanted to see me."

Rosenthal sat down on the bench and looked up.

Del Fuego took one last glance in the mirror and turned for his pants. "I guess that game didn't do much for you."

"I'm afraid that what I've got isn't curable by one game, Del."

Del flapped the pants out in front of him, stepped into them one leg at a time, and tugged them to his waist. "Well, I'm sorry to hear that." But he wasn't. Not really. He did not much care about the maladies of a man he barely knew. He pulled up his zipper.

He grabbed his shoes and sat down to put them on. They were long, alligator-skin loafers and had such a high gloss that they had to be new. He was careful to use a shoehorn to get them on his feet and admired them when they were in place.

His head was still bent when Rosenthal said, "I need to talk to you about Phoenix, Del."

Del slowly straightened up. "Phoenix?" he said, but there was something wrong with his tone. In two syllables he managed to capture an entire argument: certainly he'd been to Phoenix, he knew Phoenix well, but nothing Rosenthal could possibly say about Phoenix would have anything to do with him.

"You helped out an old teammate in Phoenix, but he was the wrong guy to give a tip. Instead of making a quiet bet on his own, he passed along what you told him to a couple of characters who run a bar down there. Maybe you remember them, Ricky Purcell and Bucky Baker from Ricky's Hacienda. They remember you, Del, and what they remember they've told the FBI."

"Then I don't have much to worry about because I never told no Ricky and no Bucky nothing." He made fun of the names by the way he pronounced them. White names, he was saying.

"You told Neil to bet against the Gaters on the night he brought you into their place, and Neil told Ricky and Ricky told Bucky and these guys got together and put money down."

Del Fuego said, "Sheee," and swung his head disgustedly. When he looked back, his mouth was hanging open. His expression said that he did not know whether to be more upset with Rosenthal or the state of mankind in general. "Neil tell you I gave him a tip?"

"The tip came on the night Neil brought you to Ricky's Hacienda," Rosenthal repeated. "Ricky Purcell told me that Neil bought off a debt he owed him by telling him to take whatever odds he could get on Phoenix. Then he and Neil and Bucky Baker combined to put down more money on Seattle for your next game. Same arrangement—odds, no points. That was the end of Neil's handicapping expertise. Two tips, two games."

Del's brow lifted. His extraordinary tea-colored eyes bulged with sincerity. "So that doesn't mean Neil got a tip from anyone. He was a basketball player. He was out to our practice. He could have just seen for himself that things weren't going so good."

"These were greedy men down in Phoenix, Del. They were going to keep riding this horse, except that Neil couldn't get them a tip for the next game. You remember that one. It was against Portland. It was the one you sat out with a groin pull, the one where Jerome took your place and scored all those points. The guys in Phoenix felt it was a good thing they didn't bet, since it ended the Gaters' losing streak."

"This is what you call circumstantial evidence. Bunch of guys standing around bullshitting. Novo telling us what a tough time he was having. I may have felt sorry for the guy and said something about what I'd do if I needed some money. But I wasn't the only one talking. Earl was there. Gilbert, W.E.B., Tim. Crabbie, he was hanging around. It was just bullshit anyhow."

"Oh, you're right. Other people were there, and one of them was Gilbert Rose. Gilbert just happens to be my client, Del. And he also happens to be very unhappy in San Antonio. Wants me to do anything I can to get him back to California. So when I asked him for a little help, he was more than willing to give it. You know what he told me, Del? He told me he heard you tell Neil to 'bet the ranch' on Phoenix. Gilbert remembered that phrase, Del, because he thought Neil really did own a ranch down there in Phoenix."

The basketball player leaned forward with his elbows on his knees and looked into Rosenthal's eyes. After a moment or two he clasped his hands and dropped them down between his open thighs. The bench, even though it was in a professional basketball team's locker room, was made for more normal-sized men and his arms reached nearly to the floor. He looked almost childlike, a big boy being punished by having to sit at a little boy's desk. "I never blew a game in my life," he said.

Rosenthal was silent.

"My job is to win basketball games, right? Isn't that what you're thinking? Well, you're wrong. My real job is to win a championship for the people that pay my salary, and there isn't a soul on this earth who can point to anything I did that wasn't geared to that."

"Winning championships generally comes from winning basketball games, Del."

"Not all eighty-two of 'em." Del pursed his lips reflectively and shifted his gaze to his cubicle. "A few losses can be a good thing if they help turn the whole season around. That was all anybody really wanted anyhow, to be on top at the end."

Del's extralong, double-breasted, dark green suit jacket and his black and gold polka-dot tie hung from a hanger in front of him. Practice clothes hung from a hook. A picture of his wife and his two children was taped to the back wall. On a shelf along with his mirror were his hairbrush and a can of deodorant and a jar of cologne and a razor and shaving cream and a stack of mail and a portable CD player, and a small trophy—a token or an award that was gathering dust. On the floor were at least three sets of athletic shoes and a sweatshirt that had fallen. It was not much, not compared to some athletes' lockers, and Rosenthal wondered if Del was having similar thoughts as he surveyed the souvenirs of his season.

Del, perhaps speaking to the contents of the locker, said, "I go way back in this business, man. I know the way things go down. When I was a kid, they used to come around my playground and give me shit, guys from the summer leagues, guys from high schools. Sweat suits, sneakers, little travel bags. I got recruited to go to high schools, you know that?"

Rosenthal, who had contacts in virtually every top youth basketball camp, did indeed know that.

"My momma was a nurse's aide and people offered to get her jobs at hospitals all over L.A. and Orange County so that we would move into their districts. At fifteen I started getting offers from colleges. Not just feelers, but promises—like they'd build the whole recruiting class around me and they'd give me this and arrange for that. Then I'd be invited to these basketball camps, and there'd always be somebody there offering me something. You know what I'm saying? Trips, flights home, food money, so many sneakers and sweat suits and tickets that I couldn't do nothing but sell 'em. So what it was, it was like a job way back then."

Del's eyes moved from his cubicle to his alligator shoes. "But I knew even when I was a kid what kind of job it was. Weren't many people doing me favors, giving me things, just because I was a nice guy. Coaches need wins to keep their jobs, to get new ones, and to get paid big money. They see this boy coming and they think, 'He can get me some Ws,' and they're willing to pay for it in some way or another. Even if it's just acting

286

concerned, that kinda shit. I saw that right away, man. The players that play the best get acted the nicest to. You stop playing so well, you get hurt maybe, the coaches, the scouts, the recruiters, aren't so nice anymore. I figured that out quick."

Del was speaking to Rosenthal, but he was still looking at the alligator shoes. "By the time I signed a professional contract I understood they were paying me money to make money. They think they can make more money by getting rid of me, they'll do it in a New York minute. I been drafted and traded and moved about without nobody asking what I wanted, and I always understood that it's business. So I walk the walk they tell me to walk and I wait until my moment arrives."

Del shook his head wistfully. He did it without breaking his gaze. "That was going to be this year. Couple of weeks from now, couple of months if all went well and we made it through the play-offs, I could be the most valuable property in basketball. It was there for the taking. My contract's up and I'm at the top of my game. All I need's the team to make a showing and this was going to be my year. I could be worth three, four million to some teams next year. Maybe this one."

Del's words drifted off and then he remained quiet for so long that Rosenthal was forced to ask him what happened.

"Huh," he said, and the sound was clipped, sure, and bitter. "What happened was we got a team that's built more for Rynn Packard than for me. Some little rich dude who's playing the game for a hobby or something. Doesn't make any difference Rynn plays like he's got gum on his shoe, you see, because Booby's comfortable with that. That's the way it was when he played. Three yards and a cloud of dust."

He paused again before adding, "Only it don't work that way anymore, man. Not at this level."

"Did you talk to Booby about that?"

"Last season, I go to Booby, I say, 'Booby, you got some studs, you gotta use 'em. We can't be out there movin' half the speed of everybody else. We gotta make something happen.' Booby, he looks at me like I'm talkin' Martian or something."

Del sighed. "So I keep my mouth shut and we finish out the season and we're no better than we were the year before. But

287

I bide my time, knowing that all kinds of things could happen over the summer. And sure enough, Rohmer goes out and signs Oliver Dawkins, who is a great college player and who no doubt is going to put ol' Bill right back where he belongs—which is on the bench.''

Del's shoulders rose and fell in a show of resignation. "Only Oliver shows up fat and lazy. He's late for camp and he didn't pick up the system right away. But Booby, he's still got Earl on the bench and we could be getting a lot more action out of him than we're getting out of Bill, and nobody's doin' nothing to change things. We keep playing middlin' basketball and we're not running and Booby's not communicating and nobody's happy.''

"So you decided to change things.''

Rosenthal did not time it, but his sense was that thirty seconds passed before Del answered. "Sometimes things need changing.''

"You told me you never blew a game in your life.''

"I never did.''

"What about the Phoenix game?''

"My shot went in, didn't it? I was on the floor diving for that ball at the end, wasn't I?''

"How about the Seattle game?''

"I got hurt. Just wasn't as bad as I thought, that's all.''

There was a sound and both men jerked their heads around to see what it was.

"Who's there?'' demanded Dixon. His back was ramrod straight. His expression was as alert as a gazelle's.

Another sound, that of something being moved, occurred. Crabbie stepped into their line of vision. "Sorry,'' he said, "I thought you guys would be all through.''

They had not heard him return. Rosenthal did not know how he had gotten back in. He asked Crabbie to give them a few more minutes and Crabbie nodded. This time Rosenthal was very conscious of the door opening and closing. When he was sure they were alone again, he said, "So you decided to take your case to management by making the Gaters look as bad as possible, is that it?''

288

"Rohmer and Brandisi are businessmen. If they're not getting their wins, they're going to do something about it."

"They did. They went out and traded for Jerome."

"Yeah."

"You hadn't figured on that possibility."

"You got that right."

"And after Jerome arrived you couldn't afford to screw around anymore, so you didn't."

Del's mouth opened and spread slowly into a grin of reluctant admiration. "That Rohmer." Del glanced out of the corner of his eye to see if Rosenthal was sharing the irony with him, and the grin snapped off his face. "Don't be lookin' at me like that."

"Like what, Del?"

"Like you're doing. What's the big deal? It's not as though I stole something."

Rosenthal got to his feet. He was feeling very tired. He was feeling almost sick to his stomach. "No?"

Del Fuego Dixon jabbed a long finger at him, trying to hold him in place. "First of all, I didn't throw none of those games. They were losses with or without me. And if somebody wants to say different, my answer is let him prove it. Let you prove it. I'll deny it to the day I die."

"There are game films, Del. Videotapes."

"Nothing I'm afraid of there. Even superstars make mistakes."

"And there's all the stuff Colin Cromwell came up with."

The rigidity went out of Del's finger. He lowered it slowly. "What stuff are you talking about?" he muttered, but Rosenthal did not have to hear his question to know what he was asking.

"Colin got word of what went on in Phoenix. My guess is that one of the players who was in Ricky's with you told him. He went there not long before his death, to Ricky's Hacienda, asking questions. He never got to Neil because the FBI had already scared Neil away, but he did get to you. Makes sense. If he was looking for somebody who did something funny in the Phoenix game, you were the most logical suspect."

Del Fuego's response was nothing but a hard glare.

"He went from Phoenix to Washington, supposedly to rejoin the team. But he didn't rejoin the team and the only person he appeared to have talked to in D.C. was you, Del. Then he disappeared again. It might help clean up some confusion if you tell me where he went—and how you got him to go there."

"What . . . makes you . . . think . . . I got him to go anywhere?"

Rosenthal smiled at the menacing delivery. "Because, Del, you had had time to prepare. You knew he, or someone like him, was coming. You knew he was going to confront you and you did something about it. Something to get him off your back. What was it?"

Del Fuego shook his head as if appalled at how inaccurate one man could be.

But Rosenthal was not fazed. He actually leaned down so that Del could see his face all the clearer. Read his lips. "Gilbert told me that about two weeks after he was traded, the FBI showed up in San Antonio to interview him and Earl Putnam about what had happened that night you guys went to Ricky's Hacienda with Neil. He said the next time their team came here to San Francisco, Earl took you aside and told you all about the FBI visit. He said you got quite upset. That you even claimed you were going to do something about it. I don't know what that something was, but I do believe it got Colin to leave on another one of his little investigations, and I know that when he next reappeared, he ended up dead. Did he go too far in whatever it was you told him to do? Or not far enough?"

"What are you saying? You think I killed the little bugger? Because if that's what you're thinking, you can kiss my ass. Anybody wanted to kill Colin Cromwell after that night at Brandisi's, it'd be Curtis Clovis, your own man, and don't tell me you don't know about that. So, Mr. Lawyer-man, whyn't you get this straight? You so much as mention my name in connection with all this shit and so help me I'll tell the world about Curtis and what happened at that party."

"It wouldn't be in your best interest to let slip anything about what happened in the pool house, Del. You see, the woman you molested that night is threatening to sue everyone involved."

The anger and indignation faded from Del's face. "Say, what?"

"The FBI apparently contacted her along with everybody else

who was at the pool house with Cromwell. My guess is she had to have some excuse for being where she was, and so she said she was drunk and that you guys took advantage of her. What I was told was that she went straight from her FBI interview to a psychiatrist. He's diagnosed her as having posttraumatic stress disorder." Reynolds Rosenthal suddenly felt himself growing spiteful, and enjoying it. "You know what that is, Del?"

Del, his chin lifting, did not tell him. Instead, he demanded, "How come you know this and I don't?"

"Because I've been talking to Mrs. Brewer's attorney. They're offering to leave Curtis out of the suit if he testifies on her behalf against the rest of you."

"Curtis wouldn't do that."

"Why, because you've been such a good friend to him over the years?"

"He'd be through as a basketball player."

"He doesn't have that much longer to go anyway, and he knows it. What he does have is the money he's earned playing this year. He doesn't want to lose that in a lawsuit, and insurance doesn't cover intentional acts like sexual battery."

"She's going after our money?" Del looked as if he had been slapped.

"Her lawyer is."

"But she's rich," Del yelped. "What's she need to sue anybody for?"

Reynolds Rosenthal laughed in his face.

291

April 12

# THE *SMART FAN*

## by Marty Smart
### Atlanta, Georgia

On February 22, the San Francisco GoldenGaters roared into this city fresh from an important road victory over Cleveland. Expectations were high for at last righting their course after foundering on the shoals of mediocrity and ineptitude for most of the season. Atlanta, however, beat them by 24 points. Atlanta could have beaten them, it seemed, by almost any amount they wished because the Gaters were sloppy and tentative and lackadaisical. Outside of a brief attempt at fisticuffs on the part of the newly acquired and ever ready Jerome Crown, the Gaters showed barely a spark of desire.

Blame it on the dynamics of the road trip, on fatigue, or on the collective biorhythms of the team if you wish, the fact remains that one man was not surprised by what he witnessed. That man is a 46-year-old prison parolee from Raleigh, North Carolina, named Edwin James Maclean, or as he is known on the street, "Eddie Mac." Mr. Maclean's résumé shows convictions for pimping and drug dealing, but he is not known to be doing those things at the present, or indeed, to have any means of support whatsoever. This, however, did not stop him from occupying one of the finest seats in the house on the night of the San Francisco game. His gap-toothed visage was readily spotted by staff members of the Fenwick investigation, who viewed videotape of the game, because he was seated just eight rows behind the Gaters' bench, in the section the Omni reserves for friends and family of the visiting team.

What is significant about Eddie Mac's being in one of those seats at this particular game? Only that the ticket he was presumably holding could not have been bought at the gate, nor obtained by any other means except from the Gaters.

Who on the Gaters reserved tickets that night? The team won't say. But such protection is of questionable value in the long run. The Fenwick investigators turned this information over to the FBI, and Eddie Mac was arrested at his Raleigh home yesterday.

Knowledgeable sources say that the charges against Mr. Maclean relate to illegal gambling. Given the fact that he can be sent back to prison to serve out the sentence on his previous convictions if he has violated any of the conditions of his parole, these same knowledgeable sources say that both the government and the Fenwick investigations are anticipating Mr. Maclean's complete cooperation.

# 42

On the night of the New York game, Booby could sense the silence of the arena even before he left the locker room. When the team went out on the court, the fans stood and stared as if they were looking at zoo animals. There was no laughing and no gesturing during warm-ups. It was as though a pall settled over everyone who entered the arena, including the players, who shot their shots and ran through their lay-up drills with brisk precision, but without saying anything to each other. Then the horn sounded and the team retreated to the sidelines to suffer the "Star Spangled Banner" and await the announcements of the starting lineup.

Booby had given the names to Hack, and Hack had given them to the announcer. Booby had said nothing to the players themselves. He listened along with everyone else.

"Starting at center for your San Francisco GoldenGaters, at six-ten in his eleventh year from Jones-Henry, number forty-five, W.E.B. Pan-cake!

"At guard, in his third year from Oregon, six-foot-five-inch number twenty-four, Larry Mil-ler!

"At forward, in his second year out of UNLV, at six feet nine, number fifty-four, Zeke Wy-att!"

And then there was a slight hesitation in the announcer's voice and the surprises started. "At forward, at six-eleven, in his fifth year from Miami, num-bah double zero, Jer-ommmme Crownnn!

"And at guard, standing six feet seven, out of UC, Irvine, in his first year, making his first start as a GoldenGater, number fifty-five, Jonnieee Mar-tin!''

Everywhere in the press section people were leaning to one side or the other, whispering to their neighbors, looking at their notes. Four national television networks were represented, and the floor was lined with photographers. Their presence in such numbers gave the sense that a dangerous event was about to take place, such as the arrival of a space shuttle; but the eerie silence of the spectators reduced even them to a feeling of solemnity. And on the court, none of the Gaters said anything.

Once the game got under way things were so quiet the fans could hear the point guards calling out the plays, and Booby's shouted instructions seemed as loud as if he were using a megaphone. The sounds of the grand hall were the sounds of sneakers squeaking and backboards rattling and hands slapping skin, and when time-outs were called and the loudspeakers roared with taped music it sounded inappropriate to the point of being offensive. Like a boom box at a funeral.

Without Del Fuego Dixon and Rynn Packard, the Gaters' offensive attack was extremely limited. Still, the Gaters managed to stay within a couple of points of New York until the second period, when W.E.B. tired and Booby was forced to go to a front line of Zeke and Tim and Jerome. New York kept taking the ball inside and Jerome kept fouling.

Since six fouls meant automatic ejection, Booby should have pulled Jerome when he drew his third foul with two and a half quarters still to play. But he left him in and a minute later Jerome fouled yet again, and this time there was no question, Jerome had to come out. He knew it and looked to the bench to see if W.E.B. was on his way, but Booby still did not make the move.

The ref, a veteran, knew that Booby had to take out Jerome. He, after all, was the one who had called the four fouls. That was why he was staring at Booby the way he was. And finally Booby did what everyone was waiting for him to do. He turned to the bench. He pointed and jerked his thumb over his shoulder. Then he did it again and then a third time. W.E.B., Del Fuego Dixon, and Rynn Packard rose together and a gasp went

295

up from the crowd. Del and Rynn tore off their warm-up suits and trotted down to the scorer's table behind W.E.B., and someone in the audience, maybe one person, began to clap.

The players tapped the scorer's table one after the other. They scuffed their soles and jogged onto the floor, tugging at their waistbands. More people began to clap, a row, a section. Jerome did not head directly for the bench, but ran along the line of new entries, slapping hands with each of them. Jonnie Martin did the same, and then Tim Biltmore, who was almost to his seat, went back and did it as well.

The clapping had now swept around the arena like a wave, and as it circled, the people who were joining in were getting to their feet. There was nothing wild about the sound they were making and there was no cheering as such, but for almost a minute nearly thirty thousand hands beat steadily together and the emotion grew. When the New York player missed both the free throws he had been awarded as a result of Jerome's foul, the fans let loose with their lungs. Their collective cry was short and savage.

It died as Larry Miller passed the ball in bounds to Rynn. It picked up again as a New York guard immediately tried for a steal. Rynn spun out of his way and the crowd went, "Ooooh," and then went, "Aaaah," as he gunned the ball up court to Del, who was all alone and who calmly banked one home from eighteen feet.

Booby, standing in front of the Gaters' bench with his arms folded tightly across his rib cage, lost a certain amount of motor control as Del shot. His right hand flapped loose from under his left arm and went to his mouth. As the place exploded with joy at the sight of the ball dropping into the net, Booby's hand pulled down across his lower lip and stayed there at the very end of his chin. He tried to make it seem as though he had been seeking that position all along, resting his chin in his hand, because he knew his every movement was being watched. His upper body twisted so that he could take a quick peek into the stands. As soon as he saw what he was looking for he tried to swivel his head toward the court, but it was as though his eyes were magnetically held to their target.

Like Booby, Dale Rohmer had his arms folded in front of him. Unlike everybody around him, Dale was not clapping. His pale eyes practically burned with outrage.

Booby would have liked to have smiled. He would have liked to have given Dale Rohmer a good, hearty "Fuck you," but once again his motor control failed him. It was all he could do to turn back to the game, to lift his cupped fingers from his chin to his mouth and yell, " 'Ay to go, Del, baby!"

Del Fuego Dixon's running one-hander at the buzzer cut the New York lead to 1 at halftime, and as the teams hurried toward their respective locker rooms, the crowd treated the Gaters to a standing ovation. As Booby jogged off the floor, his entire journey was marked by fans barking questions and giving opinions. "Was it Del and Rynn who gave the ticket to the gambler, Boob?" they shouted. "Let 'em play, Boob," and, "Get your head out of your ass." But Booby answered no one, not until he got to the locker room and found Dale Rohmer waiting for him.

Halftime was filled with dancing girls and foul-shooting contests and announcements of future Gater events, and when the teams at last returned to the floor, Dale Rohmer was missing from his seat and Del Fuego Dixon and Rynn Packard were back in theirs. Booby used the same unit that had started the game to open the second half, and the same thing happened. W.E.B. came out strong and was gradually worn down. Booby sent in Tim and then Curtis and then Felix, and New York kept pulling further and further away.

The crowd grew impatient, and then abusive. When, early in the fourth quarter, Jerome picked up his fifth foul and Booby replaced him with Chris Sarantopoulis, the arena erupted with boos of disbelief. Popcorn boxes and beer cups rained down on the floor, and the game had to be stopped while the debris was cleared and the announcer begged for cooperation.

He did not get it. The fans chanted, "Del and Rynn. Del and Rynn. Del and Rynn," but those two players sat as they had sat for most of the game, at the far end of the bench next to Oliver

Dawkins, who, alone among all twelve of the Gaters, had yet to take off his warm-ups. Throughout it all, Booby Sinclair remained stoically in his seat, staring straight ahead even as he was pelted with a hot dog that left a mustard streak across the back of his sport coat.

New York won by 20 and the Gaters' brief hold on a playoff spot was over.

# 43

This time it was Crabbie who sought him out. Reynolds Rosenthal was standing with Ida Pancake off to the edge of the huge throng of people, press people mostly, who were gathered outside the Gaters' locker room door, and Marvin the guard caught his eye and beckoned him over.

"Crabbie wants you to stick around," Marvin whispered into Rosenthal's ear. "He told me if I saw you that I should let you in once everybody else's gone."

Rosenthal returned to Mrs. Pancake, but he told her nothing. Glancing around the crowd, he saw Mrs. Sinclair, who gave him a curt nod. He saw Mrs. Dawkins and she looked right through him.

Not until the game had been over for thirty minutes did Booby unlock the doors, and then the players began emerging in twos and threes.

A few of the reporters chased after W.E.B. A few chased after Del or Rynn or Oliver. They all chased after Booby.

Curtis came out with Biltmore, saw Rosenthal, and presumed the agent was waiting for him. But Rosenthal shook his head, and Curtis, catching on, veered back to Biltmore, who was moving through the people like an icebreaker, saying, "No comment, no comment," even when questions were not being put to him.

Finally, there was nobody left inside but Crabbie and nobody left outside but Rosenthal and Marvin. Rosenthal gave Marvin a bill, ten dollars this time, and Marvin twisted the door handle for him.

Crabbie, still dressed in his game clothes of bright gold slacks and a white polo shirt with a breast emblem of a basketball zooming out of the cross-span of the Golden Gate Bridge, was bent over a bench in front of Zeke Wyatt's cubicle, packing Zeke's travel bag. He managed a smile and dragged the back of his hand across his forehead as he straightened up. "Whew!"

Rosenthal smiled back. His smile was weaker, less beguiling.

"Getting ready for the road trip," Crabbie explained, floating his hand around the room. There were packed and zippered travel bags in front of nearly all the cubicles.

"I assume everybody's going," Rosenthal said in what was really a question.

"Oh," said Crabbie, sitting down on Zeke's bench. "Nobody's told me any different. But that's what I wanted to talk to you about. This is supposed to be America, you know? Man's still innocent until proven guilty. Yet, here we got a nice kid like Rynn Packard thrown into the middle of this thing just because he happened to be in the wrong place at the wrong time."

Rosenthal took a seat of his own on the bench in front of Felix's cubicle. "How do you know that, Dick?"

Crabbie spread his hands out to his sides. He made bridges of his fingers and his two arms were positioned like outriggers. "You saw for yourself that Rynn was benched today, and it wasn't Coach who did it. In fact, Rohmer came in at halftime and read Booby the riot act for putting Rynn and Del into the game. Now I don't mean to jump to any conclusions, Reynolds, but it's the very day the story comes out about somebody giving a ticket to this outlaw in Atlanta. That looks bad. At the very least, it starts rumors. A guy like Del, he can overcome rumors. But a guy like Rynn, he's not going to weather them as well." Crabbie looked pained at the thought.

"You don't think Rynn could have had anything to do with this guy Eddie Mac, is that it, Dick?"

"Oh, no," Crabbie protested. "I know he did. I saw them together—Eddie Mac, Rynn, Del, and Oliver. All of 'em sitting in Oliver's room the night before the Atlanta game. I just happen to know that Eddie Mac was Oliver's friend, and if he was getting any inside information, that's where it had to be coming from." Crabbie was convinced. He wanted Rosenthal to be convinced.

Rosenthal said, "Why is it you're telling me this, Dick?"

"Because," Crabbie said, his eyes wide, "I was hoping you'd be able to help Rynn out. You said you did some criminal-law-type stuff, and I know you've been following the investigations, so I thought maybe you'd be able to tell him what's going on. Maybe advise him as to what he should do."

"Does Rynn want somebody to advise him?"

Crabbie threw up his hands. "I don't think he has any idea what he's up against. That's why I was hoping maybe you could just go talk to him, get him to see how maybe it would be in his best interest to tell the FBI whatever he knows about Eddie Mac and that ticket he was using. I mean, he's a good kid, Reynolds, and I'd hate to see his career get ruined just because he was trying to be noble or something."

Rosenthal nodded. "Sure, Dick. I'd be glad to try to help."

Crabbie looked relieved. Then he cocked his head. "I'd probably better go with you when you see him. Just to explain why you're there and all."

"That would be best, Dick."

Crabbie pumped his head in agreement. Then he paused. "Think we could do it tonight?"

At the Laguna Arms condominiums on Broadway in the Pacific Heights district of San Francisco, a nice but not particularly fancy BMW, a 325i with a sunroof, pulled up to the garage doors. The driver could have been a stockbroker or a real estate salesman. He put down his window and reached out to insert his plastic computerized card into a slot in a box that sat on top of a little pole.

The garage door rolled upward. Two men stepped from the shadows and approached the car before it could start forward. One man wore a dark trench coat belted at the waist. The other wore a woolen jacket and bright gold pants.

The driver recognized Crabbie. He recognized the other man, but did not know his name. He said, "Hi," to both of them.

Crabbie, his hands never leaving his pants pockets, said, "Rynn, we got to talk to you."

Rynn Packard took in the features and dress of Crabbie's companion.

Crabbie, seeing this, gestured with his head, his shoulder, his arm. "This is Reynolds Rosenthal. He's a—"

"Lawyer," said Rosenthal, extending his hand.

Rynn took it. He looked at Crabbie. "Your lawyer?"

"No," said Rosenthal. "I'm here to help you."

"Well," said Rynn, "I guess I can use all the help I can get right about now."

The apartment had a lovely view of the Bay, but was rather modest in both its size and its furnishings. Rynn poured orange juice for all of them and they talked awkwardly about all the things you could see on the water from his living room and how great it would be if he had a telescope. Then they fell silent.

They took seats around a rectangular glass coffee table, Rynn and Crabbie on a rather boxlike yellow couch, Rosenthal in a matching armchair. Rosenthal started. "Rynn, I guess I don't have to tell you that your name is being linked with the worst kind of scandal that can happen to somebody in your profession."

Rynn said, "Boy, don't I know it."

Rosenthal was surprised that Rynn so readily agreed and let the young man nod his head a few times before adding, "And the reason you're being linked is because you were seen in the company of this Eddie Mac in Atlanta."

Rynn stopped nodding and looked at Crabbie. The trainer immediately opened his palms. "I haven't told anybody but Reynolds, Rynn. But I did see you, you know, in Oliver's room that night."

"Del invited me there," Rynn said, speaking first to one and then to the other. "He came up to me in the lobby of the hotel and said he and Oliver had these girls coming and that one of them specifically asked for me."

"Had you partied with those guys before, Rynn?" Rosenthal asked.

Rynn made a sound that was half snort and half laugh. He looked at Crabbie again.

"Then why did you agree this time?" Rosenthal said, interpreting.

"Because Del said that the girls would only come if I'd be there." Rynn blushed. He lowered his eyes to the floor. "And because Dale Rohmer had told me that he wanted me to do more socializing with the other guys. With Del especially. I thought he must have said something to Del, too."

"And was that the reason Del had included you?"

"I don't know why he included me."

Rosenthal waited, leaning back in his chair. Crabbie waited, leaning forward with his elbows on his knees.

"The only thing . . . he asked me, you know . . . He said the girls there, they all needed tickets for the game, and he asked me to leave mine for one called Tiffany. And I know the next night they were all sitting together, Tiffany, the other two girls, Eddie Mac, but I don't know who got whose ticket."

Rosenthal said, "Rynn, do you think Del was trying to set you up?"

Rynn screwed one eye into a squint. "Set me up for what?"

The moment was there. Rosenthal's delivery was swift and brutal. "To take the fall for the fact that he was tanking games all through January."

Rynn's head snapped back. His eyes flared wide. "I don't believe you."

Crabbie slapped Rynn's arm. "C'mon, that's why you and Del nearly got in a fight that time in Dallas."

Rynn pointed his face toward the window, toward the view of the Bay. "Why would he do that?"

"To get rid of Booby," said Rosenthal. "Del figured that if the Gaters lost enough games, Brandisi would insist that Booby be fired and they'd bring in someone who would play a more wide-open, run-and-gun style that would better fit his skills, increase his stats . . . fatten his paycheck."

"In other words," Rynn said, "somebody who would use a different point guard than me."

Rosenthal chose not to respond.

"Chees," said Rynn, and his eye was caught by Crabbie, who looked sympathetic to the point of being heartbroken.

Rosenthal picked up again, steering the conversation back on course. "Del found out that the FBI was investigating a very large and very unusual bet that had come out of Phoenix, where you guys lost a game because of something he had done. He learned the FBI had traced that bet to Neil Novaceski—remember him? Neil had been told by Del that the Gaters were going to lose to Phoenix the night before the game was played. The FBI was trying to get confirmation of that. Del saw that they were closing in on him and was trying to set up a straw man of sorts—trying to get another big bet going in a game where he would play well and somebody else would play lousy."

"That happened in Atlanta, all right."

"Did he do anything that you remember that could have messed you up?" Crabbie asked, leaning forward still more, resting his hand confidentially on Rynn's knee. "Put anything in your drink or anything like that?"

"It wasn't like that."

Crabbie looked directly into Rynn's face. "I told Reynolds what I saw late that night," he confided. "You running for the elevator with your shirt off. You were messed up on something, Rynn."

Rynn pulled his knee away. A clock somewhere in the apartment struck midnight and all three men listened to it chime itself out. A fair amount of time went by before Rynn said, "You ever go somewhere and from the moment you walk in you feel completely out of it? Well, that's what that party was like for me. Eddie Mac runs up and sticks a fresh drink in my hand practically every time I take a sip. Then the girls arrive and Oliver goes off in the bathroom with one of them, and when they come out, there's like this big cloud of smoke and they look at me and their eyes kind of click, like shutters going up and down. I'm standing around feeling like a doofus, and all I wanted to do was get the hell out of there. Except Del wouldn't hear of it."

Rynn did not look at either of the other men as he spoke.

His eyes seemed fixed on something that was not in the room. "Someone had a boom box and Del gets me dancing with this Tiffany woman, and I'm doing my best white man's shuffle and I look up one time and I see Oliver on one of the beds with his woman, and they're screwing each other right there in front of everybody else. Then I look over at Del and he's dancing with this tall woman and he's stark naked with an erection up to here." Rynn passed his hand under his chin.

Crabbie smiled encouragingly, as if Rynn were telling a good story, a dirty story.

"Everybody's having a great old time, and this Tiffany starts tugging at my shirt, and the next thing I know I'm bare chested and feeling so pale I think my skin is glowing. I'm in the middle of trying to save my pants when Eddie Mac walks up with a glass picture frame in his hands. On the glass is a metal straw and a half dozen lines of what I assume is cocaine, thick as yarn."

"Had you ever done it before?"

Rynn Packard shook his head. He rearranged his seat. "It's not that I'm a Boy Scout or anything. . . ." He waved his hand and changed the subject. "Tiffany, she does some right away, and then somehow she gets herself all wrapped around me and she gets the glass in front of my face and the straw inside my nose and all of a sudden I'm sniffing the stuff and Eddie Mac is shouting, 'Aw-right,' like I just pulled off some big accomplishment."

Crabbie glanced at Rosenthal. It was a glance filled with alarm.

"I was the only one to do it. Oliver had been doing something, but whatever it was, he did it in the bathroom and I didn't see. And Del never went near the stuff on the glass."

"So let me guess," said Rosenthal. "You got paranoid."

"I was," admitted Rynn, "paranoid before. But now I became crazy. I mean, I didn't know what to expect. I thought maybe there'd be flowers blooming out of the walls or rainbows shooting across the ceiling, but nothing really happened except I began having wild thoughts about the unbelievable things that were going on in that room, and I just wanted to get out. You can't imagine. At one point Del had two of the women on the

305

bed with him, Oliver had the other one, and then they switched. The women got up and changed from one guy to the other. That was when it got to be too much for me and I just bolted for the door."

"And ran into me on the elevator," said Crabbie, casting a side glance of confirmation toward Rosenthal.

Rynn Packard sighed.

"Was there any chance, Rynn," Crabbie asked, his voice cracking with concern, "that any of this was photographed? That anybody got any pictures of you?"

"One. That I saw."

Again, Crabbie looked to Rosenthal, who took the cue and asked, "You want to tell us what it was?"

Rynn nodded. "Eddie Mac had a camera and he was running around taking pictures of everything they were doing. He brought one to me before the Atlanta game. It showed Tiffany draped all over me, holding the straw to my nose. You could see the cocaine, plain as day. You could see the stupid grin I had on my face."

Rosenthal took his time in asking the next question. "Was that picture important enough to you that you agreed to do something Eddie Mac wanted?"

And Rynn took his time in answering. "I thought . . . I thought if it went to the commissioner's office or to Rohmer that I would be suspended, and if I was suspended that my career would be over. I mean, I'm not fooling myself. I'm no star. If Booby Sinclair thought for one minute that I was into drugs, I'd be out on the sidewalk. So I didn't say anything at all. I didn't agree to help Eddie Mac, but I didn't report him either. I just told myself, well, Atlanta is a real good team, maybe we'll just lose naturally and this guy will think I did what he wanted and give me the picture."

"But that didn't happen. I mean, you didn't do anything wrong so he didn't give you the picture." Crabbie spoke almost breathlessly.

"I didn't plan to," Rynn said. "But once the game started I couldn't seem to do anything right. I suppose all I could think about was not making mistakes, and the more I tried not to

306

screw up the worse I did. I was so terrible I was actually glad when Booby took me out. By then I was thinking that if we lost and I just stayed on the bench, everything would be all right. And that's basically what happened. I had my worst game of the year and we lost by a lot."

"And was Eddie Mac satisfied?" asked Rosenthal.

Rynn laughed, but it was a very unfunny laugh. "Who knows? I never saw or heard from the man again."

"And did that affect your play in the Miami game?"

"I know what you're thinking, Mr. Rosenthal, and that's one of the things that really bothers me. I had a good game against Miami until the last point—whatever second, and I just completely missed that foul shot. I knew I was supposed to put the ball off the rim so that time would run out, and I was so conscious of not putting it in the basket that I did something even worse. I just shot too short and missed everything."

"Which gave Miami a chance to take the ball in at half-court, put up a prayer shot, and win."

"That's right."

"Doesn't sound like the easiest way to fix a game."

"I was hoping people would realize that, anybody who questioned me."

"But the game, as far as you know, wasn't fixed, is that what you're saying?"

"Since I was the one who blew it, I can swear to you, Mr. Rosenthal, the Miami game wasn't fixed."

"And the Atlanta game?"

"As far as I know it was just one of those things."

Rosenthal nodded. He shifted about in his seat so that he was facing Crabbie more than he was facing Rynn. Crabbie's face was the image of sadness.

Rosenthal said, "So I guess that means you didn't get a bet down on that one, Dick."

Crabbie was halfway into his nod of agreement when he realized what had been said. "What?" he asked as his eyes grew wide with shock. "What?"

"You know, Dick, like you did with Neil Novaceski for the

Phoenix and Seattle games. Like you tried to do for the Portland game."

Crabbie wanted somebody to join in his protest at the absurdity of this charge. There was, however, only Rynn, and Rynn was offering no help at all.

"I don't know what you're talking about," Crabbie said.

"There were six of you who went to Ricky's Hacienda that night with Novaceski, when he got the first tip. Of the six, Gilbert and Earl were gone before the Seattle and Portland games. Someone out of the remaining four told Colin Cromwell enough about what happened to get him down to Phoenix to investigate. That had to be W.E.B., since Colin left Alabama to get there and W.E.B. was the only one with an interest in seeing him do that. Which leaves you and Del and Tim."

Crabbie gathered himself together. He did it physically, hoisting himself to the edge of the couch and smiling his way from one man to the other. "To do what? To tip off Neil? You said yourself it was Del who was throwing games—"

"When Del said something to Neil, he did it as a favor. He felt sorry for him. But Del wasn't doing what he was doing to help out gamblers or broken-down old players who were having hard times. Like I was telling Rynn, he had his own agenda, and that didn't include telephoning Neil in Arizona before every game." Rosenthal paused. "But somebody did."

"It could have been Tim," Crabbie said smartly. "He and Neil were practically best friends."

"Del said you were there when he told Neil to bet on Phoenix. How come you never said anything to anyone, Dick?"

"Well," Crabbie sputtered. He tucked in his chin and pulled his head back. "I don't remember. Guys say a lot of things, especially when they've been drinking. Heck, I was drinking that night. I got plastered and I can barely recall anything that happened."

"Sure," said Rosenthal, and Crabbie seemed to be satisfied. He looked around as if he were glad that the misunderstanding was behind them.

But Rosenthal was not done with him yet. "Except there's this other matter about calling off the bet on the Portland game when it turned out Del wasn't going to play. Who's in a better position to know about an injury than the team trainer?"

"It wasn't any secret. He—he pulled a groin muscle."

"No one saw him get hurt and there was no reason to believe he wouldn't be in there against Portland. But I'm not going to debate the point with you, Dick. The real reason I know it was you who was providing tips to Neil is because I talked with Mrs. Novaceski. Linda, isn't that her name?"

There was no answer. Crabbie merely slumped.

"She told me how Neil disappeared after the FBI showed up at their mobile home asking questions about the bets that had been made. You knew all about that, didn't you, Dick? She told you the same thing when you called up from Philadelphia looking for him on the morning of the New Jersey game."

Rosenthal turned to Rynn. He turned without really turning, just enough to let Rynn know he was addressing him with words that were meant for Crabbie. "You remember that one, don't you? Most of the boys were hung over and you had to take that long bus ride. Dick knew you weren't going to be able to play well, and you didn't."

Rynn twisted his head, seeking out Crabbie's eyes, but the trainer sat as before, shoulders slumped, eyes down, saying nothing.

"It was the closest thing you had to a sure bet since Del got scared of Jerome and stopped trying to lose," Rosenthal said. "Find Neil and make some easy money. Whatever you could pick up that way was bound to mean a lot more to you than it would to Tim Biltmore. He gets over nine hundred thousand dollars a year. What do you get? Thirty-five? Forty?"

Very slowly, Dick Crabtree lowered his head into his hands. "It looks bad for me, doesn't it?"

Rosenthal would have said that it did except he was distracted by the grunt that came from Rynn. It was a grunt of amazement, of confusion, of disbelief.

Crabbie's head jerked at the sound, but it did not lift from its basket of fingers. His voice, when it came, was muffled. "Can you help me? I mean, you're a lawyer. You were going to help Rynn—"

309

"Rynn didn't murder anyone, Dick."

Crabbie's hands pulled down from his face, leaving white trails across his pink skin.

"You knew the FBI had been to see Neil Novaceski, but you also knew he must not have admitted anything about the source of the tips. If he had, he probably wouldn't have needed to run. And besides, the FBI would have been all over you or Del. So that wasn't the part that scared you. No, the part that scared you was when Linda Novaceski said that Colin Cromwell had been there, too. Colin didn't need hard evidence or admissions or confessions. If he had enough information to get to Neil, he probably had enough to write a column that would ruin your career. You needed to find out what he knew and what he was going to do with it. The first chance you had was when he showed up in Boston and you were able to get him alone in his hotel room after the party."

Rosenthal was surprised to find himself on his feet. When had he gotten up? He was afraid he had been shouting and he tried to soften his voice. "What happened, Dick? Did you lose your temper? Was he near the open window and did you just push him? Is that the way it was? It was only six stories, but the opportunity was there. One quick shove and he was gone, and you could take all his notes, his computer discs, everything you needed before anybody could get up there to the room."

Crabbie shook his head. He did it in long, sweeping motions that carried his chinless face from one shoulder to the other. "He was my friend," he said. "He liked me. And he never would have written anything bad about me. Like you said, Reynolds, I'm the trainer. I know when people get hurt, when they're coming and when they're going. I had too much good stuff to give him."

"Except now, Crabbie, now he had the story of the century. He had a superstar fixing games, and to expose it he had to tell the part about you and Neil—"

"He didn't even know about me. And I can prove it if you'll agree to help me."

The desperation that had been in Crabbie's voice a few moments before had given way to calculation, a fact that was not lost on Reynolds Rosenthal. "How?" the lawyer asked; and Crabbie, his porcine eyes flitting from Rosenthal to Rynn and back again, said, "I did take his notes. And his computer discs. And his files. He had dirt on half the guys on the team, but he didn't have anything about me."

The room was very still for a moment. Then Rosenthal said, "But you didn't know that until after you pushed him, did you, Dick?"

Very slowly Crabbie's gaze settled on Rynn. Almost gently, he said, "He had the picture, Rynn. The one you described, or one very much like it. The gal, the cocaine, and you."

Rynn swallowed. There was a visible movement in his throat. But he was composed enough to ask the next question. "Do you know how he got it?"

"It was Del, Rynn," Rosenthal answered, not taking his own eyes off Crabbie. "He must have given it to Colin in Philadelphia to throw him off his track, just as W.E.B. gave him the information about Del to get him out of Alabama."

"He went to my hometown—"

Rosenthal spoke over him, snapping off his words to make Rynn understand that they were no longer gathering information, that now he was supposed to shut up and listen. "And that is exactly why Crabbie wanted me to come here tonight to talk with you. He wanted me to see that you had a motive, Rynn. He knew that I needed a suspect, somebody to get W.E.B. off the hook, somebody I don't represent. Since he has Colin's files, he knows the guys that were being investigated: W.E.B., Del, you. He couldn't offer up Del, not without running the risk of exposing himself. So it had to be you."

Rynn gaped at the man sitting next to him. Crabbie looked at him. Looked away. Looked back again.

"What are you staring at?" he demanded. "All of a sudden we're bosom buddies now, is that it? Where have you been the past two years, Rynn? Treating me like shit, same as all the rest of those whining, complaining, overpaid glory boys. 'Do this, Crabbie. Do that, Crabbie,' and maybe if I bow and scrape enough, you'll vote me a quarter share of the fucking play-off money—if you ever get any. I mean, I'm just your servant, right? I'm supposed to be grateful just to hang around you."

"Yet," said Rosenthal calmly, "you were so afraid you were going to lose your job that you killed a man."

"You keep saying that," Crabbie shouted, "but that wasn't the way it was."

Rosenthal inclined his head, a sign that he neither believed nor disbelieved.

Crabbie glowered. His lips clenched. "I tried to talk to him at the party, but there was too much going on. I was hoping we'd get a chance on the bus going back, but he wasn't on the bus. So when I got to the hotel, I just went up to his room. Only, when I got there, he was all worked up about something that had happened at the party. He was trying to write a column on that little portable computer of his, but he was having problems. He was drunk and his glasses were broken and he couldn't see the screen. He kept messing up and he was swearing, and I should have known that he wasn't thinking about me, but at the time I figured he was trying to avoid me. Okay?"

"Did you argue?"

"How could we argue when he wasn't even paying attention to me? I guess he thought it was no big deal, me being there. I mean, I'd gone to his room late at night lots of times when we were on the road. Only I wasn't thinking that way."

"So you got angry?"

"Yeah. I got angry."

"So what did you do?"

"The window was wide open. I imagine he had it that way because he was trying to get his head clear. I mean, it was cold that night and there was no other reason for it. So I just went over and snatched up his computer and threatened to heave the stupid thing out if he didn't stop what he was doing and start talking to me. He must have thought I meant it because he suddenly got up and ran at me." Crabbie paused. "It wasn't a fight or anything. He just was lunging for the computer, trying to get it back inside, and we were both kind of leaning out over the sill, me holding the thing away from him, Colin trying to pull his way along my arms."

The trainer ran a finger from his brow back to his ear. "And then I saw one of the halves of his glasses fall. He tried to catch it. The next thing I knew he was gone."

Crabbie held his hands up at an angle over his head. "I was still holding the computer. I couldn't even grab him."

Slowly, he put his hands down, and for a long time, all three men were silent. Then Crabbie said, "It was so unreal I didn't believe it was happening until I looked down and saw him on the street."

"And what did you do, Dick?" Rosenthal asked, his voice barely more than a whisper.

Crabbie took a slow, extraordinarily deep breath, and spoke while he exhaled, until the words and the breath ran out together. "I thought, 'Oh, my God, I've got to help him. I've got to get down there.' And then I realized that he was dead, that he had to be dead. There wasn't anything I could do for him, but I could help myself. So I just grabbed everything I could find that I thought could possibly say anything about me and I ran."

The silence resumed.

"That's the God's truth, Reynolds."

"I don't think anybody's going to believe it, Dick."

Crabbie held Rosenthal's gaze. He did it without blinking. "There's no proof I was there. I wiped off everything I touched."

"There's the work you took. The notebooks. The discs."

"If that stuff comes out, Reynolds"—Crabbie's lower lip dropped, exposing the bases of his bottom teeth—"not only does Del's career go down the drain"—he jerked his head toward his companion on the couch—"but so does Rynn's." Inching forward until he was at the very edge of the cushions, Crabbie said, "And what Colin was working on that night, what he had on the disc that was in the computer, isn't going to do your man Curtis's career any good either."

Rosenthal nodded. He had the picture. "What is it you want, Dick?"

"You to represent me."

"I can't. It would be a conflict of interest."

"Why? Because you're trying to keep charges from being brought against W.E.B.? I just want you to do the same for me, for all of us—W.E.B., Rynn, me . . . Curtis. Just keep charges from being brought, period. Everybody has an interest in that. Everybody has an interest in keeping Colin's files from being made public."

Rosenthal stood stock-still for several seconds. "I'm not a magician. I can't pull rabbits out of a hat."

"But you are the best at what you do, aren't you, Reynolds? You can do things nobody else can."

Rosenthal turned to Rynn Packard and raised one eyebrow. He let it hang there on his forehead while he waited for the young man to say something, say anything.

Rynn had to clear his throat. "Crabbie . . . Crabbie says he didn't do it, Mr. Rosenthal, and I believe him. You say things look bad for him, and I believe that, too. I'd say things look bad for all of us. In a situation like this, you ought to be able to go to the person who can do the job best."

"That's you, Reynolds," Crabbie urged. "That's why you get to charge two hundred bucks an hour."

"Two fifty," said Reynolds Rosenthal.

# Overtime

## 44

"Good evening, everybody, and welcome to 'SportsTalk,' where our guests tonight, live via telephone from their homes across the country, will be none other than Ted Brandisi, president and CEO of the Brandisi Corporation, owner of the San Francisco GoldenGaters, and Dale Rohmer, general manager of those same GoldenGaters. Before we bring on Dale and Mr. Brandisi, there are a few things that have to be said.

"The Gaters, of course, have just completed a tumultuous year, perhaps the most tumultuous any professional basketball team has ever experienced. Two of their players entered a drug rehabilitation program the day the season ended. And shortly thereafter they traded their best-known player for a draft choice and a reserve whom they had traded away earlier in the year.

"In the record book, the Gaters finished more with a whimper than a bang, losing their last three games and finishing out of the money, in ninth place in the Western Division. A closer look at that record book, however, will show that they played those last three games against three of the toughest teams in the league with virtually only nine players.

"True enough, top scorer Del Fuego Dixon, starting point guard Rynn Packard, and number one draft choice Oliver Dawkins suited up, but outside of a few minutes against New York, none of them saw any action in those final cru-

317

cial games. The reason was, quite simply, that an allega-
tion of—how should I say it?—impropriety had been made
that was thought possibly to have involved one of these
three men.

"Now, the Gaters had never finished out of the play-offs
since Ted Brandisi had taken over the team. In order to
keep that record intact, they had to win at least two of their
final three games and beat out Denver for the final play-
off spot. Without Dixon and Packard they had almost no
hope of doing that. Yet, Ted Brandisi made the choice, at
no small sacrifice to his own pocketbook I might add, to
withhold each of the players until all questions about their
conduct could be resolved—until even the appearance of
impropriety could be wiped away. I don't think a tougher
decision ever had to be made by an owner. And with that
as an introduction, I give you, ladies and gentlemen of the
listening audience, one of the most courageous, one of the
most noble, inspiring men of the entire world of sports,
Theodore 'Ted' Brandisi. Mr. Brandisi, welcome to
'SportsTalk.' "

"Thank you, Wayne. Thank you very much."

"Also with us is the man on whose broad shoulders it
fell to carry out Mr. Brandisi's decisions, a man who has
proven to be every bit as much of a team player in the
front office as he was on the court, Gaters' GM, Dale
Rohmer. Dale, thank you for joining us."

"Thank you, Wayne. It's a pleasure to be included."

"Mr. Brandisi, tell me, was it a tough decision for you to
hold those three players out?"

"Well, Wayne, it had to be done. The world of professional athletics is built on trust, and those of us in a position
of authority owe it to the fans to make sure they're getting
fair competition at all times for their entertainment dollar.
It's like with my supermarkets. If I charge my customers for
ground sirloin, I better not be giving them ground chuck or
they won't be coming back for more."

"Well put, Mr. Brandisi. But are you saying that there
were times when there wasn't fair competition?"

"Let me jump in there, Wayne. The answer is no, emphatically not. But some mistakes were made. None of those mistakes affected the integrity of the game of basketball, but the fact is, they had to be corrected and we've taken steps to do just that."

"You're referring now, Dale, of course, to the trade of Del Fuego Dixon and the entry of Oliver Dawkins and Rynn Packard into a drug treatment center."

"That's right, Wayne—Ted Brandisi, here again. Again, I want to emphasize that there was never any evidence that any of these fine young men did any harm to anyone other than themselves. But the fact of the matter is that they're not perfect—any more than you or I are perfect. They are young and impetuous, and they are subject to the same weaknesses and temptations as the rest of our nation's young people. Unfortunately, because they are talented and highly visible, they are easy targets for those who prey on weaknesses and temptation.

"So, what I am sorry to have to report is that during the course of some investigations that were going on—investigations that the Gaters have emerged from with flying colors, by the way—a couple of our players did, with commendable honesty, admit to using illegal substances."

"You're referring now to Oliver Dawkins and Rynn Packard?"

"That's right."

"But not Del Fuego Dixon."

". . . Let me explain what happened here, Wayne. I'll explain it the way it was explained to me. There was this fellow, Eddie Mac, down in Atlanta, and it turned out he was an acquaintance of one of our players—I'm not going to say which one it was. When the Gaters arrived in Atlanta, Mr. Mac arranged some sort of party that was attended by this player, who brought along a few of his teammates. During the course of the party, Mr. Mac managed to wheedle a set of complimentary tickets to our game. Giving out complimentary tickets, of course, happens all the time. But in this case, unfortunately, Mr. Mac seems to have used his knowledge of the fact that our players might have been weakened by this party of his to bet against the very people he supposedly had befriended."

319

"Now, let me interrupt here for any of our listeners out there who haven't been following the story. Eddie Mac was arrested on parole violations after he was spotted at the San Francisco–Atlanta game. Subsequently, the FBI was able to confirm that he had made a sizable bet against the Gaters. Take it from there, Mr. Brandisi."

"In any event, Wayne, when Mr. Mac was arrested, there immediately rose a question as to where he had gotten his tickets and whether that had anything to do with his bet. And when our players found out about it—well, I can tell you, they were mighty upset. They saw how, being out there in the public eye, they can't get away with things that maybe other people can. They saw how things can appear to be even worse for them than for other people. So Oliver and Rynn came forward together—even before their names had ever come up—and they said, 'Hey, we see the danger in what we were doing and we want some help.' And of course, we were only too glad to give it."

"How serious is their problem?"

"Well, according to their agent—and they both have the same agent now, a fella named Reynolds Rosenthal—Rynn's substance abuse problem is nowhere near as severe as that of Oliver. In fact, he expects Rynn to be released from the drug rehab facility in a matter of days. But we plan to have both men back and ready to play at full capacity next season."

"Now, correct me if I'm wrong, Mr. Brandisi, but isn't Mr. Rosenthal representing Dick Crabtree in the criminal investigation that's still going on in Boston in connection with the death of sportswriter Colin Cromwell?"

"I do need to correct you on that, Wayne. No criminal charges have been filed as of this time. But Crabbie has admitted that he was in the room when Colin Cromwell, who had been drinking rather heavily and who apparently had an asthma problem that may have affected his balance, fell out his window. Crabbie apparently panicked and ran from the room. Sometime later, when he learned that the authorities were suspecting that Colin may not have fallen on his own, Crabbie and his attorney came to us and fully disclosed what Crabbie knew."

"That's Mr. Rosenthal again?"

"That's right, Wayne, and we were satisfied with his evidence as to what happened and we pledged our full cooperation."

"Well, forgive me, Mr. Brandisi, but I'm a little confused here. What evidence could these people have given that would have explained why Dick Crabtree didn't tell anybody he was in the room when Cromwell fell?"

"As I understand it, Wayne, Dick Crabtree went to talk to Mr. Cromwell after both of them had been at a party—at a party. Neither one of them was feeling any pain, as we used to say, and Crabbie had a number of complaints he wished to voice concerning some of the articles Cromwell had been writing about members of the team. Dick thought, with the Gaters pushing for the play-offs, the articles were unnecessarily personal and counterproductive. The argument got heated—this is the way it was explained to us—and Cromwell went to open a window. He wore eyeglasses, a very nearsighted fellow, and—we corroborated this with numerous people who saw him earlier in the evening—his glasses had gotten stepped on at the party. Broken in two. Very nearsighted, did I mention that? Well, you add all that together with the effects of the alcohol and this asthma thing he had, and you can understand what happened. As he leaned out the window to get a breath of fresh air, one of the halves of his glasses slipped off. He went to grab for it, lost his balance, and fell. Very sad."

"You mentioned the articles Colin Cromwell was writing, Mr. Brandisi. There were rumors to the effect that none of his notes were ever found. Can you comment on that?"

"Um . . . no, I can't. . . . I don't really know anything about that, Wayne."

"Dale, how about you?"

"Don't know anything about them, Wayne."

"Well, did Crabbie or Reynolds Rosenthal ever say anything to either one of you about those notes or what happened to them?"

"No."

"Not to me."

"Okay, well, let's move over to another subject. Is Dick Crabtree still the trainer of the San Francisco GoldenGaters?"

"Well, as you know, Wayne, a man is innocent until proven guilty in this great country of ours, but as I under-stand it, Crabbie has been greatly affected by all that has taken place and has decided not to return to the team next year."

"There have been rumors, Mr. Brandisi—and forgive me if I'm trafficking in gossip here—but that some kind of deal was cut with Dick Crabtree and his lawyer in connection with the settlement of a civil lawsuit that was being brought against you and some of the members of your team as a result of certain events that took place at your home on the night Colin Cromwell died. Would you care to comment on that?"

"There's really nothing to comment on, Wayne. No such lawsuit was filed."

"Was there a settlement of some kind?"

"Like I told you, Wayne. No lawsuit was filed along the lines of whatever it is you're talking about."

"Okay, Mr. Brandisi, let's turn back then to the Del Fuego Dixon situation. You saw fit to trade him. Can you explain the reasoning behind that?"

"Well, Wayne, Del of course is a fine player, but his evaluation and our evaluation of his worth—I'm speaking monetarily now—were a little bit different. His contract was expiring and he had, frankly, priced himself out of our range."

"Yet, turning to you now, Dale, you did sign him."

"That's right, Wayne. We did sign him and then we traded him to San Antonio to get back Gilbert Rose, whose leadership we missed, and San Antonio's number one draft pick next year. That puts us in an enviable position. We'll have two number one choices, ours and theirs."

"And—Ted Brandisi here again, Wayne—assuming Oli-ver benefits from the rehab he's undergoing, we'll have available in him what we did not get this year: one of

322

college's best players, fit and ready to take on the best of the pros. It'll be almost like having three number one picks."

"But essentially what your trades amounted to this year was Del Fuego Dixon and Earl Putnam, two certain starters for San Antonio, for a second-stringer, and a guy who's still in college. Would you care to comment on that, Dale?"

"We don't see it that way, Wayne. We think Jerome Crown's potential tips the balance in our favor. We've decided to go to more of an inside game next year, and that's better suited to Jerome's style than it is to Del's. It's also best suited to the evolution we're seeing in W.E.B. Pancake's style of play, and that's important because W.E.B. provides some much needed maturity to our team. Having him with his experience is almost like having another coach out there on the floor."

"And by the way, Wayne, let me add to what Dale is saying by taking this time to make the announcement that we've just completed negotiations with W.E.B.'s agent on a two-year extension to his present contract."

"Now, correct me if I'm wrong again, Mr. Brandisi, but isn't Pancake's agent also Reynolds Rosenthal?"

"That's right, Wayne."

"And Rosenthal is the agent for Gilbert Rose as well?"

"That's right, Wayne."

"But no deal of any sort was cut with Reynolds Rosenthal?"

"That's right, Wayne."

"Okay, you mention a coach on the floor and that brings up the stories that have been circulating about Booby Sinclair. Tell me, do you expect him back next year?"

"That's something we're not prepared to comment on, Wayne. Right now, Booby and his wife and two children are on a family vacation in Europe, something they have never done before; and if, on his return to the States, he decides he might like to come back, well, we're going to sit down and talk about it then."

"It sounds to me as though it might be in Booby's best interest to have Reynolds Rosenthal represent him at that meeting."

323

"Har, har, Wayne."

"Ah, what Mr. Brandisi means to say, Wayne, is that job burnout, as you know, is a fact of life in the coaching profession, and an argument can be made that perhaps it's best for both Booby and the Gaters if he moves on to other pastures, as he's indicated he might like to do. But that remains to be decided. The important point is that we're all looking forward to next season. Don't you agree, Mr. Brandisi?"

"Dale, I can't wait. Next season's going to be our year."

"You guarantee that, Mr. Brandisi?"

"I don't have to, Wayne. Dale already has."